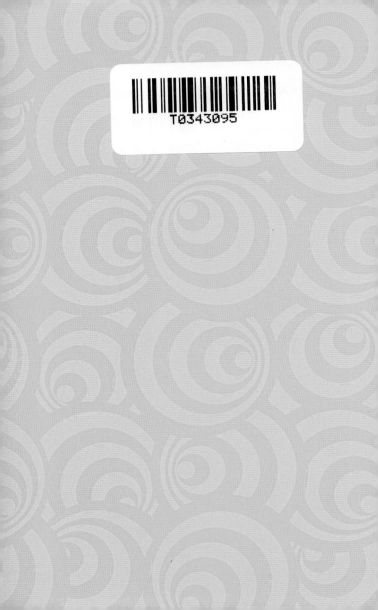

TALES OF HEROES,
GODS & MONSTERS

POLYNESIAN

STORIES & LEGENDS

FLAME TREE PUBLISHING
6 Melbray Mews, Fulham,
London SW6 3NS, United Kingdom
www.flametreepublishing.com

First published and copyright © 2025
Flame Tree Publishing Ltd

25 27 29 28 26
1 3 5 7 9 10 8 6 4 2

ISBN: 978-1-83562-279-7

Cover and pattern art was created by Flame Tree Studio, with elements courtesy of
Shutterstock.com/kurbanov/Svekloid.
Additional interior decoration courtesy Shutterstock.com/sunlight77.

Judith John (Glossary) is a writer and editor specializing in literature and history. A former
secondary school English Language and Literature teacher, she has subsequently worked
as an editor on major educational projects, including *English A: Literature* for the Pearson
International Baccalaureate series. Judith's major research interests include Romantic and
Gothic literature, and Renaissance drama.

Sources and contributors for the tales in this book include: *Polynesian Mythology & Ancient
Traditional History of the New Zealanders* by Sir George Grey, 1922; *Te Tohunga: The Ancient
Legends and Traditions of the Māoris* by W. Dittmer, with contributions by James Cowan,
1907; *Tongan Myths & Tales* by Edward Winslow Gifford, 1924; *Legends of Ma-ui – A Demi
God of Polynesia and of His Mother Hina* by W.D. Westervelt, 1910; and *Legends of Gods and
Ghosts (Hawaiian Mythology)* by W.D. Westervelt, 1915.

A copy of the CIP data for this book is available
from the British Library.
Designed and created in the UK | Printed and bound in China

COLLECTOR'S EDITIONS

TALES OF HEROES, GODS & MONSTERS

POLYNESIAN STORIES & LEGENDS

Reading List & Glossary of Terms
with a New Introduction by
ANDROMEDA WELLSPRING

FLAME TREE PUBLISHING

CONTENTS

CONTENTS

CONTENTS

TALES OF HEROES, GODS & MONSTERS

POLYNESIAN
STORIES & LEGENDS

SERIES FOREWORD

Stretching back to the oral traditions of thousands of years ago, tales of heroes and disaster, creation and conquest have been told by many different civilizations in many different ways. Their impact sits deep within our culture even though the detail in the tales themselves are a loose mix of historical record, transformed narrative and the distortions of hundreds of storytellers.

Today the language of mythology lives with us: our mood is jovial, our countenance is saturnine, we are narcissistic and our modern life is hermetically sealed from others. The nuances of myths and legends form part of our daily routines and help us navigate the world around us, with its half truths and biased reported facts.

The nature of a myth is that its story is already known by most of those who hear it, or read it. Every generation brings a new emphasis, but the fundamentals remain the same: a desire to understand and describe the events and relationships of the world. Many of the great stories are archetypes that help us find our own place, equipping us with tools for self-understanding, both individually and as part of a broader culture.

For Western societies it is Greek mythology that speaks to us most clearly. It greatly influenced the mythological heritage of the ancient Roman civilization and is the lens through which we still see the Celts, the Norse and many of the other great peoples and religions. The Greeks themselves learned much from their neighbours, the Egyptians, an older culture that became weak with age and incestuous leadership.

It is important to understand that what we perceive now as mythology had its own origins in perceptions of the divine and the rituals of the sacred. The earliest civilizations, in the crucible of the Middle East, in the Sumer of the third millennium bce, are the source to which many of the mythic archetypes can be traced. As humankind collected together in cities for the first time, developed writing and industrial scale agriculture, started to irrigate the rivers and attempted to control rather than be at the mercy of its environment, humanity began to write down its tentative explanations of natural events, of floods and plagues, of disease.

Early stories tell of Gods (or god-like animals in the case of tribal societies such as African, Native American or Aboriginal cultures) who are crafty and use their wits to survive, and it is reasonable to suggest that these were the first rulers of the gathering peoples of the earth, later elevated to god-like status with the distance of time. Such tales became more political as cities vied with each other for supremacy, creating new Gods, new hierarchies for their pantheons. The older Gods took on primordial roles and became the preserve of creation and destruction, leaving the new gods to deal with more current, everyday affairs. Empires rose and fell, with Babylon assuming the mantle from Sumeria in the 1800s bce, then in turn to be swept away by the Assyrians of the 1200s bce; then the Assyrians and the Egyptians were subjugated by the Greeks, the Greeks by the Romans and so on, leading to the spread and assimilation of common themes, ideas and stories throughout the world.

The survival of history is dependent on the telling of good tales, but each one must have the 'feeling' of truth, otherwise it will be ignored. Around the firesides, or embedded in a book or a computer, the myths and legends of the past are still the living materials of retold myth, not restricted to an exploration of origins. Now we have devices and global communications that give us unparalleled access to a diversity of traditions. We can find out about Native American, Indian, Chinese and tribal African mythology in a way that was denied to our ancestors, we can find connections, match the archaeology, religion and the mythologies of the world to build a comprehensive image of the human experience that is endlessly fascinating.

The stories in this book provide an introduction to the themes and concerns of the myths and legends of their respective cultures, with a short introduction to provide a linguistic, geographic and political context. This is where the myths have arrived today, but undoubtedly over the next millennia, they will transform again whilst retaining their essential truths and signs.

Jake Jackson
General Editor

TALES OF HEROES, GODS & MONSTERS

POLYNESIAN STORIES & LEGENDS

INTRODUCTION
& FURTHER READING

A NEW INTRODUCTION TO
POLYNESIAN STORIES & LEGENDS

How was life created? How was the land we walk upon formed? What causes the elements and makes them so dangerous? Why do we die – and where do we go after death?

These questions have been asked by humanity since time immemorial. All across the globe, ancient people wondered at their surroundings. They sought through stories to make sense of what they could not explain – stories that have become the legends and myths of today. In them, ancient cultures sought answers and explanations to the natural elements of our world. The stories they told vary around the world, but share common elements despite the barriers of distance and language.

For some, these stories are a living reality. While much of the world would describe the tales within this book as 'myths', indigenous Polynesians consider their stories sacred and a cornerstone of their culture. These stories are part of their ceremonies and continue to be passed down through oral tradition. This practice is common across the globe; it can be found in Native American cultures, among Aboriginal tribes and in Abrahamic cultures – among many, many others. Out of respect for these beliefs, the contents of this book will not be referred to as 'myths'.

THE PEOPLE OF POLYNESIA

Oral history tells of an island. Known to the Māori as Hawaiki, this island was the ancestral home of the people of Polynesia. They were a seafaring race who utilized canoes for their ocean voyages. It was these canoes that carried them during their great migration from Hawaiki. This diaspora continued over centuries of migratory voyages as people found and settled new islands, bringing their stories and beliefs with them.

While the legendary Hawaiki has not been found, archaeological evidence supports these accounts of migratory journeys. Pottery remnants from early ancestors called the Lapita have enabled archaeologists to trace their expeditions. The first islands were settled over 3,000 years ago. As populations expanded and the islands grew crowded, more people would set out on new voyages. Gradually, as Herb Kawainui Kāne observes in his work *In Search of the Ancient Polynesian Voyaging Canoe* (1998), over the course of two millennia and across countless miles of ocean new cultures and civilizations would arise. These settlements became the islands of Polynesia.

'Polynesia' stems from two Greek words: 'poly', meaning many, and 'nēsoi', meaning islands. In his article *'"Le Président des Terres Australes": Charles de Brosses and the French Enlightenment Beginnings of Oceanic Anthropology'* (2002), Tom Ryan describes how the term was first attributed to Charles de Brosses – the French scholar who, in 1756, published a compilation of accounts of voyages to the Pacific islands. The geography covered by this terminology has morphed over the centuries, at times including or excluding various island groupings. However, the vastness of this geographical division cannot be overstated; the Polynesian Triangle covers over

10 million square miles of ocean and landmass. For context, that's more square miles than all of North America.

The simplest definition, perhaps, is that Polynesia refers to the indigenous inhabitants of the islands and archipelagos of the Pacific. These inhabitants share common ethnic and linguistic characteristics, but they also represent unique and distinctive peoples with their own traits, stories and cultures.

While the history of these cultures stretches far back through time, they are alive and present today. Modern Polynesia is home to the diverse countries and territories of Samoa, Aotearoa, Hawai'i, Kūki 'Āirani, Tonga, Rapa Nui and many more. Some of these indigenous names may be more familiar to readers as New Zealand, the Cook Islands and Easter Island.

COLONIALISM

In the fifteenth and sixteenth centuries, powerful Western nations began seafaring expeditions with the intention of colonizing new land. Resources and trade routes were powerful motives for exploration. Much of Polynesia was colonized by Europeans over the course of four centuries. The colonizing countries included France, the UK, the United States and Germany, as well as Chile.

While many islands of Polynesia have been granted sovereignty in recent years, others still remain under the governance of other countries.

Colonization of the Polynesian islands brought many of the earliest written accounts of native culture. The disparate peoples of Polynesia did not have a system of writing; their histories and traditions were passed down orally. As a result, many of these histories, as well as social, religious and political norms, were transcribed by Western explorers. These resources are the oldest accounts we have for the region, but many are tainted by colonial bias.

Missionaries from several denominations settled on Polynesian islands and are responsible for several of these early histories. However, they were also the cause of religious syncretism that irrevocably changed Polynesian ceremonies and beliefs. Judeo-Christian terminology can be found in old stories, while other ceremonies were dismissed as pagan and banned outright. Their practices have now been lost to time.

SONG AND DANCE

Oral Traditions

The oral histories of Polynesia blend fact with fiction, interweaving legendary events with 'real' history. It may be easy from a Western perspective to dismiss a history without written records – yet material evidence often lends credence to oral histories. Patrick Vinton Kirch (*On the Road of the Winds*, 2017) reveals how archaeological findings, from the remains of pottery made by the Lapita people to the petroglyphs on Easter Island, offer us glimpses into the past to support these stories.

Nor were legends the only oral traditions of the Polynesian people. Māori culture values *whakapapa*, an oral genealogical record that traces the line of one's family back to its roots. *Whakapapa* can be used to examine divine origins of family lines, much as Judeo-Christian oral histories compiled in the Book of Genesis once traced families back to Adam and Eve, or Chinese genealogies traced the Imperial line back to the gods.

Story Through Song

Whakapapa are sometimes presented through *waiata* – a song or chant accompanied by simple instruments. Though these chants are known by many different names across Polynesian cultures, they are a common method for transmitting stories in each. Samuel Mānaiakalani Kamakau notes in *The Works of the People of Old* (1964) that in Hawai'i, songs such as the *Kumulipo* and the *Ea Mai Hawai'inuiākea* examine the origins of the islands and the divine connection between them and their inhabitants. *Whakapapa* may also be used to trace not only human history, but also its deep-rooted connection with the land. The Hawaiian *oli* of *hula* likewise traces the history of its people. These are just a few examples from several different cultures.

An important component of many Polynesian songs or chants is the accompanying dance. There are dances for apology songs, welcoming songs, celebrations and funerals, even songs for battles. Tongan dances such as the *faha'i-ula* feature lyrics with their roots in Samoan, revealing the interconnectedness of Polynesian cultures.

Hospitality Dances

Perhaps the best-known Polynesian dances are hospitality dances. As the name suggests, their purpose is to welcome visitors. Some of these dances are performed at important events such as weddings or coronations; others feature at parties and celebrations. More solemn dances are performed at funerals or to mark departures. The Tongan *lakalaka* is a modern reincarnation of the *me'elaufola*, a dance outlawed centuries ago by Christian missionaries. The Tahitian *'ōte'a*, the Samoan *fa'ataupati*, the Hawai'ian *hula* and the New Zealand *haka* are examples from other Polynesian cultures.

Perhaps the most famous yet misunderstood of these is the *haka*. Many consider *haka* performances to enact a war dance of sorts, showcasing physical prowess and intended to intimidate. In fact there are many different kinds of *haka*, only one version of which is intended for use by warriors in battle. Instead, as Sir Timoti Kāretu explains in *Haka! The Dance of a Noble People* (1993), the *haka* is a celebration of life, a dance with its origins in the divine; it represents the midsummer shimmer of heat in the air caused by the approach of the goddess Hine-raumati. Today *haka* live on in traditional indigenous ceremonies, as well as in performances by New Zealand rugby teams and school dance groups.

SIMILAR YET DIVERSE

'Polynesian' is in fact a blanket term used to cover many diverse peoples. Compilations that compare their cultures, languages, social roles and religions are common because there are many overlapping facets. The shared roots of language, along with similarities in stories, religion, social practices and other aspects of life, allow us to examine Polynesian culture as a whole.

Despite this, it is important to note that the peoples discussed in this book also have profound differences. Each culture has countless books dedicated to its own unique history, religion and cultural aspects. The intention of this work is not to homogenize disparate peoples, but rather to celebrate the stories they share.

The legends within this book derive from a multitude of Polynesian traditions. Similar stories are compared, with the differences between them pointed out. Sometimes Māui is credited with fishing up the islands of Hawai'i; in other stories the goddess Pele raises them from the waters. The Māori Papatūānuku is known in Hawai'i as Papahānaumoku and as Papatu'oi in Tahiti. These goddesses share similar stories despite the differences of their name.

As a result, the spellings of names may also vary. This is due both to differences between Polynesian traditions and to Anglicization. And while it is not possible to include all the legends in this work, what is here provides an intriguing glimpse into the unique lore and history of Polynesian stories.

WATER AND FIRE

Surrounded by Ocean

The ocean permeates every aspect of Polynesian life. Their stories feature countless journeys across the waves, whether migrating from their island of origin, exploring new lands or travelling to the next life. The ocean is a source of life, providing a bounty of fish and organic materials, but it can also be tempestuous. Typhoons and tropical cyclones plague the waters surrounding the Polynesian islands. Boats are lost at sea and some sailors never return.

Two of the earliest gods of Māori legend reflect these dangers, both children of the earth and sky gods. Tāwhiri-ma-tea is the god of weather and storms. When his brothers betray their parents, Tāwhiri-ma-tea swears revenge upon them. He calls up his children and gathers up their winds and waves into a mighty assault. His storms crash over the trees and topple them, drowning the beasts of the land and crushing the fish of the sea. The crops and plants are driven beneath the earth as they seek shelter. Only man stands against Tāwhiri-ma-tea, dauntless in the face of the storm.

The second god is Tangaroa. As god of the ocean, he is one of the most important deities in Māori stories, locked in perpetual opposition with his brother Tāne, god of the forests. As part of their immortal struggle, Tāne supplies mankind with wood and plant fibres to make canoes, fishhooks and nets to catch Tangaroa's children. Each time mankind sails upon the ocean, they are part of the war against Tangaroa.

Polynesian cultures recognize the beauty of the ocean. They rely upon it for food and trade, taking pride in their skill in sailing and navigation. Yet at the same time they recognize the risks inherent in each sea voyage, with the constant threat of storms and uncertain waters. This division of land and sea into two warring entities lies at the heart of many Polynesian legends.

Volcanic Activity

Volcanoes are a fact of life for many of the Polynesian islands. Several countries sit upon hotspots, with perhaps the most famous being the Hawaiian hotspot, part of the massive Hawaiian-Emperor seamount chain. This underwater chain of mountains stretches for a truly staggering distance and contains many volcanoes. Other locations include the Society hotspot, Samoa hotspot and Auckland hotspot. Numerous volcanoes congregate around these hotspots, many of them extinct or dormant. Oral history bears records of eruptions centuries before, while others have erupted in recent memory.

It is thus little wonder that volcanoes can be found across Polynesian legends. Hawai'i is home to Pele, the goddess of volcanoes. Said to dwell within the volcano Kīlauea, she is attributed with the creation of the Hawaiian islands. Māori tales tell of Rūaumoko, the youngest son of the earth and sky gods. A volcano and earthquake deity, Rūaumoko still lives in the womb of his mother Earth, his movements causing earthquakes in the land. Here, too, we see Mahuika, a goddess of fire who dwells within a mountain. Samoan lore features Mafui'e, a god of earthquakes and the keeper of fire.

Volcanoes are not always depicted as divine. The story of Taranaki, Ruapehu and Tongariro contains two male giants fighting over the favour of a female. Even in stories that do not feature volcanoes, we see hints of their presence. For instance, there are mentions of volcanic glass being used to make tools and weapons. Man and god alike use obsidian, with the goddess of death said to have teeth made of the substance.

Interestingly, these personifications of volcanic activity are not vilified in stories. Frequently presented as benevolent, they are respected, even revered. Despite the risk of eruption, Polynesian tales honour the volcanoes of their homelands – the source of the bountiful soil which surrounds them. These fiery mountains not only created the land masses settled by the people of Polynesia, but also inspired the stories they tell.

GODS AND DEMIGODS

In stories of the gods, we are able to see the joy of humanity. Faith and perseverance are rewarded; divine gifts are bestowed. It is possible for mortals to ascend to divinity, should they lead a sufficiently devout life. Should a deity be angered, however, their revenge will be swift and terrible.

In demigods we see traits of both gods and mortals. The strength, intellect and even magic of the gods combines with the hubris and foibles of mankind. The gods stand separate from their followers, infinitely beyond our reach. In demigods we are able to bridge the gap between the human and divine.

Earth and Sky

The stories of Papa and Rangi depict two lovers, split apart by force. From these two gods all life sprang. Much like the Titans of Greek mythology, they were overthrown by their children – yet they are still regarded with affection and love. Rangi is garbed in beautiful stars and wisps of cloud; Papa's devout son clothes her in lovely forests and lakes. The two are made to look their best for one another. Destined to spend an eternity apart, they constantly reach for one another. The sighs of Papa are mist rising towards the heavens; the tears of Rangi are rainfall descending to earth.

Tāne

It was the god Tāne who split Papa and Rangi apart. Despite this, he is shown to be full of filial duty, disagreeing with his siblings when they suggest killing their parents, and opting instead to separate them. He reveres both of them and grieves the necessity of their separation. It is also Tāne, ashamed of his parents' nakedness, who seeks out beautiful adornments for their bodies.

Tāne is the god of forests and of all that dwell within them. He is one of the most important deities in Polynesian culture. Many Polynesian tools are made out of wood, which is a necessity for boat-making; even their traditional cloth, *tapa*, is made from wood pulp. All of these stem from Tāne and his domain. They are believed to be gifts from the god to mankind to aid them in their battle against the ocean.

Hina

The goddess Hina is one of many important deities in the Polynesian pantheon, and her stories are told across multiple cultures and islands. In some tales, Hina is considered the mother of Māui; in others she has a different relationship with him. The desire to help Hina is the impetus for many of Māui's adventures.

Hina is considered to be a goddess of the moon. She is said to be married to the moon and sometimes dwells upon its surface. In the stories of Hawai'i, however, Hina lives instead in a cave behind a waterfall of the Wailuku river. This waterfall is associated with rainbows, sometimes accredited to Hina.

Women's chores feature in many of the stories about Hina. For instance, she is praised for her ability to make *tapa*, a thin cloth of pounded bark that is dried in the sun. Hina's *tapa* is so fine that the moon god takes her for his wife. The *tapa* she makes in the heavens are the wisps of clouds seen in the night sky.

Māui

Perhaps the best known of all Polynesian legends are those of the demigod Māui. At times a trickster, at times a hero, his exploits are told across many different Polynesian cultures (Westervelt). The spelling of Māui's name and the epithets given to him vary. In some stories, such as those of Hawai'i or New Zealand, Māui is the youngest of several brothers. In others he is an only child. At times a god, at other times a demigod, he is always legendary.

Māui is known as a shapeshifter, able to alter his form and size. He possesses a mighty fishing hook which he crafted out of the enchanted jawbone of his divine ancestor. The demigod's profound love of mischief gets him into trouble at times, but his compassion for those around him shines through in each tale.

Many of Māui's greatest tricks have resulted in great benefits for humanity.

While some cultures say that the earth and sky were split asunder by gods, others claim that it was Māui who first raised the sky. He stood beneath it and heaved the heavens upwards. This raising of the sky brought forth light and gave mankind room to stand upright.

When Māui's brothers mocked his fishing abilities, he swore that he would catch a greater fish than any of them. Using his own blood as bait, Māui then hooked islands from beneath the sea and raised them into the landmasses we know today. When his mother complained that the days were too short and she did not have enough time to do her chores, Māui caught the sun with his fishing hook and slowed its ascent across the sky. When Māui discovered fire, he tricked its keepers, stole it and gifted it to mankind. His innovation also made for more efficient ropes and traps. Māui improved upon fishing hooks and spears, adding barbs so that they could more easily ensnare their prey.

After all his exploits, Māui grew confident in his ability to overcome anything he faced. In this time death had not yet claimed any man. Māui was determined to grant himself and all mortals immortality. To do this, he journeyed to the home of Hine-nui-te-pō, goddess of night and guardian of the afterlife. Māui sought to perform a ritual to reverse birth, traversing through her womb and up through her mouth. Had he succeeded, the threat of death would have been overcome forever. However, the goddess was alerted to his presence by the noises of his companions. She awoke and crushed him with obsidian teeth. Māui's death ushered in a new era for mankind – an era in which death awaits everyone.

DEATH AND BEYOND

Surrounded by the ocean, the Polynesians were constantly travelling, carried from one island to the next by the waves. Life was a voyage, so it is not surprising that they viewed death the same way. In some traditions, the afterlife is simply another island – such as Māori legends which recognize their ancestral homeland of Hawaiki as the afterlife. The spirits of Māori who have died return to the island from which they all came. Other Polynesian cultures believe in a different underworld, but still associate it with a journey through water after death.

Different Polynesian cultures have different gods of the underworld. The underworld itself is known by several names across many different islands, sometimes being referred to as 'the Unseen Land'. In Hawai'i King Milu rules over Lua-o-Milu, while the Māori pantheon recognizes Hine-nui-te-pō as the goddess who guards the entrance to the underworld. She is also revered as a goddess of night.

The association of death with the dark of night is common across many Polynesian cultures. Epithets such as 'eternal night' or 'endless night' are used to describe the afterlife. Both ghosts and spirits are most active at night.

Ghosts fall into several categories in Polynesian legends, with Hawai'i in particular possessing a storied history of spirits and their doings. The most common are ancestor spirits, revered by their descendants. Ancestor spirits are benevolent; they have passed safely to the next life, thanks to the burial rites and offerings of their relatives.

There are also the restless dead – ghosts who have been forgotten, or whose families have made no offerings for them. They may not have been buried or had last rites performed. These ghosts are untethered, unable to return to their bodies. It is difficult for them to move on – but not impossible. Many cultures associate high cliffs over the ocean as a place for ghosts to congregate. Leaping from the cliff allows the ghost to pass into the afterlife. In Māori lore, one such location is known as Te Rerenga-Wairua – 'The Place Where the Spirits Take Their Flight'.

In some stories, it is possible to journey into the underworld and then return to life. This is a dangerous task, however, that leaves the body unoccupied and unguarded. In one story a man instructs his brothers to leave his body unburied no matter how much time goes by. His spirit journeys to the underworld, but upon his return he discovers that his brothers have buried him, leaving him unable to return to his body. The man is forced to roam as a restless ghost.

INCANTATIONS AND SORCERY

Throughout Polynesian stories we find references to incantations. Hawaiian legends especially have a long history of magic, though they can be found across cultures. This extraordinary skill may be referred to as shamanism, magic or sorcery, but is most frequently called incantations. Practitioners were known in Hawai'i as *kahunas*, the term for a master of any craft or profession. A similar word, *tohunga*, is found in Māori culture.

Sorcery and incantations may be performed by gods, demigods and mortals alike. They were perhaps most commonly utilized by those with a touch of the divine, including priests, who had a proximity and devotion to the gods. Māui uses incantations to change his shape, while his mother Hina chants incantations to give her son strength during a battle.

Incantations are invoked in these stories for a variety of reasons. They can transform a person into an insect or animal, or can bring about invisibility. Incantations are used during ocean voyages to improve the weather or to summon storms. Their uses are as diverse as the stories in which they are found.

A VOYAGE THROUGH HISTORY

Polynesian legends offer a glimpse into the past. They show us a people who valued family, duty, strength and compassion. Bravery is demonstrated through voyages undertaken centuries ago. Adventurous spirits travel to new lands and do battle with fantastical monsters. Gods walk among mortals and bless their lines with divine gifts. Ancient clans settle their homeland and expand into civilizations. History and legends co-mingle into a beautiful story still remembered today.

These stories are important not only for the history they allow us to glimpse, but also for the way in which they connect the individual with society. Families draw closer to their ancestors through genealogies. Reverence for the land is taught through stories of its creation. Respect for the ocean stems from the tales of the life it offers us.

There is a reason that Polynesian legends are still told today – a reason that they survived hundreds of years of oral retellings before finally being transcribed. It is the same reason early European settlers recorded these stories for the first time, and the same reason that you hold this book in your hands.

These stories *matter*.

They tell of values that we still hold dear. Friendship and brotherhood among tribemates. The duty and filial piety we have for our parents. A son's love for his mother. A father's grief for his slain sons. Respect for our ancestors and the importance of remembering those who came before us. A reverence for the land and the history of our people. The joy of song, of dance, of good food and companionship.

These legends seek to answer the questions that mankind is still asking, thousands of years later. Why are we here? Where do we go when we die? What lies beyond the horizon? What new lands are there to explore?

Humanity is still seeking the answers to these questions. You may find answers of your own in these stories.

Andromeda Wellspring

FURTHER READING

A Note on Resources

Many of the earliest written accounts of Polynesian culture and religion come from Western settlers. These offer a rare glimpse into a time frame before Polynesian written records, but several demonstrate ethnocentrism and are written from a colonizer's point of view. Many are still invaluable narratives and form the bulk of the stories in this book. Where possible, resources by indigenous authors have been included in the below list.

Beckwith, Martha Warren, *Hawaiian Mythology* (University of Hawai'i Press, 1982).

Drake, Tuki, *Mata Austronesia: Stories from an Ocean World* (University of Hawai'i Press, 2022).

Fischer, Steven Roger, *Island at the End of the World: The Turbulent History of Easter Island* (Reaktion Books, 2006).

Grey, Sir George, *Polynesian Mythology and Ancient Traditional History of the New Zealand Race, as Furnished by Their Priests and Chiefs* (John Murray, 1855).

Herman, B., C. Steubel and A. Kramer, *Tala o le Vavau: The Myths, Legends, and Customs of Old Samoa* (University of Hawai'i Press, 1989).

Hīroa, Te Rangi, *Vikings of the Sunrise* (Oratia Books, 2024).

Kamakau, Samuel Manaiakalani, *The Works of the People of Old: Nā Hana A Ka Po'e Kahiko* (Bishop Museum Press, 1964).

Kāne, Herb Kawainui, *In Search of the Ancient Polynesian*

Voyaging Canoe (https://archive.hokulea.com/ike/kalai_waa/kane_search_voyaging_canoe.html, 1998).

Kāretu, Sir Tīmoti, *Haka! The Dance of a Noble People* (Reed, 1993).

Kirch, Patrick Vinton, *On the Road of the Winds: An Archaeological History of the Pacific Islands Before European Contact, Revised and Expanded Edition* (University of California Press, 2017).

Māhina, ʻOkusitino, *The Tongan Traditional History Tala-Ē-Fonua: A Vernacular Ecology-Centered Historico-Cultural Concept* (Australian National University, 1992).

Ryan, Tom, *'Le Président des Terres Australes': Charles de Brosses and the French Enlightenment, Beginnings of Oceanic Anthropology 157–86* (The Journal of Pacific History, vol. 37, issue 2, 2002).

Saura, Bruno, *A Fish Named Tahiti: Myths and Power in Ancient Polynesia (Tahiti, Raʻiātea, Hawaiʻi, Aotearoa New Zealand)*, translated by Lorenz Gonschor (Maison des Sciences l'Homme du Pacifique, 2022).

Westervelt, William Drake, *Hawaiian Legends of Ghosts and Ghost-Gods* (Mutual Pub. Co., 1999).

Westervelt, William Drake, *Legends of Ma-ui – a demi god of Polynesia* (The Hawaiian Gazette Co. Ltd., 1910).

Andromeda Wellspring is the writer of MythDancer, a blog that shares world mythology with modern audiences. They majored in ancient history and have a profound love of storytelling through the ages. Under their birth name of Natasha Cover, they are the author of *Same Stories Different Storytellers: Myth Patterns Across Civilizations*, along with several works of fiction. They presented on a college panel about mythology's influence on pop culture. They live in Illinois with their husband and a menagerie of critters, and love consuming stories in all of their formats.

TALES OF CREATION

Polynesian creation legends begin with violence. The earth and sky are torn asunder, unwillingly cleaved apart from one another. From darkness, light is forced into being. Parents are overthrown by their children; brother fights brother. Despite these violent origins there is also beauty and familial devotion.

Here we see the earth described as the warm embrace of a loving mother. A loyal son collects the stars to decorate his father and the trees and lakes to clothe his mother. A demigod is welcomed into heaven, then returned to earth with his father's blessing to lead his tribe.

Here, too, we see stories of lovers ripped apart by those around them. Jealousy and anger lead to fratricide. Friends and family betray and deceive one another. The violence of man, of gods and of storms colour these early legends.

Through it all, mankind stands tall. We are introduced as the children of the gods, able to trace our lineage back to divine parents. Humanity strives and attains dominion over fish, animal, land and sea. Crops are cultivated, trees felled, tools and boats crafted. We journey across the ocean and discover new lands, settling them and creating a home.

These are the stories of creation.

THE CHILDREN OF HEAVEN AND EARTH
Ko Nga Tama A Rangi - A Tradition Relating
to the Origin of the Human Race

Men had but one pair of primitive ancestors; they sprang from the vast heaven that exists above us, and from the earth which lies beneath us. According to the traditions of our race, Rangi and Papa, or Heaven and Earth, were the source from which, in the beginning, all things originated. Darkness then rested upon the heaven and upon the earth, and they still both clave together, for they had not yet been rent apart; and the children they had begotten were ever thinking amongst themselves what might be the difference between darkness and light; they knew that beings had multiplied and increased, and yet light had never broken upon them, but it ever continued dark. Hence these sayings are found in our ancient religious services: 'There was darkness from the first division of time, unto the tenth, to the hundredth, to the thousandth', that is, for a vast space of time; and these divisions of times were considered as beings, and were each termed a Pō; and on their account there was as yet no world with its bright light, but darkness only for the beings which existed.

At last the beings who had been begotten by Heaven and Earth, worn out by the continued darkness, consulted amongst themselves, saying: 'Let us now determine what we should do with Rangi and Papa, whether it would be better to slay them or to rend them apart.' Then spoke Tū-matauenga, the fiercest of the children of Heaven and Earth: 'It is well, let us slay them.'

Then spake Tāne-mahuta, the father of forests and of all things that inhabit them, or that are constructed from trees: 'Nay, not so. It is better to rend them apart, and to let the heaven stand far above us, and the earth lie under out feet. Let the sky become as a stranger to us, but the earth remain close to us as our nursing mother.'

The brothers all consented to this proposal, with the exception of Tāwhiri-mā-tea, the father of winds and storms, and he, fearing that his kingdom was about to be overthrown, grieved greatly at the thought of his parents being torn apart. Five of the brothers willingly consented to the separation of their parents, but one of them would not agree to it.

Hence, also, these sayings of old are found in our prayers: 'Darkness, darkness, light, light, the seeking, the searching, in chaos, in chaos'; these signified the way in which the offspring of heaven and earth sought for some mode of dealing with their parents, so that human beings might increase and live.

So, also, these sayings of old time. 'The multitude, the length', signified the multitude of the thoughts of the children of Heaven and Earth, and the length of time they considered whether they should slay their parents, that human beings might be called into existence; for it was in this manner that they talked and consulted amongst themselves.

But at length their plans having been agreed on, lo, Rongo-mā-tāne, the god and father of the cultivated food of man, rises up, that he may rend apart the heavens and the earth; he struggles, but he rends them not apart. Lo, next, Tangaroa, the god and father of fish and reptiles, rises up, that he may rend apart the heavens and the earth; he also struggles, but he rends them not apart. Lo, next, Haumia-tikitiki, the god and father of the food of man which springs without cultivation, rises up and struggles, but ineffectually. Lo, then, Tū-matauenga, the god and father of fierce human beings, rises up and struggles, but he, too, fails in his efforts. Then, at last, slowly uprises Tāne-mahuta, the god and father of forests, of birds, and of insects, and he struggles with his parents; in vain he strives to rend them apart with his hands and arms. Lo, he pauses; his head is now firmly planted on his mother the earth, his feet he raises up and rests against his father the skies, he strains his back and limbs with mighty effort. Now are rent apart Rangi and Papa, and with cries and groans of woe they shriek aloud: 'Wherefore slay you thus your parents? Why commit you so dreadful a crime as to slay us, as to rend your parents apart?' But Tāne-mahuta pauses not, he regards not their shrieks and cries; far, far beneath him he presses down the earth; far, far above him he thrusts up the sky.

Hence these sayings of olden time: 'It was the fierce thrusting of Tāne which tore the heaven from the earth, so that they were rent apart, and darkness was made manifest, and so was the light.'

No sooner was heaven rent from earth than the multitude of human beings were discovered whom they had begotten, and who had hitherto lain concealed between the bodies of Rangi and Papa.

Then, also, there arose in the breast of Tāwhiri-mā-tea, the god and father of winds and storms, a fierce desire to wage war with his brothers, because they had rent apart their common parents. He from the first had refused to consent to his mother being torn from her lord and children; it was his brothers alone that wished for this separation, and desired that Papa-tu-a-nuku, or the earth alone, should be left as a parent for them.

The god of hurricanes and storms dreads also that the world should become too fair and beautiful, so he rises, follows his father to the realm above, and hurries to the sheltered hollows in the boundless skies; there he hides and clings, and nestling in this place of rest he consults long with his parent, and as the vast Heaven listens to the suggestions of Tāwhiri-mā-tea, thoughts and plans are formed in his breast, and Tāwhiri-mā-tea also understands what he should do. Then by himself and the vast Heaven were begotten his numerous brood, and they rapidly increased and grew. Ta-whiri-ma-tea despatches one of them to the westward, and one to the southward, and one to the eastward, and one to the northward; and he gives corresponding names to himself and to his progeny the mighty winds.

He next sends forth fierce squalls, whirlwinds, dense clouds, massy clouds, dark clouds, gloomy thick clouds, fiery clouds, clouds which precede hurricanes, clouds of fiery black, clouds reflecting glowing red light, clouds wildly drifting from all quarters and wildly bursting, clouds of thunder storms, and clouds hurriedly flying. In the midst of these Tāwhiri-mā-tea himself sweeps wildly on. Alas! alas! then rages the fierce hurricane; and whilst Tāne-mahuta and his gigantic forests still stand, unconscious and unsuspecting, the blast of the breath of the mouth of Tāwhiri-mā-tea smites them, the gigantic trees are snapt off right in the middle; alas! alas! they are rent to atoms, dashed to the earth, with boughs and branches torn and scattered, and lying on the earth, trees and branches all alike left for the insect, for the grub, and for loathsome rottenness.

From the forests and their inhabitants Tāwhiri-mā-tea next swoops down upon the seas, and lashes in his wrath the ocean. Ah! ah! waves steep as cliffs arise, whose summits are so lofty that to look from them would make the beholder giddy; these soon eddy in whirlpools, and Tangaroa, the god of ocean, and father of all that dwell therein, flies affrighted through his seas; but before he fled, his children consulted together how they might secure their safety, for Tangaroa had begotten Punga, and he had begotten two children, Ika-tere, the father of fish, and Tu-te-wehiwehi, or Tu-te-wanawana, the father of reptiles.

When Tangaroa fled for safety to the ocean, then Tu-te-wehiwehi and Ika-tere, and their children, disputed together as to what they should do to escape from the storms, and Tu-te-wehiwehi and his party cried aloud: 'Let us fly inland'; but Ika-tere and his party cried aloud: 'Let us fly to the sea.' Some would not obey one order, some would not obey the other, and they escaped in two parties: the party of Tu-te-wehiwehi, or the reptiles, hid themselves ashore; the party of Punga rushed to the sea. This is what, in our ancient religious services, is called the separation of Ta-whiri-ma-tea.

Hence these traditions have been handed down:

'Ika-tere, the father of things which inhabit water, cried aloud to Tu-te-wehiwehi: 'Ho, ho, let us all escape to the sea.'

'But Tu-te-wehiwehi shouted in answer: 'Nay, nay, let us rather fly inland.'

Then Ika-tere warned him, saying: 'Fly inland, then; and the fate of you and your race will be, that when they catch you, before you are cooked, they will 6inge off your scales over a lighted wisp of dry fern.'

'But Tu-te-wehiwehi answered him, saying: 'Seek safety, then, in the sea; and the future fate of your race will be, that when they serve out little baskets of cooked vegetable food to each person you will be laid upon the top of the food to give a relish to it.'

Then without delay these two races of beings separated. The fish fled in confusion to the sea, the reptiles sought safety in the forests and scrubs.'

Tangaroa, enraged at some of his children deserting him, and, being sheltered by the god of the forests on dry land, has ever since waged war on his brother Tāne, who, in return, has waged war against him.

Hence Tāne supplies the offspring of his brother Tū-matauenga with canoes, with spears and with fish-hooks made from his trees, and with nets woven from his fibrous plants, that they may destroy the offspring of Tangaroa; whilst Tangaroa, in return, swallows up the offspring of Tāne, overwhelming canoes with the surges of his sea, swallowing up the lands, trees, and houses that are swept off by floods, and ever wastes away, with his lapping waves, the shores that confine him, that the giants of the forests may be washed down and swept out into his boundless ocean, that he may then swallow up the insects, the young birds, and the various animals which inhabit them – all which things are recorded in the prayers which were offered to these gods.

Tāwhiri-mā-tea next rushed on to attack his brothers Rongo-mā-tāne and Haumia-tikitiki, the gods and progenitors of cultivated and uncultivated food; but Papa, to save these for her other children, caught them up, and hid them in a place of safety; and so well were these children of hers concealed by their mother Earth, that Tāwhiri-mā-tea sought for them in vain.

Tāwhiri-mā-tea having thus vanquished all his other brothers, next rushed against Tū-matauenga, to try his strength against his; he exerted all his force against him, but he could neither shake him nor prevail against him. What did Tū-matauenga care for his brother's wrath? He was the only one of the whole party of brothers who had planned the destruction of their parents, and had shown himself brave and fierce in war; his brothers had yielded at once before the tremendous assaults of Tāwhiri-mā-tea and his progeny – Tāne-mahuta and his offspring had been broken and torn in pieces – Tangaroa and his children had fled to the depths of the ocean or the recesses of the shore – Rongo-mā-tāne and Haumia-tikitiki had been hidden from him in the earth – but Tū-matauenga, or man, still stood erect and unshaken upon the breast of his mother Earth; and now at length the hearts of Heaven and of the god of storms became tranquil, and their passions were assuaged.

Tū-matauenga, or fierce man, having thus successfully resisted his brother, the god of hurricanes and storms, next took thought how he could turn upon his brothers and slay them, because they had not assisted him or fought bravely when Tāwhiri-mā-tea had attacked them to avenge the separation of their parents, and because they had left him alone to show his prowess in the fight. As yet death had no power over man. It was not until the birth of the children of Taranga and of Makea-tu-tara, of Māui-taha, of Māui-roto, of Māui-pae, of Māui-waho, and of Māui-tikitiki-o-Taranga, the demigod who tried to drain Hine-nui-te-pō, that death had power over men. If that goddess had not been deceived by Māui-tikitiki, men would not have died, but would in that case have lived for ever; it was from his deceiving Hine-nui-te-pō that death obtained power over mankind, and penetrated to every part of the earth.

Tū-matauenga continued to reflect upon the cowardly manner in which his brothers had acted, in leaving him to show his courage alone, and he first sought some means of injuring Tāne-mahuta, because he had not come to aid him in his combat with Tāwhiri-mā-tea, and partly because he was aware that Tāne had had a numerous progeny, who were rapidly increasing, and might at last prove hostile to him, and injure him, so he began to collect leaves of the whanake tree, and twisted them into nooses, and when his work was ended, he went to the forest to put up his snares, and hung them up – ha! ha! the children of Tāne fell before him, none of them could any longer fly or move in safety.

Then he next determined to take revenge on his brother Tangaroa, who had also deserted him in the combat; so he sought for his offspring, and found them leaping or swimming in the water; then he cut many leaves from the flax-plant, and netted nets with the flax, and dragged these, and hauled the children of Tangaroa ashore.

After that, he determined also to be revenged upon his brothers Rongo-mā-tāne and Haumia-tikitiki; he soon found them by their peculiar leaves, and he scraped into shape a wooden hoe, and plaited a basket, and dug in the earth and pulled up all kinds of plants with edible roots, and the plants which had been dug up withered in the sun.

Thus Tū-matauenga devoured all his brothers, and consumed the whole of them, in revenge for their having deserted him and left him to fight alone against Tāwhiri-mā-tea and Rangi.

When his brothers had all thus been overcome by Tū, he assumed several names, namely, Tū-ka-riri, Tū-ka-nguha, Tū-ka-taua, Tū-whaka-heke-tan-gata, Tū-mata-whā-iti, and Tū-matauenga; he assumed one name for each of his attributes displayed in the victories over his brothers. Four of his brothers were entirely deposed by him, and became his food; but one of them, Tāwhiri-mā-tea, he could not vanquish or make common, by eating him for food, so he, the last born child of Heaven and Earth, was left as an enemy for man, and still, with a rage equal to that of Man, this elder brother ever attacks him in storms and hurricanes, endeavouring to destroy him alike by sea and land.

Now, the meanings of these names of the children of the Heaven and Earth are as follows:

Tangaroa signifies fish of every kind; Rongo-mā-tāne signifies the sweet potato, and all vegetables cultivated as food; Haumia-tikitiki signifies fern root, and all kinds of food which grow wild; Tāne-mahuta signifies forests, the birds and insects which inhabit them, and all things fashioned from wood; Tāwhiri-mā-tea signifies winds and storms; and Tū-matauenga signifies man.

Four of his brothers having, as before stated, been made common, or articles of food, by Tū-matauenga, he assigned for each of them fitting incantations, that they might be abundant, and that he might easily obtain them.

Some incantations were proper to Tāne-mahuta, they were called Tāne.

Some incantations were for Tangaroa, they were called Tangaroa.

Some were for Rongo-mā-tāne, they were called Rongo-mā-tāne.

Some were for Haumia-tikitiki, they were called Haumia.

The reason that he sought out these incantations was, that his brothers might be made common by him, and serve for his food. There were also incantations for Tāwhiri-mā-tea to cause favourable winds, and prayers to the vast Heaven for fair weather, as also for mother Earth that she might produce all things abundantly. But it was the great God that taught these prayers to man. There were also many prayers and incantations composed for man, suited to the different times and circumstances of his life – prayers at the baptism of an infant; prayers for abundance of food, for wealth; prayers in illness; prayers to spirits, and for many other things.

The bursting forth of the wrathful fury of Ta-whiri-ma-tea against his brothers, was the cause of the disappearance of a great part of the dry land; during that contest a great part of mother Earth was submerged. The names of those beings of ancient days who submerged so large a portion of the earth were – Terrible-rain, Long-continued-rain, Fierce-hail-storms; and their progeny were, Mist, Heavy-dew, and Light-dew, and these together submerged the greater part of the earth, so that only a small portion of dry land projected above the sea.

From that time clear light increased upon the earth, and all the beings which were hidden between Rangi and Papa before they were separated, now multiplied upon the earth. The first beings begotten by Rangi and Papa were not like human beings; but Tū-matauenga bore the likeness of a man, as did all his brothers, as also did a Pō, a Ao, a Kore, te Kimihanga and Runuku, and thus it continued until the times of Ngainui and his generation, and of Whiro-te-tupua and his generation, and of Tiki-tawhito-ariki and his generation, and it has so continued to this day.

The children of Tū-matauenga were begotten on this earth, and they increased, and continued to multiply, until we reach at last the generation of Māui-taha, and of his brothers Māui-roto, Māui-waho, Māui-pae, and Māui-tikitiki-o-Taranga.

Up to this time the vast Heaven has still ever remained separated from his spouse the earth. Yet their mutual love still continues – the soft warm sighs of her loving bosom still ever rise up to him, ascending from the woody mountains and valleys, and men call these mists; and the vast Heaven, as he mourns through the long nights his separation from his beloved, drops frequent tears upon her bosom, and men seeing these, term them dewdrops.

TĀNE – THE CREATION OF NATURE

The Godpower of Tāne lifted his father Rangi high above the mountains – oh, high above the mountains, clad in snow he lifted him with the help of the gods who dwelled above the earth.

Ah, bare now was Rangi and naked – oh, he was beautiful and vast, but lonely and bare, and Tāne adorned him with the stars; oh, then was Rangi very beautiful indeed!

From his great work Tāne was resting upon earth while his eyes were wandering over his mother, and his heart grew sad again, for he beheld that she lay naked under the eyes of Rangi and the gods.

Ah, his love for his mother was great, and he pressed his head to her bosom and spoke: 'Oh, mother, I will not that you sorrow any more over your nakedness for I will adorn you with great beauty; do not sorrow any longer, oh mother, Papa.'

Thereupon he went into the Great Distance, and became the father of the lakes, the Water of the Many Faces; and many of these glittering faces he distributed over Papa. Faces, smiling at Rangi by day, and blushing up to him at every new morning – look my good friend, how the Moana-Rarapa is reflecting the beauty of Mahiku-rangi whilst Rangi is laughing down upon Papa out of his Eye of Day: ah, are they not lovers?

But again Tāne wandered into the Great Distance, till he found the Gentle Noise of Air; and taking her to wife, he founded the family of the Multitude of Trees. Their sons were the Totara-tree, the Manuka, the Rimu, and the Kauri-tree: ah, look at the tree under which we are resting; see the majestic beauty of the Kauri, the child of Tāne! And their daughters were the Kahiku, and the creeper and the vines.

Whilst the Multitude of Trees were growing up into maturity, Tāne rested not till he found the two sisters, the Wanderer in the Sky, and the Wanderer in the Brook, and they gave him his children, the birds.

There, friend, do you hear the sweet sounds? There? – there now; everywhere – ah, it is the black Tui; and there, do you hear the gentle noise and soft clapping of wings over our heads? It is the folk of the Kererus, the wild doves; ha, listen to their happiness! Come farther into the green shade, my good friend, that your heart may be filled with the beauty of Tāne.

Yes, my friend, when Tāne had founded these families, then he took them back to her who was still lying lonely and naked, and now he began his great work. Ah, let us wander under the shade of Tāne, that your eyes may see how the Multitude

46

of Trees are covering Papa like a beautiful garment, spreading shades and giving happiness to the children of Tiki; perceive in the wonderful garment the great god-power of Tāne-mahuta.

Close your eyes, my good friend, that Ngāwai may show to your mind the path upon which it may perceive how Tāne distributed the multitude of his children over the earth. Ah, – ha, – can you perceive how he puts their feet into the ground? Ha, ha! They will not stand! They lift their heads up to Rangi and cry, and will go whither it pleases them; ha, ha, my friend, they are rebellious, and fight with each other, and run away, for they do not like to stand and grow, and give garment and coolness to Papa, ha, ha!

Ah, can you perceive how Tāne looks upon his work of the first day, and sees the rebellion? Can you perceive his rage, the terrible rage of the god? – ha, ha!

Ah, he is wending his way back, tearing his children out of the ground and throwing them down, tearing and throwing, and then, when the sacred colour appeared again at Mahiku-rangi, he began his great work over again! Ha, ha, my friend, ha, ha, can you perceive how he began his work? Listen: he took his children and put them into the ground again, but, ha, ha, oh, he put their heads now into the ground, so that they must stand upright and stretch their feet up to Rangi; ha, ha, could they move now? – and fight? – and run away? Ah – their hair commenced to grow into the earth and took root, and their mouth drank the dew – the tears of Rangi for Papa – and sent it up into the limbs and feet as strength and life, and the feet grew long and branched off and covered themselves with leaves. Ha, my good friend!

Ah, my good friend, when Tāne saw his children now, then came joy to his heart, and all over Papa he planted his children, and they grew, and took the earth to their mother.

Oh, beautifully now was Papa dressed in her vast garment, and greater still grew the love of Rangi, and he sent the rays of his Eye of Day down upon her, and created the flowers.

O, my friend, follow Ngāwai into the darkness and the pleasures of Tāne-mahuta's creation; look, all the life of the forests and all the life in the air is his, ah, he is the great friend of man, he is the god-power of Nature.

Tāne, the great son of Rangi.

Tāne, who loved Papa.

Tāne, the friend of man.

A soft murmuring was Ngāwai's voice, murmuring to the leaves of the trees; murmuring of that what the birds had told her; murmuring to the spirits of the forest, who all are children of Tāne-mahuta.

THE DISCOVERY OF NEW ZEALAND
The Legend of Poutini and Whaiapi

Now pay attention to the cause of the contention which arose between Poutini and Whaiapu, which led them to emigrate to New Zealand. For a long time they both rested in the same place, and Hine-tu-a-hoānga, to whom the stone Whaiapu belonged, became excessively enraged with Ngahue, and with his stone Poutini.

At last she drove Ngahue out and forced him to leave the place, and Ngahue departed and went to a strange land, taking his jasper. When Heni-tu-a-hoānga saw that he was departing with his precious stone, she followed after them, and Ngahue arrived at Tūhua with his stone, and Hine-tu-a-hoānga arrived and landed there at the same time with him, and began to drive him away again. Then Ngahue went to seek a place where his jasper stones might remain in peace, and he found in the sea this island Aotearoa (the northern island of New Zealand), and he thought he would land there.

Then he thought again, lest he and his enemy should be too close to one another, and should quarrel again, that it would be better for him to go farther off with his jasper, a very long way off. So he carried it off with him, and they coasted along, and at length arrived at Arahura (on the west coast of the middle island), and he made that an everlasting resting-place for his jasper; then he broke off a portion of his jasper, and took it with him and returned, and as he coasted along he at length reached Wairere (believed to be upon the east coast of the northern island), and he visited Whangaparāoa and Tauranga, and from thence he returned direct to Hawaiki, and reported that he had discovered a new country which produced the moa and jasper in abundance. He now manufactured sharp axes from his jasper; two axes were made from it, Tutauru and Hau-hau-te-rangi. He manufactured some portions of one piece of it into images for neck ornaments, and some portions into ear ornaments; the name of one of these ear ornaments was Kaukaumatua, which was recently in the possession of Te Heuheu, and was only lost in 1846, when he was killed with so many of his tribe by a landslip. The axe Tutauru was only lately lost by Purahokura and his brother Reretai, who were descended from Tama-ihu-toroa. When Ngahue returning, arrived again in Hawaiki, he found them all engaged in war, and when they heard his description of the beauty of this country of Aotea, some of them determined to come here.

Construction of Canoes to Emigrate to New Zealand

They then felled a totara tree in Rarotonga, which lies on the other side of Hawaiki, that they might build the Arawa from it. The tree was felled, and thus the canoe was hewn out from it and finished. The names of the men who built this canoe were, Rata, Wahie-roa, Ngahue, Parata, and some other skilful men, who helped to hew out the Arawa and to finish it.

Preparations to Emigrate

A chief of the name of Hotu-roa, hearing that the Arawa was built, and wishing to accompany them, came to Tama-te-kapua and asked him to lend him his workmen to hew out some canoes for him too, and they went and built and finished the Tainui and some other canoes.

The workmen above mentioned are those who built the canoes in which our forefathers crossed the ocean to this island, to Aotea-roa. The names of the canoes were as follows: the Arawa was first completed, then Tainui, then Matatua, and Tākitumu, and Kura-hau-pō, and Toko-maru, and Matawhaorua. These are the names of the canoes in which our forefathers departed from Hawaiki, and crossed to this island. When they had lashed the topsides on to the Tainui, Rata slew the son of Manaia, and hid his body in the chips and shavings of the canoes. The names of the axes with which they hewed out these canoes were Hauhau-te-Rangi, and Tutauru. Tutauru was the axe with which they cut off the head of Uenuku.

All these axes were made from the block of green stone brought back by Ngahue to Hawaiki, which was called 'The fish of Ngahue'. He had previously come to these islands from Hawaiki, when he was driven out from thence by Hine-tu-a-hoānga, whose fish or stone was Obsidian. From that cause Ngahue came to these islands; the canoes which afterwards arrived here came in consequence of his discovery.

THE VOYAGE TO NEW ZEALAND

When the canoes were built and ready for sea, they were dragged afloat, the separate lading of each canoe was collected and put on board, with all the crews. Tama-te-kapua then remembered that he had no skilful priest on board his canoe, and he thought the best thing he could do was to outwit Ngātoro-i-rangi, the chief who had command of the Tainui. So just as his canoe shoved off, he called out to Ngātoro: 'I say, Ngātoro, just come on board my canoe, and perform the necessary religious rites for me.' Then the priest Ngātoro came on board, and Tama-te-kapua said to him: 'You had better also call your wife, Kearoa on board, that she may make the canoe clean or common, with an offering of sea-weed to be laid in the canoe instead of an offering of fish, for you know the second fish caught in a canoe, or seaweed, or some substitute, ought to be offered for the females, the first for the males; then my canoe will be quite common, for all the ceremonies will have been observed, which should be followed with canoes made by priests.' Ngātoro assented to all this, and called his wife, and they both go into Tama's canoe. The very moment they were on board, Tama' called out to the men on board his canoe: 'Heave up the anchors and make sail'; and he carried off with him Ngātoro and his wife, that he might have a priest and wise man on board his canoe. Then they up with the fore-sail, the main-sail, and the mizen, and away shot the canoe. Up then came Ngātoro from below, and said:

'Shorten sail, that we may go more slowly, lest I miss my own canoe.' And Tama' replied: 'Oh, no, no; wait a little, and your canoe will follow after us.' For a short time it kept near them, but soon dropped more and more astern, and when darkness overtook them, on they sailed, each canoe proceeding on its own course.

Two thefts were upon this occasion perpetrated by Tama-te-kapua; he carried off the wife of Ruaeo, and Ngātoro and his wife, on board the Arawa. He made a fool of Ruaeo too, for he said to him: 'Oh, Rua', you, like a good fellow, just run back to the village and fetch me my axe Tutauru, I pushed it in under the sill of the window of my house.' And Rua' was foolish enough to run back to the house. Then off went Tama' with the canoe, and when Rua' came back again, the canoe was so far off that its sails did not look much bigger than little flies. So he fell to weeping for all his goods on board the canoe, and for his wife Whakaoti-rangi, whom Tama-te-kapua had carried off as a wife for himself. Tama-te-kapua committed these two great thefts when he sailed for these islands. Hence this proverb: 'A descendant of Tama-te-kapua will steal anything he can.'

When evening came on, Rua' threw himself into the water, as a preparation for his incantations to recover his wife, and he then changed the stars of evening into the stars of morning, and those of the morning into the stars of the evening, and this was accomplished. In the meantime the Arawa scudded away far out on the ocean, and Ngātoro thought to himself: 'What a rate this canoe goes at – what a vast space we have already traversed. I know what I'll do, I'll climb up upon the roof of the house which is built on the platform joining the two canoes, and try to get a glimpse of the land in the horizon, and ascertain whether we are near it, or very far off.' But in the first place he felt some suspicions about his wife, lest Tama-te-kapua should steal her too, for he had found out what a treacherous person he was. So he took a string and tied one end of it to his wife's hair, and kept the other end of the string in his hand, and then he climbed up on the roof. He had hardly got on the top of the roof when Tama' laid hold of his wife, and he cunningly untied the end of the string which Ngātoro had fastened to her hair, and made it fast to one of the beams of the canoe, and Ngātoro feeling it tight thought his wife had not moved, and that it was still fast to her. At last Ngātoro came down again, and Tama-te-kapua heard the noise of his steps as he was coming, but he had not time to get the string tied fast to the hair of Kearoa's head again, but he jumped as fast as he could into his own berth, which was next to that of Ngātoro, and Ngātoro, to his surprise, found one end of the string tied fast to the beam of the canoe.

Then he knew that his wife had been disturbed by Tama', and he asked her, saying: 'Oh, wife, has not some one disturbed you?' Then his wife replied to him: 'Cannot you tell that from the string being fastened to the beam of the canoe?' And then he asked her: 'Who was it?' And she said: 'Who was it, indeed? Could it be any one else but Tama-te-kapua?' Then her husband said to her: 'You are a noble woman indeed thus to confess this; you have gladdened my heart by this confession; I thought after Tama' had carried us both off in this way, that he would have acted generously, and not loosely in this manner; but, since he has dealt in this way, I will now have my revenge on him.'

Then that priest again went forth upon the roof of the house and stood there, and he called aloud to the heavens, in the same way that Rua' did, and he changed the stars of the evening into those of morning, and he raised the winds that they should blow upon the prow of the canoe, and drive it astern, and the crew of the canoe were at their wits' end, and quite forgot their skill as seamen, and the canoe drew straight into the whirlpool, called 'The throat of Te Parata', and dashed right into that whirlpool.

The canoe became engulphed by the whirlpool, and its prow disappeared in it. In a moment the waters reached the first bailing place in the bows, in another second they reached the second bailing place in the centre, and the canoe now appeared to be going down into the whirlpool head foremost; then up started Hei, but before he could rise they had already sunk far into the whirlpool. Next the rush of waters was heard by Ihenga, who slept forward, and he shouted out: 'Oh, Ngātoro, oh, we are settling down head first. The pillow of your wife Kearoa has already fallen from under her head!' Ngātoro sat astern listening; the same cries of distress reached him a second time. Then up sprang Tama-te-kapua, and he in despair shouted out: 'Oh, Ngātoro, Ngātoro, aloft there! Do you hear?' The canoe is gone down so much by the bow, that Kearoa's pillow has rolled from under her head.' The priest heard them, but neither moved nor answered until he heard the goods rolling from the decks and splashing into the water; the crew meanwhile held on to the canoe with their hands with great difficulty, some of them having already fallen into the sea.

When these things all took place, the heart of Ngātoro was moved with pity, for he heard, too, the shrieks and cries of the men, and the weeping of the women and children. Then up stood that mighty man again, and by his incantations changed the aspect of the heavens, so that the storm ceased, and he repeated another incantation to draw the canoe back out of the whirlpool, that is, to lift it up again.

Lo, the canoe rose up from the whirlpool, floating rightly; but, although the canoe itself thus floated out of the whirlpool, a great part of its lading had been thrown out into the water, a few things only were saved, and remained in the canoe. A great part of their provisions were lost as the canoe was sinking into the whirlpool. Thence comes the native proverb, if they can give a stranger but little food, or only make a present of a small basket of food: 'Oh, it is the half-filled basket of Whakaoti-rangi, for she only managed to save a very small part of her provisions'. Then they sailed on, and landed at Whanga-Parāoa, in Aotea here. As they drew near to land, they saw with surprise some pōhutu–kawa trees of the sea-coast, covered with beautiful red flowers, and the still water reflected back the redness of the trees.

Then one of the chiefs of the canoe cried out to his messmates: 'See there, red ornaments for the head are much more plentiful in this country than in Hawaiki, so I'll throw my red head ornaments into the water'; and, so saying, he threw them into the sea. The name of that man was Tauninihi; the name of the red head ornament he threw into the sea was Taiwhakaea. The moment they got on shore they run to gather the pōhutukawa flowers, but no sooner did they touch them than the flowers fell to pieces; then they found out that these red head ornaments were nothing but flowers. All the chiefs on board the Arawa were then troubled that they should have been so foolish as to throw away their red head ornaments into the sea. Very shortly afterwards the ornaments of Tauninihi were found by Māhina on the beach of Mabiti. As soon as Tauninihi heard they had been picked up, he ran to Māhina to get them again, but Māhina would not give them up to him; thence this proverb for anything which has been lost and is found by another person: 'I will not give it up, 'tis the red head ornament which Māhina found.'

As soon as the party landed at Whanga-Parāoa, they planted sweet potatoes, that they might grow there; and they are still to be found growing on the cliffs at that place.

Then the crew, wearied from the voyage, wandered idly along the shore, and there they found the fresh carcase of a sperm whale stranded upon the beach. The Tainui had already arrived in the same neighbourhood, although they did not at first see that canoe nor the people who had come in it; when, however, they met, they began to dispute as to who had landed first and first found the dead whale, and as to which canoe it consequently belonged; so, to settle the question, they agreed to examine the sacred place which each party had set up to return thanks in to the gods for their safe arrival, that they might see which had been longest built; and, doing so, they found that the posts of the sacred place put up by the Arawa were quite green, whilst the posts of the sacred place set up by the Tainui had evidently been carefully dried over the fire before they had been fixed in the ground. The people who had come in the Tainui also showed part of a rope which they had made fast to its jawbone. When these things were seen, it was admitted that the whale belonged to the people who came in the Tainui, and it was surrendered to them. And the people in the Arawa, determining to separate from those in the Tainui, selected some of their crew to explore the country in a north-west direction, following the coastline. The canoe then coasted along, the land party following it along the shore; this was made up of a hundred and forty men, whose chief was Taikehu, and these gave to a place the name of Te Ranga of Taikehu.

The Tainui left Whanga-Parāoa shortly after the Arawa, and, proceeding nearly in the same direction as the Arawa, made the Gulf of Hauraki, and then coasted along to Rākau-mangamanga, or Cape Brett, and to the island with an arched passage through it, called Motukūkako, which lies off the cape; thence they ran along the coast to Whiwhia, and to Te Aukanapanapa, and to Muri-whenua, or the country near the North Cape. Finding that the land ended there, they returned again along the coast until they reached the Tamaki, and landed there, and afterwards proceeded up the creek to Tau-oma, or the portage, where they were surprised to see flocks of seagulls and oystercatchers passing over from the westward; so they went off to explore the country in that direction, and to their great surprise found a large sheet of water lying immediately behind them, so they determined to drag their canoes over the portage at a place they named Otahuhu, and to launch them again on the vast sheet of salt-water which they had found.

The first canoe which they hauled across was the Toko-maru – that they got across without difficulty. They next began to drag the Tainui over the isthmus; they hauled away at it in vain, they could not stir it; for one of the wives of Hoturoa, named Marama-kiko-hura, who was unwilling that the tired crews should proceed further on this new expedition, had by her enchantments fixed it so firmly to the earth that no human strength could stir it; so they hauled, they hauled, they excited themselves with cries and cheers, but they hauled in vain, they cried aloud in vain, they could not move it. When their strength was quite exhausted by these efforts, then another of the wives of Hoturoa, more learned in magic and incantations than Marama-kiko-hura, grieved at seeing the exhaustion and distress of her people, rose up, and chanted forth an incantation far more powerful than that of Marama-kiko-hura; then at once the canoe glided easily over the carefully laid skids, and it soon floated securely upon the harbour of Manuka. The willing crews urged on the canoes with their paddles; they soon discovered the mouth of the harbour upon the west coast, and passed out through it into the open sea; they coasted along the western coast to the southwards, and discovering the small port of Kāwhia, they entered it, and, hauling up their canoe, fixed themselves there for the time, whilst the Arawa was left at Maketu.

We now return to the Arawa. We left the people of it at Tauranga. That canoe next floated at Mōtītī ; they named that place after a spot in Hawaiki (because there was no firewood there). Next Tia, to commemorate his name, called the place now known by the name of Rangiuru, Takapu-o-tapui-ika-nui-a-Tia. Then Hei stood up and called out: 'I name that place Takapu-o-wai-tahanui-a-Hei'; the name of that place is now Otawa. Then stood up Tama-te-kapua, and pointing to the place now called the Heads of Maketu, he called out: 'I name that place Te Kuraetanga-o-te-ihu-o-Tama-te-kapua.' Next Kahu called a place, after his name, Mōtītī-nui-a-Kahu.

Ruaeo, who had already arrived at Maketu, started up. He was the first to arrive there in his canoe – the Pukeatea-wai-nui – for he had been left behind by the Arawa, and his wife Whakaoti-rangi had been carried off by Tama-te-kapua, and after the Arawa had left he had sailed in his own canoe for these islands, and landed at Maketu, and his canoe reached land first; well, he started up, cast his line into the sea, with the hooks attached to it, and they got fast in one of the beams of the Arawa, and it was pulled ashore by him (whilst the crew were asleep), and the hundred and forty men who had accompanied him stood upon the beach of Maketu, with skids all ready laid, and the Arawa was by them dragged upon the shore in the night, and left there; and Ruaeo seated himself under the side of the Arawa, and played upon his flute, and the music woke his wife, and she said: 'Dear me, that's Rua'!' – and when she looked, there he was sitting under the side of the canoe, and they passed the night together.

At last Rua' said: 'O mother of my children, go back now to your new husband, and presently I'll play upon the flute and pūtōrino, so that both you and Tama-te-kapua may hear. Then do you say to Tama-te-kapua "O! la, I had a dream in the night that I heard Rua playing a tune upon his flute", and that will make him so jealous that he will give you a blow, and then you can run away from him again, as if you were in a rage and hurt, and you can come to me.'

Then Whakaoti-rangi returned, and lay down by Tama-te-kapua, and she did everything exactly as Rua' had told her, and Tama' began to beat her (and she ran away from him). Early in the morning Rua' performed incantations, by which he kept all the people in the canoe in a profound sleep, and whilst they still slept from his enchantments, the sun rose, and mounted high up in the heavens. In the forenoon, Rua' gave the canoe a heavy blow with his club; they all started up; it was almost noon, and when they looked down over the edge of their canoe, there were the hundred and forty men of Rua' sitting under them, all beautifully dressed with feathers, as if they had been living on the Gannet Island, in the channel of Kārewa, where feathers are so abundant; and when the crew of the Arawa heard this, they all rushed upon deck, and saw Rua' standing in the midst of his one hundred and forty warriors.

Then Rua' shouted out as he stood: 'Come here, Tama-te-kapua; let us two fight the battle, you and I alone. If you are stronger than I am, well and good, let it be so; if I am stronger than you are, I'll dash you to the earth.'

Up sprang then the hero Tama-te-kapua; he held a carved two-handed sword, a sword the handle of which was decked with red feathers. Rua' held a similar weapon. Tama' first struck a fierce blow at Rua'. Rua' parried it, and it glanced harmlessly off; then Rua' threw away his sword, and seized both the arms of Tama-te-kapua; he held his arms and his sword, and dashed him to the earth. Tama' half rose, and was again dashed down; once more he almost rose, and was thrown again. Still Tama' fiercely struggled to rise and renew the fight. For the fourth time he almost rose up, then Rua', overcome with rage, took a heap of vermin (this he had prepared for the purpose, to cover Tama' with insult and shame), and rubbed them on Tama-te–kapua's head and ear, and they adhered so fast that Tama' tried in vain to get them out.

Then Rua' said: 'There, I've beaten you; now keep the woman, as a payment for the insults I've heaped upon you, and for having been beaten by me.' But Tama' did not hear a word he said; he was almost driven mad with the pain and itching, and could do nothing but stand scratching and rubbing his head; whilst Rua' departed with his hundred and forty men to seek some other dwelling-place for themselves; if they had turned against Tama' and his people to fight against them, they would have slain them all.

These men were giants – Tama-te-kapua was nine feet high, Rua' was eleven feet high; there have been no men since that time so tall as those heroes.

The only man of these later times who was as tall as these was Tū-hou-rangi: he was nine feet high; he was six feet up to the armpits. This generation have seen his bones, they used to be always set up by the priests in the sacred places when they were made high places for the sacred sacrifices of the natives, at the times the potatoes and sweet potatoes were dug up, and when the fishing season commenced, and when they attacked an enemy; then might be seen the people collecting, in their best garments, and with their ornaments, on the days when the priests exposed Tū-hou-rangi's bones to their view. At the time that the island Mokoia, in the lake of Roto-rua, was stormed and taken by the Ngā-Puhi, they probably carried those bones off, for they have not since been seen.

After the dispute between Tama-te-kapua and Rua' took place, Tama' and his party dwelt at Maketu, and their descendants after a little time spread to other places. Ngātoro-i-rangi went, however, about the country, and where he found dry valleys, stamped on the earth, and brought forth springs of water; he also visited the mountains, and placed Patupaiarehe, or fairies, there, and then returned to Maketu and dwelt there.

After this a dispute arose between Tama-te-kapua and, and in consequence of that disturbance, Tama' and Ngātoro Kahu-mata-momoe removed to Tauranga, and found Taikehu living there, and collecting food for them (by fishing), and that place was called by them Te Bang a-a-Taikehu; it lies beyond Motu-hoa; then they departed from Tauranga, and stopped at Kati-kati, where they ate food. Tama's men devoured the food very fast, whilst he kept on only nibbling his, therefore they applied this circumstance as a name for the place, and called it: 'Kati-kati-o-Tama-te-kapua', the nibbling of Tama-te kapua; then they halted at Whakahau, so called because they here ordered food to be cooked, which they did not stop to eat, but went right on with

Ngātoro, and this circumstance gave its name to the place; and they went on from place to place till they arrived at Whitianga, which they so called from their crossing the river there, and they continued going from one place to another till they came to Tangiaro, and Ngātoro stuck up a stone and left it there, and they dwelt in Moehau and Hau-raki.

They occupied those places as a permanent residence, and Tama-te-kapua died, and was buried there. When he was dying, he ordered his children to return to Maketu, to visit his relations; and they assented, and went back. If the children of Tama-te-kapua had remained at Hau-raki, that place would now have been left to them as a possession.

Tama-te-kapua, when dying, told his children where the precious ear-drop Kaukau-matua was, which he had hidden under the window of his house; and his children returned with Ngātoro to Maketu, and dwelt there; and as soon as Ngātoro arrived, he went to the waters to bathe himself, as he had come there in a state of tapu, upon account of his having buried Tama-te-kapua, and having bathed, he then became free from the tapu and clean.

Ngātoro then took the daughter of Ihenga to wife, and he went and searched for the precious ear-drop Kaukau-matua, and found it, as Tama-te-kapua had told him. After this the wife of Kahu-mata-momoe conceived a child.

At this time Ihenga, taking some dogs with him to catch kiwis with, went to Paritangi by way of Hakomiti, and kiwi was chased by one of his dogs, and caught in a lake, and the dog ate some of the fish and shellfish in the lake, after diving in the water to get them, and returned to its master carrying the captured kiwi in its mouth, and on reaching its master, it dropped the kiwi, and vomited up the raw fish and shell-fish which it had eaten.

When Ihenga saw his dog wet all over, and the fish it had vomited up, he knew there was a lake there, and was extremely glad, and returned joyfully to Maketu, and there he had the usual religious ceremonies which follow the birth of a child performed over his wife and the child she had given birth to; and when this had been done, he went to explore the country which he had previously visited with his dog.

To his great surprise he discovered a lake; it was Lake Roto-iti; he left a mark there to show that he claimed it as his own. He went farther and discovered Lake Roto-rua; he saw that its waters were running; he left there also a mark to show that he claimed the lake as his own. As he went along the side of the lake; he found a man occupying the ground; then he thought to himself that he would endeavour to gain possession of it by craft, so he looked out for a spot fit for a sacred place, where men could offer up their prayers, and for another spot fit for a sacred place, where nets could be hung up, and he found fit spots; then he took suitable stones to surround the sacred place with, and old pieces of seaweed, looking as if they had years ago been employed as offerings, and he went into the middle of the shrubbery, thick with boughs of the taha shrub, of the koromuka, and of the karamu; there he stuck up the posts of the sacred place in the midst of the shrubs, and tied bunches of flax-leaves on the posts, and having done this, he went to visit the village of the people who lived there.

They saw someone approaching and cried out:

'A stranger, a stranger, is coming here!' As soon as Ihenga heard these cries, he sat down upon the ground, and then, without waiting for the people of the place to begin the speeches, he jumped up, and commenced to speak thus: 'What theft is this, what theft is this of the people here, that they are taking away my land?' – for he saw that they had their store-houses full of prepared fern-roots and of dried fish, and shell-fish, and their heaps of fishing-nets, so as he spoke, he appeared to swell with rage, and his throat appeared to grow large from passion as he talked: 'Who authorized you to come here, and take possession of my place? Be off, be off, be off! leave alone the place of the man who speaks to you, to whom it has belonged for a very long time, for a very long time indeed.'

Then Maru-punga-nui, the son of Tua-Roto-rua, the man to whom the place really belonged, said to Ihenga: 'It is not your place, it belongs to me; if it belongs to you, where is your village, where is your sacred place, where is your net, where are your cultivations and gardens?'

Ihenga answered him: 'Come here and see them.' So they went together, and ascended a hill, and Ihenga said: 'See there, there is my net hanging up against the rocks'; but it was no such thing, it was only a mark like a net hanging up, caused by part of a cliff having slipped away; and there are the posts of the pine round my village'; but there was really nothing but some old stumps of trees; look there too at my sacred place a little beyond yours; and now come with me, and see my sacred place, if you are quite sure you see my village, and my fishing-net – come along.' So they went together, and there he saw the sacred place standing in the shrubbery, until at last he believed Ihenga, and the place was all given up to Ihenga, and he took possession of it and lived there, and the descendants of Tua-Roto-rua departed from that place, and a portion of them, under the chiefs Kawa-arero and Mata-aho, occupied the island of Mokoia, in Lake Roto-rua.

At this time Ngātoro again went to stamp on the earth, and to bring forth springs in places where there was no water, and came out on the great central plains which surround Lake Taupo, where a piece of large cloak made of kiekie-leaves was stripped off by the bushes, and the strips took root, and became large trees, nearly as large as the Kahikatea tree (they are called Painanga, and many of them are growing there still).

Whenever he ascended a hill, he left marks there, to show that he claimed it; the marks he left were fairies. Some of the generation now living have seen these spirits; they are malicious spirits. If you take embers from an oven in which food has been cooked, and use them for a fire in a house, these spirits become offended; although there be many people sleeping in that house, not one of them could escape (the fairies would, whilst they slept, press the whole of them to death).

Ngātoro went straight on and rested at Taupo, and he beheld that the summit of Mount Tongariro was covered with snow, and he was seized with a longing to ascend it, and he climbed up, saying to his companions who remained below at their encampment: 'Remember now, do not you, who I am going to leave behind, taste food from the time I leave you until I return, when we will all feast together.' Then he began to ascend the mountain, but he had not quite got to the summit when those he had left behind began to eat food, and he therefore found the greatest difficulty in reaching the summit of the mountain, and the hero nearly perished in the attempt.

At last he gathered strength, and thought he could save himself, if he prayed aloud to the gods of Hawaiki to send fire to him, and to produce a volcano upon the mountain (and his prayer was answered) and fire was given to him, and the mountain became a volcano, and it came by the way of Whakaari, or White Island, of Mau-tohora, of Okakaru, of Roto-ehu, of Roto-iti, of Roto-rua, of Tara-wera, of Pae-roa, of Orakeikorako, and of

Taupo; it came right underneath the earth, spouting up at all the above-mentioned places, and ascended right up Tongariro, to him who was sitting upon the top of the mountain, and thence the hero was revived again, and descended, and returned to Maketu, and dwelt there.

The Arawa had been laid up by its crew at Maketu, where they landed, and the people who had arrived with the party in the Arawa spread themselves over the country, examining it, some penetrating to Roto-rua, some to Taupo, some to Whanganui, some to Ruatāhuna, and no one was left at Maketu but Hei' and his son, and Tia and his son, and the usual place of residence of Ngātoro-i-rangi was on the island of Mōtītī. The people who came with the Tainui were still in Kāwhia, where they had landed.

One of their chiefs, named Raumati, heard that the Arawa was laid up at Maketu, so he started with all his own immediate dependants, and reaching Tauranga, halted there, and in the evening again pressed on towards Maketu, and reached the bank of the river, opposite that on which the Arawa was lying, thatched over with reeds and dried branches and leaves; then he slung a dart, the point of which was bound round with combustible materials, over to the other side of the river; the point of the dart was lighted, and it stuck right in the dry thatch of the roof over the Arawa, and the shed of dry stuff taking fire, the canoe was entirely destroyed.

On the night that the Arawa was burnt by Raumati, there was not a person left at Maketu; they wore all scattered in the forests, at Tapu-ika, and at Waitaha, and Ngātoro-i-rangi was at that moment at his residence on the island of Mōtītī. The pa, or fortified village at Maketu, was left quite empty, without a soul in it. The canoe was lying alone, with none to watch it; they had all gone to collect food of different kinds – it happened to be a season in which food was very abundant, and from that cause the people were all scattered in small parties about the country, fishing, fowling, and collecting food.

As soon as the next morning dawned, Raumati could see that the fortified village of Maketu was empty, and not a person left in it, so he and his armed followers at once passed over the river and entered the village, which they found entirely deserted.

At night, as the Arawa burnt, the people, who were scattered about in the various parts of the country, saw the fire, for the bright glare of the gleaming flames was reflected in the sky, lighting up the heavens, and they all thought that it was the village at Maketu that had been burnt; but those persons who were near Waitaha and close to the sea-shore near where the Arawa was, at once said: 'That must be the Arawa which is burning; it must have been accidentally set on fire by some of our friends who have come to visit us.' The next day they went to see what had taken place, and when they reached the place where the Arawa had been lying, they found it had been burnt by an enemy, and that nothing but the ashes of it were left them. Then a messenger started to all the places where the people were scattered about, to warn them of what had taken place, and they then first heard the bad news.

The children of Hou, as they discussed in their house of assembly the burning of the Arawa, remembered the proverb of their father, which he spake to them as they were on the point of leaving Hawaiki, and when he bid them farewell.

He then said to them: 'My children, Mako, O Tia, O Hei, hearken to these my words: There was but one great chief in Hawaiki, and that was Whakatauihu. Now do you, my dear children, depart in peace, and when you reach the place you are going to, do not follow after the deeds of Tu, the god of war; if you do you will perish, as if swept off by the winds, but rather follow quiet and useful occupations, then you will die tranquilly a natural death. Depart, and dwell in peace with all, leave war and strife behind you here. Depart, and dwell in peace. It is war and its evils which are driving you from hence; dwell in peace where you are going, conduct yourselves like men, let there be no quarrelling amongst you, but build up a great people.'

These were the last words which Houmai-ta-whiti addressed to his children, and they ever kept these sayings of their father firmly fixed in their hearts. 'Depart in peace to explore new homes for yourselves.'

Uenuku perhaps gave no such parting words of advice to his children, when they left him for this country, because they brought war and its evils with them from the other side of the ocean to New Zealand. But, of course, when Raumati burnt the Arawa, the descendants of Houmai-ta-whiti could not help continually considering what they ought to do, whether they should declare war upon account of the destruction of their canoe, or whether they should let this act pass by without notice. They kept these thoughts always close in mind, and impatient feelings kept ever rising up in their hearts. They could not help saying to one another: 'It was upon account of war and its consequences, that we deserted our own country, that we left our fathers, our homes, and our people, and war and evil are following after us here. Yet we cannot remain patient under such an injury, every feeling urges us to revenge this wrong.'

At last they made an end of deliberation, and unanimously agreed that they would declare war, to obtain compensation for the evil act of Raumati in burning the Arawa; and then commenced the great war which was waged between those who arrived in the Arawa and those who arrived in the Tainui.

THE CREATION OF THE STARS

Te Ra, the day-eye of Rangi is closing, and sends a last glowing look over the peacefully dreaming Moana-rarapa, the Lake of the Glittering Water.

Softly murmurs the lake and reflects the sacred Red with which Tāne once adorned the heaven, whilst over his floating colours black swans are drifting like dream-thoughts over a beautiful face. Slowly dying away in blue, deep blue and pure, is the last breath of day silently departing into the heavens.

A canoe is putting off the shore, and voices of children are heard leading it light-hearted with mirth and laughter and splashing of water over the lake, which looks clear and glittering green up to the stars. Softly now breathes the air, and the mirror is gone – the day has departed.

Muttering departs Hupene, our old friend, in dread of the darkness; with his mat he is covering our shoulders and he murmurs these words:

'Remember, while you are watching the stars on the night-mat of Rangi, and know, great is the power of the god Tāne-mahuta, and his are the stars. Remember, his are the stars.'

Bright shimmer the stars through the summer night, and the earth breathes freshness and sleep, leading the heart to rest, and it yet filling with longing; but from the heaven descends hope, promising the new day and the future.

Tāne once commenced his great wandering to find adornment for his father, the heaven, whom he beheld standing high over Papa, naked by day and lonely and cold by night, and he spoke:

'O, father Rangi, my heart is looking upon you in sorrow, for you are lonely and cold, and I will go in quest for adornments which shall make you beautiful to the eyes of Papa and her children.' Thereupon he went on his way, and, whilst he was wandering through the ten heavens, he found Te-Kura, the Red Colour, and that he took back with him upon the earth. Here he rested for seven days and seven nights, and, when his strength was growing again, he commenced his work, and covered the heaven with the beautiful red colour. But behold, when he had finished this great work and descended again to earth, he let his eyes wander over the red sky, which was stretching now over Papa, and he found that this adornment was not worthy of his great father, and full of sorrow he took it away again leaving some of it only at Mahiku-rangi, the End of Heaven. He beheld now, when Rangi was closing his great eye, sending it down into the Pō, or when he called for it again in the mornings so that it burst forth out of the Gate of Day, that the beauty of his father at Mahiku-Rangi was wonderful, but ever and ever it disappeared by day and by night.

Seven days and seven nights he was watching the dying away and bursting forth again of Rangi's beauty, and then out of his sorrow he sang these words up to his father: 'Oh, Rangi, still you are cold and dark and lonely from the first night, to the second night, to the tenth night, when your daughter Te-mārama ascends again out of the Source of Living Water, so that you look down upon Papa silent and sorrowful. What adornment can I find for you, that you may be happy and beautiful, and gladden the heart of Papa, your loved one?'

After he had spoken these words he wandered forth again upon his mighty search, and all over the world he wandered, and farther and farther still he wandered, till he came to Tawhiti-nui, the Great Distance; and farther still, till at last he came to Te-Po, the Lower World. Here he found Hine-a-te-ao, the Daughter of the Light; she is the guardian of the Gates of the Lower World, and, tired from his long journey, he slept in her house.

In the darkness of night he beheld two beautiful stars shining forth; they were the children of Ira, and their names were Lonely South, and Shore of Heaven, the morning star, and his heart was glad over their beauty, so that his eyes could not sleep, and could not but rest upon them all the night.

In the morning he called Hine-a-te-ao, and showed her the two beautiful stars shimmering forth out of the darkness of the Pō, and asked for them, for nothing could be more beautiful he thought as an adornment for his Father Rangi. Hine-a-te-ao answered: 'Go, son, and take the stars!' And again he pleaded: 'Oh, Hine, Daughter of the Light, show me the road that I may go and take the stars.' And Hine-a-te-ao answered: 'O, son, far is the way indeed! Go to the House of Tupu-renga-o-te-Pō , the Growing Night: he is the guardian over the two stars, and his house is standing at Mahiku-rangi. There ask for the two stars, whose names are Toko-meha and Te-pae-tai-o-te-rangi; go and take the stars for your father Rangi.'

After Tāne had rested, and for seven days and seven nights strengthened himself through powerful incantations and many Karakias, he went on his way to Mahiku-rangi, to the House of the Guardian of the Stars, Tupu.

When at last he had found Tupu, he pictured the sorrows and the nakedness of his father, and asked him to give the beautiful stars to Rangi, and Tupu answered: 'Oh, Tāne, son of Rangi and Papa, the stars which you behold shimmering yonder are the sacred holders of the world; they are Hira-utu, Fish by the Land, Hira-tai, Fish of the Sea; Parinuku, Cliff by the Earth, and Pari-rangi, Cliff of the Heavens. Yes, it is my wish that you may adorn Rangi with yonder stars.' And he gave him the Four Sacred Holders of the World, the stars of the four points of the compass, and then he gave him the five stars, Ao-tahi, Puaka and Tuku-rua, Tama-re-reti and Te-waka-a-tama-rereti.

All these stars Tāne took away with him and fastened the four sacred stars in the four corners of Rangi; with the other five he formed a cross in the South.

Many more stars brought Tupu, and Tāne distributed them over Rangi from the summit of the mountains whilst still the Sun was standing high in the heavens.

And again sorrow filled his heart when his eyes looked upon his work, for again he found that the adornment was not worthy of his father Rangi.

But at last he had finished his labour and that was about the time when the Sun was again entering the Gate of Night. Resting upon Papa, he watched the beautiful sacred red appear again at Mahiku-rangi, and, when with the departing sun darkness again filled the world, his wandering eyes perceived how star upon star commenced to live and shine forth, till at last Rangi in wonderful beauty was stretching over Papa, and his heart was full of joy and happiness, and he sang: 'O, father Rangi, your beauty is indescribable; in truth you are now the ariki of Papa, and all her children will love you!'

Thus had spoken the old friend on the shores of the glittering Moana-rarapa.

THE FIRST TU'I TONGA

There first appeared on the earth the human offspring of a worm or grub, and the head of the worm became Tu'i Tonga. His name was Kōhai and he was the first Tu'i Tonga in the world. The descendants of the worm became very numerous.

A large casuarina tree grew on the island of Toonangakava, between the islands of Mataaho and Talakite in the lagoon of Tongatapu. This great casuarina tree reached to the sky, and a god came down from the sky by this great tree. This god was Tangaloa Eitumatupua.

When he came down there was a woman fishing. Her name was Ilaheva and also Vaepopua. The god from the sky came to her and caught her, and they cohabited. Their sleeping place was called Mohenga.

The god ascended to the sky by the big casuarina, but again returned to the woman. They went and slept on the island of Talakite. They overslept and the day dawned. There flew by a tern, called tala, and found them. The tern cried and the god Eitumatupua awoke. He called the woman Ilaheva: 'Wake! it is day. The tern has seen us, because we overslept. Wake! It is day.' So that island was called Talakite (Tern-saw) in commemoration of the tern finding them. Another island was called Mataaho (Eye-of-day).

The god returned to the sky, but came back to the woman and they cohabited. The woman Ilaheva became pregnant and gave birth to a male child. The woman tended the child on earth, but the god dwelt in the sky. After a time the god returned and asked the woman about their child.

'Ilaheva, what is our child?' Ilaheva answered: 'A male child.' Then said the god: 'His name shall be Ahoeitu (Day-has-dawned).'

Moreover, the god asked the woman: 'Is the soil of your land clay or sand?' The woman replied: 'My place is sandy.' Then said the god: 'Wait until I throw down a piece of clay from the sky, to make a garden for the boy Ahoeitu, and also a yam for the garden of our child.'

So the god poured down the mount (near Maufanga, Tongatapu) called Holohiufi (Pour-the-yam), and brought down the yam from the sky. The name of the yam was *heketala* (slip-tern). That was the garden he brought down.

The god returned to the sky, while the woman and child remained on earth, on their land called Popua (the land to the east of Maufanga in Tongatapu, on which rises the hill Holohiufi). The mother and son lived together until the child Ahoeitu was big. Ahoeitu asked his mother: 'Vaepopua, who is my father? Tell me so that I may go some time and see him.' And the mother told him that his father was in the sky. 'What is his name?' the boy asked. 'It is Eitumatupua,' replied the mother.

The boy grew big and one day he told his mother: 'I want to go to the sky, so that I can see my father, but there is nothing for me to go in.' His mother instructed him: 'Go and climb the great casuarina, for that is the road to the sky; and see you father.' She gave him a tapa loin cloth and anointed his head with oil. When he was ready, he asked: 'How will I know my father, as I am not acquainted with his dwelling place in the sky?' His mother replied: 'You will go to the sky and proceed along the big wide road. You will see you father catching pigeons on the mound by the road.'

Ahoeitu climbed the great casuarina tree and reached the sky. He went along the road as his mother had directed, found the mound, and saw his father catching pigeons. When his father saw him approaching, he sat down because he was overpowered at seeing his son. Ahoeitu spoke when he saw his father sit down, as if paying respect to him, his own son. That is why he spoke at once to his father, saying: 'Lord, stand up. Do not sit down.'

The lad went to his father and they pressed noses and cried. Then the father asked him: 'Where have you come from?' 'I have come from earth, sent by Ilaheva, my mother, to seek you, my father Eitumatupua.' His father responded: 'Here am I,' and he put forth his hand and drew his son's head to him and again they pressed noses and cried. The god was overpowered at the realization that here was his son. Leaving the pigeon catching, they went to Eitumatupua's residence, to the house of Ahoeitu's father. There they had kava and food.

That day the celestial sons of Eitumatupua were having an entertainment. They were playing the game called *sikaulutoa* (played with a reed throwing-stick with a head of toa or casuarina wood). The god sent Ahoeitu to his brothers, saying: 'You had better go to the entertainment of your brothers, which they are having on the road in the green (*malae*).' So Ahoeitu went and looked on at the game of throwing reeds at the casuarina trunk. The people saw the lad and all gazed at him with one accord. They liked him, because he was very handsome and well formed. All of the people at the entertainment wondered who he was and whence he had come. His brothers were immediately jealous of him.

Some of the people said that they knew that he was the son of Eituma-tupua, who has just come to the sky from the earth. Then all the people of the entertainment knew, and also his brothers knew that this lad was their brother. The brothers were very angry and jealous that it should be said that this strange lad was the son of their father. They, therefore, sprang upon and tore him to pieces, then cooked and ate him. (Some accounts say his flesh was eaten uncooked.) His head was left over, so they threw it among the plants called hoi. This caused one kind of hoi to become bitter. There is another kind that is sweet. The bitter kind became so because Ahoeitu's head was thrown into it. That kind of *hoi* is not eaten, because it is poisonous.

After a little while Ahoeitu's father, Eitumatupua, said to a woman: 'Go, woman, and seek the lad at the entertainment, so that he may eat, lest he become hungry.' The woman went at once to the entertainment and asked: 'Where is Ahoeitu? The lad is wanted to come and eat.' The people answered: 'He was here walking around and observing the sika game.' They searched, but could not find him at the entertainment. So the woman returned to Eitumatupua and reported: 'The lad is not to be found.'

Eitumatupua suspected that Ahoeitu's brothers had killed the lad. Therefore, he sent a message for them to come. He asked them: 'Where is the lad?' and they lied, saying: 'We do not know.' Then their father said: 'Come and vomit.' A big wooden bowl was brought. They were told to tickle their throats, so that they would vomit up the flesh of the lad and also the blood; in fact, all the parts they had eaten. They all had their throats tickled and they vomited, filling the wooden bowl.

They were then asked: 'Where is his head?' The murderers replied: 'We threw it into the bush, into the *hoi* bush.' Then the god Eitumatupua sent a messenger to seek the head of Ahoeitu. They also collected his bones and put them together with his head into the bowl and poured water on to the flesh and blood. Then were plucked and brought the leaves of the *nonufiafia* tree. The leaves of this tree placed on a sick person possess the virtue of bringing immediate recovery, even if the person is nigh unto death. So the *nonufiafia*, or the Malay apple (*Eugenia malaccensis*), leaves were covered over the remains of Ahoeitu, and the bowl containing them was taken and put behind the house. They visited the bowl continually and, after a time, poured out the water. The flesh of his body had become compact. They visited the bowl again and again and at last found him sitting up in it.

Then they told Eitumatupua that Ahoeitu was alive, for he was sitting up. They were told to bring him into the house, into the presence of his father. Then Eitumatupua spoke, ordering that the brothers of Ahoeitu, who ate him, be brought. Their father then addressed them.

'You have killed Ahoeitu. He shall descend as the ruler of Tonga, while you, his brothers, remain here.' But the brothers loved Ahoeitu, as they had just realized that he was their real brother and had one father with them. Therefore, they pleaded with their father to be allowed to accompany Ahoeitu, a plea which was finally granted.

Ahoeitu returned to earth and became Tu'i Tonga, the first (divine) Tu'i Tonga of the world. The Tu'i Tonga who originated from the offspring of the worm were displaced.

Ahoeitu's brothers followed and joined him. They were Talafale, Matakehe, Maliepo, Tui Loloko, and Tui Folaha. Eitumatupua told Talafale that he was to go to the earth, but that he would not be Tu'i Tonga, as he was a murderer. He was, however, to be called Tui Faleua. Eitumatupua said that Maliepo and Matakehe were to go to guard the Tu'i Tonga. Tui Loloko and Tui Folaha were to govern. Should a Tu'i Tonga die, they were to have charge of all funerary arrangements, just as though it were the funeral of the Tui Langi (King of the Sky), Eitumatupua.

It is the descendants of Ahoeitu, he who was murdered in the sky, who have successively been Tu'i Tonga. The descendants of Talafale are the Tui Pelehake. The descendants of Matakehe are not known, having become extinct. The descendants of Maliepo are called Lauaki. The descendants of Tui Loloko are still called Tui Loloko.

The Tu'i Tonga and their families are of the highest rank, because Ahoeitu came originally from the sky. He was the first chief appointed from the sky, the Tu'i Tonga of all the world of brown people as far as Uea (Wallis Island), the ruler of the world. His divine origin makes his descendants real chiefs. In fact, it became customary to ask of one who is proud or thinks himself a chief: 'Is he a chief? Did he descend from the sky?'

The son of Ahoeitu was Lolofakangalo, and he became Tu'i Tonga when Ahoeitu died; and the son of Lolofakangalo was Fangaoneone and he became the third Tu'i Tonga. The son of Fangaoneone was Lihau, and he was the fourth Tu'i Tonga. The son of Lihau was Kofutu; he was the fifth Tu'i Tonga. Kaloa, the son of Kofutu, was the sixth Tu'i Tonga. His son Mau-hau was the seventh Tu'i Tonga. Then followed Apuanea, Afulunga, Momo, and Tu'i-tā-tui. It was Tu'i-tā-tui who erected the Haamonga-a-Māui, or Burden-of-Māui (the well-known trilithon of Tongatapu).

The following account concerns the Tu'i Tonga Tu'i-tā-tui and what he did on the raised platform house (*fale fatataki* or *fatafehi*). His sister went to him. Her name was Latutama and she was female Tu'i Tonga. Her attendant followed her to Tu'i-tā-tui's house. After his sister arrived Tu'i-tā-tui ascended to his platform and then he began his lies, for, behold, he had desire for his sister to go up to the platform, so that they might have sexual intercourse. From above he said to his sister below: 'Here is a vessel coming, a vessel from Haapai very likely; a very large vessel.'

And Latutama answered: 'Oh, it is your lies.' 'It is not my lies,' retorted Tu'i-tā-tui. 'Come up and see the vessel yourself.' Then his sister climbed up and sat with him on the platform, while her attendant remained below, and Tu'i-tā-tui and his sister had sexual intercourse. That was the way of that Tu'i Tonga, and it was known to the attendant.

They dwelt together at their place of abode in Hahake (eastern Tongatapu), the name of which was Heketā (near the modern village of Niutoua). The trilithon called the Burden-of-Māui and Tu'i-tā-tui's terraced stone tomb are situated there. There was also there the Olotele (or dwelling-place of the Tu'i Tonga) and the course for the game played by the Tu'i Tonga with the sikaulutoa (a reed throwing-stick with a head of toa, or casuarina wood).

The sons of Tu'i-tā-tui were Talaatama and Talaihaapepe. When Tu'i-tā-tui died, his son Talaatama succeeded him.

Then Talaatama spoke to his brother Talaihaapepe concerning the undesirability of Heketā as a place of residence. Said he: 'Let us move and leave this dwelling place, because of our love for our two vessels; lest here they go aground and be broken to pieces, for this is a very bad anchorage.' His brother Talaihaapepe replied: 'It is true, but where will we go?' And Talaatama answered: 'To Fangalongonoa (fanga, shore; longonoa, quiet), lest our vessels get wrecked.' That is the reason why they moved their vessels to Fangalongonoa and made their dwelling near by. The place where they dwelt was called Mua. They took their two vessels with them. The name of one vessel was 'Akiheuho', and the name of the other vessel was 'Tongafuesia'.

That is the reason why Laufilitonga dwells at Mua. It is the dwelling place prepared by Talaatama and Talaihaapepe. It was they who first moved from Hahake (referring to Heketā on the northeast coast of Tongatapu) and it was they who prepared Mua. And all of the Tuʻi Tonga who have succeeded them have dwelt there, even unto Laufilitonga, the present Tuʻi Tonga.

When Talaatama died, he was succeeded by Tuʻi Tonga Nui Tama Tou. This was not a person, but a piece of *tou* (*Cordia aspera*) wood which Talai-haapepe caused to be set up as Tuʻi Tonga, for he did not himself wish to become Tuʻi Tonga immediately after his brother Talaatama. It being Talaihaapepe's desire that a dummy Tuʻi Tonga be enthroned, the piece of tou wood was dressed in tapa and fine mats and duly appointed. A royal wife (*moheofo*), too, was appointed for the Tama Tou. After it had been three years Tuʻi Tonga, the vault stones were cut for the tomb and the Tama Tou was buried in the vault. Then it was pretended that his wife was pregnant, so that she might give birth to a Tuʻi Tonga. The fictitious child was none other than the wily Talaihaapepe, the brother of Talaatama, who was then proclaimed Tuʻi Tonga. A proclamation was made to the people of the land that the Tuʻi Tonga's wife (the moheofo) had given birth to a son whose father was the recently deceased Tuʻi Tonga Tama Tou. The truth of the matter was that it was really Talaihaapepe, who was at once proclaimed Tuʻi Tonga.

These are the things that those three Tuʻi Tonga, Tuʻi-tā-tui, Talaatama and Talaihaapepe, did.

Then followed in succession the Tuʻi Tonga Talakaifaiki, Talafapite, Tuʻi Tonga Maakatoe, Tuʻi Tonga i Puipui and Havea.

Havea was assassinated. He died and his body was cut in two and his head and chest floated on shore. He was murdered while having his bath, and the name of the expanse of water where he bathed is Tolopona. It is by the roadside at a place called Alakifonua (modern village of Alaki, Tongatapu island). After his head and chest floated on shore, a gallinule (*Porphyrio vitiensis*) called *kalae* came and pecked the face of the dead chief. In consequence that beach was called Houmakalae. When Lufe, the chief of the dead Tu'i Tonga's mother's family, learned of the king's death, he said: 'The Tu'i Tonga is dead. He has died a bad death, for he is cut in two. Come and kill me and join my buttocks and legs to the Tu'i Tonga's trunk, so that the corpse may be complete.' His relatives obeyed him. They slew him to make the Tu'i Tonga's body complete and then buried the remains. Thus it was done for the Tu'i Tonga Havea who was slain.

Another Tu'i Tonga was Tatafueikimeimua; another was Lomiaetupua; another Tu'i Tonga was Havea (II), who was shot by a Fijian man called Tuluvota; he was shot through the head and he died.

Another Tu'i Tonga was Takalaua. His wife was a woman called Vae. When she was born, she had a head like a pigeon's head, and her parents deserted her. Her father's name was Leasinga and her mother's name was Leamata. They left her at the island of Ata (near Tongatapu), while they sailed to Haapai.

Ahe, the chief of the island of Ata, went down to look at the place where the boat had been beached, and he said, 'Perhaps the canoe went last night.' He walked about near the place where the canoe landed, and he saw something moving. It was covered with a piece of tapa. Behold, a woman had given birth to a girl child and deserted her, because she and her husband disliked the infant and were afraid of their child. Her parents were Leasinga and Leamata. Because she had a head like a pigeon's, they decided to abandon her. The chief of Ata went and unwrapped the moving bundle, and said: 'It is a girl with a pigeon's head.'

He took her, did the chief of the island, and fed and cared for her, and adopted her as his daughter, and called her Vae. She lived and grew big, and the beak of the bird was shed, and her head, like a pigeon's, was changed. She grew very beautiful, and she was brought to Mua as a wife for the Tuʻi Tonga Takalaua. The woman who was born with the pigeon's head bore children to Takalaua, the Tuʻi Tonga. Her first son was Kauulufonuafekai, and her second son was Moungamotua, and the third was Melinoatonga, and the fourth was Lotauai, and the fifth was Latutoevave; that child talked from his mother's womb. Those were all Vaelaveamata's children to the Tuʻi Tonga Takalaua.

Vae had five male children, some were grown up and some were still young when their father Takalaua the Tuʻi Tonga was murdered. His children, Kauulufonuafekai, Moungamotua and his other sons, were very angry over their father's murder, and they said: 'Let us go and seek the two murderers.'

They made war on Tongatapu and conquered it, and the two murderers fled to Eua. And Kauulufonuafekai and his people entered a vessel and pursued the two murderers, whose names were Tamasia and Malofafa, to Eua. They fought the people of Eua, and conquered them, and the two fugitives fled to Haapai. Kauulufonuafekai and his brothers sailed in pursuit to Haapai. Haapai was waiting ready for war with the avengers, and they fought and Haapai was conquered. The two murderers then fled to Vavau, and Kauulufonuafekai pursued, and conquered Vavau. Again the two murderers fled, this time to Niuatoputapu. Kauulufonuafekai pursued, and fought and conquered Niuatoputapu. Thence the two murderers fled to Niuafoou. Still they were pursued. Kauulufonuafekai fought and conquered Niuafoou also. The two murderers again fled, but whither?

Kauulufonuafekai went to Futuna to seek them, and fought and conquered Futuna.

Kauulufonuafekai had spoken in the vessel to his brothers and warriors: 'Do you think my bravery is my own, or is it a god (*faahikehe*) that blesses me and makes me brave?' And his brothers, warriors, and people in the vessel all answered: 'What man in the world is strong in his own body, and brave in his own mind, if not blessed by a god? You are brave and strong, because a god blesses you. That is the reason why you are strong and brave.' Kauulufonuafekai replied: 'I am not brave because of the help of a god. My bravery is the bravery of a man.' Then his brothers said to him: 'It is not. You are brave and strong from a god.' Kauulufonuafekai replied: 'I will divide my body into two parts when we go and fight at Futuna. I will leave my back for the god to bless and protect, while I guard my front myself, and if I am wounded in front, it will be a sign that I am brave and strong because a god blesses me; but should I be wounded in my back, it will be a sign that it is my own bravery, and that a god has nothing to do with it.'

They went and fought the Futunans, who attempted to drive the Tongan vessel away. Then the Tongans in turn chased the Futunans on the sea and drove their warriors inland. But they were fighting for nothing, for the murderers were not at Futuna; they were at Uea. Thus Futuna was fought for nought, as it was thought that the murderers were there. They fought Futuna and the warriors from the vessel of Kauulufonuafekai, chased the people of Futuna, and caused them to flee. Kauulufonuafekai ran up the road in pursuit. A man in ambush speared Kauulufonuafekai through his back into his chest. The chief turned and clubbed the man who had speared him. And Kauulufonuafekai, returning, said: 'I told you. Don't you say that I am brave through a god. Here I am wounded in the place that was left for the god to guard. I am not wounded from my front. My wound came from my back, which I left for him to guard; therefore I am not brave and strong from any god. It is my own bravery and the strength of this world. Come and we will go on board the vessel.'

They went on board and sailed, but one of their brothers, Lotauai, was left behind at Futuna, for the people of Futuna had captured him. They did not kill him, but they let him live.

The vessel of Kauulufonuafekai sailed, and after voyaging for five days Kauulufonuafekai said: 'Let us return to Futuna, because I have love for my brother, who is detained there; and my wound is itching, because it wants to fight.' So they returned and Futuna saw the vessel coming, and the Futunans spoke to the lad, the brother of the chief, whom they had taken and they called his name: 'Lotauai! The vessel is returning; the brave chief is coming again.' And Lotauai, the lad that they held, said: 'I told you that the chief would return with his warriors. It is for love of me, because you hold me prisoner. Had the chief and his warriors come for love of me, and come and found me dead, you having killed me, Futuna would indeed have died (been exterminated). But I am alive, so no one will be killed and you will not be punished.'

Then the people of Futuna said to the lad: 'Lotauai, what can we do to live!' They were afraid that the chief would come and kill them.

The chief's brother said: 'Come and put on fine mats (ngafingafi), and pluck leaves from the chestnut (ifi) tree and put them round your neck. That is the thing to do to live, for it is the recognized Tongan way of begging mercy. Come and sit with bowed head at my back, while I sit in front, so that the chief that you are afraid of will see that I am still alive. That is the means by which you will live. Also prepare for his reception; cook food, and bring kava. After we have pacified the chief by sueing for mercy, then bring the kava and food, then we (Tongans) will drink it and go away.' The vessel arrived and the people of the land came with loin mats (*ngafingafi*) round them, and chestnut leaves around their necks. And came the brave chief, and found his young brother still alive. And his young brother told the chief: 'The people of the land are sueing for mercy, to live, because they are afraid.' Kauulufonuafekai replied: 'They live, and I am thankful that my brother still lives.'

Then the kava and food were brought by the people of Futuna. They had kava with the chief and made friends. Then Kauulufonuafekai gave a Tongan boat to the people of Futuna, and said: 'I have no wealth (tapa and mats) to give you, but here is a present for you, that I give you: Any vessel coming from Tonga is yours, but do not kill its people. All goods that are brought in it from Tonga are to be your present. That is my payment to you, because you allowed my brother, whom you took, to live, and I received a wound from you in the fight. That is why I give you the goods from the Tongan vessels.' Hence comes the meaning of the expression: 'Vete fakafutuna, to seize like the Futunans.'

Then the vessel left to go and seek the murderers in Fiji. Kauulufonuafekai went and fought the different islands of Fiji, but the two murderers were not found in Fiji. They returned from Fiji and went to Uea, and fought and conquered Uea.

The two murderers were not able to flee from Uea, but were overtaken there, for they were prisoners held for sacrifice. When the Uea people came to sue for mercy, after they were conquered in the fight, the two murderers came with them. Kauulufonuafekai did not know the faces of the two murderers, but he knew their names. When the Uea people came to sue for pardon they all had long hair; but the two murderers, who came with them, had short hair which was just beginning to grow, their heads having been shaven. The chief knew them by their short hair, as all the Ueans had long hair. The chief called: 'Tamasia!' for that was the name of one. He answered: 'I am here.' Then the chief called out the name of the other one: 'Malofafa!' and he answered: 'I am here.' The chief then said: 'What a long time you have been. Thanks to the god that you fled and that you are still alive. Come, you two Tongan men, we will sail for Tonga.'

The vessel conveyed the two men to Tonga. There Kauulufonuafekai commanded that the two murderers should be brought and cut up alive as food for Takalaua's funeral kava. They were brought and cut up, and after they were cut up, their pieces were collected and burned in the fire.

It is said that Kauulufonuafekai had had their teeth pulled out at Uea, and then he had thrown them a string of dry kava, that he had worn round his neck most of the time since he had left Tonga. Upon throwing the dry kava to them, he told them to chew it. They tried to chew, with their bleeding gums, but were not able in the least to chew. After a very long, long time of thus giving them pain, from the morning of one day to the next day, Kauulufonuafekai told them to enter the vessel for them to leave for Tonga.

Takalaua, the Tuʻi Tonga that was murdered, was buried, and Kauulufonuafekai was appointed Tuʻi Tonga. He, the child of the woman with the pigeon's head, was Tuʻi Tonga. The brother of Kauulufonuafekai, Moungamotua, was appointed Tui Haatakalaua (*tui*, king; *haa*, family; Takalaua, his father's name) and he went and lived at 'Kauhalalalo' in Fonuamotu near

Loamanu (at Mua, Tongatapu), in order to rule from there the land. And he was to be called Tui Haatakalaua. Moungamotua was the first Tui Haatakalaua, the brother of Kauulufonuafekai, the Tu'i Tonga.

Kauulufonuafekai was the first to arrange that the apaapa, or master of ceremonies in the kava ring, should sit at a distance, not near to him, because he was afraid of being murdered, as his father, the Tu'i Tonga Takalaua, was murdered. Therefore the kava ring was formed so that the people in it sat at a distance from the chief. He instructed some of his brothers to sit at his back to guard him lest he should be murdered. The name given to those brothers that sat behind him, was *huhueiki* (*huhu*, to suspect; *eiki*, chief).

Another Tu'i Tonga was Vakafuhu; another was Puipuifatu; another was called Kauulufonua; another Tu'i Tonga was Tapuosi I, and another Tu'i Tonga was Uluakimata I, (Telea). His vessel was called Lomipeau (*lomi*, keep under; *peau*, waves). That was the ship that often went to Uea to cut and load stones for the terraces (*paepae*) of the royal tombs. Paepae o Telea is the name of the graveyard of the Tu'i Tonga Telea. Fatafehi he was the son of Telea; his mother was Mataukipa. Another Tu'i Tonga was Tapuosi II, and another Tu'i Tonga was Uluakimata II His sons were the Tu'i Tonga Tui Pulotu I and his brother, Tokemoana. The latter was appointed Tui Haauluakimata (*tui*, ruler; *haa*, family; *Uluaki-mata*, his father's name). Their sister Sinaitakala, was the female Tu'i Tonga; Fatani was their brother, also Faleafu, all of one father.

The son of Tui Pulotu was Fakanaanaa and he was Tu'i Tonga; another Tu'i Tonga was Tui Pulotu II; and another Tu'i Tonga was Maulupekotofa. The son of Pau was Fatafehi Fuanunuiava, and the son of Fuanu-nuiava was Laufilitonga, the Tu'i Tonga that is alive in the world. That is the end of the Tu'i Tonga. The old Tu'i Tonga, the offspring of the Worm, are gone. The list of female Tu'i Tonga is not given, but only the list of the male Tu'i Tonga.

Here are their names in order: (1) Ahoeitu, (2) Lolofakangalo, (3) Fangaoneone, (4) Lihau, (5) Kofutu, (6) Kaloa, (7) Mauhau, (8) Apuanea, (9) Afulunga, (10) Momo, (11) Tu'i-tā-tui, (12) Talaatama, (13) Tu'i Tonga Nui Tama Tou, (14) Talaihaapepe, (15) Talakaifaiki, (16) Talafapite, (17) Tu'i Tonga Maakatoe, (18) Tu'i Tonga i Puipui, (19) Havea I, (20) Tatafueikimeimua, (21) Lomiaetupua, (22) Havea II, (23) Takalaua, (24) Kauulufonuafekai, (25) Vakafuhu, (26) Puipuifatu, (27) Kauulufonua, (28) Tapuosi I, (29) Uluakimata I (Telea), (30) Fatafehi, (31) Tapuosi II, (32) Uluakimata II, (33) Tui Pulotu I, (34) Fakanaanaa, (35) Tui Pulotu II, (36), Pau, (37) Maulupekotofa, (38) Fatafehi Fuanunuiava, (39) Laufilitonga.

The Tu'i Tonga Uluakimata, he who was called Telea, had many wives. One of his wives was Talafaiva. She was said, by the people of Mua who saw her, to be the most beautiful of women, for there was not another woman in the world so beautiful as she – she was unsurpassed. She was also a very great chief, for both her parents were chiefs. There was not another woman of such high rank, or so beautiful, or so well formed. She was the only woman called by all the world *fakatouato* (chief by both parents). Talafaiva brought fifty other wives (*fokonofo*) to Telea. The second wife of Telea was Nanasilapaha, and she brought fifty other wives to Telea. The third wife of Telea was Mataukipa and she brought one hundred other wives to Telea.

Mataukipa was the wife that always received the tail of the

fish, and rump of the pig every day. 'Why is the head of the fish, and the head of the pig, and the middle cut of the fish, and back of the pig always taken to Talafaiva and Nanasilapaha?' This was the question which troubled Mataukipa, so she decided to confer with her father. 'I will go to my father, Kauulufonuahuo (head-of-the-land-cultivators), and ask him if it is good or bad this thing that the Tu'i Tonga is doing to me.' So she carried her child on her back and went to the place called Mataliku, where Kauulufonuahuo dwelt. He was an industrious gardener, growing yams, bananas, *kape* (a root like the taro), taro, *ufilei* (a small sweet yam), *hoi* (fruit tree), and large bread fruit trees.

Her father saw his daughter coming, and went to greet her. 'You have come. Who is with you?' His daughter, Mataukipa, answered: 'Only we two.' Then the father asked: 'Why was there no one to come with you? Why only you two? Are you angry?' and Mataukipa replied: 'No!' Her father said: 'You stay here while I go and prepare some food, then I will take you back to Mua.'

They had their kava prepared twice. Then the people went and prepared the oven and baked yams and a pig. Afterwards the daughter spoke to her father: 'Why are the Tu'i Tonga's wishes like that?' she asked, and her father inquired: 'How?' His daughter replied: 'When our fish and pig is brought, the two women always eat the head and back of the pig, and the head and middle part of the fish, and I always get the tail of the fish and the rump of the pig.'

The father of the woman laughed, and made this reply to the woman: 'And are you grieved at it?' The woman answered: 'I am grieved at it.'

The father replied to the woman: 'Don't be grieved. Your portion is the rump of the pig and the tail of the fish, because the land will come eventually to your children. They will be rulers.'

The woman's mind was at peace after her father's explanation as to why she always was given the tail of the fish and rump of the pig, but before that she was jealous of the two women, and thought: 'The chief loves the two women more than me.' Consequently she was jealous.

They returned to her place and the woman was content, because of the explanation of her father, and they all lived together. When the Tu'i Tonga Telea died, the woman Mataukipa had a son called Fatafehi, and a daughter called Sinaitakala-i-langi-leka. Fatafehi was appointed Tu'i Tonga and Sinaitakala became female Tu'i Tonga. Thus what Mataukipa's father had told her came true; her son became Tu'i Tonga and her daughter female Tu'i Tonga and her descendants were Tu'i Tonga, the last being Laufili-tonga.

The Tu'i Tonga Telea dwelt in the bush, because he preferred it, and was more at home there, especially on the weather shore of Vavau. Each of his dwelling places and sleeping places at the weather shore of Vavau has a name, and each place is named after the thing he did at that place.

Telea and his wife Talafaiva came and dwelt on the island of Euakafa. Their house was built on the top of the mountain, and a reed fence was erected round the place. There was a big tree called *foui* growing there, and Talafaiva told Telea: 'It is not a nice tree. You had better have it cut down.' But Telea answered: 'Oh, leave it. It is all right.'

They had dwelt there for some time, when a man called Lolomanaia came from a place called Makave (in Vavau island). His vessel landed at the place where Telea dwelt, because Lolomanaia was in love with Talafaiva. He ascended and waited till it was dark. When it was dark he went to the place of Telea. He pushed the gate to see if it was closed or open. When he pushed it he found that it was closed, and he tried and tried to find some way to get inside the fence. He went round outside of the fence and found the big tree that Talafaiva had told Telea to cut down. He climbed the tree and thereby gained access to the enclosure. He slept with the woman Talafaiva, the wife of Tu'i Tonga Telea. After they had slept he tattooed a black mark on her abdomen, to annoy Telea, for him (Telea) to know that he (Lolomanaia) had committed adultery with his wife.

Telea slept with Talafaiva in the day, and he saw what had been done to his wife's abdomen. Telea asked her: 'Who, Talafaiva, has tattooed your stomach?' Talafaiva replied: 'It is true! Chief, will you pardon me? It was Lolomanaia who came to me. Don't you be angry, because you know I told you, on the day that the fence was made for our enclosure, to cut down the big foui tree, because the tree was badly placed, and you said to leave it. The man climbed up it and came to me. His name was Lolomanaia.' Telea was very wroth and arose and went out. He called his man servant by name. 'Uka! Come here, for me to tell you. Go and beat Talafaiva. She has had intercourse with a man.'

Uka took a club, and went with it to her. Telea did not know that he was really going to kill Talafaiva. He only meant that he should beat her. After Telea's wrath cooled, he found that Uka had really killed Talafaiva, and that she was dead. The beautiful and well formed woman was dead. Uka came to report to Telea, and Telea asked: 'Have you beaten Tala-faiva?' and Uka, the man servant, answered: 'I have beaten her.' The chief asked: 'And how is she?' Uka replied: 'She is dead,' and Telea asked: 'Is she quite dead?' and Uka replied: 'She is quite dead.' Again Telea asked: 'Is she quite dead, my wife Talafaiva?' and Uka made reply: 'She is quite dead.'

Telea was grief stricken: 'Oh! oh! my misplaced confidence! I did not mean that you should really go and kill her. I only meant for you to beat her a little because I was angry. I really loved my wife, whom you have killed. You are an old fool!' Telea went and wept over Talafaiva, who was really dead, for a night and a day.

Then Telea the Tu'i Tonga said: 'We will go and cut stones for a vault for Talafaiva.' So they went and cut the stones for the vault, and made the vault. Then Talafaiva was buried in the vault. The grave yard with the vault standing in it is on Euakafa island. The big casuarina tree at the graveyard is called Talafaiva. That is all about Talafaiva, the wife of Telea, about her ways and the meaning of what we hear about her. After Talafaiva's death Telea went to Tonga (Tongatapu) and lived there and died there.

The stones for the vault of this Tu'i Tonga Telea were cut at Uea, and the terrace stones were cut there also. This is the Tu'i Tonga that owned the vessel called Lomipeau, and this is the vessel that brought the stones for his vault and the terrace round it.

THE ART OF NETTING LEARNED BY KAHUKURA FROM THE FAIRIES
(Ko Te Korero Mo Nga Patupaiarehe)

Once upon a time, a man of the name of Kahukura wished to pay a visit to Rangiaowhia, a place lying far to the northward, near the country of the tribe called Te Rarawa. Whilst he lived at his own village, he was continually haunted by a desire to visit that place. At length he started on his journey, and reached Rangiaowhia, and as he was on his road, he passed a place where some people had been cleaning mackerel, and he saw the inside of the fish lying all about the sand on the seashore: surprised at this, he looked about at the marks, and said to himself: 'Oh, this must have been done by some of the people of the district.' But when he came to look a little more narrowly at the footmarks, he saw that the people who had been fishing had made them in the night-time, not that morning, nor in the day; and he said to himself: 'These are no mortals who have been fishing here – spirits must have done this; had they been men, some of the reeds and grass which they sat on in their canoe would have been lying about. 'He felt quite sure from several circumstances, that spirits or fairies had been there; and after observing everything well, he returned to the house where he was stopping. He, however, held fast in his heart what he had seen, as something very striking to tell all his friends in every direction, and as likely to be the means of gaining knowledge which might enable him to find out something new.

So that night he returned to the place where he had observed all these things, and just as he reached the spot, back had come the fairies too, to haul their net for mackerel; and some of them were shouting out: 'The net here! the net here!' Then a canoe paddled off to fetch the other in which the net was laid, and as they dropped the net into the water, they began to cry out: 'Drop the net in the sea at Rangiaowhia, and haul it at Mamaku.' These words were sung out by the fairies, as an encouragement in their work, and from the joy of their hearts at their sport in fishing.

As the fairies were dragging the net to the shore, Kahukura managed to mix amongst them, and hauled away at the rope; he happened to be a very fair man, so that his skin was almost as white as that of these fairies, and from that cause he was not observed by them. As the net came close in to the shore, the fairies began to cheer and shout: 'Go out into the sea some of you, in front of the rock, lest the nets should be entangled in

Tawatawauia a Teweteweuia', for that was the name of a rugged rock standing out from the sandy shore; the main body of the fairies kept hauling at the net, and Kahukura pulled away in the midst of them.

When the first fish reached the shore, thrown up in the ripples driven before the net as they hauled it in, the fairies had not yet remarked Kahukura, for he was almost as fair as they were. It was just at the very first peep of dawn that the fish were all landed, and the fairies ran hastily to pick them up from the sand, and to haul the net up on the beach. They did not act with their fish as men do, dividing them into separate loads for each, but every one took up what fish he liked, and ran a twig through their gills, and as they strung the fish, they continued calling out: 'Make haste, run here, all of you, and finish the work before the sun rises.'

Kahukura kept on stringing his fish with the rest of them. He had only a very short string, and, making a slip-knot at the end of it, when he had covered the string with fish, he lifted them up, but had hardly raised them from the ground when the slip-knot gave way from the weight of the fish, and off they fell; then some of the fairies ran good-naturedly to help him to string his fish again, and one of them tied the knot at the end of the string for him, but the fairy had hardly gone after knotting it, before Kahukura had unfastened it, and again tied a slip-knot at the end; then he began stringing his fish again, and when he had got a great many on, up he lifted them, and off they slipped as before. This trick he repeated several times, and delayed the fairies in their work by getting them to knot his string for him, and put his fish on it. At last full daylight broke, so that there was light enough to distinguish a man's face, and the fairies saw that Kahukura was a man; then they dispersed in confusion, leaving their fish and their net, and abandoning their canoes, which were nothing but stems of the flax. In a moment the fairies started for their own abodes; in their hurry, as has just been said, they abandoned their net, which was made of rushes; and off the good people fled as fast as they could go. Now was first discovered the stitch for netting a net, for they left theirs with Kahukura, and it became a pattern for him. He thus taught his children to make nets, and by them the Māori race were made acquainted with that art, which they have now known from very remote times.

THE BATTLE OF THE GIANTS
The Giants

Once the volcanoes Taranaki, Ruapehu and Tongariro dwelled together. That was the time when Tongariro in her wonderful beauty had captured the fiery hearts of the two giants, so that their joy filled the heavens with majestic outbursts and covered the earth with their dark-glowing heart-blood of fiery lava and molten stones.

Softly then answered the gently ascending steam-column of Tongariro, smiling and swaying, gold-bordered by the setting sun; smiling at both her suitors.

Ah, Tongariro was a woman!

Both, the straight and simple Taranaki and the rugged and strong Ruapehu, their cloud-piercing heads covered with spotless snow, or adorned in their passion-glowing lava-streams, were beloved by Tongariro; but the snows of the winter and the suns of the summer came and went from the first time, to the hundredth time, to the thousandth time, and still Tongariro was undecided whom she would prefer for a husband.

She became the sacred mountain of the Māori people; her beauty captured the hearts of all, so that she became the possessor of the highest tapu, and no foot dared walk upon her, and only the eyes of the new-born were directed towards her; and the eyes of the departing rested full love upon her beauty, whilst they wandered to the Reinga.

The eyes of generations upon generations of man.

Beautiful to behold from all the lands was the great love of the giants; now all covered with glittering snow, now hiding in the clouds and bursting forth, covered with strange and wonderful beauty; now girdling their bodies with clouds and lifting their endless heads into the golden heavens; and now again breaking forth into terrible passions, covering the earth with blackness.

Ah, Tongariro roused the passions of the giants: she made the volcanoes tremble! Their blood of fire and boiling stones shook them, the thundering of their voices, roaring insults at each other, made the earth tremble. Streams of lightning pierced the nights, and black smoke of deadly hate darkened the days, and the ears of man were filled with the roaring hate of the giants, and their wondering eyes beheld the beauty of Tongariro, smiling at both!

At last the two rivals decided to fight for Tongariro!

Now followed days of silence. The giants stood there grim and silent to the world, but they were gathering strength, and were melting stones in their insides, and lit terrible fires, their powerful weapons. So they stood silent and grim; the sun gilding their beautiful garments of snow, and Tongariro smiled at them with her graceful swaying column of steam; and the Māori people looked wonderingly upon the peaceful landscape.

Then a rolling grew in the nights, and rolling filled the days;

louder and louder, night after night, day after day – a terrible groaning, damp and deep. Suddenly a crashing thunder shook the earth, and bursting forth from the mouth of Ruapehu a fiery mass of molten stones and black hate and fury fell upon Taranaki, covering him with a terrible coat of fire, whilst the flying winds howled and the melted snow-waters fled thundering down into the valleys.

A beautiful straight form gave the mass of fire and ashes to Taranaki – but he shook in terrible rage! He tore himself out of the ground, shaking the earth and breaking the lands asunder; he tried to fly at Ruapehu, to kill him with his weight. But Ruapehu made the water of his lake, high up in the snows, boil, and, hurling it down, it filled all the rends Taranaki had made in the earth, and burned all the inside of the earth and of Taranaki himself. He now, tearing the air with his roaring cries of pain and thundering howling of rage, threw a tremendous mass of stones at his enemy, and broke the highest cone, the loftiest peak of Ruapehu, so that his looks were not so majestic, and his reach not so far into the skies.

Ruapehu now, in deadly hate, swallowed his broken cone and melted it; he lit terrible fires in his inside, which spread to the lake Roto-aira, so that it rose and boiled, the steam covering all the world and blinding Taranaki. Then Ruapehu filled himself with the boiling water, and, throwing it out of his mouth down upon Taranaki, it filled all the crevices, and it lifted him, for he himself had loosened his bonds with the earth; and now, darkening day into night, he sent the molten mass of his swallowed cone against his enemy, so that he was compelled to retreat: blinded by steam, burned in his inside by the boiling water, and covered with the molten mass of the cone of Ruapehu he himself had broken.

He groaned, and rose, and tumbled, and shook himself; and he felt for a way to the sea to cool his burning pain; howling in unbearable pain he had to run, in order to get out of reach of Ruapehu, deeply hollowing his path through the lands. But his conqueror, Ruapehu, melting all his ice and snow, sent it as boiling water into this deep path, that his enemy might not come back again, for his strength also was exhausted.

On to the sea went Taranaki, and, when his pain had left him a little, he looked back at his conqueror, and saw how his three peaks were again covered with fresh snow, and how he was now the supreme lord over all the lands and the husband of Tongariro. They two were now the arikis over all the land; but it was waste now, and dead, for the terrible fight had killed all the people and the living beings all around. Once more a burst of black anger broke forth from Taranaki, and again it was answered by a wonderful swaying and smiling steam-column from Tongariro; and then he went and wandered along the coast till he had found a place for his sorrow. There he stands now, brooding on revenge.

'And my people know that one day he will come back in a straight line, to fight Ruapehu again; and none of my people will ever live or be buried in that lime; for one day he will come back to fight for Tongariro – who knows?'

But the path of Taranaki to the sea is now the Wanganui River.

THE ORIGIN OF KAVA

This is the story of how kava grew.

It is said that there was once a chief called Loau, whose

ancestors resided in Lifuka, and for whom the district of Haaloau in Lifuka is named. It is said that his dwelling had eight enclosures or fences and that a great number of people lived there.

Whilst Loau resided at Haamea, a man called Fevanga paid a visit to Loau. The name of Fevanga's wife was Fefafa. After residing some time with Loau, Fevanga told him that he would like to go to Eueiki to see his relatives and that he would soon return again. To this the chief agreed.

Fevanga went to the island of Eueiki and stopped there with his wife. They had a daughter who was a leper. Time went on and still Fevanga tarried in Eueiki. Loau missed Fevanga and finally decided to go to Eueiki himself, so he had his dependants prepare for the voyage. A large rowing canoe (*tafaanga*) was launched and away they went to Eueiki. They arrived there at dusk. Loau ordered that the canoe be carried to Fevanga's home and put close to a large *kape* plant (*Arum costatum*), with the outrigger on top of the kape.

Fevanga came down to greet his visitors and they responded, saying: 'Happy to see you in good health in this island.' Loau sat down with his back to the big *kape*, whilst Fevanga searched for food. Fevanga's search was not fruitful, for Eueiki was suffering from famine at the time. Nevertheless, he fired his earth oven and at the same time suggested to Loau that, if he would not mind going down to the beach, he would find it cooler there. Fevanga was desirous that Loau should move in order that he might dig up the kape plant to roast.

After Loau had accommodatingly removed to the beach, Fevanga dug up the big *kape* plant and put it in the oven. He then killed his leperous daughter and roasted her together with the kape. Shortly after Loau and his men returned, the oven was opened, and the food set before Loau. Loau issued orders that the head of Fevanga's unfortunate daughter be cut off and buried in one place, while the body was to be buried in another place. Loau told Fevanga to take notice that two plants would grow from the head and that he was to care for them. Farewells were said and Loau returned to Tongatapu.

Fevanga remained in Eueiki to care for the plants, as it was his duty to take them to Loau in Haamea when they had reached maturity. They proved to be kava and sugar cane. He watched them carefully and, one day when they were nearly full grown, he saw a rat gnawing the kava. After eating the kava, the rat chewed the sugar cane. All the Tongan people drink the kava and eat the sugar cane, because the rat ate the kava first and then the sugar cane. Then Fevanga knew that the time had arrived to pull up the two plants and take them to Tongatapu for a meeting of the chiefs.

When Loau saw Fevanga approaching with the plants he cried: 'This is the kava of Fevanga and Fefafa from Faimata. A single chief for the *olovaha* (i.e., the plain underside of the kava bowl which is towards the presiding chief at a kava party), and many for the *apaapa* (the place occupied by other chiefs at a kava party). Husk of the coconut for cleaning the kava root.' A bowl was brought and a *matapule* directed a person from the *toua* (the place occupied in a kava party by the people as opposed to the aloft, the place of the chiefs) to make kava. Coconut husks were used to gather the pieces of kava in, as it was split. Then it was given to the people sitting in the toua to be chewed. After being chewed, it was placed in the bowl, mixed, and served. Directions were issued to chop the sugar cane, which was used as a relish (the yam, banana, or other food eaten at a kava drinking ceremony) with the kava.

The place where the kava grew is still to be seen in Eueiki even unto this day.

THE ORIGIN OF THE MAGELLAN CLOUDS

Once upon a time there was living at Vaini, in Tongatapu, a great chief called Maafu, whose descendants are living to this day. It was Maafu's habit to bathe every evening in a water hole known as Tufatakale, so called because close by there lived at one time a man and a woman whose names were Tufa and Kale. Maafu, being a cleanly person, used to take a piece of coconut husk with him as a sort of scrubbing brush. After he had finished with it, he always threw it on a flat stone at the side of the water hole.

Living in the immediate vicinity was a huge female lizard, who, after Maafu's evening bath, always came and swallowed the piece of coconut husk. Time went on and a most astonishing thing occurred. The lizard gave birth to twins – not lizards – but to all appearance, shape, and size, human beings. She called them Maafu Toka and Maafu Lele.

Years rolled by and the two boys had almost reached manhood, when one day they went to their mother and said: 'We are tired of living here by ourselves. Tell us who our father is and we will go to him and live with him.' The old lizard realized that it was of no use trying to keep hidden any longer two such fine, healthy and happy youths. So with a sad heart she rubbed them all over with scented oil, dressed their hair and hung sweet smelling garlands of flowers and leaves round their necks. Her directions were that they were to take a certain road and at the end of it, where it opened out into the town, they would see a large house, outside of which a number of people would be sitting drinking kava. They were not to go up at once, but were to watch and see to whom the greatest respect was being paid. Then, after the kava drinking was over, they were to approach the person to whom the greatest respect had been shown. That person would be Maafu, their father.

The boys bade their mother farewell. By carrying out her instructions they soon found the house and saw the kava drinking ceremony. It did not take them long to recognize their father, but they waited at a little distance until the kava-drinking was finished. Then they approached the party. While they were drawing near, the people turned to each other and asked who the two young men of such handsome appearance were. But none knew them and then conjectures were made as to whether a canoe had arrived from Haapai or Vavau.

The two lads went straight to where Maafu was sitting and when close to him, sat down cross-legged on the ground in a respectful manner and waited for him to take notice of them. After an interval Maafu addressed them: 'Young men, we do not know who you are, nor whence you have come. Please inform us.' Their only reply was that he was their father. He did not dispute the fact; indeed, he did not even ask who was their mother, because he was afraid that she would want to come and live with them too.

So the boys grew up to manhood with Maafu, but, owing to their unnatural origin, they were the very incarnation of mischief. Besides they were fleeter of foot than ordinary mortals and excelled in all athletic exercises, especially spear throwing. Although on one occasion they broke the leg of one of Maafu's nephews, this did not worry Maafu so much as the fact that they used him (Maafu) as a target for their spear throwing, each endeavoring to throw his spear as close as possible without hitting the old man. Maafu at last determined to get rid of the two youths, but in such a manner that he did not appear to be the perpetrator of the deed.

With this end in view Maafu called the lads to him one morning and explained that he wanted them to get him some water from a certain water hole called Atavahea, which was far away. They were to get the water at high noon, as it was sweetest then. He did not tell them, however, that there was a huge duck living there and that persons going to get water at high noon had never returned.

It was just noon when the boys reached their destination. One stood on the bank, while the other waded into the pond with the empty coconut shells. Hardly had he reached the middle, when the sky became overcast and a rushing sound like a roaring wind was heard. Glancing up, the lad in the water saw a huge duck making straight for him. With admirable quickness he ducked and, as the bird passed over him, his fist shot out with lightning rapidity and with such force as to break the duck's wing. Then the lad seized the duck by the neck and held it up to his brother's view, calling out: 'Here is a fine duck for Maafu.' The boys filled the coconut shells with water and returned to Vaini. It was in no pleasant frame of mind that old Maafu witnessed their return. Nevertheless, he hid his feelings and thanked them for the water and the bird.

Next morning Maafu sent the boys to another water hole called Muihātafa, which lay in an opposite direction to Atavahea, and from which they were to bring him water. The water, however, must be obtained from the bottom of the pond, as water from that part of the pond had an especially fine flavor. Maafu did not tell the lads that in this water hole there lurked a huge parrot fish. Straightway the lads went and on their arrival at the water hole, one waded in and dived down to the bottom of the pond. Hardly had he reached the bottom when he saw an enormous parrot fish (*humu*) rushing at him with gaping jaws. Without a moment's hesitation, he thrust his arm down its throat. Rising to the surface he held it up to his brother's view, exclaiming: 'Here is a fine fish for Maafu.'

The two young men returned to Vaini with the water and the fish. When Maafu saw them approaching he lost all patience and said angrily to them: 'I am tired and disgusted with the way you have been behaving yourselves. You have been most mischievous, breaking my nephew's leg and endangering my life on several occasions. I have come to the conclusion to give you each a plantation (*api*) far from this town, so that you will not be able to worry us any further.'

The lads, realizing what Maafu's feelings were, replied: 'Do not trouble to do that. We will go of our own accord and so far away that you cannot reach us. We will take our duck and our fish and go up to the sky and live there. Should you want to see us, you will only have to look up on a dark night, and if we want to see you, we will only have to look down.' So the lads went to the sky and are there to this day. Navigators know that should they steer their course by the stars Maafu Toka and Maafu Lele, it will bring them to Vaini. These stars are known to astronomy as the Magellan clouds.

TALES OF MĀUI

The exploits of the demigod Māui are best described as legendary. A larger-than-life figure, Māui can be found in the stories of many Polynesian cultures. He is a trickster, a thief and a braggart, but can also be brave and compassionate. While the stories of Māui vary from one culture to another, each paints the picture of a mischievous hero who seeks to help those around him. Every Herculean labour this demigod undertakes benefits mankind.

Following a fishing dispute with his brothers, it is Māui who fishes up the islands of Polynesia. To aid his mother, he catches the sun and extends the length of the day. Māui also uses his skills in shapeshifting and trickery to steal fire and gift it to mankind. Some stories credit him with the slaying of a giant eel or dragon; others claim that it was Māui who raised the sky and brought the earth out of primeval darkness. In his final adventure, Māui seeks to overcome death itself.

While many of Māui's exploits rely upon his strength and shapeshifting, his stories also highlight his quick mind and ingenuity. He certainly thinks outside the box, finding solutions that others could not. Māui's cleverness and inventiveness are showcased in his many legends.

MĀUI'S HOME

'Akalana was the man;
Hina-a-ke-ahi was the wife;
Māui First was born;
Then Māui-waena;
Māui Kiikii was born;
Then Māui of the malo.'

Queen Liliuokalani's Family Chant

Four brothers, each bearing the name of Māui, belong to Hawaiian legend. They accomplished little as a family, except on special occasions when the youngest of the household awakened his brothers by some unexpected trick which drew them into unwonted action. The legends of Hawai'i, Tonga, Tahiti, New Zealand and the Hervey group make this youngest Māui 'the discoverer of fire' or 'the ensnarer of the sun' or 'the fisherman who pulls up islands' or 'the man endowed with magic,' or 'Māui with spirit power.' The legends vary somewhat, of course, but not as much as might be expected when the thousands of miles between various groups of islands are taken into consideration.

Māui was one of the Polynesian demigods. His parents belonged to the family of supernatural beings. He himself was possessed of supernatural powers and was supposed to make use of all manner of enchantments. In New Zealand antiquity a Māui was said to have assisted other gods in the creation of man. Nevertheless Māui was very human. He lived in thatched houses, had wives and children, and was scolded by the women for not properly supporting his household.

The time of his sojourn among men is very indefinite. In Hawaiian genealogies Māui and his brothers were placed among the descendants of Ulu and 'the sons of Kii,' and Māui was one of the ancestors of Kamehameha, the first king of the united Hawaiian Islands. This would place him in the seventh or eighth century of the Christian era. But it is more probable that Māui belongs to the mist-land of time. His mischievous pranks with the various gods would make him another Mercury living in any age from the creation to the beginning of the Christian era.

The Hervey Island legends state that Māui's father was 'the supporter of the heavens' and his mother 'the guardian of the road to the invisible world.'

In the Hawaiian chant, Akalana was the name of his father. In other groups this was the name by which his mother was known. Kanaloa, the god, is sometimes known as the father of Māui. In Hawai'i Hina was his mother. Elsewhere Ina, or Hina, was the grandmother, from whom he secured fire.

The Hervey Island legends say that four mighty ones lived in the old world from which their ancestors came. This old world bore the name Avaiki, which is the same as Hawa-ii, or Hawai'i. The four gods were Māuike, Ra, Ru, and Bua-Taranga.

It is interesting to trace the connection of these four names with Polynesian storytelling. Māuike is the same as the demigod of New Zealand, Mafuike. On other islands the name is spelled Māuika, Mafuika, Mafuia, Mafuie, and Mahuika. Ra, the sun god of Egypt, is the same as Ra in New Zealand and La (sun) in Hawai'i. Ru, the supporter of the heavens, is probably the Ku of Hawai'i, and the Tu of New Zealand and other islands, one of the greatest of the gods worshipped by the ancient Hawaiians. The fourth mighty one from Ava-ika was a woman, Bua-taranga, who guarded the path to the underworld. Talanga in Samoa, and Akalana in Hawai'i were the same as Taranga. Pua-kalana (the Kalana flower) would probably be the same in Hawaiian as Bua-taranga in the language of the Society Islands.

Ru, the supporter of the Heavens, married Bua-taranga, the guardian of the lower world. Their one child was Māui. The legends of Raro-Tonga state that Māui's father and mother were the children of Tangaroa (Kanaloa in Hawaiian), the great god worshipped throughout Polynesia. There were three Māui brothers and one sister, Ina-ika (Ina, the fish).

The New Zealand legends relate the incidents of the babyhood of Māui.

Māui was prematurely born, and his mother, not caring to be troubled with him, cut off a lock of her hair, tied it around him and cast him into the sea. In this way the name came to him, Māui-Tiki-Tiki, or 'Māui formed in the topknot.' The waters bore him safely. The jelly fish enwrapped and mothered him. The god of the seas cared for and protected him. He was carried to the god's house and hung up in the roof that he might feel the warm air of the fire, and be cherished into life. When he was old enough, he came to his relations while they were all gathered in the great House of Assembly, dancing and making merry. Little Māui crept in and sat down behind his brothers. Soon his mother called the children and found a strange child, who proved that he was her son, and was taken in as one of the family. Some of the brothers were jealous, but the eldest addressed the others as follows:

'Never mind; let him be our dear brother. In the days of peace remember the proverb, "When you are on friendly terms, settle your disputes in a friendly way; when you are at war, you must redress your injuries by violence". It is better for us, brothers, to be kind to other people. These are the ways by which men gain influence – by laboring for abundance of food to feed others, by collecting property to give to others, and by similar means by which you promote the good of others.'

Thus, according to the New Zealand story related by Sir George Grey, Māui was received in his home.

Māui's home was placed by some of the Hawaiian tales at Kauiki, a foothill of the great extinct crater Haleakala, on the Island of Māui. It was here he lived when the sky was raised to its present position. Here was located the famous fort around which many battles were fought during the years immediately preceding the coming of Captain Cook. This fort was held by warriors of the Island of Hawai'i a number of years. It was from this home that Māui was supposed to have journeyed when he climbed Mt. Haleakala to ensnare the sun.

And yet most of the Hawaiian legends place Māui's home by the rugged black lava beds of the Wailuku river near Hilo on the island Hawai'i. Here he lived when he found the way to make fire by rubbing sticks together, and when he killed Kuna, the great eel, and performed other feats of valor. He was supposed to cultivate the land on the north side of the river. His mother, usually known as Hina, had her home in a lava cave under the beautiful Rainbow Falls, one of the fine scenic attractions of Hilo. An ancient demigod, wishing to destroy this home, threw a great mass of lava across the stream below the falls. The rising water was fast filling the cave.

Hina called loudly to her powerful son Māui. He came quickly and found that a large and strong ridge of lava lay across the stream. One end rested against a small hill. Māui struck the rock on the other side of the hill and thus broke a new pathway for the river. The water swiftly flowed away and the cave remained as the home of the Māui family.

According to the King Kalakaua family legend, translated by Queen Liliuokalani, Māui and his brothers also made this place their home. Here he aroused the anger of two uncles, his mother's brothers, who were called 'Tall Post' and 'Short Post,' because they guarded the entrance to a cave in which the Māui family probably had its home.

'They fought hard with Māui, and were thrown, and red water flowed freely from Māui's forehead. This was the first shower by Māui.' Perhaps some family discipline followed this knocking down of door posts, for it is said:

'They fetched the sacred Awa bush,
Then came the second shower by Māui;
The third shower was when the elbow of Awa was broken;
The fourth shower came with the sacred bamboo.'

Māui's mother, so says a New Zealand legend, had her home in the underworld as well as with her children. Māui determined to find the hidden dwelling place. His mother would meet the children in the evening and lie down to sleep with them and then disappear with the first appearance of dawn. Māui remained awake one night, and when all were asleep, arose quietly and stopped up every crevice by which a ray of light could enter. The morning came and the sun mounted up – far up in the sky. At last his mother leaped up and tore away the things which shut out the light.

'Oh, dear; oh, dear! She saw the sun high in the heavens; so she hurried away, crying at the thought of having been so badly treated by her own children.'

Māui watched her as she pulled up a tuft of grass and disappeared in the earth, pulling the grass back to its place.

Thus Māui found the path to the underworld. Soon he transformed himself into a pigeon and flew down, through the cave, until he saw a party of people under a sacred tree, like those growing in the ancient first Hawai'i. He flew to the tree and threw down berries upon the people. They threw back stones. At last he permitted a stone from his father to strike him, and he fell to the ground. 'They ran to catch him, but lo! the pigeon had turned into a man.'

Then his father 'took him to the water to be baptized' (possibly a modern addition to the legend). Prayers were offered and ceremonies passed through. But the prayers were incomplete and Māui's father knew that the gods would be angry and cause Māui's death, and all because in the hurried baptism a part of the prayers had been left unsaid. Then Māui returned to the upper world and lived again with his brothers.

Māui commenced his mischievous life early, for Hervey Islanders say that one day the children were playing a game dearly loved by Polynesians – hide-and-seek. Here a sister enters into the game and hides little Māui under a pile of dry sticks. His brothers could not find him, and the sister told them where to look. The sticks were carefully handled, but the child could not be found. He had shrunk himself so small that he was like an insect under some sticks and leaves. Thus early he began to use enchantments.

Māui's home, at the best, was only a sorry affair. Gods and demigods lived in caves and small grass houses. The thatch rapidly rotted and required continual renewal. In a very short time the heavy rains beat through the decaying roof. The home was without windows or doors, save as low openings in the ends or sides allowed entrance to those willing to crawl through. Off on one side would be the rude shelter, in the shadow of which Hina pounded the bark of certain trees into wood pulp and then into strips of thin, soft wood-paper, which bore the name of 'Tapa cloth.' This cloth Hina prepared for the clothing of Māui and his brothers. Tapa cloth was often treated to a coat of cocoa-nut, or candle-nut oil, making it somewhat waterproof and also more durable.

Here Māui lived on edible roots and fruits and raw fish, knowing little about cooked food, for the art of fire making was not yet known. In later years Māui was supposed to live on the eastern end of the island of Māui, and also in another home on the large island Hawai'i, on which he discovered how to make fire by rubbing dry sticks together. Māui was the Polynesian Mercury. As a little fellow he was endowed with peculiar powers, permitting him to become invisible or to change his human form into that of an animal. He was ready to take anything from any one by craft or force. Nevertheless, like the thefts of Mercury, his pranks usually benefited mankind.

It is a little curious that around the different homes of Māui, there is so little record of temples and priests and altars. He lived too far back for priestly customs. His story is a survivor of the days when of church and civil government there was none and worship of the gods was practically unknown, but every man was a law unto himself, and also to the other man, and quick retaliation followed any injury received.

MĀUI THE FISHERMAN

'Oh the great fish hook of Māui!
Manai-i-ka-lani 'Made fast to the heavens' – its name;

An earth-twisted cord ties the hook.
Engulfed from the lofty Kauiki. Its bait the red billed Alae,
The bird made sacred to Hina.
It sinks far down to Hawai'i,
Struggling and painfully dying.
Caught is the land under the water,
Floated up, up to the surface,
But Hina hid a wing of the bird
And broke the land under the water.
Below, was the bait snatched away
And eaten at once by the fishes,
The Ulua of the deep muddy places.'
Chant of Kualii, about AD 1700

One of Māui's homes was near Kauiki, a place well known throughout the Hawaiian Islands because of its strategic importance. For many years it was the site of a fort around which fierce battles were fought by the natives of the island of Māui, repelling the invasions of their neighbors from Hawai'i.

Haleakala (the House of the Sun), the mountain from which Māui the demigod snared the sun, looks down ten thousand feet upon the Kauiki headland. Across the channel from Haleakala rises Mauna Kea, 'The White Mountain' – the snow-capped – which almost all the year round rears its white head in majesty among the clouds.

In the snowy breakers of the surf which washes the beach below these mountains, are broken coral reefs – the fishing grounds of the Hawaiians. Here near Kauiki, according to some Hawaiian legends, Māui's mother Hina had her grass house and made and dried her kapa cloth. Even to the present day it is one of the few places in the islands where the kapa is still pounded into sheets from the bark of the hibiscus and kindred trees.

Here is a small bay partially reef-protected, over which year after year the moist clouds float and by day and by night crown the waters with rainbows – the legendary sign of the home of the deified ones. Here when the tide is out the natives wade and swim, as they have done for centuries, from coral block to coral block, shunning the deep resting places of their dread enemy, the shark, sometimes esteemed divine. Out on the edge of the outermost reef they seek the shellfish which cling to the coral, or spear the large fish which have been left in the beautiful little lakes of the reef. Coral land is a region of the sea coast abounding in miniature lakes and rugged valleys and steep mountains. Clear waters with every motion of the tide surge in and out through sheltered caves and submarine tunnels, according to an ancient Hawaiian song –

> 'Never quiet, never failing, never sleeping,
> Never very noisy is the sea of the sacred caves.'

Sea mosses of many hues are the forests which drape the hillsides of coral land and reflect the colored rays of light which pierce the ceaselessly moving waves. Down in the beautiful little lakes, under overhanging coral cliffs, darting in and out through the fringes of seaweed, the purple mullet and royal red fish flash before the eyes of the fisherman. Sometimes the many-tinted glorious fish of paradise reveal their beauties, and then again a school of black and gold citizens of the reef follow the tidal waves around projecting crags and through the hidden tunnels from lake to lake, while above the fisherman follows spearing or snaring as best he can. Māui's brothers were better fishermen than he. They sought the deep sea beyond the reef and the larger fish. They made hooks of bone or of mother of pearl, with a straight, slender, sharp-pointed piece leaning backward at a sharp angle. This was usually a consecrated bit of bone or mother of pearl, and was supposed to have peculiar power to hold fast any fish which had taken the bait.

These bones were usually taken from the body of some one who while living had been noted for great power or high rank. This sharp piece was tightly tied to the larger bone or shell, which formed the shank of the hook. The sacred barb of Māui's hook was a part of the magic bone he had secured from his ancestors in the underworld – the bone with which he struck the sun while lassooing him and compelling him to move more slowly through the heavens.

'Earth-twisted' – fibres of vines – twisted while growing, was the cord used by Māui in tying the parts of his magic hook together.

Long and strong were the fish lines made from the olona fibre, holding the great fish caught from the depths of the ocean. The fibres of the olona vine were among the longest and strongest threads found in the Hawaiian Islands.

Such a hook could easily be cast loose by the struggling fish, if the least opportunity were given. Therefore it was absolutely necessary to keep the line taut, and pull strongly and steadily, to land the fish in the canoe.

Māui did not use his magic hook for a long time. He seemed to understand that it would not answer ordinary needs. Possibly the idea of making the supernatural hook did not occur to him until he had exhausted his lower wit and magic upon his brothers.

It is said that Māui was not a very good fisherman. Sometimes his end of the canoe contained fish which his brothers had thought were on their hooks until they were landed in the canoe.

Many times they laughed at him for his poor success, and he retaliated with his mischievous tricks.

'E!' he would cry, when one of his brothers began to pull in, while the other brothers swiftly paddled the canoe forward. 'E!' See we both have caught great fish at the same moment. Be careful now. Your line is loose. 'Look out! Look out!'

All the time he would be pulling his own line in as rapidly as possible. Onward rushed the canoe. Each fisherman shouting to encourage the others. Soon the lines by the tricky manipulation of Māui would be crossed. Then as the great fish was brought near the side of the boat Māui the little, the mischievous one, would slip his hook toward the head of the fish and flip it over into the canoe – causing his brother's line to slacken for a moment. Then his mournful cry rang out: 'Oh, my brother, your fish is gone. Why did you not pull more steadily? It was a fine fish, and now it is down deep in the waters.' Then Māui held up his splendid catch (from his brother's hook) and received somewhat suspicious congratulations. But what could they do, Māui was the smart one of the family.

Their father and mother were both members of the household of the gods. The father was 'the supporter of the heavens' and the mother was 'the guardian of the way to the invisible world,' but pitifully small and very few were the gifts bestowed upon their children. Māui's brothers knew nothing beyond the average home life of the ordinary Hawaiian, and Māui alone was endowed with the power to work miracles. Nevertheless the student of Polynesian legends learns that Māui is more widely known than almost all the demigods of all nations as a discoverer of benefits for his fellows, and these physical rather than spiritual. After many fishing excursions Māui's brothers seemed to have wit enough to understand his tricks, and thenceforth they refused to take him in their canoe when they paddled out to the deep-sea fishing grounds. Then those who depended upon Māui to supply their daily needs murmured against his poor success. His mother scolded him and his brothers ridiculed him.

In some of the Polynesian legends it is said that his wives and children complained because of his laziness and at last goaded him into a new effort.

The ex-Queen Liliuokalani, in a translation of what is called 'the family chant,' says that Māui's mother sent him to his father for a hook with which to supply her need.

> 'Go hence to your father,
> 'Tis there you find line and hook.
> This is the hook – 'Made fast to the heavens' –
> 'Manaia-ka-lani' – 'tis called.
> When the hook catches land
> It brings the old seas together.
> Bring hither the large Alae,
> The bird of Hina.'

When Māui had obtained his hook, he tried to go fishing with his brothers. He leaped on the end of their canoe as they pushed out into deep water. They were angry and cried out: 'This boat is too small for another Māui.' So they threw him off and made him swim back to the beach. When they returned from their day's work, they brought back only a shark. Māui told them if he had been with them better fish would have been upon their hooks – the Ulua, for instance, or, possibly, the Pimoe – the king of fish. At last they let him go far out outside the harbor of Kipahula to a place opposite Ka Iwi o Pele, 'The bone of Pele,' a peculiar piece of lava lying near the beach at Hana on the eastern side of the island of Māui. There they fished, but only sharks were caught. The brothers ridiculed Māui, saying: 'Where are the Ulua, and where is Pimoe?'

Then Māui threw his magic hook into the sea, baited with one of the Alae birds, sacred to his mother Hina. He used the incantation, 'When I let go my hook with divine power, then I get the great Ulua.'

The bottom of the sea began to move. Great waves arose, trying to carry the canoe away. The fish pulled the canoe two days, drawing the line to its fullest extent. When the slack began to come in the line, because of the tired fish, Māui called for the brothers to pull hard against the coming fish. Soon land rose out of the water. Māui told them not to look back or the fish would be lost. One brother did look back – the line slacked, snapped, and broke, and the land lay behind them in islands.

One of the Hawaiian legends also says that while the brothers were paddling in full strength, Māui saw a calabash floating in the water. He lifted it into the canoe, and behold! his beautiful sister Hina of the sea. The brothers looked, and the separated islands lay behind them, free from the hook, while Cocoanut Island – the dainty spot of beauty in Hilo harbor – was drawn up – a little ledge of lava – in later years the home of a cocoanut grove.

The better, the more complete, legend comes from New Zealand, which makes Māui so mischievous that his brothers refuse his companionship – and therefore, thrown on his own resources, he studies how to make a hook which shall catch something worth while. In this legend Māui is represented as making his own hook and then pleading with his brothers to let him go with them once more. But they hardened their hearts against him, and refused again and again.

Māui possessed the power of changing himself into different forms. At one time while playing with his brothers he had concealed himself for them to find. They heard his voice in a corner of the house – but could not find him. Then under the mats on the floor, but again they could not find him. There was only an insect creeping on the floor. Suddenly they saw their little brother where the insect had been. Then they knew he had been tricky with them. So in these fishing days he resolved to go back to his old ways and cheat his brothers into carrying him with them to the great fishing grounds.

Sir George Grey says that the New Zealand Māui went out to the canoe and concealed himself as an insect in the bottom of the boat so that when the early morning light crept over the waters and his brothers pushed the canoe into the surf they could not see him. They rejoiced that Māui did not appear, and paddled away over the waters.

They fished all day and all night and on the morning of the next day, out from among the fish in the bottom of the boat came their troublesome brother.

They had caught many fine fish and were satisfied, so thought to paddle homeward; but their younger brother plead with them to go out, far out, to the deeper seas and permit him to cast his hook. He said he wanted larger and better fish than any they had captured.

So they paddled to their outermost fishing grounds – but this did not satisfy Māui –

'Farther out on the waters,
O! my brothers,
I seek the great fish of the sea.'

It was evidently easier to work for him than to argue with him – therefore far out in the sea they went. The home land disappeared from view; they could see only the outstretching waste of waters. Māui urged them out still farther. Then he drew his magic hook from under his malo or loin-cloth. The brothers wondered what he would do for bait. The New Zealand legend says that he struck his nose a mighty blow until the blood gushed forth. When this blood became clotted, he fastened it upon his hook and let it down into the deep sea.

Down it went to the very bottom and caught the under world. It was a mighty fish – but the brothers paddled with all their might and main and Māui pulled in the line. It was hard rowing against the power which held the hook down in the sea depths – but the brothers became enthusiastic over Māui's large fish, and were generous in their strenuous endeavors. Every muscle was strained and every paddle held strongly against the sea that not an inch should be lost. There was no sudden leaping and darting to and fro, no 'give' to the line; no 'tremble' as when a great fish would shake itself in impotent wrath when held captive by a hook. It was simply a struggle of tense muscle against an immensely heavy dead weight. To the brothers there came slowly the feeling that Māui was in one of his strange moods and that something beyond their former experiences with their tricky brother was coming to pass.

At last one of the brothers glanced backward. With a scream of intense terror he dropped his paddle. The others also looked.

Then each caught his paddle and with frantic exertion tried to force their canoe onward. Deep down in the heavy waters they pushed their paddles. Out of the great seas the black, ragged head of a large island was rising like a fish – it seemed to be chasing them through the boiling surf. In a little while the water became shallow around them, and their canoe finally rested on a black beach.

Māui for some reason left his brothers, charging them not to attempt to cut up this great fish. But the unwise brothers thought they would fill the canoe with part of this strange thing which they had caught. They began to cut up the back and put huge slices into their canoe. But the great fish – the island – shook under the blows and with mighty earthquake shocks tossed the boat of the brothers, and their canoe was destroyed. As they were struggling in the waters, the great fish devoured them. The island came up more and more from the waters – but the deep gashes made by Māui's brothers did not heal – they became the mountains and valleys stretching from sea to sea.

White of New Zealand says that Māui went down into the underworld to meet his great ancestress, who was one side dead and one side alive. From the dead side he took the jawbone, made a magic hook, and went fishing. When he let the hook down into the sea, he called:

> *'Take my bait. O Depths!*
> *Confused you are. O Depths!*
> *And coming upward.'*

Thus he pulled up Ao-tea-roa – one of the large islands of New Zealand. On it were houses, with people around them. Fires were burning. Māui walked over the island, saw with wonder the strange men and the mysterious fire. He took fire in his hands and was burned. He leaped into the sea, dived deep, came up with the other large island on his shoulders. This island he set on fire and left it always burning. It is said that the name for New Zealand given to Captain Cook was Te ika o Māui, 'The fish of Māui.' Some New Zealand natives say that he fished up the island on which dwelt 'Great Hina of the Night,' who finally destroyed Māui while he was seeking immortality.

One legend says that Māui fished up apparently from New Zealand the large island of the Tongas. He used this chant:

'O Tonga-nui!
Why art Thou
Sulkily biting, biting below?
Beneath the earth
The power is felt,
The foam is seen,
Coming.
O thou loved grandchild
Of Tangaroa-meha.'

This is an excellent poetical description of the great fish delaying the quick hard bite. Then the island comes to the surface and Māui, the beloved grandchild of the Polynesian god Kanaloa, is praised.

It was part of one of the legends that Māui changed himself into a bird and from the heavens let down a line with which he drew up land, but the line broke, leaving islands rather than a mainland. About two hundred lesser gods went to the new islands in a large canoe. The greater gods punished them by making them mortal.

Turner, in his book on Samoa, says there were three Māuis, all brothers. They went out fishing from Rarotonga. One of the brothers begged the 'goddess of the deep rocks' to let his hooks catch land. Then the island Manahiki was drawn up. A great wave washed two of the Māuis away. The other Māui found a great house in which eight hundred gods lived. Here he made his home until a chief from Rarotonga drove him away. He fled into the sky, but as he leaped he separated the land into two islands.

Other legends of Samoa say that Tangaroa, the great god, rolled stones from heaven. One became the island of Savaii, the other became Upolu. A god is sometimes represented as passing over the ocean with a bag of sand. Wherever he dropped a little sand islands sprang up.

Payton, the earnest and honored missionary of the New Hebrides Islands, evidently did not know the name Māuitikitiki, so he spells the name of the fisherman Ma-tshi-ktshi-ki, and gives the tale of the fishing up of the various islands. The natives said that Māui left footprints on the coral reefs of each island where he stood straining and lifting in his endeavors to pull up each other island. He threw his line around a large island intending to draw it up and unite it with the one on which he stood, but his line broke. Then he became angry and divided into two parts the island on which he stood. This same Māui is recorded by Mr. Payton as being in a flood which put out one volcano – Māui seized another, sailed across to a neighboring island and piled it upon the top of the volcano there, so the fire was placed out of reach of the flood.

In the Hervey Group of the Tahitian or Society Islands the same story prevails and the natives point out the place where the hook caught and a print was made by the foot in the coral reef. But they add some very legendary details. Māui's magic fish hook is thrown into the skies, where it continuously hangs, the curved tail of the constellation which we call Scorpio. Then one of the gods becoming angry with Māui seized him and threw him also among the stars. There he stays looking down upon his people. He has become a fixed part of the scorpion itself.

Hawaiian storytelling sometimes represents Māui as trying to draw the islands together while fishing them out of the sea. When they had pulled up the island of Kauai they looked back and were frightened. They evidently tried to rush away from the new monster and thus broke the line. Māui tore a side out of the small crater Kaula when trying to draw it to one of the other islands. Three aumakuas, three fishes supposed to be spirit-gods, guarded Kaula and defeated his purpose. At Hawai'i Cocoanut Island broke off because Māui pulled too hard. Another place near Hilo on the large island of Hawai'i where the hook was said to have caught is in the Wailuku river below Rainbow Falls.

Māui went out from his home at Kauiki, fishing with his brothers. After they had caught some fine fish the brothers desired to return, but Māui persuaded them to go out farther. Then when they became tired and determined to go back, he made the seas stretch out and the shores recede until they could see no land. Then drawing the magic hook, he baited it with the Alae or sacred mud hen belonging to his Mother Hina. Queen Liliuokalani's family chant has the following reference to this story:

> 'Māui longed for fish for Hina-akeahi
>   (Hina of the fire, his mother),
>   Go hence to your father,

There you will find line and hook.
Manaiakalani is the hook.
Where the islands are caught,
The ancient seas are connected.
The great bird Alae is taken,
The sister bird,
Of that one of the hidden fire of Māui.'

Māui evidently had no scruples against using anything which would help him carry out his schemes. He indiscriminately robbed his friends and the gods alike.

Down in the deep sea sank the hook with its struggling bait, until it was seized by 'the land under the water.'

But Hina the mother saw the struggle of her sacred bird and hastened to the rescue. She caught a wing of the bird, but could not pull the Alae from the sacred hook. The wing was torn off. Then the fish gathered around the bait and tore it in pieces. If the bait could have been kept entire, then the land would have come up in a continent rather than as an island. Then the Hawaiian group would have been unbroken. But the bait broke – and the islands came as fragments from the under world.

Māui's hook and canoe are frequently mentioned in the legends. The Hawaiians have a long rock in the Wailuku river at Hilo which they call Māui's canoe. Different names were given to Māui's canoe by the Māoris of New Zealand. 'Vine of Heaven,' 'Prepare for the North,' 'Land of the Receding Sea.' His fish hook bore the name 'Plume of Beauty.'

On the southern end of Hawke's Bay, New Zealand, there is a curved ledge of rocks extending out from the coast. This is still called by the Māoris 'Māui's fish-hook,' as if the magic hook had been so firmly caught in the jaws of the island that Māui could not disentangle it, but had been compelled to cut it off from his line.

There is a large stone on the sea coast of North Kohala on the island of Hawai'i which the Hawaiians point out as the place where Māui's magic hook caught the island and pulled it through the sea.

In the Tonga Islands, a place known as Hounga is pointed out by the natives as the spot where the magic hook caught in the rocks. The hook itself was said to have been in the possession of a chief-family for many generations.

Another group of Hawaiian legends, very incomplete, probably referring to Māui, but ascribed to other names, relates that a fisherman caught a large block of coral. He took it to his priest. After sacrificing, and consulting the gods, the priest advised the fisherman to throw the coral back into the sea with incantations. While so doing this block became Hawai'i-loa. The fishing continued and blocks of coral were caught and thrown back into the sea until all the islands appeared. Hints of this legend cling to other island groups as well as to the Hawaiian Islands. Fornander credits a fisherman from foreign lands as thus bringing forth the Hawaiian Islands from the deep seas. The reference occurs in part of a chant known as that of a friend of Pāao – the priest who is supposed to have come from Samoa to Hawai'i in the eleventh century. This priest calls for his companions:

'Here are the canoes. Get aboard.
Come along, and dwell on Hawai'i with the green back.
A land which was found in the ocean,
A land thrown up from the sea –

From the very depths of Kanaloa,
The white coral, in the watery caves,
That was caught on the hook of the fisherman.'

The god Kanaloa is sometimes known as a ruler of the underworld, whose land was caught by Māui's hook and brought up in islands. Thus in the legends the thought has been perpetuated that some one of the ancestors of the Polynesians made voyages and discovered islands.

In the time of Umi, King of Hawai'i, there is the following record of an immense bone fish-hook, which was called the 'fish-hook of Māui:'

'In the night of Muku (the last night of the month), a priest and his servants took a man, killed him, and fastened his body to the hook, which bore the name Manai-a-ka-lani, and dragged it to the heiau (temple) as a 'fish,' and placed it on the altar.'

This hook was kept until the time of Kamehameha I. From time to time he tried to break it, and pulled until he perspired.

Peapea, a brother of Kaahumanu, took the hook and broke it. He was afraid that Kamehameha would kill him. Kaahumanu, however, soothed the king, and he passed the matter over. The broken bone was probably thrown away.

MĀUI LIFTING THE SKY

Māui's home was for a long time enveloped by darkness. The heavens had fallen down, or, rather, had not been separated from the earth. According to some legends, the skies pressed so closely and so heavily upon the earth that when the plants began to grow, all the leaves were necessarily flat. According to other legends, the plants had to push up the clouds a little, and thus caused the leaves to flatten out into larger surface, so that they could better drive the skies back and hold them in place. Thus the leaves became flat at first, and have so remained through all the days of mankind. The plants lifted the sky inch by inch until men were able to crawl about between the heavens and the earth, and thus pass from place to place and visit one another.

After a long time, according to the Hawaiian legends, a man, supposed to be Māui, came to a woman and said: 'Give me a drink from your gourd calabash, and I will push the heavens higher.' The woman handed the gourd to him. When he had taken a deep draught, he braced himself against the clouds and lifted them to the height of the trees. Again he hoisted the sky and carried it to the tops of the mountains; then with great exertion he thrust it upwards once more, and pressed it to the place it now occupies. Nevertheless dark clouds many times hang low along the eastern slope of Māui's great mountain – Haleakala – and descend in heavy rains upon the hill Kauwiki; but they dare not stay, lest Māui the strong come and hurl them so far away that they cannot come back again.

A man who had been watching the process of lifting the sky ridiculed Māui for attempting such a difficult task. When the clouds rested on the tops of the mountains, Māui turned to punish his critic. The man had fled to the other side of the island. Māui rapidly pursued and finally caught him on the sea coast, not many miles north of the town now known as Lahaina. After a brief struggle the man was changed, according to the story, into a great black rock, which can be seen by any traveller who desires to localize the legends of Hawai'i.

In Samoa Tiitii, the latter part of the full name of Māuikiikii, is used as the name of the one who braced his feet against the rocks and pushed the sky up. The footprints, some six feet long, are said to be shown by the natives.

Another Samoan story is almost like the Hawaiian legend. The heavens had fallen, people crawled, but the leaves pushed up a little; but the sky was uneven. Men tried to walk, but hit their heads, and in this confined space it was very hot. A woman rewarded a man who lifted the sky to its proper place by giving him a drink of water from her cocoanut shell.

A number of small groups of islands in the Pacific have legends of their skies being lifted, but they attribute the labor to the great eels and serpents of the sea.

One of the Ellice group, Niu Island, says that as the serpent began to lift the sky the people clapped their hands and shouted 'Lift up!' 'High!' 'Higher!' But the body of the serpent finally broke into pieces which became islands, and the blood sprinkled its drops on the sky and became stars.

One of the Samoan legends says that a plant called daiga, which had one large umbrella-like leaf, pushed up the sky and gave it its shape.

The Vatupu, or Tracey Islanders, said at one time the sky and rocks were united. Then steam or clouds of smoke rose from the rocks, and, pouring out in volumes, forced the sky away from the earth. Man appeared in these clouds of steam or smoke. Perspiration burst forth as this man forced his way through the heated atmosphere. From this perspiration woman was formed. Then were born three sons, two of whom pushed up the sky. One, in the north, pushed as far as his arms would reach. The one in the south was short and climbed a hill, pushing as he went up, until the sky was in its proper place.

The Gilbert Islanders say the sky was pushed up by men with long poles.

The ancient New Zealanders understood incantations by which they could draw up or discover. They found a land where the sky and the earth were united. They prayed over their stone axe and cut the sky and land apart. 'Hau-hau-tu' was the name of the great stone axe by which the sinews of the great heaven above were severed, and Langi (sky) was separated from Papa (earth).

The New Zealand Māoris were accustomed to say that at first the sky rested close upon the earth and therefore there was utter darkness for ages. Then the six sons of heaven and earth, born during this period of darkness, felt the need of light and discussed the necessity of separating their parents – the sky from the earth – and decided to attempt the work.

Rongo (Hawaiian god Lono) the 'father of food plants,' attempted to lift the sky, but could not tear it from the earth. Then Tangaroa (Kanaloa), the 'father of fish and reptiles,' failed. Haumia Tiki-tiki (Māui Kiikii), the 'father of wild food plants,' could not raise the clouds. Then Tu (Hawaiian Ku), the 'father of fierce men,' struggled in vain. But Tāne (Hawaiian Kane), the 'father of giant forests,' pushed and lifted until he thrust the sky far up above him. Then they discovered their descendants – the multitude of human beings who had been living on the earth concealed and crushed by the clouds. Afterwards the last son, Tāwhiri (father of storms), was angry and waged war against his brothers. He hid in the sheltered hollows of the great skies. There he begot his vast brood of winds and storms with which he finally drove all his brothers and their descendants into hiding places on land and sea. The New Zealanders mention the names of the canoes in which their ancestors fled from the old home Hawaiki.

Tu (father of fierce men) and his descendants, however, conquered wind and storm and have ever since held supremacy.

The New Zealand legends also say that heaven and earth have never lost their love for each other. 'The warm sighs of earth ever ascend from the wooded mountains and valleys, and men call them mists. The sky also lets fall frequent tears which men term dewdrops.'

The Manihiki islanders say that Māui desired to separate the sky from the earth. His father, Ru, was the supporter of the heavens. Māui persuaded him to assist in lifting the burden. Māui went to the north and crept into a place, where, lying prostrate under the sky, he could brace himself against it and push with great power. In the same way Ru went to the south and braced himself against the southern skies. Then they made the signal, and both pressed 'with their backs against the solid blue mass.' It gave way before the great strength of the father and son. Then they lifted again, bracing themselves with hands and knees against the earth. They crowded it and bent it upward. They were able to stand with the sky resting on their shoulders. They heaved against the bending mass, and it receded rapidly. They quickly put the palms of their hands under it; then the tips of their fingers, and it retreated farther and farther. At last, 'drawing themselves out to gigantic proportions, they pushed the entire heavens up to the very lofty position which they have ever since occupied.'

But Māui and Ru had not worked perfectly together; therefore the sky was twisted and its surface was very irregular. They determined to smooth the sky before they finished their task, so they took large stone axes and chipped off the rough protuberances and ridges, until by and by the great arch was cut out and smoothed off. They then took finer tools and chipped and polished until the sky became the beautifully finished blue dome which now bends around the earth.

The Hervey Island tale, as related by W.W. Gill, states that Ru, the father of Māui, came from Avaiki (Hawa-iki), the underworld or abode of the spirits of the dead. He found men crowded down by the sky, which was a mass of solid blue stone. He was very sorry when he saw the condition of the inhabitants of the earth, and planned to raise the sky a little. So he planted stakes of different kinds of trees. These were strong enough to hold the sky so far above the earth 'that men could stand erect and walk about without inconvenience.' This was celebrated in one of the Hervey Island songs:

> 'Force up the heavens,
> O, Ru!
> And let the space be clear.'

For this helpful deed Ru received the name 'The supporter of the heavens.' He was rather proud of his achievement and was gratified because of the praise received. So he came sometimes and looked at the stakes and the beautiful blue sky resting on them. Māui, the son, came along and ridiculed his father for thinking so much of his work. Māui is not represented, in the legends, as possessing a great deal of love and reverence for his relatives provided his affection interfered with his mischief; so it was not at all strange that he laughed at his father. Ru became angry and said to Māui: 'Who told youngsters to talk? Take care of yourself, or I will hurl you out of existence.'

Māui dared him to try it. Ru quickly seized him and 'threw him to a great height.' But Māui changed himself to a bird and sank back to earth unharmed.

Then he changed himself back into the form of a man, and, making himself very large, ran and thrust his head between the old man's legs. He pried and lifted until Ru and the sky around him began to give. Another lift and he hurled them both to such a height that the sky could not come back.

Ru himself was entangled among the stars. His head and shoulders stuck fast, and he could not free himself. How he struggled, until the skies shook, while Māui went away. Māui was proud of his achievement in having moved the sky so far away. In this self-rejoicing he quickly forgot his father.

Ru died after a time. 'His body rotted away and his bones, of vast proportions, came tumbling down from time to time, and were shivered on the earth into countless fragments. These shattered bones of Ru are scattered over every hill and valley of one of the islands, to the very edge of the sea.'

Thus the natives of the Hervey Islands account for the many pieces of porous lava and the small pieces of pumice stone found occasionally in their islands. The 'bones' were very light and greatly resembled fragments of real bone. If the fragments were large enough they were sometimes taken and worshipped as gods. One of these pieces, of extraordinary size, was given to Mr. Gill when the natives were bringing in a large collection of idols. 'This one was known as 'The Light Stone,' and was worshipped as the god of the wind and the waves. Upon occasions of a hurricane, incantations and offerings of food would be made to it.'

Thus, according to different Polynesian legends, Māui raised the sky and made the earth inhabitable for his fellow men.

MĀUI AND TUNA

When Māui returned from the voyages in which he discovered or 'fished up' from the ocean depths new islands, he gave deep thought to the things he had found. As the islands appeared to come out of the water he saw they were inhabited. There were houses and stages for drying and preserving food. He was greeted by barking dogs. Fires were burning, food cooking and people working. He evidently had gone so far away from home that a strange people was found. The legend which speaks of the death of his brothers, 'eaten' by the great fish drawn up from the floor of the sea, may very easily mean that the new people killed and ate the brothers.

Māui apparently learned some new lessons, for on his return he quickly established a home of his own, and determined to live after the fashion of the families in the new islands.

Māui sought Hina-a-te-lepo, 'daughter of the swamp,' and secured her as his wife. The New Zealand tribes tell legends which vary in different localities about this woman Hina. She sometimes bore the name Rau-kura – 'The red plume.'

She cared for his thatched house as any other Polynesian woman was in the habit of doing. She attempted the hurried task of cooking his food before he snared the sun and gave her sufficient daylight for her labors.

They lived near the bank of a river from which Hina was in the habit of bringing water for the household needs.

One day she went down to the stream with her calabash. She was entwined with wreaths of leaves and flowers, as was the custom among Polynesian women. While she was standing on the bank, Tuna-roa, 'the long eel,' saw her. He swam up to the bank and suddenly struck her and knocked her into the water and covered her with slime from the blow given by his tail.

Hina escaped and returned to her home, saying nothing to Māui about the trouble. But the next day, while getting water, she was again overthrown and befouled by the slime of Tuna-roa.

Then Hina became angry and reported the trouble to Māui.

Māui decided to punish the long eel and started out to find his hiding place. Some of the New Zealand legends as collected by White, state that Tuna-roa was a very smooth skinned chief, who lived on the opposite bank of the stream, and, seeing Hina, had insulted her.

When Māui saw this chief, he caught two pieces of wood over which he was accustomed to slide his canoe into the sea. These he carried to the stream and laid them from bank to bank as a bridge over which he might entice Tuna-roa to cross.

Māui took his stone axe, Ma-Tori-Tori, 'the severer,' and concealed himself near the bank of the river.

When 'the long eel' had crossed the stream, Māui rushed out and killed him with a mighty blow of the stone axe, cutting the head from the body.

Other legends say that Māui found Tuna-roa living as an eel in a deep water hole, in a swamp on the sea-coast of Tata-a, part of the island Ao-tea-roa. Other stories located Tuna-roa in the river near Māui's home.

Māui saw that he could not get at his enemy without letting off the water which protected him.

Therefore into the forest went Māui, and with sacred ceremonies, selected trees from the wood of which he prepared tools and weapons.

Meanwhile, in addition to the insult given to Hina, Tuna-roa had caught and devoured two of Māui's children, which made Māui more determined to kill him.

Māui made the narrow spade (named by the Māoris of New Zealand the 'ko,' and by the Hawaiians 'o-o') and the sharp spears, with which to pierce either the earth or his enemy. These spears and spades were consecrated to the work of preparing a ditch by which to draw off the water protecting 'the long eel.'

The work of trench-making was accomplished with many incantations and prayers. The ditch was named 'the sacred digging,' and was tabooed to all other purposes except that of catching Tuna-roa.

Across this ditch Māui stretched a strong net, and then began a new series of chants and ceremonies to bring down an abundance of rain. Soon the flood came and the overflowing waters rushed down the sacred ditch. The walls of the deep pool gave way and 'the long eel' was carried down the trench into the waiting net. Then there was commotion. Tuna-roa was struggling for freedom.

Māui saw him and hastened to grasp his stone axe, 'the severer.' Hurrying to the net, he struck Tuna-roa a terrible blow, and cut off the head. With a few more blows, he cut the body in pieces. The head and tail were carried out into the sea. The head became fish and the tail became the great conger-eel. Other parts of the body became sea monsters. But some parts which fell in fresh water became the common eels. From the hairs of the head came certain vines and creepers among the plants.

After the death of Tuna-roa the offspring of Māui were in no danger of being killed and soon multiplied into a large family.

Another New Zealand legend related by White says that Māui built a sliding place of logs, over which Tuna-roa must pass when coming from the river.

Māui also made a screen behind which he could secrete himself while watching for Tuna-roa.

He commanded Hina to come down to the river and wait on the bank to attract Tuna-roa. Soon the long eel was seen in the water swimming near to Hina. Hina went to a place back of the logs which Māui had laid down.

Tuna-roa came towards her, and began to slide down the skids.

Māui sprang out from his hiding place and killed Tuna-roa with his axe, and cut him in pieces.

The tail became the conger-eel. Parts of his body became freshwater eels. Some of the blood fell upon birds and always after marked them with red spots. Some of the blood was thrown into certain trees, making this wood always red. The muscles became vines and creepers.

From this time the children of Māui caught and ate the eels of both salt and fresh water. Eel traps were made, and Māui taught the people the proper chants or incantations to use when catching eels.

This legend of Māui and the long eel was found by White in a number of forms among the different tribes of New Zealand, but does not seem to have had currency in many other island groups.

In Turner's 'Samoa' a legend is related which was probably derived from the Māui stories and yet differs in its romantic results. The Samoans say that among their ancient ones dwelt a woman named Sina. Sina among the Polynesians is the same as Hina – the 'h' is softened into 's'. She captured a small eel and kept it as a pet. It grew large and strong and finally attacked and bit her. She fled, but the eel followed her everywhere. Her father came to her assistance and raised high mountains between the eel and herself. But the eel passed over the barrier and pursued her. Her mother raised a new series of mountains. But again the eel surmounted the difficulties and attempted to seize Sina. She broke away from him and ran on and on. Finally she wearily passed through a village. The people asked her to stay and eat with them, but she said they could only help her by delivering her from the pursuing eel. The inhabitants of that village were afraid of the eel and refused to fight for her. So she ran on to another place. Here the chief offered her a drink of water and promised to kill the eel for her. He prepared awa, a stupefying drink, and put poison in it. When the eel came along the chief asked him to drink. He took the awa and prepared to follow Sina. When he came to the place where she was the pains of death had already seized him. While dying he begged her to bury his head by her home. This she did, and in time a plant new to the islands sprang up. It became a tree, and finally produced a cocoanut, whose two eyes could continually look into the face of Sina.

Tuna, in the legends of Fiji, was a demon of the sea. He lived in a deep sea cave, into which he sometimes shut himself behind closed doors of coral. When he was hungry, he swam through the ocean shadows, always watching the restless surface. When a canoe passed above him, he would throw himself swiftly through the waters, upset the canoe, and seize some of the boatmen and devour them. He was greatly feared by all the fishermen of the Fijian coasts.

Roko – a mo-o or dragon god – in his journey among the islands, stopped at a village by the sea and asked for a canoe and boatmen. The people said: 'We have nothing but a very old canoe out there by the water.' He went to it and found it in a very bad condition. He put it in the water, and decided that he could use it. Then he asked two men to go with him and paddle, but they refused because of fear, and explained this fear by telling the story of the water demon, who continually sought the destruction of this canoe, and also their own death. Roko encouraged them to take him to wage battle with Tuna, telling them he would destroy the monster. They paddled until they were directly over Tuna's cave. Roko told them to go off to one side and wait and watch, saying: 'I am going down to see this Tuna. If you see red blood boil up through the water, you may be sure that Tuna has been killed. If the blood is black, then you will know that he has the victory and I am dead.'

Roko leaped into the water and went down – down to the door of the cave. The coral doors were closed. He grasped them in his strong hands and tore them open, breaking them in pieces. Inside he found cave after cave of coral, and broke his way through until at last he awoke Tuna. The angry demon cried: 'Who is that?' Roko answered: 'It is I, Roko, alone. Who are you?'

Tuna aroused himself and demanded Roko's business and who guided him to that place. Roko replied: 'No one has guided me. I go from place to place, thinking that there is no one else in the world.'

Tuna shook himself angrily. 'Do you think I am nothing? This day is your last.'

Roko replied: 'Perhaps so. If the sky falls, I shall die.'

Tuna leaped upon Roko and bit him. Then came the mighty battle of the coral caves. Roko broke Tuna into several pieces – and the red blood poured in boiling bubbles upward through the clear ocean waters, and the boatmen cried: 'The blood is red – the blood is red – Tuna is dead by the hand of Roko.'

Roko lived for a time in Fiji, where his descendants still find their home. The people use this chant to aid them in difficulties:

'My load is a red one.

'It points in front to Kawa (Roko's home).

'Behind, it points to Dolomo – (a village on another island).'

In the Hawaiian legends, Hina was Māui's mother rather than his wife, and Kuna (Tuna) was a mo-o, a dragon or gigantic lizard possessing miraculous powers.

Hina's home was in the large cave under the beautiful Rainbow Falls near the city of Hilo. Above the falls the bed of the river is along the channel of an ancient lava flow. Sometimes the water pours in a torrent over the rugged lava, sometimes it passes through underground passages as well as along the black river bed, and sometimes it thrusts itself into boiling pools.

Māui lived on the northern side of the river, but a chief named Kuna-moo – a dragon – lived in the boiling pools. He attacked Hina and threw a dam across the river below Rainbow Falls, intending to drown Hina in her cave. The great ledge of rock filled the river bed high up the bank on the Hilo side of the river. Hina called on Māui for aid. Māui came quickly and with mighty blows cut out a new channel for the river – the path it follows to this day. The waters sank and Hina remained unharmed in her cave.

The place where Kuna dwelt was called Wai-kuna – the Kuna water. The river in which Hina and Kuna dwelt bears the name Wailuku – 'the destructive water.' Māui went above Kuna's home and poured hot water into the river. This part of the story could easily have arisen from a lava outburst on the side of the volcano above the river. The hot water swept in a flood over Kuna's home. Kuna jumped from the boiling pools over a series of small falls near his home into the river below. Here the hot water again scalded him and in pain he leaped from the river to the bank, where Māui killed him by beating him with a club. His body was washed down the river over the falls under which Hina dwelt, into the ocean.

The story of Kuna or Tuna is a legend with a foundation in the enmity between two chiefs of the long ago, and also in a desire to explain the origin of the family of eels and the invention of nets and traps.

MĀUI THE SKILLFUL

A ccording to the New Zealand legends there were six Māuis – the Hawaiians counted four. They were a band of brothers. The older five were known as 'the forgetful Māuis.' The tricky and quick-witted youngest member of the family was called Māui te atamai – 'Māui the skillful.'

He was curiously accounted for in the New Zealand underworld. When he went down through the long cave to his ancestor's home to find fire, he was soon talked about. 'Perhaps this is the man about whom so much is said in the upper world.' His ancestress from whom he obtained fire recognized him as the man called 'the deceitful Māui.' Even his parents told him once, 'We know you are a tricky fellow – more so than any other man.' One of the New Zealand fire legends while recording his flight to the underworld and his appearance as a bird, says: 'The men tried to spear him, and to catch him in nets. At last they cried out, "Maybe you are the man whose fame is great in the upper world." At once he leaped to the ground and appeared in the form of a man.'

He was not famous for inventions, but he was always ready to improve upon anything which was already in existence. He could take the sun in hand and make it do better work. He could tie the moon so that it had to swim back around the island to the place in the ocean from which it might rise again, and go slowly through the night.

His brothers invented a slender, straight and smooth spear with which to kill birds. He saw the fluttering, struggling birds twist themselves off the smooth point and escape. He made a good light bird spear and put notches in it and kept most of the birds stuck. His brothers finally examined his spear and learned the reason for its superiority. In the same way they learned how to spear fish. They could strike and wound and sometimes kill – but they could not with their smooth spears draw the fish from the waters of the coral caves. But Māui the youngest made barbs, so that the fish could not easily shake themselves loose. The others soon made their spears like his.

The brothers were said to have invented baskets in which to trap eels, but many eels escaped. Māui improved the basket by secretly making an inside partition as well as a cover, and the eels were securely trapped. It took the brothers a long time to learn the real difference between their baskets and his. One of the family made a basket like his and caught many eels. Then Māui became angry and chanted a curse over him and bewildered him, then changed him into a dog.

The Manahiki Islanders have the legend that Māui made the moon, but could not get good light from it. He tried experiments and found that the sun was quite an improvement. The sun's example stimulated the moon to shine brighter.

Once Māui became interested in tattooing and tried to make a dog look better by placing dark lines around the mouth. The legends say that one of the sacred birds saw the pattern and then marked the sky with the red lines sometimes seen at sunrise and sunset. A Hawaiian legend says that Māui tattooed his arm with a sacred name and thus that arm was strong enough to hold the sun when he lassoed it. There is a New Zealand legend in which Māui is made one of three gods who first created man and then woman from one of the man's ribs.

The Hawaiians dwelling in Hilo have many stories of Māui. They say that his home was on the northern bank of the Wailuku River. He had a strong staff made from an ohia tree (the native apple tree). With this he punched holes through the lava, making natural bridges and boiling pools, and new channels for its sometimes obstructed waters, so that the people could go up or down the river more easily. Near one of the natural bridges is a figure of the moon carved in the rocks, referred by some of the natives to Māui.

Māui is said to have taught his brothers the different kinds of fish nets and the use of the strong fibre of the olona, which was much better than cocoanut threads.

The New Zealand stories relate the spear-throwing contests of Māui and his brothers. As children, however, they were not allowed the use of wooden spears. They took the stems of long, heavy reeds and threw them at each other, but Māui's reeds were charmed into stronger and harder fibre so that he broke his mother's house and made her recognize him as one of her children. He had been taken away as soon as he was born by the gods to whom he was related. When he found his way back home his mother paid no attention to him. Thus by a spear thrust he won a home.

The brothers all made fish hooks, but Māui the youngest made two kinds of hooks – one like his brothers' and one with a sharp barb. His brothers' hooks were smooth so that it was difficult to keep the fish from floundering and shaking themselves off, but they noticed that the fish were held by Māui's hook better than by theirs. Māui was not inclined to devote himself to hard work, and lived on his brothers as much as possible – but when driven out by his wife or his mother he would catch more fish than the other fishermen. They tried to examine his hooks, but he always changed his hooks so that they could not see any difference between his and theirs. At such times they called him the mischievous one and tried to leave him behind while they went fishing. They were, however, always ready to give him credit for his improvements. They dealt generously with him when they learned what he had really accomplished. When they caught him with his barbed hook they forgot the past and called him 'ke atamai' – the skillful.

The idea that fish hooks made from the jawbones of human beings were better than others, seemed to have arisen at first from the angle formed in the lower jawbone. Later these human fish hooks were considered sacred and therefore possessed of magic powers. The greater sanctity and power belonged to the bones which bore more especial relation to the owner. Therefore Māui's 'magic hook,' with which he fished up islands, was made from the jawbone of his ancestress Mahuika. It is also said that in order to have powerful hooks for everyday fishing he killed two of his children. Their right eyes he threw up into the sky to become stars. One became the morning and the other the evening star.

The idea that the death of any members of the family must not stand in the way of obtaining magical power, has prevailed throughout Polynesia.

From this angle in the jawbone Māui must have conceived the idea of making a hook with a piece of bone or shell which should be fastened to the large bone at a very sharp angle, thus making a kind of barb. Hooks like this have been made for ages among the Polynesians.

Māui and his brothers went fishing for eels with bait strung on the flexible rib of a cocoanut leaf. The stupid brothers did not fasten the ends of the string. Therefore the eels easily slipped the bait off and escaped. But Māui made the ends of his string fast, and captured many eels.

The little things which others did not think about were the foundation of Māui's fame. Upon these little things he built his courage to snare the sun and seek fire for mankind.

In a New Zealand legend, quoted by Edward Tregear, Māui is called Māui-maka-walu, or 'Māui with eyes eight.' This eight-eyed Māui would be allied to the Hindoo deities who with their eight eyes face the four quarters of the world – thus possessing both insight into the affairs of men and foresight into the future.

Fornander, the Hawaiian ethnologist, says: 'In Hawaiian storytelling, Kamapuaa, the demigod opponent of the goddess Pele, is described as having eight eyes and eight feet; and in the legends Maka-walu, 'eight-eyed,' is a frequent epithet of gods and chiefs.' He notes this coincidence with the appearance of some of the principal Hindoo deities as having some bearing upon the origin of the Polynesians. It may be that a comparative study of the legends of other islands of the Pacific by some student will open up other new and important facts.

In Tahiti, on the island Raiatea, a high priest or prophet lived in the long, long ago. He was known as Māui the prophet of Tahiti. He was probably not Māui the demigod. Nevertheless he was represented as possessing very strange prophetical powers.

According to the historian Ellis, who previous to 1830 spent eight years in the Society and Hawaiian Islands, this prophet Māui clearly prophesied the coming of an outriggerless canoe from some foreign land. An outrigger is a log which so balances a canoe that it can ride safely through the treacherous surf.

The chiefs and prophets charged him with stating the impossible.

He took his wooden calabash and placed it in a pool of water as an illustration of the way such a boat should float.

Then with the floating bowl before him he uttered the second prophecy, that boats without line to tie the sails to the masts, or the masts to the ships, should also come to Tahiti.

When English ships under Captain Wallis and Captain Cook, in the latter part of the eighteenth century, visited these islands, the natives cried out, 'O the canoes of Māui – the outriggerless canoes.'

Passenger steamships, and the men-of-war from the great nations, have taught the Tahitians that boats without sails and masts can cross the great ocean, and again they have recurred to the words of the prophet Māui, and have exclaimed, 'O the boats without sails and masts.' This rather remarkable prophecy could easily have occurred to Māui as he saw a wooden calabash floating over rough waters.

Māui's improvement upon nature's plan in regard to certain birds is also given in the legends as a proof of his supernatural powers.

White relates the story as follows: 'Māui requested some birds to go and fetch water for him. The first one would not obey, so he threw it into the water. He requested another bird to go – and it refused, so he threw it into the fire, and its feathers were burnt. But the next bird obeyed, but could not carry the water, and he rewarded it by making the feathers of the fore part of its head white. Then he asked another bird to go, and it filled its ears with water and brought it to Māui, who drank, and then pulled the bird's legs and made them long in payment for its act of kindness.'

Diffenbach says: 'Māui, the Adam of New Zealand, left the cat's cradle to the New Zealanders as an inheritance.' The name 'Whai' was given to the game. It exhibited the various steps of creation according to Māori storytelling. Every change in the cradle shows some act in creation. Its various stages were called 'houses.' Diffenbach says again: 'In this game of Māui they are great proficients. It is a game like that called cat's cradle in Europe. It is intimately connected with their ancient traditions and in the different figures which the cord is made to assume whilst held on both hands, the outline of their different varieties of houses, canoes or figures of men and women are imagined to be represented.' One writer connects this game with witchcraft, and says it was brought from the underworld. Some parts of the puzzle show the adventures of Māui, especially his attempt to win immortality for men.

In New Zealand it was said Māui found a large, fine-grained stone block, broke it in pieces, and from the fragments learned how to fashion stone implements.

White also tells the New Zealand legend of Māui and the winds.

'Māui caught and held all the winds save the west wind. He put each wind into a cave, so that it might not blow. He sought in vain for the west wind, but could not find from whence it came. If he had found the cave in which it stayed he would have closed the entrance to that cave with rocks. When the west wind blows lightly it is because Māui has got near to it, and has nearly caught it, and it has gone into its home, the cave, to escape him. When the winds of the south, east, and north blow furiously it is because the rocks have been removed by the stupid people who could not learn the lessons taught by Māui. At other times Māui allows these winds to blow in hurricanes to punish that people, and also that he may ride on these furious winds in search of the west wind.'

In the Hawaiian legends Māui is represented as greatly interested in making and flying kites. His favorite place for the sport was by the boiling pools of the Wailuku river near Hilo. He had the winds under his control and would call for them to push his kites in the direction he wished. His incantation calling up the winds is given in this Māui proverb –

'Strong wind come,
Soft wind come.'

White in his 'Ancient History of the Māoris,' relates some of Māui's experiences with the people whom he found on the islands brought up from the underworld. On one island he found a sand house with eight hundred gods living in it. Apparently Māui discovered islands with inhabitants, and was reported to have fished them up out of the depths of the ocean. Fishing was sailing over the ocean until distant lands were drawn near or 'fished up.'

Māui walked over the islands and found men living on them and fires burning near their homes. He evidently did not know much about fire, for he took it in his hands. He was badly burned and rushed into the sea. Down he dived under the cooling waters and came up with one of the New Zealand islands on his shoulders. But his hands were still burning, so wherever he held the island it was set on fire.

These fires are still burning in the secret recesses of the volcanoes, and sometimes burst out in flowing lava. Then Māui paid attention to the people whom he had fished up. He tried to teach them, but they did not learn as he thought they should. He quickly became angry and said, 'It is a waste of light for the sun to shine on such stupid people.' So he tried to hold his hands between them and the sun, but the rays of the sun were too many and too strong; therefore, he could not shut them out. Then he tried the moon and managed to make it dark a part of the time each month. In this way he made a little trouble for the stupid people.

There are other hints in the legends concerning Māui's desire to be revenged upon any one who incurred his displeasure. It was said that Māui for a time lived in the heavens above the earth. Here he had a foster brother Maru. The two were cultivating the fields. Maru sent a snowstorm over Māui's field. (It would seem as if this might be a Polynesian memory of a cold land where their ancestors knew the cold winter, or a lesson learned from the snow-caps of high mountains.) At any rate, the snow blighted Māui's crops. Māui retaliated by praying for rain to destroy Maru's fields.

But Maru managed to save a part of his crops. Other legends make Māui the aggressor. At the last, however, Māui became very angry. The foster parents tried to soothe the two men by saying, 'Live in peace with each other and do not destroy each other's food.' But Māui was implacable and lay in wait for his foster brother, who was in the habit of carrying fruit and grass as an offering to the gods of a temple situated on the summit of a hill. Here Māui killed Maru and then went away to the earth.

This legend is told by three or four different tribes of New Zealand and is very similar to the Hebrew story of Cain and Abel. At this late day it is difficult to say definitely whether or not it owes its origin to the early touch of Christianity upon New Zealand when white men first began to live with the natives. It is somewhat similar to stories found in the Tonga Islands and also in the Hawaiian group, where a son of the first gods, or rather of the first men, kills a brother. In each case there is the shadow of the Biblical idea. It seems safe to infer that such legends are not entirely drawn from contact with Christian civilization. The natives claim that these stories are very ancient, and that their fathers knew them before the white men sailed on the Pacific.

MĀUI'S KITE FLYING

Maui the demigod was sometimes the Hercules of Polynesia. His exploits were fully as marvelous as those of the hero of classic mythology. He snared the sun. He pulled up islands from the ocean depths. He lifted the sky into its present position and smoothed its arched surface with his stone axe. These stories belong to all Polynesia.

There are numerous less important local tales, some of them peculiar to New Zealand, some to the Society Islands and some to the Hawaiian group.

One of the old native Hawaiians says that in the long, long ago the birds were flying around the homes of the ancient people. The flutter of their wings could be heard and the leaves and branches moved when the motion of the wings ceased and the wanderers through the air found resting places. Then came sweet music from the trees and the people marvelled. Only one of all mankind could see the winged warblers. Māui, the demigod, had clear vision. The swift-flying wings covered with red or gold he saw. The throats tinted many colors and reflecting the sunlight with diamond sparks of varied hues he watched while they trembled with the melody of sweet bird songs. All others heard but did not see. They were blind and yet had open vision.

Sometimes the iiwi (a small red bird) fluttered in the air and uttered its shrill, happy song, and Māui saw and heard. But the bird at that time was without color in the eyes of the ancient people and only the clear voice was heard, while no speck of bird life flecked the clear sky overhead.

At one time a god from one of the other islands came to visit Māui. Each boasted of and described the beauties and merits of his island. While they were conversing, Māui called for his friends the birds. They gathered around the house and fluttered among the leaves of the surrounding trees. Soon their sweet voices filled the air on all sides. All the people wondered and worshipped, thinking they heard the fairy or menehune people. It was said that Māui had painted the bodies of his invisible songsters and for a long time had kept the delight of their flashing colors to himself. But when the visitor had rejoiced in the mysterious harmonies, Māui decided to take away whatever veil shut out the sight of these things beautiful, that his bird friends might be known and honored ever after. So he made the birds reveal themselves perched in the trees or flying in the air. The clear eyes of the god first recognized the new revelation, then all the people became dumb before the sweet singers adorned in all their brilliant tropical plumage.

The beautiful red birds, iiwi and akakani, and the birds of glorious yellow feathers, the ōō and the mamo, were a joy to both eye and ear and found high places in Hawaiian legend and story, and all gave their most beautiful feathers for the cloaks and helmets of the chiefs.

The Māoris of New Zealand say that Māui could at will change himself into a bird and with his feathered friends find a home in leafy shelters. In bird form he visited the gods of the underworld. His capricious soul was sensitive to the touch of all that mysterious life of nature.

With the birds as companions and the winds as his servants Māui must soon have turned his inventive mind to kite-making.

The Hawaiian traditional tales are perhaps the only ones of the Pacific Ocean which give to any of the gods the pleasure and excitement of kite flying. Māui, after repeated experiments, made a large kite for himself. It was much larger than any house of his time or generation. He twisted a long line from the strong fibres of the native plant known as the olona. He endowed both kite and string with marvelous powers and launched the kite up toward the clouds. It rose very slowly. The winds were not lifting it into the sky.

Māui remembered that an old priest lived in Waipio valley, the largest and finest valley of the large island, Hawai'i, on which he made his home.

This priest had a covered calabash in which he compelled the winds to hide when he did not wish them to play on land and sea. The priest's name was Kaleiioku, and his calabash was known as ipu-makani-a ka maumau, 'the calabash of the perpetual winds.' Māui called for the priest who had charge of the winds to open his calabash and let them come up to Hilo and blow along the Wailuku river. The natives say that the place where Māui stood was marked by the pressure of his feet in the lava rocks of the river bank as he braced himself to hold the kite against the increasing force of the winds which pushed it towards the sky. Then the enthusiasm of kite flying filled his youthful soul and he cried aloud, screaming his challenge along the coast of the sea toward Waipio –

> *'O winds, winds of Waipio,*
> *In the calabash of Kaleiioku.*
> *Come from the ipu-makani,*
> *O wind, the wind of Hilo,*
> *Come quickly, come with power.'*

Then the priest lifted the cover of the calabash of the winds and let the strong winds of Hilo escape. Along the sea coast they rushed until as they entered Hilo Bay they heard the voice of Māui calling –

> *'O winds, winds of Hilo,*
> *Hasten and come to me.'*

With a tumultuous rush the strong winds turned toward the mountains. They forced their way along the gorges and palisades of the Wailuku river. They leaped into the heavens, making a fierce attack upon the monster which Māui had sent into the sky. The kite struggled as it was pushed upward by the hands of the fierce winds, but Māui rejoiced. His heart was uplifted by the joy of the conflict in which his strength to hold was pitted against the power of the winds to tear away. And again he shouted toward the sea –

> 'O winds, the winds of Hilo,
> Come to the mountains, come.'

The winds which had been stirring up storms on the face of the waters came inland. They dashed against Māui. They climbed the heights of the skies until they fell with full violence against their mighty foe hanging in the heavens.

The kite had been made of the strongest kapa (paper cloth) which Māui's mother could prepare. It was not torn, although it was bent backward to its utmost limit. Then the strain came on the strong cord of olona fibre. The line was stretched and strained as the kite was pushed back. Then Māui called again and again for stronger winds to come. The cord was drawn out until the kite was far above the mountains. At last it broke and the kite was tossed over the craters of the volcanoes to the land of the district of Ka-u on the other side of the island.

Then Māui was angry and hastily leaped over the mountains, which are nearly fourteen thousand feet in altitude. In a half dozen strides he had crossed the fifty or sixty miles from his home to the place where the kite lay. He could pass over many miles with a single step. His name was Māui-Mama, 'Māui the Swift.' When Māui returned with his kite he was more careful in calling the winds to aid him in his sport.

The people watched their wise neighbor and soon learned that the kite could be a great blessing to them. When it was soaring in the sky there was always dry and pleasant weather. It was a day for great rejoicing. They could spread out their kapa cloth to dry as long as the kite was in the sky. They could carry out their necessary work without fear of the rain. Therefore when any one saw the kite beginning to float along the mountain side he would call out joyfully, 'E! Māui's kite is in the heavens.' Māui would send his kite into the blue sky and then tie the line to the great black stones in the bed of the Wailuku river.

Māui soon learned the power of his kite when blown upon by a fierce wind. With his accustomed skill he planned to make use of his strong servant, and therefore took the kite with him on his journeys to the other islands, using it to aid in making swift voyages. With the wind in the right direction, the kite could pull his double canoe very easily and quickly to its destination.

Time passed, and even the demigod died. The fish hook with which he drew the Hawaiian Islands up from the depths of the sea was allowed to lie on the lava by the Wailuku river until it became a part of the stone. The double canoe was carried far inland and then permitted to petrify by the river side. The two stones which represent the double canoe now bear the name 'Waa-Kauhi,' and the kite has fallen from the sky far up on the mountain side, where it still rests, a flat plot of rich land between Mauna Kea and Mauna Loa.

MĀUI SNARING THE SUN

'Māui became restless and fought the sun
With a noose that he laid.

And winter won the sun,
And summer was won by Māui.'
Queen Liliuokalani's Family Chant

A very unique legend is found among the widely scattered Polynesians. The story of Māui's 'Snaring the Sun' was told among the Māoris of New Zealand, the Kanakas of the Hervey and Society Islands, and the ancient natives of Hawai'i. The Samoans tell the same story without mentioning the name of Māui. They say that the snare was cast by a child of the sun itself.

The Polynesian stories of the origin of the sun are worthy of note before the legend of the change from short to long days is given.

The Tongan Islanders, according to W.W. Gill, tell the story of the origin of the sun and moon. They say that Vatea (Wakea) and their ancestor Tongaiti quarreled concerning a child – each claiming it as his own. In the struggle the child was cut in two. Vatea squeezed and rolled the part he secured into a ball and threw it away, far up into the heavens, where it became the sun. It shone brightly as it rolled along the heavens, and sank down to Avaiki (Hawai'i), the nether world. But the ball came back again and once more rolled across the sky. Tongaiti had let his half of the child fall on the ground and lie there, until made envious by the beautiful ball Vatea made.

At last he took the flesh which lay on the ground and made it into a ball. As the sun sank he threw his ball up into the darkness, and it rolled along the heavens, but the blood had drained out of the flesh while it lay upon the ground, therefore it could not become so red and burning as the sun, and had not life to move so swiftly. It was as white as a dead body, because its blood was all gone; and it could not make the darkness flee away as the sun had done. Thus day and night and the sun and moon always remain with the earth.

The legends of the Society Islands say that a demon in the west became angry with the sun and in his rage ate it up, causing night. In the same way a demon from the east would devour the moon, but for some reason these angry ones could not destroy their captives and were compelled to open their mouths and let the bright balls come forth once more. In some places a sacrifice of some one of distinction was needed to placate the wrath of the devourers and free the balls of light in times of eclipse.

The moon, pale and dead in appearance, moved slowly; while the sun, full of life and strength, moved quickly. Thus days were very short and nights were very long. Mankind suffered from the fierceness of the heat of the sun and also from its prolonged absence. Day and night were alike a burden to men. The darkness was so great and lasted so long that fruits would not ripen.

After Māui had succeeded in throwing the heavens into their place, and fastening them so that they could not fall, he learned that he had opened a way for the sun-god to come up from the lower world and rapidly run across the blue vault. This made two troubles for men – the heat of the sun was very great and the journey too quickly over. Māui planned to capture the sun and punish him for thinking so little about the welfare of mankind.

As Rev. A.O. Forbes, a missionary among the Hawaiians, relates, Māui's mother was troubled very much by the heedless haste of the sun. She had many kapa-cloths to make, for this was the only kind of clothing known in Hawai'i, except sometimes a woven mat or a long grass fringe worn as a skirt. This native cloth was made by pounding the fine bark of certain trees with wooden mallets until the fibres were beaten and ground into a wood pulp. Then she pounded the pulp into thin sheets from which the best sleeping mats and clothes could be fashioned. These kapa cloths had to be thoroughly dried, but the days were so short that by the time she had spread out the kapa the sun had heedlessly rushed across the sky and gone down into the underworld, and all the cloth had to be gathered up again and cared for until another day should come. There were other troubles. 'The food could not be prepared and cooked in one day. Even an incantation to the gods could not be chanted through ere they were overtaken by darkness.'

This was very discouraging and caused great suffering, as well as much unnecessary trouble and labor. Many complaints were made against the thoughtless sun.

Māui pitied his mother and determined to make the sun go lower that the days might be long enough to satisfy the needs of men. Therefore, he went over to the northwest of the island on which he lived. This was Mt. Iao, an extinct volcano, in which lies one of the most beautiful and picturesque valleys of the Hawaiian Islands. He climbed the ridges until he could see the course of the sun as it passed over the island. He saw that the sun came up the eastern side of Mt. Haleakala. He crossed over the plain between the two mountains and climbed to the top of Mt. Haleakala. There he watched the burning sun as it came up from Koolau and passed directly over the top of the mountain. The summit of Haleakala is a great extinct crater twenty miles in circumference, and nearly twenty-five hundred feet in depth. There are two tremendous gaps or chasms in the side of the crater wall, through which in days gone by the massive bowl poured forth its flowing lava. One of these was the Koolau, or eastern gap, in which Māui probably planned to catch the sun.

Mt. Hale-a-ka-la of the Hawaiian Islands means House-of-the-sun. 'La,' or 'Ra,' is the name of the sun throughout parts of Polynesia. Ra was the sun-god of ancient Egypt. Thus the antiquities of Polynesia and Egypt touch each other, and today no man knows the full reason thereof.

The Hawaiian legend says Māui was taunted by a man who ridiculed the idea that he could snare the sun, saying, 'You will never catch the sun. You are only an idle nobody.'

Māui replied, 'When I conquer my enemy and my desire is attained, I will be your death.'

After studying the path of the sun, Māui returned to his mother and told her that he would go and cut off the legs of the sun so that he could not run so fast.

His mother said: 'Are you strong enough for this work?' He said, 'Yes.' Then she gave him fifteen strands of well-twisted fibre and told him to go to his grandmother, who lived in the great crater of Haleakala, for the rest of the things in his conflict with the sun. She said: 'You must climb the mountain to the place where a large wiliwili tree is standing. There you will find the place where the sun stops to eat cooked bananas prepared by your grandmother. Stay there until a rooster crows three times; then watch your grandmother go out to make a fire and put on food. You had better take her bananas. She will look for them and find you and ask who you are. Tell her you belong to Hina.'

When she had taught him all these things, he went up the mountain to Kaupo to the place Hina had directed. There was a large wiliwili tree. Here he waited for the rooster to crow. The name of that rooster was Kalauhele-moa. When the rooster had crowed three times, the grandmother came out with a bunch of bananas to cook for the sun. She took off the upper part of the bunch and laid it down. Māui immediately snatched it away. In a moment she turned to pick it up, but could not find it. She was angry and cried out: 'Where are the bananas of the sun?' Then she took off another part of the bunch, and Māui stole that. Thus he did until all the bunch had been taken away. She was almost blind and could not detect him by sight, so she sniffed all around her until she detected the smell of a man. She asked: 'Who are you? To whom do you belong?' Māui replied: 'I belong to Hina.' 'Why have you come?' Māui told her, 'I have come to kill the sun. He goes so fast that he never dries the tapa Hina has beaten out.'

The old woman gave a magic stone for a battle axe and one more rope. She taught him how to catch the sun, saying: 'Make a place to hide here by this large wiliwili tree. When the first leg of the sun comes up, catch it with your first rope, and so on until you have used all your ropes. Fasten them to the tree, then take the stone axe to strike the body of the sun.'

Māui dug a hole among the roots of the tree and concealed himself. Soon the first ray of light – the first leg of the sun – came up along the mountain side. Māui threw his rope and caught it. One by one the legs of the sun came over the edge of the crater's rim and were caught. Only one long leg was still hanging down the side of the mountain. It was hard for the sun to move that leg. It shook and trembled and tried hard to come up. At last it crept over the edge and was caught by Māui with the rope given by his grandmother.

When the sun saw that his sixteen long legs were held fast in the ropes, he began to go back down the mountain side into the sea. Then Māui tied the ropes fast to the tree and pulled until the body of the sun came up again. Brave Māui caught his magic stone club or axe, and began to strike and wound the sun, until he cried: 'Give me my life.' Māui said: 'If you live, you may be a traitor. Perhaps I had better kill you.' But the sun begged for life. After they had conversed a while, they agreed that there should be a regular motion in the journey of the sun. There should be longer days, and yet half the time he might go quickly as in the winter time, but the other half he must move slowly as in summer. Thus men dwelling on the earth should be blessed.

Another legend says that he made a lasso and climbed to the summit of Mt. Haleakala. He made ready his lasso, so that when the sun came up the mountain side and rose above him he could cast the noose and catch the sun, but he only snared one of the sun's larger rays and broke it off. Again and again he threw the lasso until he had broken off all the strong rays of the sun.

Then he shouted exultantly, 'Thou art my captive; I will kill thee for going so swiftly.'

Then the sun said, 'Let me live and thou shalt see me go more slowly hereafter. Behold, hast thou not broken off all my strong legs and left me only the weak ones?'

So the agreement was made, and Māui permitted the sun to pursue his course, and from that day he went more slowly.

Māui returned from his conflict with the sun and sought for Moemoe, the man who had ridiculed him. Māui chased this man around the island from one side to the other until they had passed through Lahaina (one of the first mission stations in 1828). There on the seashore near the large black rock of the legend of Māui lifting the sky he found Moemoe. Then they left the seashore and the contest raged up hill and down until Māui slew the man and 'changed the body into a long rock, which is there to this day, by the side of the road going past Black Rock.'

Before the battle with the sun occurred Māui went down into the underworld, according to the New Zealand tradition, and remained a long time with his relatives. In some way he learned that there was an enchanted jawbone in the possession of some one of his ancestors, so he waited and waited, hoping that at last he might discover it.

After a time he noticed that presents of food were being sent away to some person whom he had not met.

One day he asked the messengers, 'Who is it you are taking that present of food to?'

The people answered, 'It is for Muri, your ancestress.'

Then he asked for the food, saying, 'I will carry it to her myself.'

But he took the food away and hid it. 'And this he did for many days,' and the presents failed to reach the old woman.

By and by she suspected mischief, for it did not seem as if her friends would neglect her so long a time, so she thought she would catch the tricky one and eat him. She depended upon her sense of smell to detect the one who had troubled her. As Sir George Grey tells the story: 'When Māui came along the path carrying the present of food, the old chiefess sniffed and sniffed until she was sure that she smelt some one coming. She was very much exasperated, and her stomach began to distend itself that she might be ready to devour this one when he came near.

Then she turned toward the south and sniffed and not a scent of anything reached her. Then she turned to the north, and to the east, but could not detect the odor of a human being. She made one more trial and turned toward the west. Ah! then came the scent of a man to her plainly and she called out, 'I know, from the smell wafted to me by the breeze, that somebody is close to me."

Māui made known his presence and the old woman knew that he was a descendant of hers, and her stomach began immediately to shrink and contract itself again.

Then she asked, 'Art thou Māui?'

He answered, 'Even so,' and told her that he wanted 'the jawbone by which great enchantments could be wrought.'

Then Muri, the old chiefess, gave him the magic bone and he returned to his brothers, who were still living on the earth.

Then Māui said: 'Let us now catch the sun in a noose that we may compel him to move more slowly in order that mankind may have long days to labor in and procure subsistence for themselves.'

They replied, 'No man can approach it on account of the fierceness of the heat.'

According to the Society Island legend, his mother advised him to have nothing to do with the sun, who was a divine living creature, 'in form like a man, possessed of fearful energy,' shaking his golden locks both morning and evening in the eyes of men. Many persons had tried to regulate the movements of the sun, but had failed completely.

But Māui encouraged his mother and his brothers by asking them to remember his power to protect himself by the use of enchantments.

The Hawaiian legend says that Māui himself gathered cocoanut fibre in great quantity and manufactured it into strong ropes. But the legends of other islands say that he had the aid of his brothers, and while working learned many useful lessons. While winding and twisting they discovered how to make square ropes and flat ropes as well as the ordinary round rope. In the

Society Islands, it is said, Māui and his brothers made six strong ropes of great length. These he called aeiariki (royal nooses).

The New Zealand legend says that when Māui and his brothers had finished making all the ropes required they took provisions and other things needed and journeyed toward the east to find the place where the sun should rise. Māui carried with him the magic jawbone which he had secured from Muri, his ancestress, in the underworld.

They traveled all night and concealed themselves by day so that the sun should not see them and become too suspicious and watchful. In this way they journeyed, until 'at length they had gone very far to the eastward and had come to the very edge of the place out of which the sun rises. There they set to work and built on each side a long, high wall of clay, with huts of boughs of trees at each end to hide themselves in.'

Here they laid a large noose made from their ropes and Māui concealed himself on one side of this place along which the sun must come, while his brothers hid on the other side.

Māui seized his magic enchanted jawbone as the weapon with which to fight the sun, and ordered his brothers to pull hard on the noose and not to be frightened or moved to set the sun free.

'At last the sun came rising up out of his place like a fire spreading far and wide over the mountains and forests.

He rises up.

His head passes through the noose.

The ropes are pulled tight.

Then the monster began to struggle and roll himself about, while the snare jerked backwards and forwards as he struggled. Ah! was not he held fast in the ropes of his enemies.

Then forth rushed that bold hero Māui with his enchanted weapon. The sun screamed aloud and roared. Māui struck him fiercely with many blows. They held him for a long time. At last they let him go, and then weak from wounds the sun crept very slowly and feebly along his course.'

In this way the days were made longer so that men could perform their daily tasks and fruits and food plants could have time to grow.

The legend of the Hervey group of islands says that Māui made six snares and placed them at intervals along the path over which the sun must pass. The sun in the form of a man climbed up from Avaiki (Hawaiki). Māui pulled the first noose, but it slipped down the rising sun until it caught and was pulled tight around his feet.

Māui ran quickly to pull the ropes of the second snare, but that also slipped down, down, until it was tightened around the knees. Then Māui hastened to the third snare, while the sun was trying to rush along on his journey. The third snare caught around the hips. The fourth snare fastened itself around the waist. The fifth slipped under the arms, and yet the sun sped along as if but little inconvenienced by Māui's efforts.

Then Māui caught the last noose and threw it around the neck of the sun, and fastened the rope to a spur of rock. The sun struggled until nearly strangled to death and then gave up, promising Māui that he would go as slowly as was desired. Māui left the snares fastened to the sun to keep him in constant fear.

'These ropes may still be seen hanging from the sun at dawn and stretching into the skies when he descends into the ocean at night. By the assistance of these ropes he is gently let down into Avaiki in the evening, and also raised up out of shadow-land in the morning.'

Another legend from the Society Islands is related by Mr. Gill:

Māui tried many snares before he could catch the sun. The sun was the Hercules, or the Samson, of the heavens. He broke the strong cords of cocoanut fibre which Māui made and placed around the opening by which the sun climbed out from the underworld. Māui made stronger ropes, but still the sun broke them every one.

Then Māui thought of his sister's hair, the sister Inaika, whom he cruelly treated in later years. Her hair was long and beautiful. He cut off some of it and made a strong rope. With this he lassoed or rather snared the sun, and caught him around the throat. The sun quickly promised to be more thoughtful of the needs of men and go at a more reasonable pace across the sky.

A story from the American Indians is told in Hawai'i's Young People, which is very similar to the Polynesian legends.

An Indian boy became very angry with the sun for getting so warm and making his clothes shrink with the heat. He told his sister to make a snare. The girl took sinews from a large deer, but they shriveled under the heat. She took her own long hair and made snares, but they were burned in a moment. Then she tried the fibres of various plants and was successful. Her brother took the fibre cord and drew it through his lips. It stretched and became a strong red cord. He pulled and it became very long. He went to the place of sunrise, fixed his snare, and caught the sun. When the sun had been sufficiently punished, the animals of the earth studied the problem of setting the sun free. At last a mouse as large as a mountain ran and gnawed the red cord. It broke and the sun moved on, but the poor mouse had been burned and shriveled into the small mouse of the present day.

A Samoan legend says that a woman living for a time with the sun bore a child who had the name 'Child of the Sun.' She wanted gifts for the child's marriage, so she took a long vine, climbed a tree, made the vine into a noose, lassoed the sun, and made him give her a basket of blessings.

In Fiji, the natives tie the grasses growing on a hilltop over which they are passing, when traveling from place to place. They do this to make a snare to catch the sun if he should try to go down before they reach the end of their day's journey.

This legend is a misty memory of some time when the Polynesian people were in contact with the short days of the extreme north or south. It is a very remarkable exposition of a fact of nature perpetuated many centuries in lands absolutely free from such natural phenomena.

MĀUI FINDING FIRE

'Grant, oh grant me thy hidden fire,
O Banyan Tree.
Perform an incantation,
Utter a prayer
To the Banyan Tree.
Kindle a fire in the dust
Of the Banyan Tree.'
Translation of ancient Polynesian chant

A mong students of mythology certain characters in the legends of the various nations are known as 'culture heroes.' Mankind has from time to time learned exceedingly useful lessons and has also usually ascribed the new knowledge to some noted person in the national mythology. These legendary benefactors who have brought these practical benefits to men are placed among the 'hero-gods.' They have been teachers or 'culture heroes' to mankind.

Probably the fire finders of the different nations are among the best remembered of all these benefactors. This would naturally be the case, for no greater good has touched man's physical life than the discovery of methods of making fire.

Prometheus, the classical fire finder, is most widely known in literature. But of all the helpful gods, Māui, the mischievous Polynesian, is beyond question the hero of the largest numbers of nations scattered over the widest extent of territory. Prometheus belonged to Rome, but Māui belonged to the length and breadth of the Pacific Ocean. Theft or trickery, the use of deceit of some kind, is almost inseparably connected with fire finding all over the world. Prometheus stole fire from Jupiter and gave it to men together with the genius to make use of it in the arts and sciences. He found the rolling chariot of the sun, secretly filled his hollow staff with fire, carried it to earth, put a part in the breast of man to create enthusiasm or animation, and saved the remainder for the comfort of mankind to be used with the artist skill of Minerva and Vulcan. In Brittany the golden or fire-crested wren steals fire and is red-marked while so doing. The animals of the North American Indians are represented as stealing fire sometimes from the cuttle fish and sometimes from one another. Some swiftly flying bird or fleet-footed coyote would carry the stolen fire to the home of the tribe.

The possession of fire meant to the ancients all that wealth means to the family of today. It meant the possession of comfort. The gods were naturally determined to keep this wealth in their own hands. For any one to make a sharp deal and cheat a god of fire out of a part of this valuable property or to make a courageous raid upon the fire guardian and steal the treasure, was easily sufficient to make that one a 'culture hero.' As a matter of fact a prehistoric family without fire would go to any length in order to get it. The fire finders would naturally be the hero-gods and stealing fire would be an exploit rather than a crime.

It is worth noting that in many tales not only was fire stolen, but birds marked by red or black spots among their feathers were associated with the theft.

It would naturally be supposed that the Hawaiians living in a volcanic country with ever-flowing fountains of lava, would connect their fire tales with some volcano when relating the story of the origin of fire. But like the rest of the Polynesians, they found fire in trees rather than in rivers of melted rock. They must have brought their fire legends and fire customs with them when they came to the islands of active volcanoes.

Flint rocks as fire producers are not found in Hawaiian storytelling, nor in the stories from the island groups related to the Hawaiians. Indians might see the fleeing buffalo strike fire from the stones under his hard hoofs. The Tartars might have a god to teach them 'the secret of the stone's edge and the iron's hardness.' The Peruvians could very easily form a legend of their mythical father Guamansuri finding a way to make fire after he had seen the sling stones, thrown at his enemies, bring forth sparks of fire from the rocks against which they struck. The thunder and the lightning of later years were the sparks and the crash of stones hurled among the cloud mountains by the mighty gods.

In Australia the story is told of an old man and his daughter who lived in great darkness. After a time the father found the doorway of light through which the sun passed on his journey. He opened the door and a flood of sunshine covered the earth. His daughter looked around her home and saw numbers of serpents. She seized a staff and began to kill them. She wielded it so vigorously that it became hot in her hands. At last it broke, but the pieces rubbed against each other and flashed into sparks and flames. Thus it was learned that fire was buried in wood.

Flints were known in Europe and Asia and America, but the Polynesian looked to the banyan and kindred trees for the hidden sparks of fire. The natives of De Peyster's Island say that their ancestors learned how to make fire by seeing smoke rise from crossed branches rubbing together while trees were shaken by fierce winds.

In studying the Māui tales of the Pacific it is necessary to remember that Polynesians use 't' and 'k' without distinguishing them apart, and also as in the Hawaiian Islands an apostrophe (') is often used in place of 't' or 'k'. Therefore the Māui Ki-i-k-i'i of Hawai'i becomes the demigod Tiki-tiki of the Gilbert Islands – or the Ti'i-ti'i of Samoa or the Tiki of New Zealand – or other islands of the great ocean. We must also remember that in the Hawaiian legends Kalana is Māui's father. This in other groups becomes Talanga or Kalanga or Karanga. Kanaloa, the great god of most of the different Polynesians, is also sometimes called the Father of Māui. It is not strange that some of the exploits usually ascribed to Māui should be in some places transferred to his father under one name or the other. On one or two groups Mafuia, an ancestress of Māui, is mentioned as finding the fire. The usual legend makes Māui the one who takes fire away from Mafuia. The story of fire finding in Polynesia sifts itself to Māui under one of his widely accepted names, or to his father or to his ancestress – with but very few exceptions. This fact is important as showing in a very marked manner the race relationship of a vast number of the islanders of the Pacific world. From the Marshall Islands, in the west, to the Society Islands of the east; from the Hawaiian Islands in the north to the New Zealand group in the south, the footsteps of Māui the fire finder can be traced.

The Hawaiian story of fire finding is one of the least marvelous of all the legends. Hina, Māui's mother, wanted fish. One morning early Māui saw that the great storm waves of the sea had died down and the fishing grounds could be easily reached. He awakened his brothers and with them hastened to the beach. This was at Kaupo on the island of Māui. Out into the gray shadows of the dawn they paddled. When they were far from shore they began to fish. But Māui, looking landward, saw a fire on the mountain side.

'Behold,' he cried. 'There is a fire burning. Whose can this fire be?'

'Whose, indeed?' his brothers replied.

'Let us hasten to the shore and cook our food,' said one.

They decided that they had better catch some fish to cook before they returned. Thus, in the morning, before the hot sun drove the fish deep down to the dark recesses of the sea, they fished until a bountiful supply lay in the bottom of the canoe.

When they came to land, Māui leaped out and ran up the mountain side to get the fire. For a long, long time they had been without fire. The great volcano Haleakala above them had become extinct – and they had lost the coals they had tried to keep alive. They had eaten fruits and uncooked roots and the shell fish broken from the reef – and sometimes the great raw fish from the far-out ocean. But now they hoped to gain living fire and cooked food.

But when Māui rushed up toward the cloudy pillar of smoke he saw a family of birds scratching the fire out. Their work was finished and they flew away just as he reached the place.

Māui and his brothers watched for fire day after day – but the birds, the curly-tailed Alae (or the mud-hens) made no fire. Finally the brothers went fishing once more – but when they looked toward the mountain, again they saw flames and smoke. Thus it happened to them again and again.

Māui proposed to his brothers that they go fishing leaving him to watch the birds. But the Alae counted the fishermen and refused to build a fire for the hidden one who was watching them. They said among themselves, 'Three are in the boat and we know not where the other one is, we will make no fire today.'

So the experiment failed again and again. If one or two remained or if all waited on the land there would be no fire – but the dawn which saw the four brothers in the boat, saw also the fire on the land.

Finally Māui rolled some kapa cloth together and stuck it up in one end of the canoe so that it would look like a man. He then concealed himself near the haunt of the mud-hens, while his brothers went out fishing. The birds counted the figures in the boat and then started to build a heap of wood for the fire.

Māui was impatient – and just as the old Alae began to select sticks with which to make the flames he leaped swiftly out and caught her and held her prisoner. He forgot for a moment that he wanted the secret of fire making. In his anger against the wise bird his first impulse was to taunt her and then kill her for hiding the secret of fire.

But the Alae cried out: 'If you are the death of me – my secret will perish also – and you cannot have fire.'

Māui then promised to spare her life if she would tell him what to do.

Then came the contest of wits. The bird told the demigod to rub the stalks of water plants together. He guarded the bird and tried the plants. Water instead of fire ran out of the twisted stems. Then she told him to rub reeds together – but they bent and broke and could make no fire. He twisted her neck until she was half dead – then she cried out: 'I have hidden the fire in a green stick.'

Māui worked hard, but not a spark of fire appeared. Again he caught his prisoner by the head and wrung her neck, and she named a kind of dry wood. Māui rubbed the sticks together, but they only became warm. The neck twisting process was resumed – and repeated again and again, until the mud-hen was almost dead – and Māui had tried tree after tree. At last Māui found fire. Then as the flames rose he said: 'There is one more thing to rub.' He took a fire stick and rubbed the top of the head of his prisoner until the feathers fell off and the raw flesh appeared. Thus the Hawaiian mud-hen and her descendants have ever since had bald heads, and the Hawaiians have had the secret of fire making.

Another Hawaiian legend places the scene of Māui's contest with the mud-hens a little inland of the town of Hilo on the Island of Hawai'i. There are three small extinct craters very near each other known as The Halae Hills. One, the southern or Puna side of the hills, is a place called Pohaku-nui. Here dwelt two brother birds of the Alae family. They were gods. One had the power of fire making. Here at Pohaku-nui they were accustomed to kindle a fire and bake their dearly loved food – baked bananas. Here Māui planned to learn the secret of fire. The birds had kindled the fire and the bananas were almost done, when the elder Alae called to the younger: 'Be quick, here comes the swift son of Hina.'

The birds scratched out the fire, caught the bananas and fled. Māui told his mother he would follow them until he learned the secret of fire. His mother encouraged him because he was very strong and very swift. So he followed the birds from place to place as they fled from him, finding new spots on which to make their fires. At last they came to Waianae on the island Oahu. There he saw a great fire and a multitude of birds gathered around it, chattering loudly and trying to hasten the baking of the bananas. Their incantation was this: 'Let us cook quick. Let us cook quick. The swift child of Hina will come.'

Māui's mother Hina had taught him how to know the fire-maker. 'If you go up to the fire, you will find many birds. Only one is the guardian. This is the small, young Alae. His name is Alae-iki: Only this one knows how to make fire.' So whenever Māui came near to the fire-makers he always sought for the little Alae. Sometimes he made mistakes and sometimes almost captured the one he desired. At Waianae he leaped suddenly among the birds. They scattered the fire, and the younger bird tried to snatch his banana from the coals and flee, but Māui seized him and began to twist his neck. The bird cried out, warning Māui not to kill him or he would lose the secret of fire altogether. Māui was told that the fire was made from a banana stump. He saw the bananas roasting and thought this was reasonable. So, according to directions, he began to rub together pieces of the banana. The bird hoped for an unguarded moment when he might escape, but Māui was very watchful and was also very angry when he found that rubbing only resulted in squeezing out juice. Then he twisted the neck of the bird and was told to rub the stem of the taro plant. This also was so green that it only produced water. Then he was so angry that he nearly rubbed the head of the bird off – and the bird, fearing for its life, told the truth and taught Māui how to find the wood in which fire dwelt.

They learned to draw out the sparks secreted in different kinds of trees. The sweet sandalwood was one of these fire trees. Its Hawaiian name is 'Ili-ahi' – the 'ili' (bark) and 'ahi' (fire), the bark in which fire is concealed.

A legend of the Society Islands is somewhat similar. Ina (Hina) promised to aid Māui in finding fire for the islanders. She sent him into the underworld to find Tangaroa (Kanaloa). This god Tangaroa held fire in his possession – Māui was to know him by his tattooed face. Down the dark path through the long caves Māui trod swiftly until he found the god. Māui asked him for fire to take up to men. The god gave him a lighted stick and sent him away. But Māui put the fire out and went back again after fire. This he did several times, until the wearied giver decided to teach the intruder the art of fire making. He called a white duck to aid him. Then, taking two sticks of dry wood, he gave the under one to the bird and rapidly moved the upper stick across the under until fire came. Māui seized the upper stick, after it had been charred in the flame, and burned the head of the bird back of each eye. Thus were made the black spots which mark the head of the white duck. Then arose a quarrel between Tangaroa and Māui – but Māui struck down the god, and, thinking he had killed him, carried away the art of making fire. His father and mother made inquiries about their relative – Māui hastened back to the fire fountain and made the spirit return to the body – then, coming back to Ina, he bade her goodbye and carried the fire sticks to the upper world. The Hawaiians, and probably others among the

Polynesians, felt that any state of unconsciousness was a form of death in which the spirit left the body, but was called back by prayers and incantations. Therefore, when Māui restored the god to consciousness, he was supposed to have made the spirit released by death return into the body and bring it back to life.

In the Samoan legends as related by G. Turner, the name Ti'iti'i is used. This is the same as the second name found in Māui Ki'i-ki'i. The Samoan legend of Ti'iti'i is almost identical with the New Zealand fire story of Māui, and is very similar to the story coming from the Hervey Islands from Savage Island and also from the Tokelau and other island groups. The Samoan story says that the home of Mafuie the earthquake god was in the land of perpetual fire. Māui's or Ti'iti'i's father Talanga (Kalana) was also a resident of the underworld and a great friend of the earthquake god.

Ti'iti'i watched his father as he left his home in the upper world. Talanga approached a perpendicular wall of rock, said some prayer or incantation – and passed through a door which immediately closed after him. (This is a very near approach to the 'open sesame' of the *Arabian Nights* stories.)

Ti'iti'i went to the rock, but could not find the way through. He determined to conceal himself the next time so near that he could hear his father's words.

After some days he was able to catch all the words uttered by his father as he knocked on the stone door –

> 'O rock! divide.
> I am Talanga,
> I come to work
> On my land
> Given by Mafuie.'

Ti'iti'i went to the perpendicular wall and imitating his father's voice called for a rock to open. Down through a cave he passed until he found his father working in the underworld.

The astonished father, learning how his son came, bade him keep very quiet and work lest he arouse the anger of Mafuie. So for a time the boy labored obediently by his father's side.

In a little while the boy saw smoke and asked what it was. The father told him that it was the smoke from the fire of Mafuie, and explained what fire would do.

The boy determined to get some fire – he went to the place from which the smoke arose and there found the god, and asked him for fire. Mafuie gave him fire to carry to his father. The boy quickly had an oven prepared and the fire placed in it to cook some of the taro they had been cultivating. Just as everything was ready an earthquake god came up and blew the fire out and scattered the stones of the oven.

Then Ti'iti'i was angry and began to talk to Mafuie. The god attacked the boy, intending to punish him severely for daring to rebel against the destruction of the fire.

What a battle there was for a time in the underworld! At last Ti'iti'i seized one of the arms of Mafuie and broke it off. He caught the other arm and began to twist and bend it.

Mafuie begged the boy to spare him. His right arm was gone. How could he govern the earthquakes if his left arm were torn off also? It was his duty to hold Samoa level and not permit too many earthquakes. It would be hard to do that even with one arm – but it would be impossible if both arms were gone.

Ti'iti'i listened to the plea and demanded a reward if he should spare the left arm. Mafuie offered Ti'iti'i one hundred wives. The boy did not want them.

Then the god offered to teach him the secret of fire finding to take to the upper world.

The boy agreed to accept the fire secret, and thus learned that the gods in making the earth had concealed fire in various trees for men to discover in their own good time, and that this fire could be brought out by rubbing pieces of wood together.

The people of Samoa have not had much faith in Mafuie's plea that he needed his left arm in order to keep Samoa level. They say that Mafuie has a long stick or handle to the world under the islands – and when he is angry or wishes to frighten them he moves this handle and easily shakes the islands. When an earthquake comes, they give thanks to Ti'iti'i for breaking off one arm – because if the god had two arms they believe he would shake them unmercifully.

One legend of the Hervey Islands says that Māui and his brothers had been living on uncooked food – but learned that their mother sometimes had delicious food which had been cooked. They learned also that fire was needed in order to cook their food. Then Māui wanted fire and watched his mother.

Māui's mother was the guardian of the way to the invisible world. When she desired to pass from her home to the other world, she would open a black rock and pass inside. Thus she went to Hawaiki, the underworld. Māui planned to follow her, but first studied the forms of birds that he might assume the body of the strongest and most enduring. After a time he took the shape of a pigeon and, flying to the black rock, passed through the door and flew down the long dark passageway.

After a time he found the god of fire living in a bunch of banyan sticks. He changed himself into the form of a man and demanded the secret of fire.

The fire god agreed to give Māui fire if he would permit himself to be tossed into the sky by the god's strong arms.

Māui agreed on condition that he should have the right to toss the fire god afterwards.

The fire-god felt certain that there would be only one exercise of strength – he felt that he had everything in his own hands – so readily agreed to the tossing contest. It was his intention to throw his opponent so high that when he fell, if he ever did fall, there would be no antagonist uncrushed.

He seized Māui in his strong arms and, swinging him back and forth, flung him upward – but the moment Māui left his hands he changed himself into a feather and floated softly to the ground.

Then the boy ran swiftly to the god and seized him by the legs and lifted him up. Then he began to increase in size and strength until he had lifted the fire god very high. Suddenly he tossed the god upward and caught him as he fell – again and again – until the bruised and dizzy god cried enough, and agreed to give the victor whatever he demanded.

Māui asked for the secret of fire-producing. The god taught him how to rub the dry sticks of certain kinds of trees together, and, by friction, produce fire, and especially how fire could be produced by rubbing fire sticks in the fine dust of the banyan tree.

A Society Island legend says Māui borrowed a sacred red pigeon, belonging to one of the gods, and, changing himself into a dragon fly, rode this pigeon through a black rock into Avaiki (Hawaiki), the fire-land of the underworld. He found the god of fire, Mau-ika, living in a house built from a banyan tree. Mau-ika taught Māui the kinds of wood into which when fire went out on the earth a fire goddess had thrown sparks in order to preserve fire. Among these were the 'au' (Hawaiian hau), or 'the lemon hibiscus' – the 'argenta,' the 'fig' and the 'banyan.' She taught him also how to make fire by swift motion when rubbing the sticks of these trees. She also gave him coals for his present need.

But Māui was viciously mischievous and set the banyan house on fire, then mounted his pigeon and fled toward the upper world. But the flames hastened after him and burst out through the rock doors into the sunlit land above – as if it were a volcanic eruption.

The Tokelau Islanders say that Talanga (Kalana) known in other groups of islands as the father of Māui, desired fire in order to secure warmth and cooked food. He went down, down, very far down in the caves of the earth. In the lower world he found Mafuika – an old blind woman, who was the guardian of fire. He told her he wanted fire to take back to men. She refused either to give fire or to teach how to make it. Talanga threatened to kill her, and finally persuaded her to teach how to make fire in any place he might dwell – and the proper trees to use, the fire-yielding trees. She also taught him how to cook food – and also the kind of fish he should cook, and the kinds which should be eaten raw. Thus mankind learned about food as well as fire.

The Savage Island legend adds the element of danger to Māui's mischievous theft of fire. The lad followed his father one day and saw him pull up a bunch of reeds and go down into the fire-land beneath. Māui hastened down to see what his father was doing. Soon he saw his opportunity to steal the secret of fire. Then he caught some fire and started for the upper world.

His father caught a glimpse of the young thief and tried to stop him.

Māui ran up the passage through the black cave – bushes and trees bordered his road.

The father hastened after his son and was almost ready to lay hands upon him, when Māui set fire to the bushes. The flames spread rapidly, catching the underbrush and the trees on all sides and burst out in the face of the pursuer. Destruction threatened the underworld, but Māui sped along his way. Then he saw that the fire was chasing him. Bush after bush leaped into flame and hurled sparks and smoke and burning air after him. Choked and smoke-surrounded, he broke through the door of the cavern and found the fresh air of the world. But the flames followed him and swept out in great power upon the upper world a mighty volcanic eruption.

The New Zealand legends picture Māui as putting out, in one night, all the fires of his people. This was serious mischief, and Māui's mother decided that he should go to the underworld and see his ancestress, Mahuika, the guardian of fire, and get new fire to repair the injury he had wrought. She warned him against attempting to play tricks upon the inhabitants of the lower regions.

Māui gladly hastened down the cave-path to the house of Mahuika, and asked for fire for the upper world. In some way he pleased her so that she pulled off a finger nail in which fire was burning and gave it to him. As soon as he had gone back to a place where there was water, he put the fire out and returned to Mahuika, asking another gift, which he destroyed. This he did for both hands and feet until only one nail remained. Māui wanted this. Then Mahuika became angry and threw the last finger nail on the ground. Fire poured out and laid hold of everything. Māui ran up the path to the upper world, but the fire was swifter-footed. Then Māui changed himself into an eagle and flew high up into the air, but the fire and smoke still followed him. Then he saw water and dashed into it, but it was too hot. Around him the forests were blazing, the earth burning and the sea boiling. Māui, about to perish, called on the gods for rain. Then floods of water fell and the fire was checked. The great rain fell on Mahuika and she fled, almost drowned. Her stores of fire were destroyed, quenched by the storm. But in order to save fire for the use of men, as she fled she threw sparks into different kinds of trees where the rain could not reach them, so that when fire was needed it might be brought into the world again by rubbing together the fire sticks.

The Chatham Islanders give the following incantation, which they said was used by Māui against the fierce flood of fire which was pursuing him:

> 'To the roaring thunder;
> To the great rain – the long rain;
> To the drizzling rain – the small rain;
> To the rain pattering on the leaves.
> These are the storms – the storms
> Cause them to fall;
> To pour in torrents.'

The legend of Savage Island places Māui in the role of fire-maker. He has stolen fire in the underworld. His father tries to catch him, but Māui sets fire to the bushes by the path until a great conflagration is raging which pursues him to the upper world.

Some legends make Māui the fire-teacher as well as the fire-finder. He teaches men how to use hardwood sticks in the fine dry dust on the bark of certain trees, or how to use the fine fibre of the palm tree to catch sparks.

In Tahiti the fire god lived in the 'Hale-a-o-a,' or House of the Banyan. Sometimes human sacrifices were placed upon the sacred branches of this tree of the fire god.

In the Bowditch or Fakaofa Islands the goddess of fire when conquered taught not only the method of making fire by friction but also what fish were to be cooked and what were to be eaten raw.

Thus some of the stories of Māui, the mischievous, finding fire are told by the side of the inrolling surf, while natives of many islands, around their poi bowls, rest in the shade of the far-reaching boughs and thick foliage of the banyan and other fire-producing trees.

MĀUI SEEKING IMMORTALITY

Climb up, climb up,
To the highest surface of heaven,
To all the sides of heaven.

Climb then to thy ancestor,
The sacred bird in the sky,
To thy ancestor Rehua
In the heavens.
New Zealand kite incantation

The story of Māui seeking immortality for the human race is one of the finest traditional tales in the world. For pure imagination and pathos it is difficult to find any tale from Grecian or Latin literature to compare with it. In Greek and Roman fables gods suffered for other gods, and yet none were surrounded with such absolutely harrowing experiences as those through which the demigod Māui of the Pacific Ocean passed when he entered the gates of death with the hope of winning immortality for mankind.

The really remarkable group of legends which cluster around Māui is well concluded by the story of his unselfish and heroic battle with death.

The different islands of the Pacific have their Hades, or abode of dead. It is, with very few exceptions, down in the interior of the earth. Sometimes the tunnels left by currents of melted lava are the passages into the home of departed spirits. In Samoa there are two circular holes among the rocks at the west end of the island Savaii. These are the entrances to the underworld for chiefs and people. The spirits of those who die on the other islands leap into the sea and swim around the land from island to island until they reach Savaii. Then they plunge down into their heaven or their hades.

The Tongans had a spirit island for the home of the dead. They said that some natives once sailed far away in a canoe and found this island. It was covered with all manner of beautiful fruits, among which rare birds sported. They landed, but the trees were shadows. They grasped but could not hold them. The fruits and the birds were shadows. The men ate, but swallowed nothing substantial. It was shadow-land. They walked through all the delights their eyes looked upon, but found no substance. They returned home, but ever seemed to listen to spirits calling them back to the island. In a short time all the voyagers were dead.

There is no escape from death. The natives of New Zealand say: 'Man may have descendants, but the daughters of the night strangle his offspring'; and again: 'Men make heroes, but death carries them away.'

There are very few legends among the Polynesians concerning the death of Māui. And these are usually fragmentary, except among the Māoris of New Zealand.

The Hawaiian legend of the death of Māui is to the effect that he offended some of the greater gods living in Waipio valley on the Island of Hawai'i. Kanaloa, one of the four greatest gods of Hawai'i, seized him and dashed him against the rocks. His blood burst from the body and colored the earth red in the upper part of the valley. The Hawaiians in another legend say that Māui was chasing a boy and girl in Honolii gulch, Hawai'i. The girl climbed a breadfruit tree. Māui changed himself into an eel and stretched himself along the side of the trunk of the tree. The tree stretched itself upward and Māui failed to reach the girl. A priest came along and struck the eel and killed it, and so Māui died. This is evidently a changed form of the legend of Māui and the long eel. Another Hawaiian fragment approaches very near to the beautiful New Zealand story. The Hawaiians said that Māui attempted to tear a mountain apart. He wrenched a great hole in the side. Then the elepaio bird sang and the charm was broken. The cleft in the mountain could not be enlarged. If the story could be completed it would not be strange if the death of Māui came with this failure to open the path through the mountain.

The Hervey Islands say that after Māui fished up the islands his hook was thrown into the heavens and became the curved tail of the constellation of stars which we know as 'The Scorpion.' Then the people became angry with Māui and threw him up into the sky and his body is still thought to be hanging among the stars of the scorpion.

The Samoans, according to Turner, say that Māui went fishing and tried to catch the land under the seas and pull it to the surface. Finally an island appeared, but the people living on it were angry with Māui and drove him away into the heavens.

As he leaped from the island it separated into two parts. Thus the Samoans account for the origin of two of their islands and also for the passing away of Māui from the earth.

The natives of New Zealand have many stories concerning the death of Māui. Each tribe tells the story with such variations as would be expected when the fact is noted that these tribes have preserved their individuality through many generations. The substance of the story, however, is the same.

In Māui's last days he longed for the victory over death. His innate love of life led him to face the possibility of escaping and overcoming the relentless enemy of mankind and thus bestow the boon of deathlessness upon his fellow men. He had been successful over and over again in his contests with both gods and men. When man was created, he stood erect, but, according to a Hawaiian story, had jointless arms and limbs. A web of skin connected and fastened tightly the arms to the body and the legs to each other. 'Māui was angry at this motionless statue and took him and broke his legs at ankle, knee and hip and then, tearing them and the arms from the body, destroyed the web. Then he broke the arms at the elbow and shoulder. Then man could move from place to place, but he had neither fingers or toes.' Here comes the most ancient Polynesian statement of the theory of evolution: 'Hunger impelled man to seek his food in the mountains, where his toes were cut out by the brambles in climbing, and his fingers were also formed by the sharp splinters of the bamboo while searching with his arms for food in the ground.'

It was not strange that Māui should feel self-confident when considering the struggle for immortality as a gift to be bestowed upon mankind. And yet his father warned him that his time of failure would surely come.

White, who has collected many of the stories and legends of New Zealand, states that after Māui had ill-treated Mahu-ika, his grandmother, the goddess and guardian of fire in the underworld, his father and mother tried to teach him to do differently. But he refused to listen. Then the father said:

'You heard our instructions, but please yourself and persist for life or death.'

Māui replied: 'What do I care? Do you think I shall cease? Rather I will persist forever and ever.'

Then his father said: 'There is one so powerful that no tricks can be of any avail.'

Māui asked: 'By what shall I be overcome?' The answer was that one of his ancestors, Hine-nui-te-pō (Great Hine of the Night), the guardian of life, would overcome him.

When Māui fished islands out of the deep seas, it was said that Hine made her home on the outer edge of one of the outermost islands. There the glow of the setting sun lighted the thatch of her house and covered it with glorious colors. There Great Hine herself stood flashing and sparkling on the edge of the horizon.

Māui, in these last days of his life, looked toward the west and said: 'Let us investigate this matter and learn whether life or death shall follow.'

The father replied: 'There is evil hanging over you. When I chanted the invocation of your childhood, when you were made sacred and guarded by charms, I forgot a part of the ceremony. And for this you are to die.'

Then Māui said, 'Will this be by Hine-nui-te-pō? What is she like?'

The father said that the flashing eyes they could see in the distance were dark as greenstone, the teeth were as sharp as volcanic glass, her mouth was large like a fish, and her hair was floating in the air like sea-weed.

One of the legends of New Zealand says that Māui and his brothers went toward the west, to the edge of the horizon, where they saw the goddess of the night. Light was flashing from her body. Here they found a great pit – the home of night. Māui entered the pit – telling his brothers not to laugh. He passed through and turning about started to return. The brothers laughed and the walls of night closed in around him and held him till he died.

The longer legend tells how Māui after his conversation with his father, remembered his conflict with the moon. He had tied her so that she could not escape, but was compelled to bathe in the waters of life and return night after night lest men should be in darkness when evening came.

Māui said to the goddess of the moon: 'Let death be short. As the moon dies and returns with new strength, so let men die and revive again.'

But she replied: 'Let death be very long, that man may sigh and sorrow. When man dies, let him go into darkness, become like earth, that those he leaves behind may weep and wail and mourn.'

Māui did not lay aside his purpose, but, according to the New Zealand story, 'did not wish men to die, but to live forever. Death appeared degrading and an insult to the dignity of man. Man ought to die like the moon, which dips in the life-giving waters of Kane and is renewed again, or like the sun, which daily sinks into the pit of night and with renewed strength rises in the morning.'

Māui sought the home of Hine-nui-te-pō – the guardian of life. He heard her order her attendants to watch for any one approaching and capture all who came walking upright as a man. He crept past the attendants on hands and feet, found the place of life, stole some of the food of the goddess and returned home. He showed the food to his brothers and persuaded them to go with him into the darkness of the night of death. On the way he changed them into the form of birds. In the evening they came to the house of the goddess on the island long before fished up from the seas.

Māui warned the birds to refrain from making any noise while he made the supreme effort of his life. He was about to enter upon his struggle for immortality. He said to the birds: 'If I go into the stomach of this woman, do not laugh until I have gone through her, and come out again at her mouth; then you can laugh at me.'

His friends said: 'You will be killed.' Māui replied: 'If you laugh at me when I have only entered her stomach I shall be killed, but if I have passed through her and come out of her mouth I shall escape and Hine-nui-te-pō will die.'

His friends called out to him: 'Go then. The decision is with you.'

Hine was sleeping soundly. The flashes of lightning had all ceased. The sunlight had almost passed away and the house lay in quiet gloom. Māui came near to the sleeping goddess. Her large, fish-like mouth was open wide. He put off his clothing and prepared to pass through the ordeal of going to the hidden source of life, to tear it out of the body of its guardian and carry it back with him to mankind. He stood in all the glory of savage manhood. His body was splendidly marked by the tattoo-bones, and now well oiled shone and sparkled in the last rays of the setting sun.

He leaped through the mouth of the enchanted one and entered her stomach, weapon in hand, to take out her heart, the vital principle which he knew had its home somewhere within her being. He found immortality on the other side of death. He turned to come back again into life when suddenly a little bird (the Pata-tai) laughed in a clear, shrill tone, and Great Hine, through whose mouth Māui was passing, awoke. Her sharp, obsidian teeth closed with a snap upon Māui, cutting his body in the centre. Thus Māui entered the gates of death, but was unable to return, and death has ever since been victor over rebellious men. The natives have the saying:

'If Māui had not died, he could have restored to life all who had gone before him, and thus succeeded in destroying death.'

Māui's brothers took the dismembered body and buried it in a cave called Te-ana-i-hana, 'The cave dug out,' possibly a prepared burial place.

Māui's wife made war upon the spirits, the gods, and killed as many as she could to avenge her husband's death. One of the old native poets of New Zealand, in chanting the story to Mr. White, said: 'But though Māui was killed, his offspring survived. Some of these are at Hawa-i-i-ki and some at Aotea-roa (New Zealand), but the greater part of them remained at Hawa-i-ki. This history was handed down by the generations of our ancestors of ancient times, and we continue to rehearse it to our children, with our incantations and genealogies, and all other matters relating to our race.'

> 'But death is nothing new,
> Death is, and has been ever since old Māui died.
> Then Pata-tai laughed loud
> And woke the goblin-god,
> Who severed him in two, and shut him in,
> So dusk of eve came on.'

Māori death chant, New Zealand

THE OAHU LEGENDS OF MĀUI

Several Māui legends have been located on the island of Oahu. They were given by Mr. Kaaia to Mr. T.G. Thrum, the publisher of what is well known in the Hawaiian Islands as 'Thrum's Annual.' He has kindly furnished them for added interest to the present volume. The legends have a distinctly local flavor confined entirely to Oahu. It has seemed best to reserve them for a chapter by themselves although they are chiefly variations of stories already told.

Māui and the Two Gods

This history of Māui and his grandmother Hina begins with their arrival from foreign lands. They dwelt in Kane-ana (Kane's cave), Waianae, Oahu. This is an 'ana,' or cave, at Puu-o-hulu. Hina had wonderful skill in making all kinds of tapa according to the custom of the women of ancient Hawai'i.

Māui went to the Koolau side and rested at Kaha-luu, a diving place in Koolaupoko. In that place there is a noted hill called Ma-eli-eli. This is the story of that hill. Māui threw up a pile of dirt and concealed rubbish under it. The two gods, Kane and Kanaloa, came along and asked Māui what he was doing. He said, 'What you see. You two dig on that side to the foot of the pali, (precipice) and I will go down at Kaha-luu. If you two dig through first, you may kill me. If I get through first I will kill you.'

They agreed, and began to dig and throw up the dirt. Then Māui dug three times and tossed up some of the hills of that place. Kane and Kanaloa saw that Māui was digging very fast, so they put forth very great strength and threw the dirt into a hill. Meanwhile Māui ran away to the other side of the island.

Thus by the aid of the gods the hill Ma-eli-eli was thrown up and received its name 'eli,' meaning 'dig.' 'Ma-eli-eli' meant 'the place of digging.'

How They Found Fire

It was said that Māui and Hina had no fire. They were often cold and had no cooked food. Māui saw flames rising in a distant place and ran to see how they were made. When he came to that place the fire was out and some birds flew away. One of them was Ka-Alae-huapi, 'the stingy Alae' – a small duck, the Hawaiian mud hen. Māui watched again and saw fire. When he went up the birds saw him coming and scattered the fire, carrying the ashes into the water; but he leaped and caught the little Alae. 'Ah!' he said, 'I will kill you, because you do not let me have fire.' The bird replied, 'If you kill me you cannot find fire.' Māui said, 'Where is fire?' The Alae said, 'Go up on the high land where beautiful plants with large leaves are standing; rub their branches.' Māui set the bird free and went inland from Hālawa and found dry land taro. He began to rub the stalks, but only juice came out like water. He had no red fire. He was very angry and said, 'If that lying Alae is caught again by me I will be its death.'

After a while he saw the fire burning and ran swiftly. The birds saw him and cried, 'The cooking is over. Here comes the swift grandchild of Hina.' They scattered the fire, threw the ashes away and flew into the water. But again Māui caught the Alae and began to kill it, saying: 'You gave me a plant full of water from which to get fire.' The bird said, 'If I die you can never find fire. I will give you the secret of fire. Take a branch of that dry tree and rub.' Māui held the bird fast in one hand while he rubbed with the other until smoke and fire came out. Then he took the fire stick and rubbed the head of the bird, making a place where red and white feathers have grown ever since.

He returned to Hina and taught her how to make fire, using the two fire sticks and how to twist coconut fibre to catch the fire when it had been kindled in wood. But the Alae was not forgotten. It was called huapi, 'stingy,' because it selfishly kept the knowledge of fire making to itself.

Māui Catching the Sun

Māui watched Hina making tapa. The wet tapa was spread on a long tapa board, and Hina began at one end to pound it into shape; pounding from one end to another. He noticed that sunset came by the time she had pounded to the middle of the board. The sun hurried so fast that she could only begin her work before the day was past.

He went to the hill Hele-a-ka-la, which means 'journey of the sun.' He thought he would catch the sun and make it move slowly. He went up the hill and waited. When the sun began to rise, Māui made himself long, stretching up toward the sky. Soon the shining legs of the sun came up the hillside. He saw Māui and began to run swiftly, but Māui reached out and caught one of the legs, saying: 'O sun, I will kill you. You are a mischief maker. You make trouble for Hina by going so fast.' Then he broke the shining leg of the sun. The sufferer said, 'I will change my way and go slowly – six months slow and six months faster.' Thus arose the saying, 'Long shall be the daily journey of the sun and he shall give light for all the people's toil.' Hina learned that she could pound until she was tired while the farmers could plant and take care of their fields. Thus also this hill received its name Hele-a-ka-la. This is one of the hills of Waianae near the precipice of the hill Puu-o-hulu.

Uniting the Islands

Māui suggested to Hina that he had better try to draw the islands together, uniting them in one land. Hina told Māui to go and see Alae-nui-a-Hina, who would tell him what to do. The Alae told him they must go to Ponaha-ke-one (a fishing place outside of Pearl Harbor) and find Ka-uniho-kahi, 'the one-toothed,' who held the land under the sea.

Māui went back to Hina. She told him to ask his brothers to go fishing with him. They consented and pushed out into the sea. Soon Māui saw a bailing dish floating by the canoe and picked it up. It was named Hina-a-ke-ka, 'Hina who fell off.' They paddled to Ponaha-ke-one. When they stopped they saw a beautiful young woman in the boat. Then they anchored and again looked in the boat, but the young woman was gone. They saw the bailing dish and threw it into the sea.

Māui-mua threw his hook and caught a large fish, which was seen to be a shark as they drew it to the surface. At once they cut the line. So also Māui-hope and Māui-waena. At last Māui threw his hook Manai-i-ka-lani into the sea. It went down, down into the depths. Māui cried, 'Hina-a-ke-ka has my hook in her hand. By her it will be made fast.' Hina went down with the hook until she met Ka-uniho-kahi. She asked him to open his mouth, then threw the hook far inside and made it fast. Then she pulled the line so that Māui should know that the fish was caught. Māui fastened the line to the outrigger of the canoe and asked his brothers to paddle with all diligence, and not look back. Long, long, they paddled and were very tired. Then Māui took a paddle and dipped deep in the sea. The boat moved more swiftly through the sea. The brothers looked back and cried, 'There is plenty of land behind us.' The charm was broken. The hook came out of 'the one-toothed,' and the raised islands sank back into their place. The native say, 'The islands are now united to America. Perhaps Māui has been at work.'

Māui and Pea-Pea the Eight-Eyed

Māui had been fishing and had caught a great fish upon which he was feasting. He looked inland and saw his wife, Kumu-lama, seized and carried away by Pea-pea-maka-walu, 'Pea-pea the eight-eyed.' This is a legend derived from the stories of many islands in which Lupe or Rupe (pigeon) changed himself into a bird and flew after his sister Hina who had been carried on the back of a shark to distant islands. Sometimes as a man and sometimes as a bird he prosecuted his search until Hina was found.

Māui pursued Pea-pea, but could not catch him. He carried Māui's wife over the sea to a far away island. Māui was greatly troubled but his grandmother sent him inland to find an old man who would tell him what to do. Māui went inland and looking down toward Waipahu saw this man Ku-olo-kele. He was humpbacked. Māui threw a large stone and hit the 'hill on the back' knocked it off and made the back straight. The old man lifted up the stone and threw it to Waipahu, where it lies to this day. Then he and Māui talked together. He told Māui to go and catch birds and gather ti leaves and fibres of the ie-ie vine, and fill his house. These things Māui secured and brought to him. He told Māui to go home and return after three days.

Ku-olo-kele took the ti leaves and the ie-ie threads and made the body of a great bird which he covered with bird feathers. He fastened all together with the ie-ie. This was done in the first day. The second day he placed food inside and tried his bird and it flew all right. 'Thus,' as the Hawaiians say, 'the first flying ship was made in the time of Māui.' This is a modern version of Rupe changing himself into a bird.

On the third day Māui came and saw the wonderful bird body thoroughly prepared for his journey. Māui went inside. Ku-olo-kele said, 'When you reach that land, look for a village. If the people are not there look to the beach. If there are many people, your wife and Pea-pea the eight-eyed will be there. Do not go near, but fly out over the sea. The people will say, 'O, the strange bird;' but Pea-pea will say, 'This is my bird. It is tabu.' You can then come to the people.'

Māui pulled the ie-ie ropes fastened to the wings and made them move. Thus he flew away into the sky. Two days was his journey before he came to that strange island, Moana-liha-i-ka-wao-kele. It was a beautiful land. He flew inland to a village, but there were no people; according to the ancient chant:

> 'The houses of Lima-loa stand,
> But there are no people;
> They are at Mana.'

The people were by the sea. Māui flew over them. He saw his wife, but he passed on flying out over the sea, skimming like a sea bird down to the water and rising gracefully up to the sky. Pea-pea called out, 'This is my bird. It is tabu.' Māui heard and came to the beach. He was caught and placed in a tabu box. The servants carried him up to the village and put him in the chief's sleeping house, when Pea-pea and his people returned to their homes.

In the night Pea-pea and Māui's wife lay down to sleep. Māui watched Pea-pea, hoping that he would soon sleep. Then he would kill him. Māui waited. One eye was closed, seven eyes were opened. Then four eyes closed, leaving three. The night was almost past and dawn was near. Then Māui called to Hina with his spirit voice, 'O Hina, keep it dark.' Hina made the gray dawn dark in the three eyes and two closed in sleep. The last eye was weary, and it also slept. Then Māui went out of the bird body and cut off the head of Pea-pea and put it inside the bird. He broke the roof of the house until a large opening was made. He took his wife, Kumu-lama, and flew away to the island of Oahu. The winds blew hard against the flying bird. Rain fell in torrents around it, but those inside had no trouble.

'Thus Māui returned with his wife to his home in Oahu. The story is pau (finished).'

TALES OF HINA

Hina is an ancient goddess – one of the first to appear in Polynesian legends. She is associated with several women's tasks, but especially with the making of cloth, or tapa. Many Polynesian cultures know her as the mother of Māui; in others she appears as his wife and in yet others a divine ancestor. Whatever their relationship, it is Māui's love for Hina that drives him to undertake many of his tasks. When a dragon torments Hina, he answers her call for protection. When she does not have enough time for her daily chores, he slows down the sun to give her more time. Their feelings for one another are those of love and respect.

In Polynesian legends many physical locations and landmarks are associated with Hina. In some stories she is said to live behind a waterfall of the Wailuku river, described as beautiful and shimmering with rainbows. Hina's connection with prisms and rainbows is a common theme in her stories.

The moon also has many associations with Hina. She is said to be married to the moon and sometimes to dwell on its surface. In some stories, it is Hina's tapa-making skill that captures the attention of her husband. Her tapa is so fine that it spreads out across the night sky as wisps of cloud.

HINA OF HILO

Hina is not an uncommon name in Hawaiian genealogies. It is usually accompanied by some adjective which explains or identifies the person to whom the name is given. In Hawai'i the name Hina is feminine. This is also true throughout all Polynesia except in a few cases where Hina is reckoned as a man with supernatural attributes. Even in these cases it is apparent that the legend has been changed from its original form as it has been carried to small islands by comparatively ignorant people when moving away from their former homes.

Hina is a Polynesian goddess whose story is very interesting – one worthy of study when comparing the legends of the island groups of the Pacific. The Hina of Hilo is the same as the goddess of that name most widely known throughout Polynesia – and yet her legends are located by the ancient Hawaiians in Hilo, as if that place were her only home. The legends are so old that the Hawaiians have forgotten their origin in other lands. The stories were brought with the immigrants who settled on the Hilo coast. Thus the stories found their final location with the families who brought them. There are three Hawaiian Hinas practically distinct from each other, although a supernatural element is connected with each one. Hina who was stolen from Hawai'i by a chief of the Island of Molokai was an historical character, although surrounded by legendary stories. Another Hina, who was the wife of Kuula, the fish god, was pre-eminently a local deity, having no real connection with the legends of the other islands of the Pacific, although sometimes the stories told concerning her have not been kept entirely distinct from the legends of the Hina of Hilo.

The Hilo Hina was the true legendary character closely connected with all Polynesia. The stories about her are of value not simply as legends, but as traditions closely uniting the Hawaiian Islands with the island groups thousands of miles distant. The Wailuku river, which flows through the town of Hilo, has its own peculiar and weird beauty. For miles it is a series of waterfalls and rapids. It follows the course of an ancient lava flow, sometimes forcing its way under bridges of lava, thus forming what are called boiling pots, and sometimes pouring in massive sheets over the edges of precipices which never disintegrate. By the side of this river Hina's son Māui had his lands. In the very bed of the river, in a cave under one of the largest falls, Hina made her own home, concealed from the world by the silver veil of falling water and lulled to sleep by the continual roar of the flood falling into the deep pool below. By the side of this river, the legends say, she pounded her tapa and prepared her food. Here were the small, graceful mamake and the coarser wauke trees, from which the bark was stripped with which she made tapa cloth. Branches were cut or broken from these and other trees whose bark was fit for the purpose. These branches were well soaked until the bark was removed easily. Then the outer bark was scraped off, leaving only the pliable inner bark. The days were very short and there was no time for rest while making tapa cloth. Therefore, as soon as the morning light reddened the clouds, Hina would take her calabash filled with water to pour upon the bark, and her little bundle of round clubs (the *hohoa*) and her four-sided mallets (the *i-e-kuku*) and hasten to the sacred spot where, with chants and incantations, the tapa was made.

The bark was well soaked in the water all the days of the process of tapa making. Hina took small bundles of the wet inner bark and laid them on the kua or heavy tapa board, pounding them together into a pulpy mass with her round clubs. Then using the four-sided mallets, she beat this pulp into thin sheets. Beautiful tapa, soft as silk, was made by adding pulpy mass to pulpy mass and beating it day after day until the fibres were lost and a sheet of close-woven bark cloth was formed. Although Hina was a goddess and had a family possessing miraculous power, it never entered the mind of the Hawaiian legend tellers to endow her with ease in producing wonderful results. The legends of the Southern Pacific Islands show more imagination. They say that Ina (Hina) was such a wonderful artist in making beautiful tapas that she was placed in the skies, where she beat out glistening fine tapas, the white and glorious clouds. When she stretches these cloud sheets out to dry, she places stones along the edges, so that the fierce winds of the heavens shall not blow them away. When she throws these stones aside, the skies reverberate with thunder. When she rolls her cloud sheets of tapa together, the folds glisten with flashes of light and lightning leaps from sheet to sheet.

The Hina of Hilo was grieved as she toiled because after she had pounded the sheets out so thin that they were ready to be dried, she found it almost impossible to secure the necessary aid of the sun in the drying process. She would rise as soon as she could see and hasten to spread out the tapa made the day before. But the sun always hurried so fast that the sheets could not dry. He leaped from the ocean waters in the earth, rushed across the heavens and plunged into the dark waters again on the other side of the island before she could even turn her tapas so that they might dry evenly. This legend of very short days is strange because of its place not only among the stories of Hawai'i but also because it belongs to practically all the tropical islands of the Pacific Ocean. In Tahiti the legends said that the sun rushed across the sky very rapidly. The days were too short for fruits to ripen or for work to be finished. In Samoa the 'mats' made by Sina had no time to dry. The ancestors of the Polynesians sometime somewhere must have been in the region of short days and long nights. Hina found that her incantations had no influence with the sun. She could not prevail upon him to go slower and give her more time for the completion of her task. Then she called on her powerful son, Māui-ki-i-ki-i, for aid.

Some of the legends of the Island of Māui say that Hina dwelt by the sea coast of that island near the high hill Kauwiki at the foot of the great mountain Haleakala, House of the Sun, and that there, facing the southern skies under the most favorable conditions for making tapa, she found the days too short for the tapa to dry. At the present time the Hawaiians point out a long, narrow stone not far from the surf and almost below the caves in which the great queen Kaahumanu spent the earliest days of her childhood. This stone is said to be the kua or tapa board on which Hina pounded the bark for her cloth. Other legends of that same island locate Hina's home on the northeast coast near Pōhakuloa.

The Hilo legends, however, do not deem it necessary that Hina and Māui should have their home across the wide channel which divides the Island Hawai'i from the Island of Māui in order to wage war successfully with the inconsiderate sun. Hina remained in her home by the Wailuku river, sometimes resting in her cave under Rainbow Falls, and sometimes working on the river bank, trusting her powerful son Māui to make the swiftly passing lord of day go more slowly.

Māui possessed many supernatural powers. He could assume the form of birds or insects. He could call on the winds to do his will, or he could, if he wished, traverse miles with a single stride. It is interesting to note that the Hilo legends differ as to the way in which Māui the man passed over to Māui the island. One legend says that he crossed the channel, miles wide, with a single step. Another says that he launched his canoe and with a breath the god of the winds placed him on the opposite coast, while another story says that Māui assumed the form of a white chicken, which flew over the waters to Haleakala. Here he took ropes made from the fibre of trees and vines and lassoed the sun while it climbed the side of the mountain and entered the great crater which hollows out the summit. The sun came through a large gap in the eastern side of the crater, rushing along as rapidly as possible. Then Māui threw his lassoes one after the other over the sun's legs (the rays of light), holding him fast and breaking off some of them. With a magic club Māui struck the face of the sun again and again. At last, wounded and weary, and also limping on its broken legs, the sun promised Māui to go slowly forevermore.

'La' among the Polynesians, like the word 'Ra' among the Egyptians, means 'sun' or 'day' or 'sun-god' – and the mountain where the son of Hina won his victory over the monster of the heavens has long borne the name Hale-a-ka-la, or House of the Sun.

Hina of Hilo soon realized the wonderful deed which Māui had done. She spread out her fine tapas with songs of joy and cheerily performed the task which filled the hours of the day. The comfort of sunshine and cooling winds came with great power into Hina's life, bringing to her renewed joy and beauty.

HINA AND THE WAILUKU RIVER

There are two rivers of rushing, tumbling rapids and waterfalls in the Hawaiian Islands, both bearing the name of Wailuku. One is on the Island of Māui, flowing out of a deep gorge in the side of the extinct volcano Iao. Yosemite-like precipices surround this majestically walled crater. The name Iao means 'asking for clouds.' The head of the crater-valley is almost always covered with great masses of heavy rain clouds. Out of the crater the massed waters rush in a swift-flowing stream of only four or five miles, emptying into Kahului harbor. The other Wailuku river is on the Island of Hawai'i. The snows melt on the summits of the two great mountains, Mauna Kea and Mauna Loa. The water seeps through the porous lava from the eastern slope of Mauna Loa and the southern slope of Mauna Kea, meeting where the lava flows of centuries from each mountain have piled up against each other. Through the fragments of these volcanic battles the waters creep down the mountain side toward the sea.

At one place, a number of miles above the city of Hilo, the waters were heard gurgling and splashing far below the surface. Water was needed for the sugar plantations, which modern energy has established all along the eastern coast of the large island. A tunnel was cut into the lava, the underground stream was tapped – and an abundant supply of water secured and sluiced down to the large plantations below. The head waters of the Wailuku river gathered from the melting snow of the mountains found these channels, which centred at last in the bed of a very ancient and very interesting lava flow. Sometimes breaking forth in a large, turbulent flood, the stream forces its way over and around the huge blocks of lava which mark the course of the eruption of long ago. Sometimes it courses in a tunnel left by the flowing lava and comes up from below in a series of boiling pools. Then again it falls in majestic sheets over high walls of worn precipices. Several large falls and some very picturesque smaller cascades interspersed with rapids and natural bridges give to this river a beauty peculiarly its own. The most weird of all the rough places through which the Wailuku river flows is that known as the basin of Rainbow Falls near Hilo. Here Hina, the moon goddess of the Polynesians, lived in a great open cave, over which the falls hung their misty, rainbow-tinted veil. Her son Māui, the mighty demigod of Polynesia, supposed by some writers to be the sun-god of the Polynesians, had extensive lands along the northern bank of the river. Here among his cultivated fields he had his home, from which he went forth to accomplish the wonders attributed to him in the legends of the Hawaiians.

Below the cave in which Hina dwelt the river fought its way through a narrow gorge and then, in a series of many small falls, descended to the little bay, where its waters mingled with the surf of the salt sea. Far above the cave, in the bed of the river, dwelt Kuna. The district through which that portion of the river runs bears to this day the name 'Wai-kuna' or 'Kuna's river.' When the writer was talking with the natives concerning this part of the old legend, they said 'Kuna is not a Hawaiian word. It means something like a snake or a dragon, something we do not have in these islands.' This, they thought, made the connection with the Hina legend valueless until they were shown that Tuna (or kuna) was the New Zealand name of a reptile which attacked Hina and struck her with his tail like a crocodile, for which Māui killed him. When this was understood, the Hawaiians were greatly interested to give the remainder of this legend and compare it with the New Zealand story. In New Zealand there are several statements concerning Tuna's dwelling place. He is sometimes represented as coming from a pool to attack Hina and sometimes from a distant stream, and sometimes from the river by which Hina dwelt. The Hawaiians told of the annoyances which Hina endured from Kuna while he lived above her home in the Wailuku. He would stop up the river and fill it with dirt as when the freshets brought down the debris of the storms from the mountain sides. He would throw logs and rolling stones into the stream that they might be carried over the falls and drive Hina from her cave. He had sought Hina in many ways and had been repulsed again and again until at last hatred took the place of all more kindly feelings and he determined to destroy the divine chiefess.

Hina was frequently left with but little protection, and yet from her home in the cave feared nothing that Kuna could do. Precipices guarded the cave on either side, and any approach of an enemy through the falling water could be easily thwarted. So her chants rang out through the river valley even while floods swirled around her, and Kuna's missiles were falling over the rocky bed of the stream toward her. Kuna became very angry and, uttering great curses and calling upon all his magic forces to aid him, caught a great stone and at night hurled it into the gorge of the river below Hina's home, filling the river bed from bank to bank. 'Ah, Hina! Now is the danger, for the river rises. The water cannot flow away. Awake! Awake!'

Hina is not aware of this evil which is so near. The water rises and rises, higher and higher. 'Auwe! Auwe! Alas, alas, Hina must perish!' The water entered the opening of the cave and began to creep along the floor. Hina cannot fly, except into the very arms of her great enemy, who is waiting to destroy her. Then Hina called for Māui. Again and again her voice went out from the cave. It pierced through the storms and the clouds which attended Kuna's attack upon her. It swept along the side of the great mountain. It crossed the channel between the islands of Hawai'i and Māui. Its anguish smote the side of the great mountain Haleakala, where Māui had been throwing his lassoes around the sun and compelling him to go more slowly. When Māui heard Hina's cry for help echoing from cliff to cliff and through the ravines, he leaped at once to rush to her assistance.

Some say that Hina, the goddess, had a cloud servant, the 'ao-ōpua,' the 'warning cloud,' which rose swiftly above the falls when Hina cried for aid and then, assuming a peculiar shape, stood high above the hills that Māui might see it. Down the mountain he leaped to his magic canoe. Pushing it into the sea with two mighty strokes of his paddle he crossed the sea to the mouth of the Wailuku river. Here even to the present day lies a long double rock, surrounded by the waters of the bay, which the natives call Ka waa o Māui, 'The canoe of Māui.' It represents to Hawaiian thought the magic canoe with which Māui always sailed over the ocean more swiftly than any winds could carry him. Leaving his canoe, Māui seized the magic club with which he had conquered the sun after lassoing him, and rushed along the dry bed of the river to the place of danger. Swinging the club swiftly around his head, he struck the dam holding back the water of the rapidly rising river.

'Ah! Nothing can withstand the magic club. The bank around one end of the dam gives way. The imprisoned waters leap into the new channel. Safe is Hina the goddess.'

Kuna heard the crash of the club against the stones of the river bank and fled up the river to his home in the hidden caves by the pools in the river bed. Māui rushed up the river to punish Kuna-mo-o for the trouble he had caused Hina. When he came to the place where the dragon was hidden under deep waters, he took his magic spear and thrust it through the dirt and lava rocks along one side of the river, making a long hole, through which the waters rushed, revealing Kuna-mo-o's hiding place. This place of the spear thrust is known among the Hawaiians as Ka puka a Māui, 'the door made by Māui.' It is also known as 'The natural bridge of the Wailuku river.'

Kuna-mo-o fled to his different hiding places, but Māui broke up the river bed and drove the dragon out from every one, following him from place to place as he fled down the river. Apparently this is a legendary account of earthquakes. At last Kuna-mo-o found what seemed to be a safe hiding place in a series of deep pools, but Māui poured a lava flow into the river. He threw red-hot burning stones into the water until the pools were boiling and the steam was rising in clouds. Kuna uttered incantation after incantation, but the water scalded and burned him. Dragon as he was, his hard, tough skin was of no avail. The pain was becoming unbearable. With cries to his gods he leaped from the pools and fled down the river. The waters of the pools are no longer scalding, but they have never lost the tumbling, tossing, foaming, boiling swirl which Māui gave to them when he threw into them the red-hot stones with which he hoped to destroy Kuna, and they are known today as 'The Boiling Pots.'

Some versions of the legend say that Māui poured boiling water in the river and sent it in swift pursuit of Kuna, driving him from point to point and scalding his life out of him. Others say that Māui chased the dragon, striking him again and again with his consecrated weapons, following Kuna down from falls to falls until he came to the place where Hina dwelt. Then, feeling that there was little use in flight, Kuna battled with Māui. His struggles were of no avail. He was forced over the falls into the stream below. Hina and her women encouraged Māui by their chants and strengthened him by the most powerful incantations with which they were acquainted. Great was their joy when they beheld Kuna's ponderous body hurled over the falls. Eagerly they watched the dragon as the swift waters swept him against the dam with which he had hoped to destroy Hina; and when the whirling waves caught him and dashed him through the new channel made by Māui's magic club, they rejoiced and sang the praise of the mighty warrior who had saved them. Māui had rushed along the bank of the river with tremendous strides overtaking the dragon as he was rolled over and over among the small waterfalls near the mouth of the river. Here Māui again attacked Kuna, at last beating the life out of his body. 'Moo-Kuna' was the name given by the Hawaiians to the dragon. 'Moo' means anything in lizard shape, but Kuna was unlike any lizard known in the Hawaiian Islands. Moo Kuna is the name sometimes given to a long black stone lying like an island in the waters between the small falls of the river. As one who calls attention to this legendary black stone says: 'As if he were not dead enough already, every big freshet in the stream beats him and pounds him and drowns him over and over as he would have drowned Hina.' A New Zealand legend relates a conflict of incantations, somewhat like the filling in of the Wailuku river by Kuna, and the cleaving of a new channel by Māui with the different use of means. In New Zealand the river is closed by the use of powerful incantations and charms and reopened by the use of those more powerful.

In the Hervey Islands, Tuna, the god of eels, loved Ina (Hina) and finally died for her, giving his head to be buried. From this head sprang two cocoanut trees, bearing fruit marked with Tuna's eyes and mouth.

In Samoa the battle was between an owl and a serpent. The owl conquered by calling in the aid of a friend.

This story of Hina apparently goes far back in the traditions of Polynesians, even to their ancient home in Hawaiki, from which it was taken by one branch of the family to New Zealand and by another to the Hawaiian Islands and other groups in the Pacific Ocean. The dragon may even be a remembrance of the days when the Polynesians were supposed to dwell by the banks of the River Ganges in India, when crocodiles were dangerous enemies and heroes saved families from their destructive depredations.

HINA, THE WOMAN IN THE MOON

The Wailuku river has by its banks far up the mountain side some of the most ancient of the various interesting picture rocks of the Hawaiian Islands. The origin of the Hawaiian picture writing is a problem still unsolved, but the picture rocks of the Wailuku river are called 'na kii o Māui,' 'the Māui pictures.' Their antiquity is beyond question.

The most prominent figure cut in these rocks is that of the crescent moon. The Hawaiian legends do not attempt any direct explanation of the meaning of this picture writing. The traditions of the Polynesians both concerning Hina and Māui look to Hina as the moon goddess of their ancestors, and in some measure the Hawaiian stories confirm the traditions of the other island groups of the Pacific.

Fornander, in his history of the Polynesian race, gives the Hawaiian story of Hina's ascent to the moon, but applies it to a Hina the wife of a chief called Aikanaka rather than to the Hina of Hilo, the wife of Akalana, the father of Māui. However, Fornander evidently found some difficulty in determining the status of the one to whom he refers the legend, for he calls her 'the mysterious wife of Aikanaka.' In some of the Hawaiian legends Hina, the mother of Māui, lived on the southeast coast of the Island of Māui at the foot of a hill famous in Hawaiian story as Kauiki. Fornander says that this 'mysterious wife' of Aikanaka bore her children Puna and Huna, the latter a noted sea-rover among the Polynesians, at the foot of this hill Kauiki. It can very easily be supposed that a legend of the Hina connected with the demigod Māui might be given during the course of centuries to the other Hina, the mother of Huna. The application of the legend would make no difference to anyone were it not for the fact that the story of Hina and her ascent to the moon has been handed down in different forms among the traditions of Samoa, New Zealand, Tonga, Hervey Islands, Fate Islands, Nauru and other Pacific island groups. The Polynesian name of the moon, Māhina or Masina, is derived from Hina, the goddess mother of Māui. It is even possible to trace the name back to 'Sin,' the moon god of the Assyrians.

The moon goddess of Ponape was Ina-maram (Hawaiian Hina-malamalama, 'Hina giving light').

In the Paumotan Islands an eclipse of the sun is called Higa-higa-hana (Hina-hiua-hana), 'The act (hana) of Hina – the moon.'

In New Zealand moonless nights were called 'Dark Hina.'

In Tahiti it is said there was war among the gods. They cursed the stars. Hina saved them, although they lost a little light. Then they cursed the sea, but Hina preserved the tides. They cursed the rivers, but Hina saved the springs – the moving waters inland, like the tides in the ocean.

The Hawaiians say that Hina and her maidens pounded out the softest, finest kapa cloth on the long, thick kapa board at the foot of Kauiki. Incessantly the restless sea dashed its spray over the picturesque groups of splintered lava rocks which form the Kauiki headland. Here above the reach of the surf still lies the long, black stone into which the legends say Hina's kapa board was changed. Here Hina took the leaves of the hala tree and, after the manner of the Hawaiian women of the ages past, braided mats for the household to sleep upon, and from the nuts of the kukui trees fashioned the torches which were burned around the homes of those of high chief rank.

At last she became weary of her work among mortals. Her family had become more and more troublesome. It was said that her sons were unruly and her husband lazy and shiftless. She looked into the heavens and determined to flee up the pathway of her rainbow through the clouds.

The Sun was very bright and Hina said, 'I will go to the Sun.' So she left her home very early in the morning and climbed up, higher, higher, until the heat of the rays of the sun beat strongly upon her and weakened her so that she could scarcely crawl along her beautiful path. Up a little higher and the clouds no longer gave her even the least shadow. The heat from the sun was so great that she began to feel the fire shriveling and torturing her. Quickly she slipped down into the storms around her rainbow and then back to earth. As the day passed her strength came back, and when the full moon rose through the shadows of the night she said, 'I will climb to the moon and there find rest.'

But when Hina began to go upward her husband saw her and called to her: 'Do not go into the heavens.' She answered him: 'My mind is fixed; I will go to my new husband, the moon.' And she climbed up higher and higher. Her husband ran toward her. She was almost out of reach, but he leaped and caught her foot. This did not deter Hina from her purpose. She shook off her husband, but as he fell he broke her leg so that the lower part came off in his hands. Hina went up through the stars, crying out the strongest incantations she could use. The powers of the night aided her. The mysterious hands of darkness lifted her, until she stood at the door of the moon. She had packed her calabash with her most priceless possessions and had carried it with her even when injured by her cruel husband. With her calabash she limped into the moon and found her abiding home. When the moon is full, the Hawaiians of the long ago, aye and even today, look into the quiet, silvery light and see the goddess in her celestial home, her calabash by her side.

The natives call her now Lono-moku, 'the crippled Lono.' From this watch tower in the heavens she pointed out to Kahai, one of her descendents, the way to rise up into the skies. The ancient chant thus describes his ascent:

'The rainbow is the path of Kahai.
Kahai rose. Kahai bestirred himself.
Kahai passed on the floating cloud of Kane.
Perplexed were the eyes of Alihi.

> *Kahai passed on the glancing light.*
> *The glancing light on men and canoes.*
> *Above was Hanaiakamalama' (Hina).*

Thus under the care of his ancestress Hina, Kahai, the great sea-rover, made his ascent in quest of adventures among the immortals.

In the Tongan Islands the legends say that Hina remains in the moon watching over the 'fire-walkers' as their great protecting goddess.

The Hervey Island traditions say that the Moon (Marama) had often seen Hina and admired her, and at last had come down and caught her up to live with himself. The moonlight in its glory is called Ina-motea, 'the brightness of Ina.'

The story as told on Atiu Island (one of the Society group) is that Hina took her human husband with her to the moon, where they dwelt happily for a time, but as he grew old she prepared a rainbow, down which he descended to the earth to die, leaving Hina forevermore as 'the woman in the moon.' The Savage Islanders worshipped the spirits of their ancestors, saying that many of them went up to the land of Sina, the always bright land in the skies. To the natives of Niue Island, Hina has been the goddess ruling over all tapa making. They say that her home is 'Motu a Hina,' 'the island of Hina,' the home of the dead in the skies.

The Samoans said that the Moon received Hina and a child, and also her tapa board and mallet and material for the manufacture of tapa cloth. Therefore, when the moon is shining in full splendor, they shade their eyes and look for the goddess and the tools with which she fashions the tapa clouds in the heavens.

The New Zealand legend says that the woman went after water in the night. As she passed down the path to the spring the bright light of the full moon made the way easy for her quick footsteps, but when she had filled her calabash and started homeward, suddenly the bright light was hidden by a passing cloud and she stumbled against a stone in the path and fell to the ground, spilling the water she was carrying. Then she became very angry and cursed the moon heartily. Then the moon became angry and swiftly swept down upon her from the skies, grasping her and lifting her up. In her terrible fight she caught a small tree with one hand and her calabash with the other. But oh! the strong moon pulled her up with the tree and the calabash and there in the full moon they can all be traced when the nights are clear.

Pleasant or Nauru Island, in which a missionary from Central Union Church, Honolulu, is laboring, tells the story of Gigu, a beautiful young woman, who has many of the experiences of Hina. She opened the eyes of the Mother of the Moon as Hina, in some of the Polynesian legends, is represented to have opened the eyes of one of the great goddesses, and in reward is married to Maraman, the Moon, with whom she lives ever after, and in whose embrace she can always be seen when the moon is full. Gigu is Hina under another and more guttural form of speech. Maraman is the same as Malama, one of the Polynesian names for the moon.

GHOSTS OF THE HILO HILLS

The legends about Hina and her famous son Māui and her less widely known daughters are common property among the natives of the beautiful little city of Hilo. One of these legends of more than ordinary interest finds its location in the three small hills back of Hilo toward the mountains.

These hills are small craters connected with some ancient lava flow of unusual violence. The eruption must have started far up on the slopes of Mauna Loa. As it sped down toward the sea it met some obstruction which, although overwhelmed, checked the flow and caused a great mass of cinders and ashes to be thrown out until a large hill with a hollow crater was built up, covering many acres of ground.

Soon the lava found another vent and then another obstruction and a second and then a third hill were formed nearer the sea. These hills or extinct craters bear the names Halai, Opeapea and Puu Honu. They are not far from the Wailuku river, famous for its picturesque waterfalls and also for the legends which are told along its banks. Here Māui had his lands overlooking the steep bluffs. Here in a cave under the Rainbow Falls was the home of Hina, the mother of Māui, according to the Hawaiian stories. Other parts of the Pacific sometimes make Hina Māui's wife, and sometimes a goddess from whom he descended. In the South Sea legends Hina was thought to have married the moon. Her home was in the skies, where she wove beautiful tapa cloths (the clouds), which were bright and glistening, so that when she rolled them up flashes of light (cloud lightning) could be seen on the earth. She laid heavy stones on the corners of these tapas, but sometimes the stones rolled off and made the thunder. Hina of the Rainbow Falls was a famous tapa maker whose tapa was the cause of Māui's conflict with the sun.

Hina had several daughters, four of whose names are given: Hina Ke Ahi, Hina Ke Kai, Hina Mahuia, and Hina Kuluua.

Each name marked the peculiar 'mana' or divine gift which Hina, the mother, had bestowed upon her daughters.

Hina Ke Ahi meant the Hina who had control of fire. This name is sometimes given to Hina the mother. Hina Ke Kai was the daughter who had power over the sea. She was said to have been in a canoe with her brother Māui when he fished up Cocoanut Island, his line breaking before he could pull it up to the mainland and make it fast. Hina Kuluua was the mistress over the forces of rain. The winds and the storms were supposed to obey her will. Hina Mahuia is peculiarly a name connected with the legends of the other island groups of the Pacific. Mahuia or Mafuie was a god or goddess of fire all through Polynesia.

The legend of the Hilo hills pertains especially to Hina Ke Ahi and Hina Kuluua. Hina the mother gave the hill Halai to Hina Ke Ahi and the hill Puu Honu to Hina Kuluua for their families and dependents.

The hills were of rich soil and there was much rain. Therefore, for a long time, the two daughters had plenty of food for themselves and their people, but at last the days were like fire and the sky had no rain in it. The taro planted on the hillsides died. The bananas and sugar cane and sweet potatoes withered and the fruit on the trees was blasted. The people were faint because of hunger, and the shadow of death was over the land. Hina Ke Ahi pitied her suffering friends and determined to provide food for them. Slowly her people labored at her command. Over they went to the banks of the river course, which was only the bed of an ancient lava stream, over which no water was flowing; the famished laborers toiled, gathering and carrying back whatever wood they could find, then up the mountain side to the great koa and ohia forests, gathering their burdens of fuel according to the wishes of their chiefess.

Their sorcerers planted charms along the way and uttered incantations to ward off the danger of failure. The priests offered sacrifices and prayers for the safe and successful return of the burden-bearers. After many days the great quantity of wood desired by the goddess was piled up by the side of the Halai Hill.

Then came the days of digging out the hill and making a great imu or cooking oven and preparing it with stones and wood. Large quantities of wood were thrown into the place. Stones best fitted for retaining heat were gathered and the fires kindled. When the stones were hot, Hina Ke Ahi directed the people to arrange the imu in its proper order for cooking the materials for a great feast. A place was made for sweet potatoes, another for taro, another for pigs and another for dogs. All the form of preparing the food for cooking was passed through, but no real food was laid on the stones. Then Hina told them to make a place in the imu for a human sacrifice. Probably out of every imu of the long ago a small part of the food was offered to the gods, and there may have been a special place in the imu for that part of the food to be cooked. At any rate Hina had this oven so built that the people understood that a remarkable sacrifice would be offered in it to the gods, who for some reason had sent the famine upon the people.

Human sacrifices were frequently offered by the Hawaiians even after the days of the coming of Captain Cook. A dead body was supposed to be acceptable to the gods when a chief's house was built, when a chief's new canoe was to be made or when temple walls were to be erected or victories celebrated. The bodies of the people belonged to the will of the chief. Therefore it was in quiet despair that the workmen obeyed Hina Ke Ahi and prepared the place for sacrifice. It might mean their own holocaust as an offering to the gods. At last Hina Ke Ahi bade the laborers cease their work and stand by the side of the oven ready to cover it with the dirt which had been thrown out and piled up by the side. The people stood by, not knowing upon whom the blow might fall.

But Hina Ke Ahi was 'Hina the kind,' and although she stood before them robed in royal majesty and power, still her face was full of pity and love. Her voice melted the hearts of her retainers as she bade them carefully follow her directions.

'O my people. Where are you? Will you obey and do as I command? This imu is my imu. I shall lie down on its bed of burning stones. I shall sleep under its cover. But deeply cover me or I may perish. Quickly throw the dirt over my body. Fear not the fire. Watch for three days. A woman will stand by the imu. Obey her will.'

Hina Ke Ahi was very beautiful, and her eyes flashed light like fire as she stepped into the great pit and lay down on the burning stones. A great smoke arose and gathered over the imu. The men toiled rapidly, placing the imu mats over their chiefess and throwing the dirt back into the oven until it was all thoroughly covered and the smoke was quenched.

Then they waited for the strange, mysterious thing which must follow the sacrifice of this divine chiefess.

Halai hill trembled and earthquakes shook the land round about. The great heat of the fire in the imu withered the little life which was still left from the famine. Meanwhile Hina Ke Ahi was carrying out her plan for securing aid for her people. She could not be injured by the heat for she was a goddess of fire. The waves of heat raged around her as she sank down through the stones of the imu into the underground paths which belonged to the spirit world. The legend says that Hina made her appearance in the form of a gushing stream of water which would always supply the want of her adherents. The second day passed. Hina was still journeying underground, but this time she came to the surface as a pool named Moe Waa (canoe sleep) much nearer the sea. The third day came and Hina caused a great spring of sweet water to burst forth from the sea shore in the very path of the ocean surf. This received the name Auauwai. Here Hina washed away all traces of her journey through the depths. This was the last of the series of earthquakes and the appearance of new water springs. The people waited, feeling that some more wonderful event must follow the remarkable experiences of the three days. Soon a woman stood by the imu, who commanded the laborers to dig away the dirt and remove the mats. When this was done, the hungry people found a very great abundance of food, enough to supply their want until the food plants should have time to ripen and the days of the famine should be over.

The joy of the people was great when they knew that their chiefess had escaped death and would still dwell among them in comfort. Many were the songs sung and stories told about the great famine and the success of the goddess of fire.

The second sister, Hina Kuluua, the goddess of rain, was always very jealous of her beautiful sister Hina Ke Ahi, and many times sent rain to put out fires which her sister tried to kindle. Hina Ke Ahi could not stand the rain and so fled with her people to a home by the seaside.

Hina Kuluua (or Hina Kuliua as she was sometimes known among the Hawaiians) could control rain and storms, but for some reason failed to provide a food supply for her people, and the famine wrought havoc among them. She thought of the stories told and songs sung about her sister and wished for the same honor for herself. She commanded her people to make a great imu for her in the hill Puu Honu. She knew that a strange power belonged to her and yet, blinded by jealousy, forgot that rain and fire could not work together. She planned to furnish a great supply of food for her people in the same way in which her sister had worked.

The oven was dug. Stones and wood were collected and the same ghostly array of potatoes, taro, pig and dog prepared as had been done before by her sister.

The kahunas or priests knew that Hina Kuluua was going out of her province in trying to do as her sister had done, but there was no use in attempting to change her plans. Jealousy is self-willed and obstinate and no amount of reasoning from her dependents could have any influence over her.

The ordinary incantations were observed, and Hina Kuluua gave the same directions as those her sister had given. The imu was to be well heated. The make-believe food was to be put in and a place left for her body. It was the goddess of rain making ready to lie down on a bed prepared for the goddess of fire. When all was ready, she lay down on the heated stones and the oven mats were thrown over her and the ghostly provisions. Then the covering of dirt was thrown back upon the mats and heated stones, filling the pit which had been dug. The goddess of rain was left to prepare a feast for her people as the goddess of fire had done for her followers.

On Lava Beds

Some of the legends have introduced the demigod Māui into this story. The natives say that Māui came to 'burn' or 'cook the rain' and that he made the oven very hot, but that the goddess of rain escaped and hung over the hill in the form of a cloud. At least this is what the people saw – not a cloud of smoke over the imu, but a rain cloud. They waited and watched for such evidences of underground labor as attended the passage of Hina Ke Ahi through the earth from the hill to the sea, but the only strange appearance was the dark rain cloud. They waited three days and looked for their chiefess to come in the form of a woman. They waited another day and still another and no signs or wonders were manifest. Meanwhile Māui, changing himself into a white bird, flew up into the sky to catch the ghost of the goddess of rain which had escaped from the burning oven. Having caught this spirit, he rolled it in some kapa cloth which he kept for food to be placed in an oven and carried it to a place in the forest on the mountain side where again the attempt was made to 'burn the rain,' but a great drop escaped and sped upward into the sky. Again Māui caught the ghost of the goddess and carried it to a pali or precipice below the great volcano Kilauea, where he again tried to destroy it in the heat of a great lava oven, but this time the spirit escaped and found a safe refuge among kukui trees on the mountain side, from which she sometimes rises in clouds which the natives say are the sure sign of rain.

Whether this Māui legend has any real connection with the two Hinas and the famine we do not surely know. The legend ordinarily told among the Hawaiians says that after five days had passed the retainers decided on their own responsibility to open the imu. No woman had appeared to give them directions. Nothing but a mysterious rain cloud over the hill. In doubt and fear, the dirt was thrown off and the mats removed. Nothing was found but the ashes of Hina Kuluua. There was no food for her followers and the goddess had lost all power of appearing as a chiefess. Her bitter and thoughtless jealousy brought destruction upon herself and her people. The ghosts of Hina Ke Ahi and Hina Kuluua sometimes draw near to the old hills in the form of the fire of flowing lava or clouds of rain while the old men and women tell the story of the Hinas, the sisters of Māui, who were laid upon the burning stones of the imus of a famine.

TALES OF GODS

'When the borders of mist-land are crossed, a
rich store of folk-lore with a historical foundation is
discovered. Chiefs and gods mingle together…'
William Drake Westervelt, from 'Legends of
Gods & Ghosts (Hawaiian Mythology)'

Polynesian stories blend fact and fiction, mingling history and legend together. Their tales of gods showcase the triumph of humanity; the otherworldliness of divinity highlights mortal strength and resilience.

In these tales devoted sons set out to avenge their father and rescue their mother. Heaven regards the eldest brother's efforts so highly that a goddess descends to take him as her husband. When his mortal foibles drive her away, his tenacity and perseverance prove his worthiness to win her back.

When a priest's children are killed, he seeks the aid of the gods. Even the most bloodthirsty deity is impressed by his devotion and agrees to assist him. The father's determination sees his quest victorious, with his enemy cast into a shark-infested sea.

These legends are filled with fantastic journeys across the ocean and heavens. Magical bananas endlessly replenish. Gods walk alongside men. A journey does not end, even in death. These are stories of magic and wonder, and especially of human perseverance.

THE LEGEND OF TĀWHAKI

Now quitting the deeds of Māui, let those of Tāwhaki be recounted. He was the son of Hema and Urutonga, and he had a younger brother named Karilii. Tāwhaki having taken Hinepiripiri as a wife, he went one day with his brothers-in-law to fish, from a flat reef of rocks which ran far out into the sea; he had four brothers-in-law, two of these when tired of fishing returned towards their village, and he went with them; when they drew near the village, they attempted to murder him, and thinking they had slain him, buried him; they then went on their way to the village, and when they reached it, their young sister said to them: 'Why, where is your brother-in-law?' and they replied: 'Oh, they're all fishing.' So the young wife waited until the other two brothers came back, and when they reached the village they were questioned by their young sister, who asked: 'Where is your brother-in-law?' and the two who had last arrived, answered her: 'Why, the others all went home together long since.' So the young wife suspected that they had killed her husband, and ran off at once to search for him; and she found where he had been buried, and on examining him ascertained that he had only been insensible, and was not quite dead; then with great difficulty she got him upon her back, and carried him home to their house, and carefully washed his wounds, and staunched the bleeding.

Tāwhaki, when he had a little recovered, said to her: 'Fetch some wood, and light a fire for me'; and as his wife was going to do this, he said to her; If you see any tall tree growing near you, fell it, and bring that with you for the fire.' His wife went, and saw a tree growing such as her husband spoke of; so she felled it, and put it upon her shoulder, and brought it along with her; and when she reached the house, she put the whole tree upon the fire without chopping it into pieces; and it was this circumstance that led her to give the name of Wahieroa (long-log-of-wood-for-the-fire) to their first son, for Tāwhaki had told her to bring this log of wood home, and to call the child after it, that the duty of avenging his father's wrongs might often be recalled to his mind.

As soon as Tāwhaki had recovered from his wounds, he left the place where his faithless brothers-in-law lived, and went away taking all his own warriors and their families with him, and built a fortified village upon the top of a very lofty mountain, where he could easily protect himself; and they dwelt there. Then he called aloud to the Gods, his ancestors, for revenge, and they let the floods of heaven descend, and the earth was overwhelmed by the waters and all human beings perished, and the name given to that event was 'The overwhelming of the Mataaho,' and the whole of that race perished.

When this feat was accomplished, Tāwhaki and his younger brother next went to seek revenge for the death of their father. It was a different race who had carried off and slain the father of Tāwhaki; the name of that race was the Ponaturi – the country they inhabited was underneath the waters, but they had a large house on the dry land to which they resorted to sleep at night; the name of that large house was 'Mānawa-Tāne'.

The Ponaturi had slain the father of Tāwhaki and carried off his body, but his father's wife they had carried off alive and kept as a captive. Ta-whaki and his younger brother went upon their way to seek out that people and to revenge themselves upon them. At length they reached a place from whence they could see the house called Mānawa-Tāne. At the time they arrived near the house there was no one there but their mother, who was sitting near the door; but the bones of their father were hung up inside the house under its high sloping roof. The whole tribe of the Ponaturi were at that time in their country under the waters, but at the approach of night they would return to their house, to Mānawa-Tāne.

Whilst Tāwhaki and his younger brother Karihi were coming along still at a great distance from the house, Tāwhaki began to repeat an incantation, and the bones of his father, Hema, felt the influence of this, and rattled loudly together where they hung under the roof of the house, for gladness, when they heard Tāwhaki repeating his incantations as he came along, for they knew that the hour of revenge had now come. As the brothers drew nearer, their mother, Urutonga, heard the voice of Tāwhaki, and she wept for gladness in front of her children, who came repeating incantations upon their way. And when they reached at length the house, they wept over their mother, over old Urutonga. When they had ended weeping, their mother said to them:

My children, hasten to return hence, or you will both certainly perish. The people who dwell here are a very fierce and savage race.' Karihi said to her: 'How low will the sun have descended when those you speak of return home?' And she replied: 'They will return here when the sun sinks beneath the ocean.' Then Karihi asked her: 'What did they save you alive for?' And she answered: 'They saved me alive that I might watch for the rising of the dawn; they make me ever sit watching here at the door of the house, hence this people have named me 'Tatau', or 'the door'; and they keep on throughout the night calling out to me:

'Ho, Tatau, there! is it dawn yet?' And then I call out in answer: 'No, no, it is deep night – it is lasting night – it is still night; compose yourselves to sleep, sleep on.'

Karihi then said to his mother: 'Cannot we hide ourselves somewhere here?'

Their mother answered: 'You had better return; you cannot hide yourselves here, the scent of you will be perceived by them.'

'But', said Karihi, 'we will hide ourselves away in the thick thatch of the house.'

Their mother, however, answered: ''Tis of no use, you cannot hide yourselves there.'

All this time Tāwhaki sat quite silent; but Karihi said: 'We will hide ourselves here, for we know incantations which will render us invisible to all.'

On hearing this, their mother consented to their remaining, and attempting to avenge their father's death. So they climbed up to the ridge-pole of the house, upon the outside of the roof, and made holes in the thick layers of reeds which formed the thatch of the roof, and crept into them and covered themselves up; and their mother called to them, saying: 'When it draws near dawn, come down again, and stop up every chink in the house, so that no single ray of light may shine in.'

At length the day closed, and the sun sank below the horizon, and the whole of that strange tribe left the water in a body, and ascended to the dry land; and, according to their custom from time immemorial, they sent one of their number in front of them, that he might carefully examine the road, and see that there were no hidden foes lying in wait for them either on the way or in their house. As Boon as this scout arrived at the threshold of the house, he perceived the scent of Tāwhaki and Karihi; so he lifted up his nose and turned sniffing all round the inside of the house. As he turned about, he was on the point of discovering that strangers were hidden there, when the rest of the tribe (whom long security had made careless) came hurrying on, and crowding into the house in thousands, so that from the denseness of the crowd the scent of the strange men was quite lost. The Ponaturi then stowed themselves away in the house until it was entirely filled up with them, and by degrees they arranged themselves in convenient places, and at length all fell fast asleep.

At midnight Tāwhaki and Karihi stole down from the roof of the house, and found that their mother had crept out of the door to meet them, so they sat at the doorway whispering together.

Karihi then asked his mother: 'Which is the best way for us to destroy these people who are sleeping here?' And their mother answered: 'You had better let the sun kill them, its rays will destroy them.'

Having said this, Tatau crept into the house again; presently an old man of the Ponaturi called out to her: 'Ho, Tatau, Tatau, there; is it dawn yet?' And she answered: 'No, no, it is deep night – it is lasting night; 'tis still night; sleep soundly, sleep on.'

When it was very near dawn, Tatau whispered to her children, who were still sitting just outside the door of the house: 'See that every chink in the doorway and window is stopped, so that not a ray of light can penetrate here.'

Presently another old man of the Ponaturi called out again: 'Ho, Tatau there, is not it near dawn yet?' And she answered: 'No, no, it is night; it is lasting night; 'tis still night; sleep soundly, sleep on.'

This was the second time that Tatau had thus called out to them.

At last dawn had broken – at last the sun had shone brightly upon the earth, and rose high in the heavens; and the old man again called out: 'Ho, Tatau there; is not it dawn yet?' And she answered: 'Yes.' And then she called out to her children: 'Be quick, pull out the things with which you have stopped up the window and the door.'

So they pulled them out, and the bright rays of the sun came streaming into the house, and the whole of the Ponaturi perished before the light; they perished not by the hand of man, but withered before the sun's rays.

When the Ponaturi had been all destroyed, Tāwhaki and Karihi carefully took down their father's bones from the roof of the house, and burnt them with fire, and together with the bodies of all those who were in the house, who had perished, scorched by the bright rays of the sun; they then returned again to their own country, taking with them their mother, and carefully carrying the bones of their father.

The fame of Tāwhaki's courage in thus destroying the race of Ponaturi, and a report also of his manly beauty, chanced to reach the ears of a young maiden of the heavenly race who live above in the skies; so one night she descended from the heavens to visit Tāwhaki, and to judge for herself, whether these reports were true. She found him lying sound asleep, and after gazing on him for some time, she stole to his side and laid herself down by him. He, when disturbed by her, thought that it was only some female of this lower world, and slept again; but before dawn the young girl stole away again from his side, and ascended once more to the heavens. In the early morning Tāwhaki awoke and felt all over his sleeping place with both his hands, but in vain, he could nowhere find the young girl.

From that time Tangotango, the girl of the heavenly race, stole every night to the side of Tāwhaki and lo, in the morning she was gone, until she found that she had conceived a child, who was afterwards named Arahuta; then full of love for Tāwhaki, she disclosed herself fully to him and lived constantly in this world with him, deserting, for his sake, her friends above; and he discovered that she who had so loved him belonged to the race whose home is in the heavens.

Whilst thus living with him, this girl of the heavenly race, his second wife, said to him: 'Oh, Tāwhaki, if our baby so shortly now to be born, should prove a son, I will wash the little tiling before it is baptized; but if it should be a little girl then you shall wash it.' When the time came Tangotango had a little girl, and before it was baptized Tāwhaki took it to a spring to wash it, and afterwards held it away from him as if it smelt badly, and said: 'Faugh, how badly the little thing smells.' Then Tangotango, when she heard this said of her own dear little baby, began to sob and cry bitterly, and at last rose up from her place with her child, and began to take flight towards the sky, but she paused for one minute with one foot resting upon the carved figure at the end of the ridge-pole of the house above the door. Then Tāwhaki rushed forward, and springing up tried to catch hold of his young wife, but missing her, he entreatingly besought her: 'Mother of my child, oh return once more to me?' But she in reply called down to him: 'No, no, I shall now never return to you again.'

Tāwhaki once more called up to her: 'At least, then, leave me some one remembrance of you.'

Then his young wife called down to him: 'These are my parting words of remembrance to you – take care that you lay not hold with your hands of the loose root of the creeper, which dropping from aloft sways to and fro in the air; but rather lay fast hold on that which hanging down from on high has again struck its fibres into the earth.' Then she floated up into the air, and vanished from his sight.

Tāwhaki remained plunged in grief, for his heart was torn by regrets for his wife and his little girl. One moon had waned after her departure, when Tāwhaki, unable longer to endure such sufferings, called out to his younger brother, to Karihi, saying: 'Oh, brother, shall we go and search for my little girl?' And Karihi consented, saying: 'Yes, let us go.' So they departed, taking two slaves with them as companions for their journey.

When they reached the pathway along which they intended to travel, Tāwhaki said to the two slaves who were accompanying himself and his brother: 'You being unclean or unconsecrated persons must be careful when we come to the place where the road passes the fortress of Tōngāmeha, not to look up at it for it is enchanted, and some evil will befall you if you do.' They then went along the road, and when they came to the place mentioned by Tāwhaki, one of the slaves looked up at the fortress, and his eye was immediately torn out by the magical arts of Tōngāmeha, and he perished. Tāwhaki and Karihi then went upon the road accompanied by only one slave. They at last reached the spot where the ends of the tendrils which hung down from heaven reached the earth, and they there found an old ancestress of theirs who was quite blind, and whose name was Matakerepō. She was appointed to take care of the tendrils, and she sat at the place where they touched the earth, and held the ends of one of them in her hands.

This old lady was at the moment employed in counting some taro roots, which she was about to have cooked, and as she was blind she was not aware of the strangers who stole quietly and silently up to her. There were ten taro roots lying in a heap before her. She began to count them, one, two, three, four, five, six, seven, eight, nine. Just at this moment Tāwhaki quietly slipped away the tenth, the old lady felt about everywhere for it, but she could not find it. She thought she must have made some mistake, and so began to count her taro over again very carefully. One, two, three, four, five, six, seven, eight. Just then Tāwhaki had slipped away the ninth. She was now quite surprised, so she counted them over again quite slowly, one, two, three, four, five, six, seven, eight; and as she could not find the two that were missing, she at last guessed that somebody was playing a trick upon her, so she pulled her weapon out, which she always sat upon to keep it safe, and standing up turned round, feeling about her as she moved, to try if she could find Tāwhaki and Karihi; but they very gently stooped down to the ground and lay close there, so that her weapon passed over them, and she could not feel anybody; when she had thus swept her weapon all round her, she sat down and put it under her again. Karihi then struck her a blow upon the face, and she, quite frightened, threw up her hands to her face, pressing them on the place where she had been struck, and crying out: 'Oh! who did that?' Tāwhaki then touched both her eyes, and, lo, she was at once restored to sight, and saw quite plainly, and she knew her grandchildren and wept over them.

When the old lady had finished weeping over them, she asked: 'Where are you going to?' And Tāwhaki answered: 'I go to seek my little girl.' She replied: 'But where is she?' He answered: 'Above there, in the skies.' Then she replied: 'But what made her go to the skies?' And Tāwhaki answered: 'Her mother came from heaven. She was the daughter of Watitiri-mata-ka-taka.' The old lady then pointed to the tendrils, and said to them: 'Up there, then, lies your road; but do not begin the ascent so late in the day, wait until tomorrow, for the morning, and then commence to climb up.' He consented to follow this good advice, and called out to his slave: 'Cook some food for us.' The slave began at once to cook food, and when it was dressed, they all partook of it and slept there that night.

At the first peep of dawn Tāwhaki called out to his slave: 'Cook some food for us, that we may have strength to undergo the fatigues of this great journey'; and when their meal was finished, Tāwhaki took his slave, and presented him to Matakerepō, as an acknowledgment for her great kindness to them.

His old ancestress then called out to him, as he was starting: 'There lies the ascent before you, lay fast hold of the tendrils with your hands, and climb on; but when you get midway between heaven and earth, take care not to look down upon this lower world again, lest you become charmed and giddy, and fall down. Take care, also, that you do not by mistake lay hold of a tendril which swings loose; but rather lay hold of one which hanging down from above, has again firmly struck root into the earth.'

Just at that moment Karihi made a spring at the tendrils to catch them, and by mistake caught hold of a loose one, and away he swung to the very edge of the horizon, but a blast of wind blew forth from thence, and drove him back to the other side of the skies; on reaching that point, another strong land wind swept him right up heavenwards, and down he was blown again by the currents of air from above: then just as he reached near the earth again, Tāwhaki called out: 'Now, my brother, loose your hands: now is the time!' – and he did so, and, lo, he stood upon the earth once more; and the two brothers wept together over Karihi's narrow escape from destruction. And when they had ceased lamenting, Tāwhaki, who was alarmed lest any disaster should overtake his younger brother, said to him: 'It is my desire that you should return home, to take care of our families and our dependants.' Thereupon Karihi at once returned to the village of their tribe, as his eldest brother directed him.

Tāwhaki now began to climb the ascent to heaven, and his old ancestress, Matakerepō, called out to him as he went up: 'Hold fast, my child; let your hands hold tight.' And Tāwhaki made use of, and kept on repeating, a powerful incantation as he climbed up to the heavens, to preserve him from the dangers of that difficult and terrible road.

At length he reached the heavens, and pulled himself up into them, and then by enchantments he disguised himself, and changed his handsome and noble appearance, and assumed the likeness of a very ugly old man, and he followed the road he had at first struck upon, and entered a dense forest into which it ran, and still followed it until he came to a place in the forest where his brothers-in-law, with a party of their people, were hewing canoes from the trunks of trees; and they saw him, and little thinking who he was, called out: 'Here's an old fellow will make a nice slave for us'; but Tāwhaki went quietly on, and when he reached them he sat down with the people who were working at the canoes.

It now drew near evening, and his brothers-in-law finished their work, and called out to him: 'Ho! old fellow, there! – you just carry these heavy axes home for us, will you?' He at once consented to do this, and they gave him the axes. The old man then said to them: 'You go on in front, do not mind, I am old and heavy laden, I cannot travel fast.' So they started off, the old man following slowly behind. When his brothers-in-law and their people were all out of sight, he turned back to the canoe, and taking an axe just axed the canoe rapidly along from the bow to the stern, and lo, one side of the canoe was finished. Then he took the axe again, and ran it rapidly along the other side of the canoe, from the bow to the stem, and lo, that side also was beautifully finished.

He then walked quietly along the road again, like an old man, carrying the axes with him, and went on for some time without seeing anything; but when he drew near the village, he found two women from the village in the forest gathering firewood, and as soon as they saw him, one of them observed to her companion: 'I say here is a curious-looking old fellow, is he not?' – and her companion exclaimed: 'He shall be our slave'; to which the first answered: 'Make him carry the firewood for us, then.' So they took Tāwhaki, and laid a load of firewood upon his back, and made him carry that as well as the axes, so was this mighty chief treated as a slave, even by female slaves.

When they all reached the village, the two women called out: 'We've caught an old man for a slave.' Then Tangotango exclaimed in reply: 'That's right bring him along with you, then; he'll do for all of us.' Little did his wife Tangotango think that the slave they were so insulting, and whom she was talking about in such a way, was her own husband Tāwhaki.

When Tāwhaki saw Tangotango sitting at a fireplace near the upper end of the house with their little girl, he went straight up to the place, and all the persons present tried to stop him, calling out: 'Ho! ho! take care what you are doing; do not go there; you will become tapued from sitting near Tangotango.' But the old man, without minding them, went rapidly straight on, and carried his load of firewood right up to the very fire of Tangotango. Then they all said: 'There, the old fellow is tapu; it is his own fault.' But Tangotango had not the least idea that this was Tāwhaki; and yet there were her husband and herself seated, the one upon the one side, the other upon the opposite side of the very same fire.

They all stopped in the house until the sun rose next morning; then at daybreak his brothers-in-law called out to him: 'Holloa, old man, you bring the axes along, do you hear.' So the old man took up the axes, and started with them, and they all went off together to the forest, to work at dubbing out their canoes. When they reached them, and the brothers-in-law saw the canoe which Tāwhaki had worked at, they looked at it with astonishment, saying: 'Why, the canoe is not at all as we left it; who can have been working at it?' At last, when their wonder was somewhat abated, they all sat down, and set to work again to dub out another canoe, and worked until evening, when they again called out to the old man as on the previous one: 'Holloa, old fellow, come here, and carry the axes back to the village again.' As before, he said: 'Yes', and when they started he remained behind, and after the others were all out of sight he took an axe, and began again to axe away at the canoe they had been working at; and having finished his work he returned again to the village, and once more walked straight up to the fire of Tangotango, and remained there until the sun rose upon the following morning.

When they were all going at early dawn to work at their canoes as usual, they again called out to Tāwhaki: 'Holloa, old man, just bring these axes along with you'; and the old man went patiently and silently along with them, carrying the axes on his shoulder. When they reached the canoe they were about to work at, the brothers-in-law were quite astonished on seeing it, and shouted out: 'Why, here again, this canoe, too, is not at all as it was when we left it; who can have been at work at it?' Having wondered at this for some time, they at length sat down and set to again to dub out another canoe, and laboured away until evening, when a thought came into their minds that they would hide themselves in the forest, and wait to see who it was came every evening to work at their canoe; and Tāwhaki overheard them arranging this plan.

They therefore started as if they were going home, and when they had got a little way they turned off the path on one side, and hid themselves in the thick clumps of bushes, in a place from whence they could see the canoes. Then Tāwhaki, going a little way back into the forest, stripped off his old cloaks, and threw them on one side, and then repeating the necessary incantations he put off his disguise, and took again his own appearance, and made himself look noble and handsome, and commenced his work at the canoe. Then his brothers-in-law, when they saw him so employed, said one to another: 'Ah, that must be the old man whom we made a slave of who is working away at our canoe'; but again they called to one another and said: 'Come here, come here, just watch, why he is not in the least like that old man.' Then they said amongst themselves: 'This must be a demigod'; and without showing themselves to him, they ran off to the village, and as soon as they reached it they asked their sister Tangotango to describe her husband for them; and she described his appearance as well as she could, representing him just like the man they had seen: and they said to her: 'Yes, that must be he; he is exactly like him you have described to us.' Their sister replied: 'Then that chief must certainly be your brother-in-law.'

Just at this moment Tāwhaki reappeared at the village, having again disguised himself, and changed his appearance into that of an ugly old man. But Tangotango immediately questioned him, saying: 'Now tell me, who are you?' Tāwhaki made no reply, but walked on straight towards her. She asked him again: 'Tell me, are you Tāwhaki?' He murmured 'Humph!' in assent, still walking on until he reached the side of his wife, and then he snatched up his little daughter, and, holding her fast in his arms, pressed her to his heart. The persons present all rushed out of the court-yard of the house to the neighbouring court-yards, for the whole place was made tapu by Tāwhaki, and murmurs of gratification and surprise arose from the people upon every side at the splendour of his appearance, for in the days when he had been amongst them as an old man his figure was very different from the resplendent aspect which he presented on this day.

Then he retired to rest with his wife, and said to her: 'I came here that our little daughter might be made to undergo the ceremonies usual for the children of nobles, to secure them good fortune and happiness in this life'; and Tangotango consented.

When in the morning the sun arose, they broke out an opening through the end of the house opposite to the door, that the little girl's rank might be seen by her being carried out that way instead of through the usual entrance to the house; and they repeated the prescribed prayers when she was carried through the wall out of the house.

The prayers and incantations being finished, lightnings flashed from the arm-pits of Tāwhaki; then they carried the little girl to the water, and plunged her into it, and repeated a baptismal incantation over her.

Tāwhaki is said to still dwell in the skies, and is worshipped as a god, and thunder and lightning are said to be caused by his footsteps when he moves.

KALAI-PAHOA, THE POISON-GOD

The Bishop Museum of Honolulu has one of the best as well as one of the most scientifically arranged collections of Hawaiian curios in the world. In it are images of many of the gods of long ago. One of these is a helmeted head made of wicker-work, over which has been woven a thick covering of beautiful red feathers bordered with yellow feathers. This was the mighty war-god of the great Kamehameha. Another is a squat rough image, crudely carved out of wood. This was Kamehameha's poison-god.

The ancient Hawaiians were acquainted with poisons of various kinds. They understood the medicinal qualities of plants and found some of these strong enough to cause sickness and even death. One of the Hawaiian writers said: 'The opihi-awa is a poison shell-fish. These are bitter and deadly and can be used in putting enemies to death. Kalai-pahoa is also a tree in which there is the power to kill.'

Kamehameha's poison-god was called Kalai-pahoa, because it was cut from that tree which grew in the upland forest on the island of Molokai.

A native writer says there was an antidote for the poison from Kalai-pahoa, and he thus describes it: 'The war-god and the poison-god were not left standing in the temples like the images of other gods, but after being worshipped were wrapped in kapa and laid away.

'When the priest wanted Kalai-pahoa he was taken down and anointed with cocoanut-oil and wrapped in a fresh kapa cloth. Then he was set up above the altar and a feast prepared before him, awa to drink, and pig, fish, and poi to eat.

'Then the priest who had special care of this god would scrape off a little from the wood, and put it in an awa cup, and hold the cup before the god, chanting a prayer for the life of the king, the government, and the people. One of the priests would then take the awa cup, drink the contents, and quickly take food.

'Those who were watching would presently see a red flush creep over his cheeks, growing stronger and stronger, while the eyes would become glassy and the breath short like that of a dying man. Then the priest would touch his lips to the stick, Mai-ola, and have his life restored. Mai-ola was a god who had another tree. When Kalai-pahoa entered his tree on Molokai, Mai-ola entered another tree and became the enemy of the poison-god.'

The priests of the poison-god were very powerful in the curious rite called pule-ana-ana, or praying to death. The Hawaiians said: 'Perhaps the priests of Kalai-pahoa put poison in bananas or in taro. It was believed that they scraped the body of the image and put the pieces in the food of the one they wished to pray to death. There was one chief who was very skilful in waving kāhilis, or feather fans, over any one and shaking the powder of death into the food from the moving feathers. Another would have scrapings in his cloak and would drop them into whatever food his enemy was eating.' The spirit of death was supposed to reside in the wood of the poison-god.

A very interesting legend was told by the old people to their children to explain the coming of medicinal and poisonous properties into the various kinds of trees and plants. These stories all go back to the time when Milu died and became the king of ghosts. They say that after the death of Milu the gods left Waipio Valley on the island of Hawai'i and crossed the channel to the island of Māui.

These gods had all kinds of power for evil, such as stopping the breath, chilling or burning the body, making headaches or pains in the stomach, or causing palsy or lameness or other injuries, even inflicting death.

Pua and Kapo, who from ancient times have been worshipped as goddesses having medicinal power, joined the party when they came to Māui. Then all the gods went up Mauna Loa, a place where there was a large and magnificent forest with fine trees, graceful vines and ferns, and beautiful flowers. They all loved this place, therefore they became gods of the forest.

Near this forest lived Kane-ia-kama, a high chief, who was a very great gambler. He had gambled away all his possessions. While he was sleeping, the night of his final losses, he heard some one call, 'O Kane-ia-kama, begin your play again.' He shouted out into the darkness: 'I have bet everything. I have nothing left.'

Then the voice again said, 'Bet your bones, bet your bones, and see what will happen.'

When he went to the gambling-place the next day the people all laughed at him, for they knew his goods were all gone. He sat down among them, however, and said: 'I truly have nothing left. My treasures are all gone; but I have my bones. If you wish, I will bet my body, then I will play with you.'

The other chiefs scornfully placed some property on one side and said, 'That will be of the same value as your bones.'

They gambled and he won. The chiefs were angry at their loss and bet again and again. He always won until he had more wealth than any one on the island.

After the gambling days were over he heard again the same voice saying: 'O Kane-ia-kama, you have done all that I told you and have become very rich in property and servants. Will you obey once more?'

The chief gratefully thanked the god for the aid that he had received, and said he would obey. The voice then said: 'Perhaps we can help you to one thing. You are now wealthy, but there is a last gift for you. You must listen carefully and note all I show you.'

Then this god of the night pointed out the trees into which the gods had entered when they decided to remain for a time in the forest, and explained to him all their different characteristics. He showed him where gods and goddesses dwelt and gave their names. Then he ordered Kane-ia-kama to take offerings of pigs, fish, cocoanuts, bananas, chickens, kapas, and all other things used for sacrifice, and place them at the roots of these trees into which the gods had entered, the proper offerings for each.

The next morning he went into the forest and saw that he had received a very careful description of each tree. He observed carefully the tree shown as the home of the spirit who had become his strange helper.

Before night fell he placed offerings as commanded. As a worshipper he took each one of these trees for his god, so he had many gods of plants and trees.

For some reason not mentioned in the legends he sent woodcutters to cut down these trees, or at least to cut gods out of them with their stone axes.

They began to cut. The koko (blood) of the trees, as the natives termed the flowing sap, and the chips flying out struck some of the woodcutters and they fell dead.

Kane-ia-kama made cloaks of the long leaves of the 'ie'ie vine and tied them around his men, so that their bodies could not be touched, then the work was easily accomplished.

The chief kept these images of gods cut from the medicinal trees and could use them as he desired. The most powerful of all these gods was that one whose voice he had heard in the night. To this god he gave the name Kalai-pahoa (The-one-cut-by-the-pahoa-or-stone-axe).

One account relates that the pahoa (stone) from which the axe was made came from Kalakoi, a celebrated place for finding a very hard lava of fine grain, the very best for making stone implements.

The god who had spoken to the chief in his dream was sometimes called Kane-kulana-ula.

The gods were caught by the sacrifices of the chief while they were in their tree bodies before they could change back into their spirit bodies, therefore their power was supposed to remain in the trees.

It was said that when Kane-kulana-ula changed into his tree form he leaped into it with a tremendous flash of lightning, thus the great mana, or miraculous power, went into that tree.

The strange death which came from the god Kalai-pahoa made that god and his priest greatly feared. One of the pieces of this tree fell into a spring at Kaakee near the maika, or disc-rolling field, on Molokai. All the people who drank at that spring died. They filled it up and the chiefs ruled that the people should not keep branches or pieces of the tree for the injury of others. If such pieces were found in the possession of any one he should die. Only the carved gods were to be preserved.

Kahekili, king of Māui at the time of the accession of Kamehameha to the sovereignty of the island Hawai'i, had these images in his possession as a part of his household gods.

Kamehameha sent a prophet to ask him for one of these gods. Kahekili refused to send one, but told him to wait and he should have the poison-god and the government over all the islands.

One account records that a small part from the poison one was then given.

So, after the death of Kahekili, Kamehameha did conquer all the islands with their hosts of gods, and Kalai-pahoa, the poison-god, came into his possession.

The overthrow of idolatry and the destruction of the system of tabus came in 1819, when most of the wooden gods were burned or thrown into ponds and rivers, but a few were concealed by their caretakers. Among these were the two gods now to be seen in the Bishop Museum in Honolulu.

KAUHUHU, THE SHARK-GOD OF MOLOKAI

The story of the shark-god Kauhuhu has been told under the legend of 'Aikanaka (Man-eater),' which was the ancient name of the little harbor Pukoo, which lies at the entrance to one of the beautiful valleys of the island of Molokai. The better way is to take the legend as revealing the great man-eater in one of his most kindly aspects. The shark-god appears as the friend of a priest who is seeking revenge for the destruction of his children. Kamalo was the name of the priest. His heiau, or temple, was at Kaluaaha, a village which faced the channel between the islands of Molokai and Māui. Across the channel the rugged red-brown slopes of the mountain Eeke were lost in the masses of clouds which continually hung around its sharp peaks. The two boys of the priest delighted in the glorious revelations of sunrise and sunset tossed in shattered fragments of cloud color, and revelled in the reflected tints which danced to them over the swift channel-currents. It is no wonder that the courage of sky and sea entered into the hearts of the boys, and that many deeds of daring were done by them. They were taught many of the secrets of the temple by their father, but were warned that certain things were sacred to the gods and must not be touched. The high chief, or alii, of that part of the island had a temple a short distance from Kaluaaha, in the valley of the harbor which was called Aikanaka. The name of this chief was Kupa. The chiefs always had a house built within the temple walls as their own residence, to which they could retire at certain seasons of the year. Kupa had two remarkable drums which he kept in his house at the heiau. His skill in beating his drums was so great that they could reveal his thoughts to the waiting priests.

One day Kupa sailed far away over the sea to his favorite fishing-grounds. Meanwhile the boys were tempted to go to Kupa's heiau and try the wonderful drums. The valley of the little harbor Aikanaka bore the musical name Mapulehu. Along the beach and over the ridge hastened the two sons of Kamalo. Quickly they entered the heiau, found the high chief's house, took out his drums and began to beat upon them. Some of the people heard the familiar tones of the drums. They dared not enter the sacred doors of the heiau, but watched until the boys became weary of their sport and returned home.

When Kupa returned they told him how the boys had beaten upon his sacred drums. Kupa was very angry, and ordered his mu, or temple sacrifice seekers, to kill the boys and bring their bodies to the heiau to be placed on the altar. When the priest Kamalo heard of the death of his sons, in bitterness of heart he sought revenge. His own power was not great enough to cope with his high chief; therefore he sought the aid of the seers and prophets of highest repute throughout Molokai. But they feared Kupa the chief, and could not aid him, and therefore sent him on to another kaula, or prophet, or sent him back to consult some one the other side of his home. All this time he carried with him fitting presents and sacrifices, by which he hoped to gain the assistance of the gods through their priests. At last he came to the steep precipice which overlooks Kalaupapa and Kalawao, the present home of the lepers. At the foot of this precipice was a heiau, in which the great shark-god was worshipped. Down the sides of the precipice he climbed and at last found the priest of the shark-god. The priest refused to give assistance, but directed him to go to a great cave in the bold cliffs south of Kalawao. The name of the cave was Anao-puhi, the cave of the eel. Here dwelt the great shark-god Kauhuhu and his guardians or watchers, Waka and Mo-o, the great dragons or reptiles of Polynesian legends. These dragons were mighty warriors in the defence of the shark-god, and were his kahus, or caretakers, while he slept, or when his cave needed watching during his absence.

Kamalo, tired and discouraged, plodded along through the rough lava fragments piled around the entrance to the cave. He bore across his shoulders a black pig, which he had carried many miles as an offering to whatever power he could find to aid him. As he came near to the cave the watchmen saw him and said:

'E, here comes a man, food for the great Mano. Fish for Kauhuhu.' But Kamalo came nearer and for some reason aroused sympathy in the dragons. 'E hele! E hele!' they cried to him. 'Away, away! It is death to you. Here's the tabu place.' 'Death it may be – life it may be. Give me revenge for my sons – and I have no care for myself.' Then the watchmen asked about his trouble and he told them how the chief Kupa had slain his sons as a punishment for beating the drums. Then he narrated the story of his wanderings all over Molokai, seeking for some power strong

enough to overcome Kupa. At last he had come to the shark-god
– as the final possibility of aid. If Kauhuhu failed him, he was
ready to die; indeed he had no wish to live. The mo-o assured him
of their kindly feelings, and told him that it was a very good thing
that Kauhuhu was away fishing, for if he had been home there
would have been no way for him to go before the god without
suffering immediate death. There would have been not even an
instant for explanations. Yet they ran a very great risk in aiding
him, for they must conceal him until the way was opened by the
favors of the great gods. If he should be discovered and eaten
before gaining the aid of the shark-god, they, too, must die with
him. They decided that they would hide him in the rubbish pile
of taro peelings which had been thrown on one side when they
had pounded taro. Here he must lie in perfect silence until the
way was made plain for him to act. They told him to watch for the
coming of eight great surf waves rolling in from the sea, and then
wait from his place of concealment for some opportunity to speak
to the god because he would come in the last great wave. Soon
the surf began to roll in and break against the cliffs.

Higher and higher rose the waves until the eighth reared
far above the waters and met the winds from the shore which
whipped the curling crest into a shower of spray. It raced along
the water and beat far up into the cave, breaking into foam, out
of which the shark-god emerged. At once he took his human
form and walked around the cave. As he passed the rubbish heap
he cried out: 'A man is here. I smell him.' The dragons earnestly
denied that any one was there, but the shark-god said, 'There is
surely a man in this cave. If I find him, dead men you are. If I find
him not, you shall live.' Then Kauhuhu looked along the walls of
the cave and into all the hiding-places, but could not find him.

He called with a loud voice, but only the echoes answered, like the voices of ghosts. After a thorough search he was turning away to attend to other matters when Kamalo's pig squealed. Then the giant shark-god leaped to the pile of taro leavings and thrust them apart. There lay Kamalo and the black pig which had been brought for sacrifice.

Oh, the anger of the god!

Oh, the blazing eyes!

Kauhuhu instantly caught Kamalo and lifted him from the rubbish up toward his great mouth. Now the head and shoulders are in Kauhuhu's mouth. So quickly has this been done that Kamalo has had no time to think. Kamalo speaks quickly as the teeth are coming down upon him. 'E Kauhuhu, listen to me. Hear my prayer. Then perhaps eat me.' The shark-god is astonished and does not bite. He takes Kamalo from his mouth and says: 'Well for you that you spoke quickly. Perhaps you have a good thought. Speak.' Then Kamalo told about his sons and their death at the hands of the executioners of the great chief, and that no one dared avenge him, but that all the prophets of the different gods had sent him from one place to another but could give him no aid. Sure now was he that Kauhuhu alone could give him aid. Pity came to the shark-god as it had come to his dragon watchers when they saw the sad condition of Kamalo. All this time Kamalo had held the hog which he had carried with him for sacrifice. This he now offered to the shark-god. Kauhuhu, pleased and compassionate, accepted the offering, and said: 'E Kamalo. If you had come for any other purpose I would eat you, but your cause is sacred. I will stand as your kahu, your guardian, and sorely punish the high chief Kupa.'

Then he told Kamalo to go to the heiau of the priest who told him to see the shark-god, take this priest on his shoulders, carry him over the steep precipices to his own heiau at Kaluaaha, and there live with him as a fellow priest. They were to build a tabu fence around the heiau and put up the sacred tabu staffs of white tapa cloth. They must collect black pigs by the four hundred, red fish by the four hundred, and white chickens by the four hundred. Then they were to wait patiently for the coming of Kauhuhu. It was to be a strange coming. On the island Lanai, far to the west of the Māui channel, they should see a small cloud, white as snow, increasing until it covers the little island. Then that cloud shall cross the channel against the wind and climb the mountains of Molokai until it rests on the highest peaks over the valley where Kupa has his temple. 'At that time,' said Kauhuhu, 'a great rainbow will span the valley. I shall be in the care of that rainbow, and you may clearly understand that I am there and will speedily punish the man who has injured you. Remember that because you came to me for this sacred cause, therefore I have spared you, the only man who has ever stood in the presence of the shark-god and escaped alive.' Gladly did Kamalo go up and down precipices and along the rough hard ways to the heiau of the priest of the shark-god. Gladly did he carry him up from Kalaupapa to the mountain-ridge above. Gladly did he carry him to his home and there provide for him while he gathered together the black pigs, the red fish, and the white chickens within the sacred enclosure he had built. Here he brought his family, those who had the nearest and strongest claims upon him. When his work was done, his eyes burned with watching the clouds of the little western island Lanai. Ah, the days passed by so slowly! The weeks and the months came, so the legends say, and still Kamalo waited in patience. At last one day a white cloud appeared. It was unlike all the other white clouds he had anxiously watched during the dreary months. Over the channel it came. It spread over the hillsides and climbed the mountains and rested at the head of the valley belonging to Kupa. Then the watchers saw the glorious rainbow and knew that Kauhuhu had come according to his word.

The storm arose at the head of the valley. The winds struggled into a furious gale. The clouds gathered in heavy black masses, dark as midnight, and were pierced through with terrific flashes of lightning. The rain fell in floods, sweeping the hillside down into the valley, and rolling all that was below onward in a resistless mass toward the ocean. Down came the torrent upon the heiau belonging to Kupa, tearing its walls into fragments and washing Kupa and his people into the harbor at the mouth of the valley. Here the shark-god had gathered his people. Sharks filled the bay and feasted upon Kupa and his followers until the waters ran red and all were destroyed. Hence came the legendary name for that little harbor – Aikanaka, the place for man-eaters.

It is said in the legends that 'when great clouds gather on the mountains and a rainbow spans the valley, look out for furious storms of wind and rain which come suddenly, sweeping down the valley.' It also said in the legends that this strange storm which came in such awful power upon Kupa also spread out over the adjoining lowlands, carrying great destruction everywhere, but it paused at the tabu staff of Kamalo, and rushed on either side of the sacred fence, not daring to touch any one who dwelt therein. Therefore Kamalo and his people were spared. The legend has been called 'Aikanaka' because of the feast of the sharks on the human flesh swept down into that harbor by the storm, but it seems more fitting to name the story after the shark-god Kauhuhu, who sent mighty storms and wrought great destruction.

TUI TOFUA

The father of Tui Tofua was Vakafuhu and his mother was Langitaetaea. Vakafuhu also had some concubines who were kept in his enclosure, but Langitaetaea was the best beloved.

Vakafuhu's people were buried, when they died, in the place where Tui Tofua was wont to throw spears along the ground. The place was known as 'the burial place where spears are thrown.'

All the first born males of the people who were cared for by Vakafuhu were given to Tui Tofua as companions when they had matured. There was a considerable number of these young men and all resided together. Tui Tofua had his own separate enclosure apart from his father's and it was fenced.

One day Tui Tofua was playing at sika (throwing cane spears along the ground) with the first born. They were playing close to Vakafuhu's enclosure, where the concubines lived. Tui Tofua's spear fell within Vakafuhu's enclosure. Forthwith the concubines broke Tui Tofua's spear, at the same time making improper and amorous remarks to him. Vakafuhu was sleeping at the time, but was awakened by the unusual chattering of his women. He called to Tui Tofua, saying: 'Canst thou not go and play thy game of sika at a distance? Must thou come and play here?'

The remarks of his father made Tui Tofua quite indignant. So he left and proceeded to build a vessel of the sort known as tongiaki. In fact, it was he who built the first one.

Tui Tofua and his men embarked and, after doing so, Tui Tofua said: 'If there be one amongst you who desires to live on land, let him go at once ashore.' They answered: 'We will go overboard together, so as to show that Tofua can produce men.' But a Samoan cried: 'I will not jump overboard, as I might be changed into a shark, be noosed by the crew of a rowing canoe (*tafaanga*) and struck by the big steering oar, besides being cut to pieces and divided amongst the people who would clap their hands with joy and eat me.' In deference to his wishes the Samoan was allowed to go ashore, although first his little finger was cut off and thrown into the sea. It became a porpoise.

Then Tui Tofua instructed the Samoan: 'Go thou to our relatives and tell them to cut pieces of tapa and to weave garlands of flowers. Tell them to be at the beach of Siuatama the day after tomorrow and we will hold a festival.' The Samoan departed.

Then Tui Tofua and his men leaped into the sea. He was changed into a man-eating shark (*tenifa*) and the people with him into ordinary sharks.

Upon the day set for the festival, the relatives of the transformed men proceeded to Siuatama beach with the tapa and garlands. They waited there. They noticed that the sea was discolored. This was caused by the coming of Tui Tofua and his people. When the sharks were close to the shore, their human parents approached with their presents. However, when Tui Tofua's parents came to the water's edge, he fled, for he was annoyed and did not wish to be near his own parents. After the presentation of the gifts the sharks went their way.

After a time a fish god named Seketoa from Niuatoputapu came to Haapai. He did an immense amount of mischief in Haapai. Consequently Tui Tofua said to him: 'Do not come here again to do mischief, such as you have already done.' Seketoa retorted by challenging Tui Tofua to a fight and Tui Tofua replied that he agreed. So they set a date for the contest.

On the appointed day Seketoa set forth from Niuatoputapu. On the same day Tui Tofua collected all the rubbish from the islands of Tofua, Kao, Kotu, and Fotuhaa and hid himself in the midst of it. Seketoa came along and swallowed all the rubbish together with Tui Tofua. The latter proceeded to inflate himself once he was in Seketoa's stomach. Seketoa at once begged for mercy, to which Tui Tofua replied: 'Open your mouth and I will come out.' Tui Tofua deflated himself and came out of Seketoa's interior. He now addressed Seketoa, saying: 'Get thee hence and do not return, for I am lord of these isles and the sea surrounding them.' Seketoa returned to Niuatoputapu, his own domain, and Tui Tofua remained supreme in his own dominions.

THE STRANGE BANANA SKIN

Kukali, according to the folklore of Hawai'i, was born at Kalapana, the most southerly point of the largest island of the Hawaiian group. Kukali lived hundreds of years ago in the days of the migrations of Polynesians from one group of islands to another throughout the length and breadth of the great Pacific Ocean. He visited strange lands, now known under the general name, Kahiki, or Tahiti. Here he killed the great bird Halulu, found the deep bottomless pit in which was a pool of the fabled water of life, married the sister of Halulu, and returned to his old home. All this he accomplished through the wonderful power of a banana skin.

Kukali's father was a priest, or kahuna, of great wisdom and ability, who taught his children how to exercise strange and magical powers. To Kukali he gave a banana with the impressive charge to preserve the skin whenever he ate the fruit, and be careful that it was always under his control. He taught Kukali the wisdom of the makers of canoes and also how to select the

257

fine-grained lava for stone knives and hatchets, and fashion the blade to the best shape. He instructed the young man in the prayers and incantations of greatest efficacy and showed him charms which would be more powerful than any charms his enemies might use in attempting to destroy him, and taught him those omens which were too powerful to be overcome. Thus Kukali became a wizard, having great confidence in his ability to meet the craft of the wise men of distant islands.

Kukali went inland through the forests and up the mountains, carrying no food save the banana which his father had given him. Hunger came, and he carefully stripped back the skin and ate the banana, folding the skin once more together. In a little while the skin was filled with fruit. Again and again he ate, and as his hunger was satisfied the fruit always again filled the skin, which he was careful never to throw away or lose.

The fever of sea-roving was in the blood of the Hawaiian people in those days, and Kukali's heart burned within him with the desire to visit the far-away lands about which other men told marvelous tales and from which came strangers like to the Hawaiians in many ways.

After a while he went to the forests and selected trees approved by the omens, and with many prayers fashioned a great canoe in which to embark upon his journey. The story is not told of the days passed on the great stretches of water as he sailed on and on, guided by the sun in the day and the stars in the night, until he came to the strange lands about which he had dreamed for years.

His canoe was drawn up on the shore and he lay down for rest. Before falling asleep he secreted his magic banana in his malo, or loin-cloth, and then gave himself to deep slumber. His rest was troubled with strange dreams, but his weariness was great and his eyes heavy, and he could not arouse himself to meet the dangers which were swiftly surrounding him.

A great bird which lived on human flesh was the god of the land to which he had come. The name of the bird was Halulu. Each feather of its wings was provided with talons and seemed to be endowed with human powers. Nothing like this bird was ever known or seen in the beautiful Hawaiian Islands. But here in the mysterious foreign land it had its deep valley, walled in like the valley of the *Arabian Nights*, over which the great bird hovered looking into the depths for food. A strong wind always attended the coming of Halulu when he sought the valley for his victims.

Kukali was lifted on the wings of the bird-god and carried to this hole and quietly laid on the ground to finish his hour of deep sleep.

When Kukali awoke he found himself in the shut-in valley with many companions who had been captured by the great bird and placed in this prison hole. They had been without food and were very weak. Now and then one of the number would lie down to die. Halulu, the bird-god, would perch on a tree which grew on the edge of the precipice and let down its wing to sweep across the floor of the valley and pick up the victims lying on the ground. Those who were strong could escape the feathers as they brushed over the bottom and hide in the crevices in the walls, but day by day the weakest of the prisoners were lifted out and prepared for Halulu's feast.

Kukali pitied the helpless state of his fellow prisoners and prepared his best incantations and prayers to help him overcome the great bird. He took his wonderful banana and fed all the people until they were very strong. He taught them how to seek stones best fitted for the manufacture of knives and hatchets.

Then for days they worked until they were all well armed with sharp stone weapons.

While Kukali and his fellow prisoners were making preparation for the final struggle, the bird-god had often come to his perch and put his wing down into the valley, brushing the feathers back and forth to catch his prey.

Frequently the search was fruitless. At last he became very impatient, and sent his strongest feathers along the precipitous walls, seeking for victims.

Kukali and his companions then ran out from their hiding-places and fought the strong feathers, cutting them off and chopping them into small pieces.

Halulu cried out with pain and anger, and sent feather after feather into the prison. Soon one wing was entirely destroyed. Then the other wing was broken to pieces and the bird-god in his insane wrath put down a strong leg armed with great talons. Kukali uttered mighty invocations and prepared sacred charms for the protection of his friends.

After a fierce battle they cut off the leg and destroyed the talons. Then came the struggle with the remaining leg and claws, but Kukali's friends had become very bold. They fearlessly gathered around this enemy, hacking and pulling until the bird-god, screaming with pain, fell into the pit among the prisoners, who quickly cut the body into fragments.

The prisoners made steps in the walls, and by the aid of vines climbed out of their prison. When they had fully escaped, they gathered great piles of branches and trunks of trees and threw them into the prison until the body of the bird-god was covered. Fire was thrown down and Halulu was burned to ashes. Thus Kukali taught by his charms that Halulu could be completely destroyed.

But two of the breast feathers of the burning Halulu flew away to his sister, who lived in a great hole which had no bottom. The name of this sister was Namakaeha. She belonged to the family of Pele, the goddess of volcanic fires, who had journeyed to Hawai'i and taken up her home in the crater of the volcano Kilauea.

Namakaeha smelled smoke on the feathers which came to her, and knew that her brother was dead. She also knew that he could have been conquered only by one possessing great magical powers. So she called to his people: 'Who is the great kupua who has killed my brother? Oh, my people, keep careful watch.'

Kukali was exploring all parts of the strange land in which he had already found marvelous adventures. By and by he came to the great pit in which Namakaeha lived. He could not see the bottom, so he told his companions he was going down to see what mysteries were concealed in this hole without a bottom. They made a rope of the hau tree bark. Fastening one end around his body he ordered his friends to let him down. Uttering prayers and incantations he went down and down until, owing to counter incantations of Namakaeha's priests, who had been watching, the rope broke and he fell.

Down he went swiftly, but, remembering the prayer which a falling man must use to keep him from injury, he cried, 'O Ku! guard my life!'

In the ancient Hawaiian storytelling there was frequent mention of 'the water of life.' Sometimes the sick bathed in it and were healed. Sometimes it was sprinkled upon the unconscious, bringing them back to life. Kukali's incantation was of great power, for it threw him into a pool of the water of life and he was saved.

One of the kahunas (priests) caring for Namakaeha was a very great wizard. He saw the wonderful preservation of Kukali and became his friend. He warned Kukali against eating anything that was ripe, because it would be poison, and even the most powerful charms could not save him.

Kukali thanked him and went out among the people. He had carefully preserved his wonderful banana skin, and was able to eat apparently ripe fruit and yet be perfectly safe.

The kahunas of Namakaeha tried to overcome him and destroy him, but he conquered them, killed those who were bad, and entered into friendship with those who were good.

At last he came to the place where the great chiefess dwelt. Here he was tested in many ways. He accepted the fruits offered him, but always ate the food in his magic banana. Thus he preserved his strength and conquered even the chiefess and married her. After living with her for a time he began to long for his old home in Hawai'i. Then he persuaded her to do as her relative Pele had already done, and the family, taking their large canoe, sailed away to Hawai'i, their future home.

PUNA AND THE DRAGON

Two images of goddesses were clothed in yellow kapa cloth and worshipped in the temples. One was Kiha-wahine, a noted dragon-goddess, and the other was Haumea, who was also known as Papa, the wife of Wakea, a great ancestor-god among the Polynesians.

Haumea is said to have taken as her husband, Puna, a chief of Oahu. He and his people were going around the island. The surf was not very good, and they wanted to find a better place. At last they found a fine surf-place where a beautiful woman was floating on the sea.

She called to Puna, 'This is not a good place for surf.' He asked, 'Where is there a place?' She answered, 'I know where there is one, far outside.' She desired to get Puna. So they swam way out in the sea until they were out of sight nor could they see the sharp peaks of the mountains. They forgot everything else but each other. This woman was Kiha-wahine.

The people on the beach wailed, but did not take canoes to help them. They swam over to Molokai. Here they left their surf-boards on the beach and went inland. They came to the cave house of the woman. He saw no man inside nor did he hear any voice, all was quiet.

Puna stayed there as a kind of prisoner and obeyed the commands of the woman. She took care of him and prepared his food. They lived as husband and wife for a long time, and at last his real body began to change.

Once he went out of the cave. While standing there he heard voices, loud and confused. He wanted to see what was going on, but he could not go, because the woman had laid her law on him, that if he went away he would be killed.

He returned to the cave and asked the woman, 'What is that noise I heard from the sea?' She said: 'Surf-riding, perhaps, or rolling the maika stone. Some one is winning and you heard the shouts.' He said, 'It would be fine for me to see the things you have mentioned.' She said, 'Tomorrow will be a good time for you to go and see.'

In the morning he went down to the sea to the place where the people were gathered together and saw many sports.

While he was watching, one of the men, Hinole, the brother of his wife, saw him and was pleased. When the sports were through he invited Puna to go to their house and eat and talk.

Hinole asked him, 'Whence do you come, and what house do you live in?' He said, 'I am from the mountains, and my house is a cave.' Hinole meditated, for he had heard of the loss of Puna at Oahu. He loved his brother-in-law, and asked, 'How did you come to this place?' Puna told him all the story. Then Hinole told him his wife was a goddess. 'When you return and come near to the place, go very easily and softly, and you will see her in her real nature, as a mo-o, or dragon; but she knows all that you are doing and what we are saying. Now listen to a parable. Your first wife, Haumea, is the first born of all the other women. Think of the time when she was angry with you. She had been sporting with you and then she said in a tired way, "I want the water." You asked, "What water do you want?" She said, "The water from Poliahu of Mauna Kea." You took a water-jar and made a hole so that the water always leaked out, and then you went to the pit of Pele. That woman Pele was very old and blear-eyed, so that she could not see you well, and you returned to Haumea. She was that wife of yours. If you escape this mo-o wife she will seek my life. It is my thought to save your life, so that you can look into the eyes of your first wife.'

The beautiful dragon-woman had told him to cry with a loud voice when he went back to the cave. But when Puna was going back he went slowly and softly, and saw his wife as a dragon, and understood the words of Hinole. He tried to hide, but was trembling and breathing hard.

His wife heard and quickly changed to a human body, and cursed him, saying: 'You are an evil man coming quietly and hiding, but I heard your breath when you thought I would not know you. Perhaps I will eat your eyes. When you were talking with Hinole you learned how to come and see me.'

The dragon-goddess was very angry, but Puna did not say anything. She was so angry that the hair on her neck rose up, but it was like a whirlwind, soon quiet and the anger over. They dwelt together, and the woman trusted Puna, and they had peace.

One day Puna was breathing hard, for he was thirsty and wanted the water of the gods.

The woman heard his breathing, and asked, 'Why do you breathe like this?' He said: 'I want water. We have dwelt together a long time and now I need the water.' 'What water is this you want?' He said, 'I must have the water of Poliahu of Mauna Kea, the snow covered mountain of Hawai'i.'

She said, 'Why do you want that water?' He said: 'The water of that place is cold and heavy with ice. In my youth my good grandparents always brought water from that place for me. Wherever I went I carried that water with me, and when it was gone more would be brought to me, and so it has been up to the time that I came to dwell with you. You have water and I have been drinking it, but it is not the same as the water mixed with ice, and heavy. But I would not send you after it, because I know it is far away and attended with toil unfit for you, a woman.'

The woman bent her head down, then lifted her eyes, and said: 'Your desire for water is not a hard thing to satisfy. I will go and get the water.'

Before he had spoken of his desire he had made a little hole in the water-jar, as Hinole had told him, that the woman might spend a long time and let him escape.

She arose and went away. He also arose and followed. He found a canoe and crossed to Māui. Then he found another boat going to Hawai'i and at last landed at Kau.

He went up and stood on the edge of the pit of Pele. Those who were living in the crater saw him, and cried out, 'Here is a man, a husband for our sister.' He quickly went down into the crater and dwelt with them. He told all about his journey. Pele heard these words, and said: 'Not very long and your wife will be here coming after you, and there will be a great battle, but we will not let you go or you will be killed, because she is very angry against you. She has held you, the husband of our sister Haumea. She should find her own husband and not take what belongs to another. You stay with us and at the right time you can go back to your wife.'

Kiha-wahine went to Poliahu, but could not fill the water-jar. She poured the water in and filled the jar, but when the jar was lifted it became light. She looked back and saw the water lying on the ground, and her husband far beyond at the pit of Pele. Then she became angry and called all the dragons of Molokai, Lanai, Māui, Kahoolawe, and Hawai'i.

When she had gathered all the dragons she went up to Kilauea and stood on the edge of the crater and called all the people below, telling them to give her the husband. They refused to give Puna up, crying out: 'Where is your husband? This is the husband of our sister; he does not belong to you, O mischief-maker.'

Then the dragon-goddess said, 'If you do not give up this man, of a truth I will send quickly all my people and fill up this crater and capture all your fires.' The dragons threw their drooling saliva in the pit, and almost destroyed the fire of the pit where Pele lived, leaving Ka-moho-alii's place untouched.

Then the fire moved and began to rise with great strength, burning off all the saliva of the dragons. Kiha-wahine and the rest of the dragons could not stand the heat even a little while, for the fire caught them and killed a large part of them in that place. They tried to hide in the clefts of the rocks. The earthquakes opened the rocks and some of the dragons hid, but fire followed the earthquakes and the fleeing dragons. Kiha-wahine ran and leaped down the precipice into a fish-pond called by the name of the shadow, or aka, of the dragon, Loko-aka (the shadow lake).

So she was imprisoned in the pond, husbandless, scarcely escaping with her life. When she went back to Molokai she meant to kill Hinole, because she was very angry for his act in aiding Puna to escape. She wanted to punish him, but Hinole saw the trouble coming from his sister, so arose and leaped into the sea, becoming a fish in the ocean.

When he dove into the sea Kiha-wahine went down after him and tried to find him in the small and large coral caves, but could not catch him. He became the Hinalea, a fish dearly loved by the fishermen of the islands. The dragon-goddess continued seeking, swimming swiftly from place to place.

Ounauna saw her passing back and forth, and said, 'What are you seeking, O Kiha-wahine?' She said, 'I want Hinole.' Ounauna said: 'Unless you listen to me you cannot get him, just as when you went to Hawai'i you could not get your husband from Pele. You go and get the vine inalua and come back and make a basket and put it down in the sea. After a while dive down and you will find that man has come inside. Then catch him.'

The woman took the vine, made the basket, came down and put it in the sea. She left it there a little while, then dove down. There was no Hinole in the basket, but she saw him swimming along outside of the basket. She went up, waited awhile, came down again and saw him still swimming outside.

This she did again and again, until her eyes were red because she could not catch him. Then she was angry, and went to Ounauna and said: 'O slave, I will kill you to-day. Perhaps you told the truth, but I have been deceived, and will chase you until you die.'

Ounauna said: 'Perhaps we should talk before I die. I want you to tell me just what you have done, then I will know whether you followed directions. Tell me in a few words. Perhaps I forgot something.'

The dragon said, 'I am tired of your words and I will kill you.' Then Ounauna said, 'Suppose I die, what will you do to correct any mistakes you have made?'

Then she told how she had taken vines and made a basket and used it. Ounauna said: 'I forgot to tell you that you must get some sea eggs and crabs, pound and mix them together and put them inside the basket. Put the mouth of the basket down. Leave it for a little while, then dive down and find your brother inside. He will not come out, and you can catch him.' This is the way the Hinalea is caught to this day.

After she had caught her brother she took him to the shore to kill him, but he persuaded her to set him free. This she did, compelling him ever after to retain the form of the fish Hinalea.

Kiha-wahine then went to the island of Māui and dwelt in a deep pool near the old royal town of Lahaina.

After Pele had her battle with the dragons, and Puna had escaped according to the directions of Hinole, he returned to Oahu and saw his wife, Haumea, a woman with many names, as if she were the embodiment of many goddesses.

After Puna disappeared, Kou became the new chief of Oahu. Puna went to live in the mountains above Kalihi-uka. One day

Haumea went out fishing for crabs at Heeia, below the precipice of Koolau, where she was accustomed to go.

Puna came to a banana plantation, ate, and lay down to rest. He fell fast asleep and the watchmen of the new chief found him. They took his loin-cloth, and tied his hands behind his back, bringing him thus to Kou, who killed him and hung the body in the branches of a breadfruit-tree. It is said that this was at Wai-kaha-lulu just below the steep diving rocks of the Nuuanu stream.

When Haumea returned from gathering moss and fish to her home in Kalihi-uka, she heard of the death of her husband. She had taken an akala vine, made a pa-u, or skirt, of it, and tied it around her when she went fishing, but she forgot all about it, and as she hurried down to see the body of her husband, all the people turned to look at her, and shouted out, 'This is the wife of the dead man.'

She found Puna hanging on the branches. Then she made that breadfruit-tree open. Leaving her pa-u on the ground where she stood, she stepped inside the tree and bade it close about her and appear the same as before. The akala of which the pa-u had been made lay where it was left, took root and grew into a large vine.

The fat of the body of Puna fell down through the branches and the dogs ate below the tree. One of these dogs belonged to the chief Kou. It came back to the house, played with the chief, then leaped, caught him by the throat and killed him.

Note: This is the same legend as 'The Wonderful Breadfruit Tree' published in the 'Legends of Old Honolulu,' but the names are changed and the time is altered from the earliest days of Hawaiian lore to the almost historic period of King Kakuhihewa, whose under-chief mentioned in this legend gave the name to Old Honolulu, as for centuries it bore the name 'Kou.' The legend is new, however, in so far as it gives the account of the infatuation of Puna for Kiha-wahine, the dragon-goddess, and his final escape from her.

PASIKOLE, THE SAMOAN

Many years ago, when Tonga was peopled by gods, not men, two of them, Faingaa and Sisi, held Pasikole in bondage and made him do all sorts of heavy tasks.

One day they conceived the plan of making a journey in a novel manner and without fatigue to themselves. They commanded Pasikole to make two big baskets large enough to contain their bodies. When the baskets were completed they had Pasikole hang them at each end of a pole. They climbed in themselves and ordered Pasikole to carry them. They were sitting in the baskets in such a way that they could see naught but the sky.

Pasikole picked them up and carried them a short distance, but soon grew tired. Presently he came to a large pnko tree with a long overhanging branch. There he hung the pole with its double burden and blithely went his way. As the clouds were drifting by Faingaa and Sisi thought that they were still being carried, so they kept making encouraging remarks to Pasikole, as they thought. Time went on and they began to grumble at Pasikole for not getting to his journey's end quicker. In time the baskets got rotten and Faingaa and Sisi fell through to the ground, only to find that they had been grossly deceived.

Some time after they managed to get hold of Pasikole again and made him do their bidding. One day they decided to paddle in a canoe to Samoa. They ordered Pasikole to make the boat ready. He did so, but took the opportunity of hiding some garlands of flowers and sweet-smelling leaves in the stern of the canoe where he thought he would sit to paddle. They started, Faingaa in the bow, Sisi in the centre, and Pasikole in the stern of the canoe.

After they had paddled for a long while, Pasikole bedecked himself with the garlands unbeknown to his two enslavers who had their backs to him. Suddenly he remarked that he saw some fish and at the same instant he dived, ostensibly for the object of capturing some. When he rose to the surface, he kept out of sight of the other two by hiding under the stern of the canoe, where he remained for a long while. Then he dived again and came up between Faingaa and Sisi. They expressed astonishment at his being down so long and returning adorned with garlands. Pasikole explained: 'I have been down at the bottom of the sea. There were many people there holding a great feast and entertainment. They were so pleased to see me that they decked me with garlands. I should not have returned so quickly, but that I thought you would like to go, too.'

The other two immediately expressed an ardent desire to see the entertainment that Pasikole had been to. Then continuing, Pasikole said: 'Well, if you go, I must attire you properly, so that you will be presentable to the people at the bottom of the sea.' To this they consented and Pasikole set to work and bedecked them with his garlands, but in such a manner that their hands and feet were tied. When he had completed the job to his satisfaction, he told them to stand so that they might all dive together. They did so, but Faingaa and Sisi, being bound, were unable to swim, whilst Pasikole climbed back into the canoe and returned to Tonga a free man.

Sometimes on a dark night large shining patches are to be seen, seemingly at some depth, beneath the sea. These are said to be caused by Faingaa and Sisi struggling in the water trying to get to the surface. To this day Tongan mothers endeavor to quiet their fretful infants by saying, 'Naa, naa, I will tell Faingaa and Sisi to come to you.'

THE ORIGIN OF THE DEITY FEHULUNI

It is said that there were two parents that had nine children. And suddenly one day the eldest died. And after he was buried, then the next eldest died; and after he was buried, then the next eldest died and so on, continued day after day till the sixth was reached. And after the burial of the sixth, the man who was the seventh said: 'You remain here while I go and see what is the matter with us; for we are nearly all dead; perhaps there is some one that is carrying us off.' Thus he told them. 'I am going, and I will leave my dead body in the cave (the name of which was Makatuuua: *maka*, stone; *tuu*, appear as a spirit; *ua*, two); and should I be away a long time don't bury my body, but leave it for me to return to it.'

And he took a fine mat as a loin cloth, then he went down to Pulotu. And when he reached Pulotu he found a house and some fire that was smoking outside. Behold! it was the home of Hikuleo. And he went up to it and found a yam on the fire baking. The name of that yam was *lokolokamangavalu* (*lokoloka*, rough skin; *manga*, forked; *valu*, eight). And he broke off one of the forks (the yam had eight forks), and ate it. And Hikuleo came and turned the baking yam. Lo! one of the forks was gone. And he shouted and said, 'Who is the person that has taken the fork of my yam; just like Tui Haatala but is he not still in the world?' Then he (the intruder) again crawled forth and broke off another fork. Then again came Hikuleo and again he shouted and they repeated this, till six of the forks were taken. Then the lad appeared before Hikuleo, and said, 'It is I, Tui Haatala. I have come from the world.' It is said that Hikuleo was blind. And Hikuleo called softly, 'Come, come, why have you come to this bad place?' And then he (Hikuleo) said, 'Go to that water and bathe; and there is that cloth to wipe with; then come and we will talk.'

And he did according to Hikuleo's instructions; and he took his fine mat from earth that he had used as loin cloth, and washed it in the water. And put it on wet, and then went up and left it outside while he entered the house to talk with Hikuleo. And he told Hikuleo, 'There is something about which I have come, because we have nearly all died. We were nine in number, but there are only three of us left. Why is it, kindly tell me, that we die like that; for we die one after the other in succession and not a day passes (without a death).' And Hikuleo told him, 'All right; I have brought them to dwell with me; here we are all together, and we cannot bear for you to dwell in poverty on earth.' And he again said, 'This day it was arranged to bring you, and you have come quicker.' He had gone down before the sixth had been buried. 'But you shall return; and those that remain shall escape.'

And Tui Haatala went outside and took his fine mat which was still wet, and went up to the earth. And when he went to his body, behold they had buried it as he was so long in returning. And he cried in grief, and he took off his fine mat which was still wet, as he had brought it with him from Pulotu, and hung it on a big pandanus tree. And the fine mat dripped water, which caused a little stream which is called Maaeatanu; that stream is still in existence. And he said, 'I will not stay here; I will go and wander in other lands, and I will not go to Pulotu, because Hikuleo has said we shall dwell on earth we who are left.' And he came from Eua to Eueiki, and from there he came to Tongatapu, and from there he went to Haapai; and from there he went to Vavau; and from there he went to Samoa, and from there he went to Fiji. And he is seen at these islands, but he is never seen at Eua. And he is called by different names in the various islands. He is called by the Tongans Fehuluni (to move about); and he is called by the Samoans Moso; and he is called by another name in Fiji; but he is still Tui Haatala.

His father was Tui Haatala, and he and their mother were the first to die, and then they (his brothers) died one after the other as has been stated.

And they were the grandchildren of Hikuleo, and since then there has been no more Tui Haatala, the man that went to Pulotu was the last one. The way of their death was perplexing, one died and another was appointed, and he died and another was appointed. They were just like that. And the Tui Haatala that went to Pulotu was the last. When he went he was already appointed, and it is said that none were appointed after him; he went without dying and was to return. And it was difficult (for another) to take (his title), because he had returned but was unable to become a man because his body had been buried. And it has been so ever since.

And there are also some things about by-gone days, his (hair) lime is a big stone, which if chipped and made into a hair wash is like cooked lime.

TALES OF GHOSTS
& THE UNDERWORLD

Polynesian history is an endless saga of journeys from one place to another. In death, humans undertake their final voyage, with the afterlife portrayed in their stories as a new land. Their heroes travel into the beyond, to an 'unseen world' – from which, sometimes, they are allowed to return. One story tells of gods who travel into the afterlife, undergo a series of trials and return with spoils from beyond. Mortals who leave behind their bodies run a terrifying risk. They may be lucky enough to reunite spirit with flesh…or they may be forced to roam forever as restless ghosts.

Both ghosts and the gods of the underworld are heavily associated with night and darkness. It is during the night that spirits are most active, for good or ill. Ancestor spirits may assist their descendants; they are respected, and offerings are regularly left to them. Yet ghosts with no one to honour them are a source of danger. The restless dead have nothing to tether them to the physical plane. They must wander, unconnected, searching for a home, until they are finally able to cross to the afterlife.

This crossing is heavily associated with cliffs and plunging into the ocean below. Spirits must leap from the cliff to pass into the next life, an action reflected in Māori legends by the location's name: 'The Place Where the Spirits Take Their Flight'.

THE BOAT THAT WENT TO PULOTU

This is the story of the gods that went to Pulotu (the unseen world, the land of the departed) in a boat. There was one god whose name was Plaveatoke (Slippery Eel), another whose name was Fakafuumaka (Like-a-Big Stone), another whose name was Haelefeke (Octopus-Comes, or Walking-Octopus), and the last one's name was Lohi (Lie). These four embarked in their boat and paddled away with the intention of journeying to Pulotu.

As they were passing a part of the coast not far from their starting point a goddess named Faimalie (Take-Care or Perform-Fortunately) was standing on the beach. She called to them; 'Why are you coming here and where are you going?' The gods in the boat told her that they were going to Pulotu. Then the goddess cried: 'Come here and we will all go together.'

Then the gods in the boat said: 'We tell you that the boat is overloaded.' But Faimalie persisted, saying: 'I will go too and sit on the outrigger, or else bail the water from the boat.' The four gods in the boat held a consultation. 'What is the use of this old woman coming with us? But it might be as well to ask old Faimalie, who is very anxious to come, of what use she would be.' So the gods in the boat called out: 'Of what use would you be, old woman, you who are so anxious to accompany us?' Faimalie at once replied: 'Let me go with you. I will be of some little use.' The gods in the boat, becoming impatient, cried: 'Come then. We will go together.' They continued their voyage towards Pulotu after getting Faimalie aboard. There were thus five of them altogether and they exulted in their own strength.

At last they reached Pulotu and dragged their boat up on the beach. Then they went to the house of Hikuleo (Watching

Tail), who was out at the time and hid there. When the people of Pulotu came down to the beach, they saw the boat and asked one another: 'Whose boat is this? Perhaps it is a boat from the world.'

So they guessed until they were tired. Then someone suggested that as the boat was there its crew must be somewhere about, especially because the boat smelt as if people from the world had been in it. Several suggested: 'Well, let us search and perhaps we will find them.' So they searched and searched, but could not discover them anywhere. Then they went and told Hikuleo: 'There is a boat on the beach. We think it is a boat from the world, but we cannot find her people, or even their whereabouts.'

Their inability to find the five gods from the world is not remarkable, for the five had transformed themselves and hidden most effectually. One of them had transformed himself into a small insect and had entered one of the big posts that supported the roof. From this vantage point he was quietly watching the people of Pulotu as they searched for him and his companions. Others had gone into the ground. One was hidden in the big cross beam of the house, but Fakafuumaka (Like-a-Big-Stone) simply lay down in the doorway. When the people were searching, they paid no attention to him, saying, 'It is only a big stone.' Thus he escaped.

Hikuleo then addressed the people, saying, 'So you are tired of searching for the gods from the World. Then go, someone and tell the Haama–takikila (Those of the Piercing Eyes) to come and see what they can do. They came and glared until their eyes were nearly falling out, but were unable to find the intruders. Then they told Hikuleo: 'We have looked and looked until our eyes are sore, but we have to admit defeat.' So saying, they departed.

Then the gods that were in hiding breathed audibly in mockery of the Haamatakikila who had been looking for them so earnestly. Hearing the breathing, the people of Pulotu exclaimed at once, 'The gods must be hiding here, for they are breathing to mock us, because we cannot find them.' Again they searched but without success, until some one said, 'Let us go and get the Haafakanamunamu (Those of the Keen Scent), so that they can smell out the gods from the world, for we are tired of searching and Those of the Piercing Eyes were unable to find them.' So they called out, saying, 'Come, ye of the Keen Scent.'

Those of the Keen Scent came and smelt and sniffed in every direction, until they were tired. Then they departed, as they were unable to find the gods from the world. Again the gods in hiding breathed loudly in derision. The people of Pulotu were tired of asking each other whence the breathing came, so they called to the Guessers to come and guess and perhaps thus be able to find the hiding places of the gods from the world. The Guessers came and guessed until they were tired, but not a bit wiser as to the whereabouts of the lurking gods. Being tired of guessing they went away. Whereupon, the people of Pulotu told Faahingatelingaongo (Those-of-the-Sharp-Ears) to try. They came and listened and listened until they were weary. Then they departed.

Thereat Hikuleo said, 'Come you and lift up my palanquin. I will go and examine into these things and into the gods that seem almighty. There are people in Pulotu that are supposed to know everything and yet they are weary. In fact, we are all weary. Where is there a greater chief, or one that can compare with me?

Yet we are tired of searching for these gods from the world.'

Addressing the gods from the world, who were in hiding, Hikuleo said: 'Show yourselves to us that we may meet, for we cannot find you.' So the gods of the world showed themselves and each one spoke from his hiding place. 'It is I, Haveatoke (Slippery Eel).' Then another spoke from his hiding place: 'It is I, Fakafuumaka (Like a Big Stone).' Again, another spoke from his place of concealment: 'It is I, Haelefeke (Octopus Comes).' Then another, from his hiding place, called out: 'It is I, the Lie (Lohi).' The last one then spoke and said: 'It is I, Faimalie (Take Care).' That is how the five gods from the world introduced themselves to Hikuleo and the people of Pulotu.

Thus they met Hikuleo and the people of Pulotu and these were heard to remark: 'These gods from the world are most wonderful on account of their power. We grew weary of searching for them.' Hikuleo then said: 'Several of you go and get me a very large piece of kava and we will drink kava with the gods from the world.'

A great concourse of people went away to bring in the kava. They cut down twenty coconut trees to carry it on, so immense was the piece of kava which they brought. Some compared it with a country, so large was it. They brought the kava to Hikuleo and to the gods from the world, who returned thanks for the huge kava that had been brought to them. They remarked that they themselves were only fools and commoners (tua).

Hikuleo then spoke to the gods from the world: 'Listen to what I have to say to you, gods who have come from the world. We will drink this kava that has been brought, but if you do not drink so as to finish it, you will be murdered, for you are only common gods who have been stopping all the time in the world.

You suddenly drift into Pulotu. But is it permissible for gods who are but commoners and fools to come to Pulotu?'

The kava was cut in small pieces and chewed until it was soft; then the bowl was brought and placed ready to mix the kava. It was an enormous bowl. Some compared it with a huge open space, whilst others said it was as large as all of Haapai. The kava was then mixed and was like the sea, so enormous was the bowl.

Then the gods from the world wept, being frightened, for they were not much accustomed to kava drinking. Hikuleo addressed them sternly: 'If the kava is not finished, we will kill you.' Haveatoke, one of the gods from the world cried. Fakafuumaka, another of the mundane gods, wept also. Then another one of them, Haelefeke, likewise cried. Lohi also began to shed tears and all the four gods from the world wept together. Only the old woman, the goddess Faimalie, with a flat nose, sat quiet. She was the only god that did not weep, but sat silent while the other four lamented.

The kava was next strained and, when it was clear, it was dealt out to Haveatoke to drink first. Pie drained the cup, but it made him drunk. Again the cup was filled and brought to Fakafuumaka. He drank to the dregs and also became drunk. Again the kava was served, this time to Haelefeke and with the same effect. Once more the cup was passed and Lohi became drunk. In fact, the whole four became drunk. Faimalie, who had not had her kava, now spoke, addressing her four companions: 'How do you feel? Cannot you endure more kava? Will you be carried away by a little kava?' the four of them replied: 'We cannot possibly drink any more. Our stomachs are full and we are drunk.'

Then said Faimalie, rating her companions: 'To be sure, you did not want to take me on board. I have come because I almost compelled you to take me. You told me to remain behind, because the boat was overloaded. I was of no use anyhow, you said. But I told you that I would come and that I had a little use, even if I came only to bail the boat.

'Now you are not able to drink the kava. If I had not come, but remained behind, would you have been able to drink this kava? As it is, you are drunk. This kava is enough to make us afraid, because we cannot drink it and we will be killed very shortly.'

Then Hikuleo interrupted and ordered silence. She now said to Faimalie: 'What is it, old woman, that you are talking about? Has no kava been brought to you to drink? What does it mean?'

Faimalie replied, saying to Hikuleo in a respectful manner: 'Do not trouble. I will run and drink my kava from the bowl.' Then Faimalie stood up in order to go and drink from the great bowl the kava that had not been served to her. Bending down she drank from the middle of the bowl. She drank and drank until the kava was finished. Then she swallowed the bowl and ate the fibre strainer and the stalks of the kava. Next she ate the twenty coconut trees on which the kava had been brought. She swallowed the whole lot together with the pulverized root of the kava from which the infusion had been made. All of these did Faimalie swallow, and nothing was left.

This made Hikuleo and all of the people of Pulotu very angry and they said: 'Dear me, this boat that has come from the world is very cheeky.' Then Hikuleo commanded the people of Pulotu: 'Go and make known to all of the people in Pulotu that every man has to prepare an oven of yams, breadfruit, taro and other things. Furthermore, every man is to bring a roast pig. Thus we will pay our respects to this boat and the gods from the world.' So all of Pulotu worked at their ovens and roasted pigs, an oven and a pig to each man. The cooked food was brought to the gods from the world to show the respect of the people of Pulotu. Then Hikuleo said: 'Come and eat this. If it is not all eaten, you will be killed.'

Haveatoke, Fakafuumaka, Haelefeke, and Lohi, the whole four of them, began to weep, but Faimalie did not cry; she remained quiet. The four cried when they saw the enormous size of the pile of food. But how about eating it? That thought was what made them weep, because if the food was not finished they would be murdered.

Faimalie, the old woman with the flat nose, asked: 'What are you crying about?' The four told her: 'We are crying because our feast will not be entirely eaten. There are so many baskets of food and pigs that they are piled up almost to the sky. How are we to eat them?' Faimalie replied: 'You four come and eat first, you Haveatoke, you Fakafuumaka, you Haelefeke, and you Lohi. Is there anything you can do?' she inquired scathingly. 'You eat one basket of food and one pig. What there is left leave to me. I will go and see what I can do.' The four responded, saying: 'Very well, Faimalie. You wait a little. We will eat first and you eat afterwards, for we fear that we cannot finish the food and that we will be killed stone dead.' Faimalie's only response was: 'You eat.'

So the four started to eat, but were not able to finish even one pig. One yam each and a small piece of pork were all they were able to eat, and then they were full, surfeited in fact. Then they said to Faimalie: 'We are finished and cannot eat any more, as we are full and surfeited.' Then Faimalie, the old woman with the flat nose, replied: 'The reason you gave for not wanting to bring me from the world was that I was of no use and had better remain behind. Yet were it not for me you would have been murdered in the kava drinking a short time ago. Wait a little and I will go and eat.'

Faimalie started to eat. She ate first all the yams and pigs and they were finished. Then she ate the leaves that had covered the ovens; after that the ropes that were used to carry the baskets and the sticks by which the baskets were carried. In fact, she ate everything and nothing remained.

This made Hikuleo and all the chiefs in Pulotu very angry and they said: 'Really, this boat, that has come from the world, is exceedingly cheeky. But let us find something that they will not be able to do.' Then Hikuleo said: 'Tell Haveatoke, Fakafuumaka, Haelefeke, Lohi and Faimalie to come here, or at least one of them that is clever in any sport. We will hold a sports competition, but we will wait until our sportsmen go along. The sport that will be tried first,' said Hikuleo addressing the five gods from the world, 'is surf riding. If some one of you cannot ride the surf, you will all be killed.'

Upon hearing this the five gods from the world held a consultation, inquiring: 'Which one of us is clever in each particular sport? If we are weak in surf riding, we will be killed. Hikuleo and the chiefs of Pulotu have selected something in which we are not accomplished. If we fail we will die. The gods of Pulotu are boasting that surf riding is the sport in which they are strong.' Thus the gods from the world kept inquiring who was the cleverest in surf riding.

Then spoke Faimalie, the old woman who ate so much, saying: 'I will not be of any use, because I cannot go into the water on account of my sickness. My nose is bad and that is why I cannot go surf riding and indulge in similar sports which require diving about in the sea.' Then spoke Haveatoke (Slippery Eel), saying:

'Leave it to me. I will go and ride the surf, for that is what I can do well.'

So the two contestants, the god from Pulotu and the god from the world, went down to the sea and swam, while Hikuleo and the people of Pulotu sat and watched to see who would be first in the surf riding. The two gods rode the boiling surf. The people of Pulotu began to breathe freely, for they felt that their champion would win. They roundly abused and ridiculed the gods from the world, because they felt happy in the thought that Pulotu would be victorious in the surf riding. The two contestants dived into the surf, rose together, came in abreast, and lay on the sand. They went out again, while the people of Pulotu increased their ridicule, for they were light-hearted to think that they would be the stronger in the sport of surf riding. Again the champions went out and returned together, and so again and again they went. Suddenly, however, Haveatoke, the god from the world, made a jump at the god from Pulotu, bit the back of his neck, and killed him at once. Then he went ashore and claimed the victory and the gods of Pulotu were once more beaten.

This defeat of Pulotu made Hikuleo very angry and she said that there was no one of any use in Pulotu, for they had not been victorious in any contest. However, Hikuleo decided to have another contest and she said to the gods from the world: 'We have an expert diver. If there is one of you that can hold his breath a long time, let him come and pit himself against our man, who is long winded.' Then the gods from the world held a conference. There was not one that was used to diving or that was long winded, and if they were beaten in the contest they would be murdered. Old Faimalie said: 'I am not any use in diving, so you four settle the matter of that sport among yourselves.' Then one of them, Fakafuumaaka (Like a Big Stone), volunteered and said, 'Leave it to me to go. I will dive with the Pulotu champion.'

Fakafuumaka went at once with the Pulotu diver and they dived and remained at the bottom. Meanwhile Hikuleo and all the people of Pulotu, together with the crew of the boat from the world, Haveatoke, Haelefeke, Lohi and Faimalie, watched the diving to see who would come to the end of his breath first and rise to the surface to breathe.

So the two contestants dived and dived and remained at the bottom of the sea. For one night they dived and for two nights they dived and then they remained at the bottom of the sea for ten nights. At last a month had passed and still they were down on the bottom of the sea and neither was so short winded that he had to rise to the surface. So there they remained, when lo, the Pulotu diver's breath gave out and he made as if to go up to the surface to breathe. When Fakafuumaka perceived that his rival wanted to go up for breath, he rushed him and jumped on his head and neck and held him, in order to prevent his rising to the surface to save his life. Fakafuumaka caught him in his arms and held him until he was dead. When the victor knew that his Pulotu rival was dead and his flesh had become rotten and stinking in the sea, he then went up to the surface of the sea, having thus killed the Pulotu diver.

This defeat of the Pulotu champion angered Hikuleo and the Pulotu chiefs very much and they said: 'There is nothing good here. This small boat with only a few people has arrived and is able to overcome us. Let us choose something else.' 'But,' inquired Hikuleo, 'what other sports still remain that we can use to try conclusions with this vessel and the gods from the world?'

Then replied several Pulotu people: 'There are plenty more sports, but they are only games. We have exhausted our difficult sports, such as surf riding and diving, in which we lost two of our number. There is not one difficult sport left.'

'There remains yet one thing, our big tree,' said Hikuleo. It was a *vi* tree (*Spondias dulcis*) of enormous size, so large, in fact, that it nearly filled the whole of Pulotu with its branches, trunk, and fruit. Hikuleo continued, addressing the visitors: 'Gods from the world, which one of you is clever enough to catch and pluck the fruit which you must eat?'

Haveatoke, Fakafuumaka, Haelefeke, Lohi and Faimalie discussed the matter and said: 'Who can catch all the fruit of that huge *vi* tree? It looks exceedingly difficult.' They were afraid and in their fright they said to themselves: 'This is too much, but if we are not able to accomplish it, we are sure to be murdered.' They thought about and discussed the matter, because Hikuleo had said to them: 'When plucking the *vi* only one person may come to catch the fruit. If any falls to the ground, you gods of the world will be slain. If you catch all the fruit, you will be allowed to live, for this is the last trial in Pulotu. However, when you have plucked and caught all the fruit, you must eat it so that none remains. If it is not all finished, you will be killed.'

So they held consultation together, did the gods of the world, almost weeping, because they thought they would be unable to catch all the fruit without one falling to the ground. Then said one god, Haelefeke by name: 'Leave it to me. I will catch all of the fruit of the *vi* tree, so that not one shall fall to the ground.'

Haelefeke came forward and lay his head on the roots of the tree, face upwards. Then he put some of his tentacles up so that they held the branches in one direction, but still his tentacles went up and along the branches until all were encompassed. By this means he would be able to catch and pluck all of the fruit, so that none should fall to the ground, otherwise the five gods from the world would be slain. Then he shook the tree to make the fruit fall, but not one touched the ground, for all were caught by Haelefeke. Once more Pulotu was beaten.

Great was Pulotu's wrath and Hikuleo said: 'Come now, and eat the fruit of the *vi*. If you do not finish it, you will be killed. Understand, this is absolutely the last of your trials.' Haveatoke, Fakafuumaka, Haelefeke and Lohi commenced to eat, but they soon wearied for they were not great eaters. They said to Faimalie: 'Faimalie, you come and eat, for we ourselves do not care for the *vi* fruit. We are tired of it and besides we are full and our stomachs have turned against it. If you love us, then come.' And continued the gods to Faimalie: 'You come and finish the *vi*, for this is the last of Hikuleo's petty tyranny to us. If we are able to accomplish this feat of eating all the fruit, then we will be able to return to the world alive.' Faimalie obligingly came and finished all the fruit, then ate all the leaves, so that not one remained. Then she ate the branches and finished by devouring the whole trunk of the huge tree.

This annoyed Hikuleo and all of the chiefs of Pulotu exceedingly, so that they drove away the boat of the gods of the world and Hikuleo addressed them thus: 'Get back to the world. Do not dare to come here again and pretend to be important and to play tricks. You came, you low born ones. But where did you come from? The world. That is the place of the low commoners. Get ye hence.'

The gods from the world departed, but Faimalie came away with something, a yam she had swallowed. She buried it beneath a fire and when she lifted it out, she found that it was burnt on one side but quite raw on the other. Taking it up she put it out of sight. Another god, Lohi, stole some taro from Pulotu and hid it about his person. That was the beginning of taro in Tonga. He planted it in his island of Eua. All taro started in Eua, for it was stolen from Pulotu by Lohi.

Besides the yam, Faimalie also stole the fish known as the o. When Faimalie came back, she gave birth to the yam in the bush and that portion of the bush is known as Koloi. It is in the part of the country called Haamotuku. Faimalie went to dwell in the bush so that she might give birth. After she was delivered, the yam was called *kahokaho*. It is amongst the finest and best of yams, fit for chiefs. There are also the *manange* and *levei* and that is all of the chiefs' yams. There are a great many other sorts of yams. There are plenty of white yams, as well as purple yams, but the origin of these particular yams is in the one brought by Faimalie, as also the fish, and the taro brought by Lohi. But the yams known as the *tuaata* and the *nguata* are different. These were early yams, for they fell from the sky on to the island of Ata (near Tongatapu). Then there is the yam *heketala*, that was brought from heaven to Ilaheva and Ahoeitu by an old woman called Vaepopua. These were the earliest yams in Tonga. Faimalie came afterwards from Pulotu with the different sorts of yams and in giving birth leaned her back against a tree known as the *masikoka*. The place was called 'The Resting Place.'

This is the conclusion of the tale of the boat belonging to the gods called Haveatoke, Fakafuumaka, Haelefeke, and Lohi. The vessel came from Eua and went to Pulotu. Only four were going, but an old woman stood on the beach at the end of the island. It was she who called to the boat that there might be five persons to go to Pulotu. This is the end of the tale of the gods that went to Pulotu, their challenge, and their strength, and of the overcoming of Plikuleo and all the people of Pulotu.

HOMELESS AND DESOLATE GHOSTS

The spirits of the dead, according to a summary of ancient Hawaiian statements, were divided into three classes, each class bearing the prefix 'ao,' which meant either the enlightened or instructed class, or simply a crowd or number of spirits grouped together.

The first class, the Ao-Kuewa, were the desolate and the homeless spirits who during their residence in the body had no friends and no property.

The second class was called the Ao-Aumakuas. These were the groups of ghost-gods or spirit-ancestors of the Hawaiians. They usually remained near their old home as helpful protectors of the family to which they belonged, and were worshipped by the family.

The third class was the Ao-o-Milu. Milu was the chief god of the Underworld throughout the greater part of Polynesia. Many times the Underworld itself bore the name of Milu. The Ao-o-Milu were the souls of the departed of both the preceding classes who had performed all tasks, passed all barriers, and found their proper place in the land of the king of ghosts.

The Old Hawaiians never intelligently classified these departed spirits and sometimes mixed them together in inextricable confusion, but in the legends and remarks of early Hawaiian writers these three classes are roughly sketched. The desolate ghost had no right to call any place its home, to which it could come, over which it could watch, and around which it could hover. It had to go to the desolate parts of the islands or into a wilderness or forest.

The homeless ghost had no one to provide even the shadow of food for it. It had to go into the dark places and search for butterflies, spiders, and other insects. These were the ordinary food for all ghosts unless there were worshippers to place offerings on secret altars, which were often dedicated to gain a special power of praying other people to death. Such ghosts were well cared for, but, on the other hand, the desolate ones must wander and search until they could go down into the land of Milu.

There were several ways which the gods had prepared for ghosts to use in this journey to the Underworld. It is interesting to note that all through Polynesia as well as in the Hawaiian Islands the path for ghosts led westward.

The students of New Zealand folklore will say that this signified the desire of those about to die to return to the land of their ancestors beyond the western ocean.

The paths were called Leina-a-ka-uhane (paths-for-leaping-by-the-spirit). They were almost always on bold bluffs looking westward over the ocean. The spirit unless driven back could come to the headland and leap down into the land of the dead, but when this was done that spirit could never return to the body it had left. Frequently connected with these Leina-a-ka-uhane was a breadfruit-tree which would be a gathering-place for ghosts.

At these places there were often friendly ghosts who would help and sometimes return the spirit to the body or send it to join the Ao-Aumakuas (ancestor ghosts). At the place of descent it was said there was an owawa (ditch) through which the ghosts one by one were carried down to Pō, and Lei-lono was the gate where the ghosts were killed as they went down. Near this gateway was the Ulu-o-lei-walo, or breadfruit-tree of the spirits. This tree had two branches, one toward the east and one toward the west, both of which were used by the ghosts. One was for leaping into eternal darkness into Po-pau-ole, the other as a meeting-place with the helpful gods.

This tree always bore the name Ulu-o-lei-walo (the-quietly-calling-breadfruit-tree). On the island of Oahu, one of these was said to have been at Kaena Point; another was in Nuuanu Valley.

The desolate ghost would come to this meeting-place of the dead and try to find a ghost of the second class, the aumakuas, who had been one of his ancestors and who still had some family to watch over. Perhaps this one might entertain or help him.

If the ghost could find no one to take him, then he would try to wander around the tree and leap into the branches. The rotten, dead branches of the tree belonged to the spirits. When they broke and fell, the spirits on them dropped into the land of Milu – the underworld home of ghosts. Often the spirit could leap from these dead branches into the Underworld.

Sometimes the desolate spirit would be blown, as by the wind, back and forth, here and there, until no possible place of rest could be found on the island where death had come; then the ghost would leap into the sea, hoping to find the way to Milu through some sea-cave. Perhaps the waves would carry the ghost, or it might be able to swim to one of the other islands, where a new search would be made for some ancestor-ghost from which to obtain help. Not finding aid, it would be pushed and driven over rough, rocky places and through the wilderness until it again went into the sea. At last perhaps a way would be found into the home of the dead, and the ghost would have a place in which to live, or it might make the round through the wilderness again and again, until it could leap from a bluff, or fall from a rotten branch of the breadfruit-tree.

A great caterpillar was the watchman on the eastern side of the leaping-off place. Napaha was the western boundary. A mo-o (dragon) was the watchman on that side. If the ghost was afraid of them it went back to secure the help of the ghost-gods in order to get by. The Hawaiians were afraid that these watchmen would kill ghosts if possible.

If a caterpillar obstructed the way it would raise its head over the edge of the bluff, and then the frightened ghost would go far out of its way, and wandering around be destroyed or compelled to leap off some dead branch into eternal darkness. But if that frightened ghost, while wandering, could find a helpful ghost god, it would be kept alive, although still a wanderer over the islands.

At the field of kaupea (coral) near Barbers Point, in the desert of Puuloa, the ghost would go around among the lehua flowers, catching spiders, butterflies, and insects for food, where the ghost-gods might find them and give them aid in escaping the watchmen.

There are many places for the Leina-a-ka-uhane (leaping-off-places) and the Ulu-o-lei-walo (breadfruit-trees) on all the islands. To these places the wandering desolate ghosts went to find a way to the Underworld.

Another name for the wandering ghosts was lapu, also sometimes called Akua-hele-loa (great travellers). These ghosts were frequently those who enjoyed foolish, silly pranks. They would sweep over the old byways in troops, dancing and playing.

They would gather around the old mats where the living had been feasting, and sit and feast on imaginary food.

The Hawaiians say: 'On one side of the island Oahu, even to this day the lapu come at night. Their ghost drums and sacred chants can be heard and their misty forms seen as they hover about the ruins of the old heiaus (temples).'

The fine mists or fogs of Manoa Valley were supposed to conceal a large company of priests and their attendants while roaming among the great stones which still lie where there was a puu-honua (refuge-temple) in the early days. If any one saw these roving ghosts he was called lapu-ia, or one to whom spirits had appeared.

The Hawaiians said: 'The lapu ghosts were not supposed to watch over the welfare of the persons they met. They never went into the heavens to become black clouds, bringing rain for the benefit of their households. They did not go out after winds to blow with destructive force against their enemies. This was the earnest work of the ancestor-ghosts, and was not done by the lapu.'

Another name for ghosts was wai-lua, which referred especially to the spirit leaving the body and supposed to have been seen by some one. This wai-lua spirit could be driven back into the body by other ghosts, or persuaded to come back through offerings or incantations given by living friends, so that a dead person could become alive again.

It was firmly believed that a person could endure many deaths, and that if any one lost consciousness he was dead, and that when life stopped it was because the spirit left the body. When life was renewed it was because the spirit had returned to its former home.

The kino-wai-lua was a ghost leaving the body of a living person and returning after a time, as when any one fainted.

Besides the ghosts of the dead, the Hawaiians gave spirit power to all natural objects. Large stones were supposed to have dragon power sometimes.

AUMAKUAS, OR ANCESTOR-GHOSTS

There are two meanings to the first part of this word, for 'au' means a multitude, as in 'auwaa' (many canoes), but it may mean time and place, as in the following: 'Our ancestors thought that if there was a desolate place where no man could be found, it was the aumakua (place of many gods).' 'Makua' was the name given to the ancestors of a chief and of the people as well as to parents.

The aumakuas were the ghosts who did not go down into Pō, the land of King Milu. They were in the land of the living, hovering around the families from which they had been separated by death. They were the guardians of these families.

When any one died, many devices were employed in disposing of the body. The fact that an enemy of the family might endeavor to secure the bones of the dead for the purpose of making them into fish-hooks, arrow-heads, or spear-heads led the surviving members of a family either to destroy or to conceal the body of the dead. For if the bones were so used it meant great dishonor, and the spirit was supposed to suffer on account of this indignity.

Sometimes the flesh was stripped from the bones and cast into the ocean or into the fires of the volcanoes, that the ghost might be made a part of the family ghosts who lived in such places, and the bones were buried in some secret cave or pit, or folded together in a bundle which was thought to resemble a grasshopper, so these were called unihipili (grasshopper). The unihipili bones were used in connection with a strange belief called pule-ana-ana (praying to death).

When the body of a dead person was to be hidden, only two or three men were employed in the task. Sometimes the one highest in rank would slay his helpers so that no one except himself would know the burial-place.

The tools, the clothing, and the calabashes of the dead were unclean until certain ceremonies of purification had been faithfully performed. Many times these possessions were either placed in the burial-cave beside the body or burned so that they might be the property of the spirit in ghost-land.

The people who cared for the body had to bathe in salt water and separate themselves from the family for a time. They must sprinkle the house and all things inside with salt water. After a few days the family would return and occupy the house once more.

Usually the caretakers of a dead body would make a hole in the side of the house and push it through rather than take it through the old doorway, probably having the idea that the ghost would only know the door through which the body had gone out when alive and so could not find the new way back when the opening was closed.

After death came, the ghost crept out of the body, coming up from the feet until it rested in the eyes, and then it came out from the corner of one eye, and had a kind of wind body. It could pass around the room and out of doors through any opening it could find. It could perch like a bird on the roof of a house or in the branches of trees, or it could seat itself on logs or stones near the house. It might have to go back into the body and make it live again. Possibly the ghost might meet some old ancestor-ghosts and be led so far away that it could not return; then it must become a member of the aumakua, or ancestor-ghost, family, or wander off to join the homeless desolate ghost vagabonds.

Sometimes dead bodies were thrown into the sea with the hope that the ghost body would become a shark or an eel, or perhaps a mo-o, or dragon-god, to be worshipped with other ancestor-gods of the same class.

Sometimes the body or the bones would be cast into the crater of Kilauea, the people thinking the spirit would become a flame of fire like Pele, the goddess of volcanoes; other spirits went into the air concealed in the dark depths of the sky, perhaps in the clouds.

Here they carried on the work needed to help their families. They would become fog or mist or the fine misty rain colored by light. With these the Rainbow Maiden, Ānuenue, delighted to dwell. They often lived in the great rolling white clouds, or in the gray clouds which let fall the quiet rain needed for farming. They also lived in the fierce black thunder-clouds which sent down floods of a devastating character upon the enemies of the family to which they belonged.

There were ghost ancestors who made their homes near the places where the members of their families toiled; there were ancestor-ghosts to take care of the tapa, or kapa, makers, or the calabash or house or canoe makers. There were special ancestor-ghosts called upon by name by the farmers, the fishermen, and the bird-hunters. These ghosts had their own kuleanas, or places to which they belonged, and in which they had their own peculiar duties and privileges. They became ancestor ghost-gods and dwelt on the islands near the homes of their worshippers, or in the air above, or in the trees around the houses, or in the ocean or in the glowing fires of volcanoes. They even dwelt in human beings, making them shake or sneeze as with cold, and then a person was said to become an ipu, or calabash containing a ghost.

Sometimes it was thought that a ghost god could be seen sitting on the head or shoulder of the person to whom it belonged. Even in this twentieth century a native woman told the writer that she saw a ghost-god whispering in his ear while he was making an address. She said, 'That ghost was like a fire or a colored light.' Many times the Hawaiians have testified that they believed in the presence of their ancestor ghost-gods.

This is the way the presence of a ghost was detected: Some sound would be heard, such as a sibilant noise, a soft whistle, or something like murmurs, or some sensation in a part of the body might be felt. If an eyelid trembled, a ghost was sitting on that spot. A quivering or creepy feeling in any part of the body meant that a ghost was touching that place. If any of these things happened, a person would cry out, 'I have seen or felt a spirit of the gods.'

Sometimes people thought they saw the spirits of their ghost friends. They believed that the spirits of these friends appeared in the night, sometimes to kill any one who was in the way. The high chiefs and warriors are supposed to march and go in crowds, carrying their spears and piercing those they met unless some ghost recognized that one and called to the others, 'Alia', but if the word was 'O-i-o!' then that spirit's spear would strike death to the passer-by.

There were night noises which the natives attributed to sounds or rustling motions made by such night gods as the following:

Akua-hokio (whistling gods),
-kiei (peeping gods).
-nalo (prying gods).
-loa (long gods).
-poko (short gods).
-muki (sibilant gods).

A prayer to these read thus:

'O Akua-loa!
O Akua-poko!
O Akua-muki!
O Akua-hokio!
O Akua-kiei!
O Akua-nalo!
O All ye Gods, who travel on the dark night paths!
Come and eat.
Give life to me,
And my parents,
And my children,
To us who are living in this place. Amama.'

This prayer was offered every night as a protection against the ghosts.

The aumakuas were very laka (tame and helpful). It was said that an aumakua living in a shark would be very laka, and would come to be rubbed on the head, opening his mouth for a sacrifice. Perhaps some awa, or meat, would be placed in his mouth, and then he would go away. So also if the aumakua were a bird, it would become tame. If it were the alae (a small duck), it would come to the hand of its worshipper; if the pueo (owl), it would come and scratch the earth away from the grave of one of its worshippers, throwing the sand away with its wings, and would bring the body back to life. An owl ancestor-god would come and set a worshipper free were he a prisoner with hands and feet bound by ropes.

It made no difference whether the dead person were male or female, child or aged one, the spirit could become a ghost-god and watch over the family.

There were altars for the ancestor-gods in almost every land. These were frequently only little piles of white coral, but sometimes chiefs would build a small house for their ancestor-gods, thus making homes that the ghosts might have a kuleana, or place of their own, where offerings could be placed, and prayers offered, and rest enjoyed.

The Hawaiians have this to say about sacrifices for the aumakuas: If a mo-o, or dragon-god, was angry with its caretaker or his family and they became weak and sick, they would sacrifice a spotted dog with awa, red fish, red sugar-cane, and some of the grass growing in taro patches wrapped in yellow kapa. This they would take to the lua, or hole, where the mo-o dwelt, and fasten the bundle there. Then the mo-o would become pleasant and take away the sickness. If it were a shark-god, the sacrifice was a black pig, a dark red chicken, and some awa wrapped in new white kapa made by a virgin. This bundle would be carried to the beach, where a prayer would be offered:

> 'O aumakuas from sunrise to sunset,
> From North to South, from above and below,
> O spirits of the precipice and spirits of the sea,
> All who dwell in flowing waters,

> *Here is a sacrifice – our gifts are to you.*
> *Bring life to us, to all the family,*
> *To the old people with wrinkled skin,*
> *To the young also.*
> *This is our life,*
> *From the gods.'*

Then the farmer would throw the bundle into the sea, bury the chicken alive, take the pig to the temple, then go back to his house looking for rain. If there was rain, it showed that the aumakua had seen the gifts and washed away the wrong. If the clouds became black with heavy rain, that was well.

The offerings for Pele and Hiiaka were awa to drink and food to eat, in fact all things which could be taken to the crater.

This applies to the four great gods, Kane, Ku, Lono and Kanaloa. They are called the first of the ancestors. Each one of these was supposed to be able to appear in a number of different forms, therefore each had a number of names expressive of the work he intended or was desired to do. An explanatory adjective or phrase was added to the god's own name, defining certain acts or characteristics, thus: Kane-puaa (Kane, the pig) was Kane who would aid in stirring up the ground like a pig.

This is one of the prayers used when presenting offerings to aumakuas, 'O Aumakuas of the rising of the sun, guarded by every tabu staff, here are offerings and sacrifices – the black pig, the white chicken, the black cocoanut, the red fish – sacrifices for the gods and all the aumakuas; those of the ancestors, those of the night, and of the dawn, here am I. Let life come.'

The ancestor-gods were supposed to use whatever object they lived with. If ghosts went up into the clouds, they moved the clouds from place to place and made them assume such shape as might be fancied. Thus they would reveal themselves over their old homes.

All the aumakuas were supposed to be gentle and ready to help their own families. The old Hawaiians say that the power of the ancestor-gods was very great. 'Here is the magic power. Suppose a man would call his shark, "O Kuhai-moana! O, the One who lives in the Ocean! Take me to the land!" Then perhaps a shark would appear, and the man would get on the back of the shark, hold fast to the fin, and say: "You look ahead. Go on very swiftly without waiting." Then the shark would swim swiftly to the shore.'

The old Hawaiians had the sport called 'lua.' This sometimes meant wrestling, but usually was the game of catching a man, lifting him up, and breaking his body so that he was killed. A wrestler of the lua class would go out to a plain where no people were dwelling and call his god Kuialua. The aumakua ghost-god would give this man strength and skill, and help him to kill his adversaries.

There were many priests of different classes who prayed to the ancestor-gods. Those of the farmers prayed like this:

> 'O great black cloud in the far-off sky,
> O shadow watching shadow,
> Watch over our land.
> Overshadow our land
> From corner to corner
> From side to side.
> Do not cast your shadow on other lands
> Nor let the waters fall on the other lands.'

Also they prayed to Kane-puaa (Kane, the pig), the great aumakua of farmers:

> 'O Kane-puaa, root!
> Dig inland, dig toward the sea;
> Dig from corner to corner,
> From side to side;
> Let the food grow in the middle,
> Potatoes on the side roots,
> Fruit in the centre.
> Do not root in another place!
> The people may strike you with the spade
> Or hit you with a stone
> And hurt you. Amama.'

So also they prayed to Kukea-olo-walu (a taro aumakua god):

> 'O Kukea-olo-walu!
> Make the taro grow,
> Let the leaf spread like a banana.
> Taro for us, O Kukea!
> The banana and the taro for us.
> Pull up the taro for us, O Kukea!
> Pound the taro,
> Make the fire for cooking the pig.
> Give life to us –
> To the farmers –
> From sunrise to sunset
> From one fastened place to the other fastened place,
> Amama.'

Trees with their branches and fruit were frequently endowed

with spirit power. All the different kinds of birds and even insects, and also the clouds and winds and the fish in the seas were given a place among the spirits around the Hawaiians.

The people believed in life and its many forms of power. They would pray to the unseen forces for life for themselves and their friends, and for death to come on the families of their enemies. They had special priests and incantations for the pule-ana-ana, or praying to death, and even to the present time the supposed power to pray to death is one of the most formidable terrors to their imagination.

Menehunes, eepas and kupuas were classes of fairies or gnomes which did not belong to the ancestor-gods, or aumakuas.

The menehunes were fairy servants. Some of the Polynesian Islands called the lowest class of servants 'manahune.' The Hawaiians separated them almost entirely from the spirits of ancestors. They worked at night performing prodigious tasks which they were never supposed to touch again after the coming of dawn.

The eepas were usually deformed and defective gnomes. They suffered from all kinds of weakness, sometimes having no bones and no more power to stand than a large leaf. They were sometimes set apart as spirit caretakers of little children. Nuuanu Valley was the home of a multitude of eepas who had their temple on the western side of the valley.

Kupuas were the demons of ghost-land. They were very powerful and very destructive. No human being could withstand their attacks unless specially endowed with power from the gods. They had animal as well as human bodies and could use whichever body seemed to be most available. The dragons, or mo-os, were the most terrible kupuas in the islands.

THE DRAGON GHOST-GODS

Dragons were among the ghost-gods of the ancient Hawaiians. These dragons were called mo-o. The New Zealanders used the same names for some of their large reptile gods. They, however, spelled the word with a 'k,' calling it mo-ko, and it was almost identical in pronunciation as in meaning with the Hawaiian name. Both the Hawaiians and New Zealanders called all kinds of lizards mo-o or mo-ko; and their use of this word in traditions showed that they often had in mind animals like crocodiles and alligators, and sometimes they referred the name to any monster of great legendary powers belonging to a man-destroying class.

Mighty eels, immense sea-turtles, large fish of the ocean, fierce sharks, were all called mo-o. The most ancient dragons of the Hawaiians are spoken of as living in pools or lakes. These dragons were known also as kupuas, or mysterious characters who could appear as animals or human beings according to their wish. The saying was: 'Kupuas have a strange double body.'

There were many other kupuas besides those of the dragon family. It was sometimes thought that at birth another natural form was added, such as an egg of a fowl or a bird, or the seed of a plant, or the embryo of some animal, which when fully developed made a form which could be used as readily as the human body. These kupuas were always given some great magic power. They were wonderfully strong and wise and skilful.

Usually the birth of a kupua, like the birth of a high chief, was attended with strange disturbances in the heavens, such as reverberating thunder, flashing lightning, and severe storms which sent the abundant red soil of the islands down the mountain-sides in blood-red torrents known as ka-ua-koko (the blood rain). This name was also given to misty fine rain when shot through by the red waves of the sun.

By far the largest class of kupuas was that of the dragons. These all belonged to one family. Their ancestor was Mo-o-inanea (The Self-reliant Dragon), who figured very prominently in the Hawaiian legends of the most ancient times, such as 'The Maiden of the Golden Cloud.'

Mo-o-inanea (The Self-reliant Dragon) brought the dragons, the kupua dragons, from the 'Hidden Land of Kane' to the Hawaiian Islands. Mo-o-inanea was apparently a demigoddess of higher power even than the gods Ku, Kane, or Kanaloa. She was the great dragon-goddess of the Hawaiians, coming to the islands in the migration of the gods from Nuu-mea-lani and Kuai-he-lani to settle. The dragons and other kupuas came as spirit servants of the gods.

For a while this Mo-o-inanea lived with her brothers, the gods, at Waolani, but after a long time there were so many dragons that it was necessary to distribute them over the islands, and Mo-o-inanea decided to leave her brothers and find homes for her numerous family. So she went down to Puunui in the lower part of Nuuanu Valley and there made her home, and it is said received worship from the men of the ancient days. Here she dwelt in her dual nature – sometimes appearing as a dragon, sometimes as a woman.

Very rich clayey soil was found in this place, forced out of the earth as if by geyser action. It was greatly sought in later years by the chiefs who worshipped this goddess. They made the place tabu, and used the clay, sometimes eating it, but generally plastering the hair with it. This place was made very tabu by the late Queen Kaahumanu during her lifetime.

Mo-o-inanea lived in the pit from which this clay was procured, a place called Lua-palolo, meaning pit-of-sticky-clay. After she had come to this dwelling-place the dragons were sent out to find homes. Some became chiefs and others servants, and when by themselves were known as the evil ones. She distributed her family over all the islands from Hawai'i to Niihau. Two of these dragon-women, according to the legends, lived as guardians of the pali (precipice) at the end of Nuuanu Valley, above Honolulu. After many years it was supposed that they both assumed the permanent forms of large stones which have never lost their associations with mysterious, miraculous power.

Even as late as 1825, Mr. Bloxam, the chaplain of the English man-of-war, recorded in 'The Voyage of the Blonde' the following statement:

'At the bottom of the Parre (pali) there are two large stones on which even now offerings of fruits and flowers are laid to propitiate the Aku-wahines, or goddesses, who are supposed to have the power of granting a safe passage.'

Mr. Bloxam says that these were a kind of mo-o, or reptile, goddesses, and adds that it was difficult to explain the meaning of the name given to them, probably because the Hawaiians had nothing in the shape of serpents or large reptiles in their islands.

A native account of these stones says: 'There is a large grove of hau-trees in Nuuanu Valley, and above these lie the two forest women, Hau-ola and Ha-puu. These are now two large stones, one being about three feet long with a fine smooth back, the other round with some little rough places. The long stone is on the seaward side, and this is the Mo-o woman, Hau-ola; and the other, Ha-puu. The leaves of ferns cover Hau-ola, being laid on that stone. On the other stone, Ha-puu, are lehua flowers. These are kupuas.'

Again the old people said that their ancestors had been accustomed to bring the navel cords of their children and bury them under these stones to insure protection of the little ones from evil, and that these were the stone women of Nuuanu.

Ala-muki lived in the deep pools of the Waialua River near the place Ka-mo-o-loa, which received its name from the long journeys that dragon made over the plains of Waialua. She and her descendants guarded the paths and sometimes destroyed those who travelled that way.

One dragon lived in the Ewa lagoon, now known as Pearl Harbor. This was Kane-kua-ana, who was said to have brought the pipi (oysters) to Ewa. She was worshipped by those who gathered the shell-fish. When the oysters began to disappear about 1850, the natives said that the dragon had become angry and was sending the oysters to Kahiki, or some far-away foreign land.

Kilioe, Koe and Milolii were noted dragons on the island of Kauai. They were the dragons of the precipices of the northern coast of this island, who took the body of the high chief Lohiau and concealed it in a cave far up the steep side of the mountain. There is a very long interesting story of the love between Lohiau and Pele, the goddess of fire. In this story Pele overcame the dragons and won the love of the chief. Hiiaka, the sister of the fire-goddess, won a second victory over them when she rescued a body from the cave and brought it back to life.

On Māui, the greatest dragon of the island was Kiha-wahine. The natives had the saying, 'Kiha has mana, or miraculous power, like Mo-o-inanea.' She lived in a large deep pool on the edge of the village Lahaina, and was worshipped by the royal family of Māui as their special guardian.

There were many dragons of the island of Hawai'i, and the most noted of these were the two who lived in the Wailuku River near Hilo. They were called 'the moving boards' which made a bridge across the river.

Sometimes they accepted offerings and permitted a safe passage, and sometimes they tipped the passengers into the water and drowned them. They were destroyed by Hiiaka.

Sacred to these dragons who were scattered over all the islands were the mo-o priests and the sorcerers, who propitiated them with offerings and sacrifices, chanting incantations.

THE MAGICAL WOODEN HEAD
(Ron Ga Puhi A Puarata Raua Ko Tautōhito)

This head bewitched all persons who approached the hill where the fortress in which it was kept was situated, so that, from fear of it, no human being dared to approach the place, which was thence named the Sacred Mount.

Upon that mount dwelt Puarata and Tautōhito with their carved head, and its fame went through all the country, to the river Tarnaki, and to Kaipara, and to the tribes of Ngāpuhi, to Akau, to Waikato, to Kawhia, to Mokau, to Hauraki, and to Tauranga; the exceeding great fame of the powers of that carved head spread to every part of Aotea-roa, or the northern island of New Zealand; everywhere reports were heard, that so great were its magical powers, none could escape alive from them; and although many warriors and armies went to the Sacred Mount to try to destroy the sorcerers to whom the head belonged, and to carry it off as a genius for their own district, that its magical powers might be subservient to them, they all perished in the attempt. In short, no mortal could approach the fortress and live; even parties of people who were travelling along the forest track, to the northwards towards Muri-whenua, all died by the magical powers of that head; whether they went in large armed bodies, or simply as quiet travellers, their fate was alike – they all perished, from its magical influence, somewhere about the place where the beaten track passes over Waimatuku.

The deaths of so many persons created a great sensation in the country, and, at last, the report of these things reached a very powerful sorcerer named Hākawau, who, confiding in his magical arts, said he was resolved to go and see this magic head, and the sorcerers who owned it. So, without delay, he called upon all the genii who were subservient to him, in order that he might be thrown into an enchanted sleep, and see what his fate in this undertaking would be; and in his slumber he saw that his genius would triumph in the encounter, for it was so lofty and mighty, that in his dream its head reached the heavens, whilst its feet remained upon earth.

Having by his spells ascertained this, he at once started on his journey, and the district through which he travelled was that of Akau; and, confiding in his own enchantments, he went fearlessly to try whether his arts of sorcery would not prevail over the magic head, and enable him to destroy the old sorcerer Puarata.

He took with him one friend, and went along the sea-coast towards the Sacred Mount, and passed through Whanga-roa, and followed the sea-shore to Rangikahu and Kuhawera, and came out upon the coast again at Karoroumanui, and arrived at Maraetai;

there was a fortified village, the people of which endeavoured to detain Hākawau and his friend until they rested themselves and partook of a little food; but he said: 'We ate food on the road, a short distance behind us; we are not at all hungry or weary.' So they would not remain at Maraetai, but went straight on until they reached Putataka, and they crossed the river there, and proceeded along the beach to Rukuwai; neither did they stop there, but on they went, and at last reached Waitara.

When they got to Waitara, the friend who accompanied Hākawau began to get alarmed, and said: 'Now we shall perish here, I fear'; but they went safely on, and reached Te Weta; there the heart of Hākawau's friend began to beat again, and he said: 'I feel sure that we shall perish here'; however they passed by that place too in safety, and on they went, and at length they reached the most fatal place of all – Waimatuku. Here they smelt the stench of the carcases of the numbers who had been previously destroyed; indeed the stench was so bad that it was quite suffocating, and they both now said: 'This is a fearful place; we fear we shall perish here.' However, Hākawau kept on unceasingly working at his enchantments, and repeating incantations, which might ward off the attacks of evil genii, and which might collect good genii about them, to protect them from the malignant spirits of Puarata, lest these should injure them; thus they passed over Waimatuku, looking with horror at the many corpses strewed about the beach, and in the dense fern and bushes which bordered the path; and as they pursued their onward journey, they expected death every moment. Nevertheless they died not on the dreadful road, but went straight along the path till they came to the place where it passes over some low hills, from whence they could see the fortress which stood upon the Sacred Mount.

Here they sat down and rested, for the first time since they had commenced their journey. They had not yet been seen by the watchmen of the fortress. Then Hākawau, with his incantations, sent forth many genii, to attack the spirits who kept watch over the fortress and magic head of Puarata. Some of his good genii were sent by Hākawau in advance, whilst he charged others to follow at some distance. The incantations by the power of which these genii were sent forth by Hākawau was a Whāngai. The genii he sent in front were ordered immediately to begin the assault. As soon as the spirits who guarded the fortress of Puarata saw the others, they all issued out to attack them; the good genii then feigned a retreat the evil ones following them, and whilst they were thus engaged in the pursuit some of the thousands of good genii, who had last been sent forth by Hākawau, stormed the fortress now left without defenders; when the evil spirits, who had been led away in the pursuit, turned to protect the fortress, they found that the genii of Hākawau had already got quite close to it, and the good genii of Hākawau without trouble caught them one after the other, and thus all the spirits of the old sorcerer Puarata were utterly destroyed.

When all the evil spirits who had been subject to the old sorcerer had been thus destroyed, Hākawau walked straight up towards the fortress of this fellow, in whom spirits had dwelt as thick as men stow themselves in a canoe, and whom they had used in like manner to carry them about. When the watchmen of the fortress, to their great surprise, saw strangers coming, Puarata hurried to his magic head, to call upon it; his supplication was after this manner: 'Strangers come here! strangers come here! Two strangers come! two strangers come!' But it uttered only a low wailing sound; for since the good genii of Hākawau had destroyed the spirits who served Puarata, the old sorcerer addressed in vain his supplications to the magic head, it could no longer raise aloud its powerful voice as in former times, but uttered only low moans and wails. Could it have cried out with a loud voice, straightway Hākawau and his friend would both have perished; for thus it was, when armies and travellers had in other times passed the fortress, Puarata addressed supplications to his magic head, and when it cried out with a mighty voice, the strangers all perished as they heard it.

Hākawau and his friend had, in the meantime, continued to walk straight to the fortress. When they drew near it, Hākawau said to his friend: 'You go directly along the path that leads by the gateway into the fortress; as for me, I will show ray power over the old sorcerer, by climbing right over the parapet and palisades': and when they reached the defences of the place, Hākawau began to climb over the palisades of the gateway. When the people of the place saw this, they were much exasperated, and desired him, in an angry manner, to pass underneath the gateway, along the pathway which was common to all, and not to dare to climb over the gateway of Puarata and of Tautōhito; but Hākawau went quietly on over the gateway, without paying the least attention to the angry words of those who were calling out to him, for he felt quite sure that the two old sorcerers were not so skilful in magical arts as he was; so Hākawau persisted in going direct to all the most holy places of the fortress, where no person who had not been made sacred might enter.

After Hākawau and his friend had been for a short time in the fortress, and had rested themselves a little, the people of the place began to cook food for them; they still continued to sit resting them- selves in the fortress for a long time, and at length Hākawau said to his friend: 'Let us depart.' Directly his servant heard what his master said to him, he jumped up at once and was ready enough to be off. Then the people of the place called out to them not to go immediately, but to take some food first; but Hākawau answered: 'Oh, we ate only a little while ago; not far from here we took some food.' So Hākawau would not remain longer in the fortress, but departed, and as he started, he smote his hands on the threshold of the house in which they had rested, and they had hardly got well outside of the fortress before every soul in it was dead – not a single one of them was left alive.

TE REINGA

Like a filled sponge is the air lying over the pa, heavy and sorrowful – filled with desolate cries. Dismal wails issue from the groups which surround the dead chief, men and women howling, dancing, and distorting their faces.

The wailing lies like a cloud upon the earth, and hangs like fog around the groups. A sharp shriek pierces the air, or a shouted sentence in honour of the dead chief cuts the fog; and again everything unites into a monotonous, heart-breaking lament.

The dead chief was a Rangatira-Tohunga, and deep is the sorrow of his people from the mountains and his people from the lake. The women of his next relatives cut their breasts with sharp-edged shells, bleeding, and howling in their pain and sorrow.

Tribe upon tribe nears with dismal lament: all are received by the old women with the long-drawn, piercing cry of welcome to the Tangi. The women march in front; they have flowers wound around their heads, and wave flowers and twigs and leaves in their outstretched arms up and down, up and down – a sign of sorrow. Crying and sobbing follow the men, whose heads are bent and whose gestures betoken the deepest grief – warlike figures, with tattooed faces bestrewn with tears.

In long lines they approach. Canoe after canoe brings ever new hapus (parties), and each approaches in a long line loudly howling: louder and louder grow the howls till the hapu stands before the dead chief, who is covered with the red feather-mat of his rank; and there the whole mass of people is uniting in terrible dirge, dancing and distorting their faces, in which each new arrival joins. All nature seems to lament: the wide lake, the hills, the forests upon the hills and the cloud-covered heads of the mountains – all is united in grief.

Slowly night descends and covers the dirge in darkness.

Great was the mana of the dead Rangatira; terrible was his death; and great sorrow fills the hearts of his people.

The star-lit night is wonderfully clear, and looks down upon the dead chief in his red garment of the Rangatira, surrounded by the treasures of his people; in his hand the beautiful greenstone weapon, the famous mere Pahi-kaure.

Slowly the moon ascends over the murmuring waves of the lake, and streams peacefully her soft light down upon the thousands who are sleeping around her dead Rangatira.

Te Rēinga, the Māori Spirit-Land

The empty forms of men inhabit there;
Impassive semblances, images of air.
The Odyssey

In the extreme north of the North Island of New Zealand is the Muri-whenua, the Land's End, where the never-resting surges thunder at the feet of the bare rocky capes, and the giant sea-kelp swirls in long snaky masses round the fabled gateway to the Māori spirit-land. For here is Te Rēinga, otherwise called Te Rerenga-Wairua, or the Place where the Spirits take their Flight. Te Rēinga is a long craggy ridge that dips down to the ocean, ending in a rocky point whence the ghosts of the departed take their final plunge into the realms of darkness and oblivion. The souls (wairua) of the dead, the moment they are released from their earthly tenements, travel northwards until they arrive at the Land's End of Ao-tea-roa. As they near the Reinga, crossing sand-dune and stony cliff, treading with viewless feet the wild precipices whose bases are ever licked ravenously by the wilder ocean, the spirits bethink them of their old homes. And they pause awhile on the wind-swept heights, and gaze backwards over the long and dreary way by which they came; and they wail aloud, and lacerate themselves after the fashion of the mourners of this world, with sharp splinters of volcanic glass (mata-Tūhua), and in proof thereof these mata are to be seen there to this day by living man. They deck their heads with parépare, or mourning chaplets of green leaves, and their weird, ghostly wails for the Land of Light they are leaving mingle with the melancholy voice of the ocean winds. The long flax leaves which spring from the rocky soil on these heights above the Reinga are often found knotted and twisted together in a peculiar manner. The pakeha says this is the work of the ever restless winds and eddying gales which sweep the Land's End. But to the Māori those knotted leaves are the work of the sad spirits of their departed, tied by the ghosts as they pass along to the gates of Pō, to show their sorrowing friends the way they took in leaving this world of day. And the waterfalls cease their sound as the ghosts flit by;

Trembling the spectres glide, and plaintive vent
Thin hollow screams, along the steep descent.

Down along the narrow ridge to the tideway they move, until they reach the ghostly leaping-place, tapu to the manes of the innumerable multitude of dead. Here grew a venerable pōhutukawa tree, gnarled and knotty, with great ropy roots trailing to the tide. By these roots the spirits dropped to the sea, loosing their last grip of Ao-tea-roa to the dirge of the screaming sea-birds and the moaning waves. Below, the tossing sea-kelp opens a moment to receive the wairua, and then the dark waters close over them for ever. This is the Tatau-o-te-Pō, the Door of Death, which is the entrance to the gloomy Kingdom of Miru, the Goddess of Eternal Night.

Many an Ossianic concept, many a weird and poetic fancy, is woven by the Māoris round this haunted spot. This is a fragment of an ancient lament for the dead, sung to this day at Māori tangis:

'*E tomo, e Pa*
Ki Murimuri-te-Po,
Te Tatau-o-te-Pō.
Ko te whare tena
O Rua-Kumea,
O Rua-toia,
O Miru ra-e!
O tuhouropunga,
O kaiponu-kino.
Nana koe i maka
Ki te kopae o te whare i!'

('Enter, oh sire,
The gates of that last land,
So dread and dark;
The Gates of the Endless Night.
For that is the dwelling
Of Rua-kumea,
Of Rua-toia,
Of the grim goddess Miru,
The ever-greedy one.
'Tis she who hurleth thee
To the deep shadows of her gloomy house.')

And, again, the tribal bards, lamenting over their dead, chant this centuries-old poem:

'Now like an angry gale,
The cold death-wind pierceth me through.
O chiefs of old,
Ye have vanished from us like the moa-bird,
That ne'er is seen of man.
O lordly totara-tree!
Thou'rt fallen to the earth,
And naught but worthless shrubs remain.
I hear the waves' loud tangi
On the strand of Spirit Land,
Where souls, borne from this world of light,
Cast one last look behind.
The rolling seas surge in at Taumaha
Singing their wave-song for the dead
Who have forever vanished from our eyes.'

THE BURIAL OF TE HEU-HEU ON TONGARIRO

Dreamily is Ngāwai staring into the embers, whilst the pale new morning is crawling through the spaces between the fern-stems which form the walls of the mountain-whare (hut).

Cold and pale at first appear the long stripes painted over the floor, till they change slowly into warmer and more glowing colours, lighting up the calabashes, the nets, the paddles, and the mats, which hang on the walls smoke-blackened under the raupō roof. The stripes of daylight are able, too, to light up Ngāwai's eyes, which stare into the nearly burnt-out embers. More fiery glow the stripes, and suddenly they flood the whare with wonderful golden light: it is pure gold, through which, like music, the blue smoke ascends to the roof. Now the sunshine pours in at the door, and with it the wonderful picture of the mountain-lake, reflecting the mountain giants, to the astonished eye. And in all the beautiful world life commences again with laughter and happiness – the laughter and happiness of the parting day.

Slowly is the sun wandering his way in the skies; up to the height of midday he wanders; the shades grow longer, and Rangi-o-mohio, a very old woman, the daughter of the famous Rangatira Te Heu-heu, is still relating:

'Listen: A great procession is ascending with much noise and shouting and frolic the barren wilderness around the stone-body of Tongariro – a great procession of Tohungas, warriors, women, and children.

Ah, Iwikau the Rangatira is leader, and they carry the bones of Te Heu-heu, my father. – Ah, Te Heu-heu, he was my father! Ah, with his bones we wander and crawl and climb over the lonely wilderness. Ah, he was the Rangatira over the lands – but, my son, look upon the greatest Rangatira of all the lands: look upon the Tongariro-tapu!'

Ngāwai listens to the narrative of the old Rangi-o-mohio whilst her eyes are gazing upon the sacred Tongariro. The moon has risen over the lake, and a fine silvery gleam is glittering upon the snow of the mountain, which is sending its beautiful column of silver high up into the skies. Then once more Ngāwai looks sorrowfully back, and goes on her way to her people in the distant pa.

This is Rangi-a-mohio's story:

Iwikau, the brother of the dead Rangatira Te Heu-heu, and chief now over the tribe of the Ngāti-tū-wharetoa, is the leader of a large procession of sorrowing, weeping people of the tribe. The four greatest warriors of the tribe carried the carved box which contained the bones of Te Heu-heu; it was painted red, and adorned with white albatross-feathers.

The whole tribe had decided to give their dead Rangatira the mightiest burial-ground in all Ao-tea-roa – the crater of Tongariro-tapu!

Truly, the mountain Tongariro shall swallow the bones of the Rangatira, that they never may fall in the hands of man – perhaps enemies.

The sharp-edged coke-rocks cut the feet of the bearers, and the sulphur in the air is the deadliest foe to frolic – and what can be properly done without frolic in Māoriland? The feet of the bearers begin to bleed, the incantations of the Tohungas grow weaker; less overbearing, too, become the songs of defiance which Iwikau is shouting to the gods: silence and ghostly fright fall upon the multitude.

Deeper now are the precipices, steeper the rocks, and hellish the sulphurous fumes; but high above still towers the crater, the summit of Tongariro, the mighty grave of the Rangatira! The sacred mountain shall swallow the bones of the sacred chief – as the base of the mountain, in a frightful landslip, has swallowed his life!

Great is the conception, and bravely they try to carry it into effect beneath the mighty column of steam and sulphur which Tongariro is streaming out and which the heaven is pressing down again upon the people, in wrathful defiance of its sanctity.

Distant thunder rolls, shaking the ground, and the sulphur-fumes press fiercely beneath the broadening steam-column. Hard and heavy breathe the bearers; terror at the temerity of the undertaking, which violates the sacredness of the mountain, grows in the heart of their leader.

The vast world stretches all around, and the people who surround the dead Rangatira seem tiny and powerless as the mountain defends his sacred crater with mighty bursts of steam and smoke and rolling thunder and suffocating fumes. Overawed by terror the strength of the bearers fails: they let fall their burden upon a rock; the hearts of the bravest are trembling.

The sanctity of Tongariro-tapu cannot be violated; no, not even by the sacred bones of the Rangatira; and fear grows overpowering beneath the still high-towering, angry crater-summit.

None dares touch the remains of Te Heu-heu again; one and all let them be where they are, upon the rock, overtowered and defended by the majestic summit, with its rolling, thundering, steaming crater – and down they tumble, down, down, helter skelter, in wild and fearful fright they run, a shouting, shrieking body of men, possessed by overpowering terror of the sacred giant. Down, down.

But high up in the sacred regions of Tongariro lie bleaching the bones of the greatest Rangatira of the mountain people –

Māui Pōmare, M.D., the grandson of a famous chief, gave me, at parting, this lament composed by the wife of his ancestor:

'Behold! far off, the bright evening star
Rises – our guardian in the dark,
A gleam of light across my lonely way.
Belov'd, wer't thou the Evening Star,
Thou wouldst not, fixed, so far from me remain.
Let once again thy spirit wander back,
To soothe my slumbers on my restless couch,
And whisper in my dreams sweet words of love.
Oh! cruel Death, to damp that beauteous brow
With Night's cold softly falling dews.
Rau-i-ru, Keeper of Celestial Gates,
There comes to thee a lovely bride
Borne from me on Death's swollen tide.
Belov'd, thy wandering spirit now hath passed
By pendant roots of clinging vine
To Spirit Land, where never foot of man
Hath trod – whence none can e'er return –
Paths to the Gods which I not yet have seen.
Belov'd, if any of that host of Heaven
Dare ask of thee thy birth or rank,
Say thou art of that great tribe
Who, sacred, sprang from loins of Gods.
As stands lone Kapiti, a sea-girt isle,
And Tararua's solitary range,
So I to-day stand lonely midst my grief.
My bird with sacred wings hath flown away
Far from my ken, to Spirit Land.

I would I were a Kawau, resolute
To dive into the inmost depths of time,
To reappear at my beloved's side
Amidst the throng upon the further shore.
Belov'd, I soon will join thee there!
I come! Await me at the gates!
My spirit frets; how slow is time.'

HOW MILU BECAME THE KING OF GHOSTS

Lono was a chief living on the western side of the island Hawai'i. He had a very red skin and strange-looking eyes. His choice of occupation was farming. This man had never been sick. One time he was digging with the oo, a long sharp-pointed stick or spade. A man passed and admired him. The people said, 'Lono has never been sick.' The man said, 'He will be sick.'

Lono was talking about that man and at the same time struck his oo down with force and cut his foot. He shed much blood, and fainted, falling to the ground. A man took a pig, went after the stranger, and let the pig go, which ran to this man. The stranger was Kamaka, a god of healing. He turned and went back at the call of the messenger, taking some popolo fruit and leaves in his cloak. When he came to the injured man he asked for salt, which he pounded into the fruit and leaves and placed in coco cloth and bound it on the wound, leaving it a long time. Then he went away.

As he journeyed on he heard heavy breathing, and turning saw Lono, who said, 'You have helped me, and so I have left my lands in the care of my friends, directing them what to do, and have hastened after you to learn how to heal other people.'

The god said, 'Lono, open your mouth!' This Lono did, and the god spat in his mouth, so that the saliva could be taken into every part of Lono's body. Thus a part of the god became a part of Lono, and he became very skilful in the use of all healing remedies. He learned about the various diseases and the medicines needed for each. The god and Lono walked together, Lono receiving new lessons along the way, passing through the districts of Kau, Puna, Hilo, and then to Hamakua.

The god said, 'It is not right for us to stay together. You can never accomplish anything by staying with me. You must go to a separate place and give yourself up to healing people.'

Lono turned aside to dwell in Waimanu and Waipio Valleys and there began to practise healing, becoming very noted, while the god Kamaka made his home at Ku-kui-haele.

This god did not tell the other gods of the medicines that he had taught Lono. One of the other gods, Kalae, was trying to find some way to kill Milu, and was always making him sick. Milu, chief of Waipio, heard of the skill of Lono. Some had been sick even to death, and Lono had healed them. Therefore Milu sent a messenger to Lono who responded at once, came and slapped Milu all over the body, and said: 'You are not ill. Obey me and you shall be well.'

Then he healed him from all the sickness inside the body caused by Kalae. But there was danger from outside, so he said: 'You must build a ti-leaf house and dwell there quietly for some time, letting your disease rest. If a company should come by the house making sport, with a great noise, do not go out, because when you go they will come up and get you for your death. Do not open the ti leaves and look out. The day you do this you shall die.'

Some time passed and the chief remained in the house, but one day there was the confused noise of many people talking and shouting around his house. He did not forget the command of Lono. Two birds were sporting in a wonderful way in the sky above the forest. This continued all day until it was dark.

Then another long time passed and again Waipio was full of resounding noises. A great bird appeared in the sky resplendent in all kinds of feathers, swaying from side to side over the valley, from the top of one precipice across to the top of another, in grand flights passing over the heads of the people, who shouted until the valley re-echoed with the sound.

Milu became tired of that great noise and could not patiently obey his physician, so he pushed aside some of the ti leaves of his house and looked out upon the bird. That was the time when the bird swept down upon the house, thrusting a claw under Milu's arm, tearing out his liver. Lono saw this and ran after the bird, but it flew swiftly to a deep pit in the lava on one side of the valley and dashed inside, leaving blood spread on the stones. Lono came, saw the blood, took it and wrapped it in a piece of tapa cloth and returned to the place where the chief lay almost dead. He poured some medicine into the wound and pushed the tapa and blood inside. Milu was soon healed.

The place where the bird hid with the liver of Milu is called to this day Ke-ake-o-Milu ('The liver of Milu'). When this death had passed away he felt very well, even as before his trouble.

Then Lono told him that another death threatened him and would soon appear. He must dwell in quietness.

For some time Milu was living in peace and quiet after this trouble. Then one day the surf of Waipio became very high, rushing from far out even to the sand, and the people entered into the sport of surf-riding with great joy and loud shouts. This noise continued day by day, and Milu was impatient of the restraint and forgot the words of Lono. He went out to bathe in the surf.

When he came to the place of the wonderful surf he let the first and second waves go by, and as the third came near he launched himself upon it while the people along the beach shouted uproariously. He went out again into deeper water, and again came in, letting the first and second waves go first. As he came to the shore the first and second waves were hurled back from the shore in a great mass against the wave upon which he was riding. The two great masses of water struck and pounded Milu, whirling and crowding him down, while the surf-board was caught in the raging, struggling waters and thrown out toward the shore. Milu was completely lost in the deep water.

The people cried: 'Milu is dead! The chief is dead!' The god Kalae thought he had killed Milu, so he with the other poison-gods went on a journey to Mauna Loa. Kapo and Pua, the poison-gods, or gods of death, of the island of Māui, found them as they passed, and joined the company. They discovered a forest on Molokai, and there as kupua spirits, or ghost bodies, entered into the trees of that forest, so the trees became the kupua bodies. They were the medicinal or poison qualities in the trees.

Lono remained in Waipio Valley, becoming the ancestor and teacher of all the good healing priests of Hawai'i, but Milu became the ruler of the Underworld, the place where the spirits of the dead had their home after they were driven away from the land of the living. Many people came to him from time to time.

He established ghostly sports like those which his subjects had enjoyed before death. They played the game kilu with polished cocoanut shells, spinning them over a smooth surface to strike a post set up in the centre. He taught kōnane, a game commonly called 'Hawaiian checkers,' but more like the Japanese game of 'Go.' He permitted them to gamble, betting all the kinds of property found in ghost-land. They boxed and wrestled; they leaped from precipices into ghostly swimming-pools; they feasted and fought, sometimes attempting to slay each other. Thus they lived the ghost life as they had lived on earth. Sometimes the ruler was forgotten and the ancient Hawaiians called the Underworld by his name – Milu. The New Zealanders frequently gave their Underworld the name 'Miru.' They also supposed that the ghosts feasted and sported as they had done while living.

A VISIT TO THE KING OF GHOSTS

When any person lay in an unconscious state, it was supposed by the ancient Hawaiians that death had taken possession of the body and opened the door for the spirit to depart. Sometimes if the body lay like one asleep the spirit was supposed to return to its old home. One of the Hawaiian legends weaves their deep-rooted faith in the spirit-world into the expressions of one who seemed to be permitted to visit that ghost-land and its king. This legend belonged to the island of Māui and the region near the village Lahaina. Thus was the story told:

Ka-ilio-hae (the wild dog) had been sick for days and at last sank into a state of unconsciousness. The spirit of life crept out of the body and finally departed from the left eye into a corner of the house, buzzing like an insect. Then he stopped and looked back over the body he had left. It appeared to him like a massive mountain. The eyes were deep caves, into which the ghost looked.

Then the spirit became afraid and went outside and rested on the roof of the house. The people began to wail loudly and the ghost fled from the noise to a cocoanut-tree and perched like a bird in the branches. Soon he felt the impulse of the spirit-land moving him away from his old home. So he leaped from tree to tree and flew from place to place wandering toward Kekaa, the place from which the ghosts leave the island of Māui for their home in the permanent spirit-land – the Underworld.

As he came near this doorway to the spirit-world he met the ghost of a sister who had died long before, and to whom was given the power of sometimes turning a ghost back to its body again. She was an aumakua-ho-ola (a spirit making alive). She called to Ka-ilio-hae and told him to come to her house and dwell for a time. But she warned him that when her husband was at home he must not yield to any invitation from him to enter their house, nor could he partake of any of the food which her husband might urge him to eat. The home and the food would be only the shadows of real things, and would destroy his power of becoming alive again.

The sister said, 'When my husband comes to eat the food of the spirits and to sleep the sleep of ghosts, then I will go with you and you shall see all the spirit-land of our island and see the king of ghosts.'

The ghost-sister led Ka-ilio-hae into the place of whirlwinds, a hill where he heard the voices of many spirits planning to enjoy all the sports of their former life. He listened with delight and drew near to the multitude of happy spirits. Some were making ready to go down to the sea for the hee-nalu (surf-riding). Others were already rolling the ulu-maika (the round stone discs for rolling along the ground). Some were engaged in the mokomoko, or umauma (boxing), and the kulakulai (wrestling), and the honuhonu (pulling with hands), and the loulou (pulling with hooked fingers), and other athletic sports.

Some of the spirits were already grouped in the shade of trees, playing the gambling games in which they had delighted when alive. There was the stone kōnane-board (somewhat like checkers), and the puepue-one (a small sand mound in which was concealed some object), and the puhenehene (the hidden stone under piles of kapa), and the many other trials of skill which permitted betting.

Then in another place crowds were gathered around the hulas (the many forms of dancing). These sports were all in the open air and seemed to be full of interest.

There was a strange quality which fettered every new-born ghost: he could only go in the direction into which he was pushed by the hand of some stronger power. If the guardian of a ghost struck it on one side, it would move off in the direction indicated by the blow or the push until spirit strength and experience came and he could go alone. The newcomer desired to join in these games and started to go, but the sister slapped him on the breast and drove him away. These were shadow games into which those who entered could never go back to the substantial things of life.

Then there was a large grass house inside which many ghosts were making merry. The visitor wanted to join this great company, but the sister knew that, if he once was engulfed by this crowd of spirits in this shadow-land, her brother could never escape. The crowds of players would seize him like a whirlwind and he would be unable to know the way he came in or the way out. Ka-ilio-hae tried to slip away from his sister, but he could not turn readily. He was still a very awkward ghost, and his sister slapped him back in the way in which she wanted him to go.

An island which was supposed to float on the ocean as one of the homes of the aumakuas (the ghosts of the ancestors) had the same characteristics. The ghosts (aumakuas) lived on the shadows of all that belonged to the earth-life. It was said that a canoe with a party of young people landed on this island of dreams and for some time enjoyed the food and fruits and sports, but after returning to their homes could not receive the nourishment of the food of their former lives, and soon died. The legends taught that no ghost passing out of the body could return unless it made the life of the aumakuas tabu to itself.

Soon the sister led her brother to a great field, stone walled, in which were such fine grass houses as were built only for chiefs of the highest rank. There she pointed to a narrow passageway into which she told her brother he must enter by himself.

'This,' she said, 'is the home of Walia, the high chief of the ghosts living in this place. You must go to him. Listen to all he says to you. Say little. Return quickly. There will be three watchmen guarding this passage. The first will ask you, 'What is the fruit of your heart?' You will answer, 'Walia.' Then he will let you enter the passage.

'Inside the walls of the narrow way will be the second watchman. He will ask why you come; again answer, 'Walia,' and pass by him.

'At the end of the entrance the third guardian stands holding a raised spear ready to strike. Call to him, 'Ka-make-loa'. This is the name of his spear. Then he will ask what you want, and you must reply, 'To see the chief,' and he will let you pass.

'Then again when you stand at the door of the great house you will see two heads bending together in the way so that you cannot enter or see the king and his queen. If these heads can catch a spirit coming to see the king without knowing the proper incantations, they will throw that ghost into the Po-Milu. Watch therefore and remember all that is told you.

'When you see these heads, point your hands straight before you between them and open your arms, pushing these guards off on each side, then the ala-nui will be open for you – and you can enter.

'You will see kāhilis moving over the chiefs. The king will awake and call, 'Why does this traveller come?' You will reply quickly, 'He comes to see the Divine One.' When this is said no injury will come to you. Listen and remember and you will be alive again.'

Ka-ilio-hae did as he was told with the three watchmen, and each one stepped back, saying, 'Noa' (the tabu is lifted), and he pushed by. At the door he shoved the two heads to the side and entered the chief's house to the Ka-ikuwai (the middle), falling on his hands and knees. The servants were waving the kāhilis this way and that. There was motion, but no noise.

The chief awoke, looked at Ka-ilio-hae, and said: 'Aloha, stranger, come near. Who is the high chief of your land?'

Then Ka-ilio-hae gave the name of his king, and the genealogy from ancient times of the chiefs dead and in the spirit-world.

The queen of ghosts arose, and the kneeling spirit saw one more beautiful than any woman in all the island, and he fell on his face before her.

The king told him to go back and enter his body and tell his people about troubles near at hand.

While he was before the king twice he heard messengers call to the people that the sports were all over; any one not heeding would be thrown into the darkest place of the home of the ghosts when the third call had been sounded.

The sister was troubled, for she knew that at the third call the stone walls around the king's houses would close and her brother would be held fast forever in the spirit-land, so she uttered her incantations and passed the guard. Softly she called. Her brother reluctantly came. She seized him and pushed him outside. Then they heard the third call, and met the multitude of ghosts coming inland from their sports in the sea, and other multitudes hastening homeward from their work and sports on the land.

They met a beautiful young woman who called to them to come to her home, and pointed to a point of rock where many birds were resting. The sister struck her brother and forced him down to the seaside where she had her home and her responsibility, for she was one of the guardians of the entrance to the spirit-world.

She knew well what must be done to restore the spirit to the body, so she told her brother they must at once obey the command of the king; but the brother had seen the delights of the life of the aumakuas and wanted to stay. He tried to slip away and hide, but his sister held him fast and compelled him to go along the beach to his old home and his waiting body.

When they came to the place where the body lay she found a hole in the corner of the house and pushed the spirit through. When he saw the body he was very much afraid and tried to escape, but the sister caught him and pushed him inside the foot up to the knee. He did not like the smell of the body and tried to rush back, but she pushed him inside again and held the foot fast and shook him and made him go to the head.

The family heard a little sound in the mouth and saw breath moving the breast, then they knew that he was alive again. They warmed the body and gave a little food. When strength returned he told his family all about his wonderful journey into the land of ghosts.

MALUAE AND THE UNDERWORLD

This is a story from Manoa Valley, back of Honolulu. In the upper end of the valley, at the foot of the highest mountains on the island Oahu, lived Maluae. He was a farmer, and had chosen this land because rain fell abundantly on the mountains, and the streams brought down fine soil from the decaying forests and disintegrating rocks, fertilizing his plants.

Here he cultivated bananas and taro and sweet potatoes. His bananas grew rapidly by the sides of the brooks, and yielded large bunches of fruit from their tree-like stems; his taro filled small walled-in pools, growing in the water like water-lilies, until the roots were matured, when the plants were pulled up and the roots boiled and prepared for food; his sweet potatoes – a vegetable known among the ancient New Zealanders as ku-maru, and supposed to have come from Hawai'i – were planted on the drier uplands.

Thus he had plenty of food continually growing, and ripening from time to time. Whenever he gathered any of his food products he brought a part to his family temple and placed it on an altar before the gods Kane and Kanaloa, then he took the rest to his home for his family to eat.

He had a boy whom he dearly loved, whose name was Kaa-lii (rolling chief). This boy was a careless, rollicking child.

One day the boy was tired and hungry. He passed by the temple of the gods and saw bananas, ripe and sweet, on the little platform before the gods. He took these bananas and ate them all.

The gods looked down on the altar expecting to find food, but it was all gone and there was nothing for them. They were very angry, and ran out after the boy. They caught him eating the bananas, and killed him. The body they left lying under the trees, and taking out his ghost threw it into the Underworld.

The father toiled hour after hour cultivating his food plants, and when wearied returned to his home. On the way he met the two gods. They told him how his boy had robbed them of their sacrifices and how they had punished him. They said, 'We have sent his ghost body to the lowest regions of the Underworld,'

The father was very sorrowful and heavy hearted as he went on his way to his desolate home. He searched for the body of his boy, and at last found it. He saw too that the story of the gods was true, for partly eaten bananas filled the mouth, which was set in death.

He wrapped the body very carefully in kapa cloth made from the bark of trees. He carried it into his rest-house and laid it on the sleeping-mat. After a time he lay down beside the body, refusing all food, and planning to die with his boy. He thought if he could escape from his own body he would be able to go down where the ghost of his boy had been sent. If he could find that ghost he hoped to take it to the other part of the Underworld, where they could be happy together.

He placed no offerings on the altar of the gods. No prayers were chanted. The afternoon and evening passed slowly. The gods waited for their worshipper, but he came not. They looked down on the altar of sacrifice, but there was nothing for them.

The night passed and the following day. The father lay by the side of his son, neither eating nor drinking, and longing only for death. The house was tightly closed.

Then the gods talked together, and Kane said: 'Maluae eats no food, he prepares no awa to drink, and there is no water by him. He is near the door of the Underworld. If he should die, we would be to blame.'

Kanaloa said: 'He has been a good man, but now we do not hear any prayers. We are losing our worshipper. We in quick anger killed his son. Was this the right reward? He has called us morning and evening in his worship. He has provided fish and fruits and vegetables for our altars. He has always prepared awa from the juice of the yellow awa root for us to drink. We have not paid him well for his care.'

Then they decided to go and give life to the father, and permit him to take his ghost body and go down into Pō, the dark land, to bring back the ghost of the boy. So they went to Maluae and told him they were sorry for what they had done.

The father was very weak from hunger, and longing for death, and could scarcely listen to them.

When Kane said, 'Have you love for your child?' the father whispered: 'Yes. My love is without end.'

'Can you go down into the dark land and get that spirit and put it back in the body which lies here?'

'No,' the father said, 'no, I can only die and go to live with him and make him happier by taking him to a better place.'

Then the gods said, 'We will give you the power to go after your boy and we will help you to escape the dangers of the land of ghosts.'

Then the father, stirred by hope, rose up and took food and drink. Soon he was strong enough to go on his journey.

The gods gave him a ghost body and also prepared a hollow stick like bamboo, in which they put food, battle-weapons, and a piece of burning lava for fire.

Not far from Honolulu is a beautiful modern estate with fine roads, lakes, running brooks, and interesting valleys extending back into the mountain range. This is called by the very ancient name Moanalua (two lakes). Near the seacoast of this estate was one of the most noted ghost localities of the islands. The ghosts after wandering over the island Oahu would come to this place to find a way into their real home, the Underworld, or, as the Hawaiians usually called it, Pō.

Here was a ghostly breadfruit-tree named Lei-walo, possibly meaning 'the eight wreaths' or 'the eighth wreath' – the last wreath of leaves from the land of the living which would meet the eyes of the dying.

The ghosts would leap or fly or climb into the branches of this tree, trying to find a rotten branch upon which they could sit until it broke and threw them into the dark sea below.

Maluae climbed up the breadfruit-tree. He found a branch upon which some ghosts were sitting waiting for it to fall. His weight was so much greater than theirs that the branch broke at once, and down they all fell into the land of Pō.

He needed merely to taste the food in his hollow cane to have new life and strength. This he had done when he climbed the tree; thus he had been able to push past the fabled guardians of the pathway of the ghosts in the Upper-world. As he entered the Underworld he again tasted the food of the gods and he felt himself growing stronger and stronger.

He took a magic war-club and a spear out of the cane given by the gods. Ghostly warriors tried to hinder his entrance into the different districts of the dark land. The spirits of dead chiefs challenged him when he passed their homes. Battle after battle was fought. His magic club struck the warriors down, and his spear tossed them aside.

Sometimes he was warmly greeted and aided by ghosts of kindly spirit. Thus he went from place to place, searching for his boy, finding him at last, as the Hawaiians quaintly expressed it, 'down in the papa-ku' (the established foundation of Pō), choking and suffocating from the bananas of ghost-land which he was compelled to continually force into his mouth.

The father caught the spirit of the boy and started back toward the Upper-world, but the ghosts surrounded him. They tried to catch him and take the spirit away from him. Again the father partook of the food of the gods. Once more he wielded his war-club, but the hosts of enemies were too great. Multitudes arose on all sides, crushing him by their overwhelming numbers.

At last he raised his magic hollow cane and took the last portion of food. Then he poured out the portion of burning lava which the gods had placed inside. It fell upon the dry floor of the Underworld. The flames dashed into the trees and the shrubs of ghost-land. Fire-holes opened in the floor and streams of lava burst out.

Backward fled the multitudes of spirits. The father thrust the spirit of the boy quickly into the empty magic cane and rushed swiftly up to his home-land. He brought the spirit to the body lying in the rest-house and forced it to find again its living home.

Afterward the father and the boy took food to the altars of the gods, and chanted the accustomed prayers heartily and loyally all the rest of their lives.

THE DECEIVING OF KEWA

A poem, or mourning chant, of the Māoris of New Zealand has many references to the deeds of their ancestors in Hawaiki, which in this case surely has reference to the Hawaiian Islands. Among the first lines of this poem is the expression, 'Kewa was deceived.' An explanatory note is given which covers almost two pages of the Journal of the Polynesian Society in which the poem is published. In this note the outline of the story of the deceiving of Kewa is quite fully translated, and is substantially the same as 'The Bride from the Underworld.'

'The Deceiving of Kewa,' as the New Zealand story is called, has this record among the Māoris. 'This narrative is of old, of ancient times, very, very old. "The Deceiving of Kewa" is an old, old story.' Milu in some parts of the Pacific is the name of the place where the spirits of the dead dwell. Sometimes it is the name of the ruler of that place. In this ancient New Zealand legend it takes the place of Hiku, and is the name of the person who goes down into the depths after his bride, while the spirit-king is called Kewa, a part of the name Kewalu, which was the name of the Hawaiian bride whose ghost was brought back from the grave.

This, then, is the New Zealand legend, 'The Deceiving of Kewa.' There once lived in Hawaiki a chief and his wife. They had a child, a girl, born to them; then the mother died. The chief took another wife, who was not pleasing to the people. His anger was so great that the chief went away to the great forest of Tāne (the god Kane in Hawaiian), and there built a house for himself and his wife.

After a time a son was born to them and the father named him Miru. This father was a great tohunga (kahuna), or priest, as well as a chief. He taught Miru all the supreme kinds of knowledge, all the invocations and incantations, those for the stars, for the winds, for foods, for the sea, and for the land. He taught him the peculiar incantations which would enable him to meet all cunning tricks and enmities of man. He learned also all the great powers of witchcraft. It is said that on one occasion Miru and his father went to a river, a great river. Here the child experimented with his powerful charms. He was a child of the forest and knew the charm which could conquer the trees. Now there was a tall tree growing by the side of the river. When Miru saw it he recited his incantations. As he came to the end the tree fell, the head reaching right across the river. They left the tree lying in this way that it might be used as a bridge by the people who came to the river. Thus he was conscious of his power to correctly use the mighty invocations which his father had taught him.

The years passed and the boy became a young man. His was a lonely life, and he often wondered if there were not those who could be his companions. At last he asked his parents: 'Are we here, all of us? Have I no other relative in the world?'

His parents answered, 'You have a sister, but she dwells at a distant place.'

When Miru heard this he arose and proceeded to search for his sister, and he happily came to the very place where she dwelt. There the young people were gathered in their customary place for playing teka (Hawaiian keha). The teka was a dart which was thrown along the ground, usually the hard beach of the seashore. Miru watched the game for some time and then returned to his home in the forest. He told his father about the teka and the way it was played. Then the chief prepared a teka for Miru, selected from the best tree and fashioned while appropriate charms were repeated.

Miru threw his dart along the slopes covered by the forest and its underbrush, but the ground was uneven and the undergrowth retarded the dart. Then Miru found a plain and practised until he was very expert.

After a while he came to the place where his sister lived. When the young people threw their darts he threw his. Aha! it flew indeed and was lost in the distance. When the sister beheld him she at once felt a great desire toward him.

The people tried to keep Miru with them, pleading with him to stay, and even following him as he returned to his forest home, but they caught him not. Frequently he repeated his visits, but never stayed long.

The sister, whose name is not given in the New Zealand legends, was disheartened, and hanged herself until she was dead. The body was laid in its place for the time of wailing. Miru and his father came to the uhunga, or place of mourning. The people had not known that Miru was the brother of the one who was dead. They welcomed the father and son according to their custom. Then the young man said, 'After I leave, do not bury my sister.' So the body was left in its place when the young man arose.

He went on his way till he saw a canoe floating. He then gave the command to his companions and they all paddled away in the canoe. They paddled on for a long distance, in fact to Rerenga-wai-rua, the point of land in New Zealand from which the spirits of the dead take their last leap as they go down to the Underworld. When they reached this place they rested, and Miru let go the anchor. He then said to his companions, 'When you see the anchor rope shaking, pull it up, but wait here for me.'

The young man then leaped into the water and went down, down near the bottom, and then entered a cave. This cave was the road by which the departed spirits went to spirit-land. Miru soon saw a house standing there. It was the home of Kewa, the chief of the Underworld. Within the house was his sister in spirit form.

Miru carried with him his nets which were given magic power, with which he hoped to catch the spirit of his sister. In many ways he endeavored to induce her ghost to come forth from the house of Kewa, but she would not come. He commenced whipping his top in the yard outside, but could not attract her attention. At last he set up a swing and many of the ghosts joined in the pastime. For a long time the sister remained within, but eventually came forth induced by the attraction of the swing and by the appearance of Miru. Miru then took the spirit in his arms and began to swing.

Higher and higher they rose whilst he incited the ghosts to increase to the utmost the flight of the moari, or swing. On reaching the highest point he gathered the spirit of the sister into his net, then letting go the swing away they flew and alighted quite outside the spirit-land.

Thence he went to the place where the anchor of the floating canoe was. Shaking the rope his friends understood the signal. He was drawn up with the ghost in his net. He entered the canoe and returned home. On arrival at the settlement the people were still lamenting. What was that to him? Taking the spirit he laid it on the dead body, at the same time reciting his incantations. The spirit gradually entered the body and the sister was alive again. This is the end of the narrative, but it is of old, of ancient times, very, very old. 'The Deceiving of Kewa' is an old, old story.

In the Māori poem in which the reference to Kewa is made which brought out the above translation of one of the old New Zealand stories are also many other references to semi-historical characters and events. At the close of the poem is the following note: 'The lament is so full of references to the ancient history of the Māoris that it would take a volume to explain them all. Most of the incidents referred to occurred in Hawaiki before the migration of the Māoris to New Zealand or at least five hundred to six hundred years ago.'

Another New Zealand legend ought to be noticed in connection with the Hawaiian story of Hiku (Miru, New Zealand) seeking his sister in the Underworld. In what is probably the more complete Hawaiian story Hiku had a magic arrow which

341

flew long distances and led him to the place where his sister-wife could be found.

In a New Zealand legend a magic dart leads a chief by the name of Tama in his search for his wife, who had been carried away to spirit-land. He threw the dart and followed it from place to place until he found a wrecked canoe, near which lay the body of his wife and her companions. He tried to bring her back to life, but his incantations were not strong enough to release the spirit.

Evidently the Hawaiian legend became a little fragmentary while being transplanted from the Hawaiian Islands to New Zealand. Hiku, the young chief who overcomes Miru of the spirit-world, loses his name entirely. Kewalu, the sister, also loses her name, a part of which, Kewa, is given to the ruler of the Underworld, and the magic dart is placed in the hands of Tama in an entirely distinct legend which still keeps the thought of the wife-seeker. There can scarcely be any question but that the original legend belongs to the Hawaiian Islands, and was carried to New Zealand in the days of the sea-rovers.

A GLOSSARY OF
MYTH & FOLKLORE

Aaru Heavenly paradise where the blessed go after death.

Ab Heart or mind.

Abiku (Yoruba) Person predestined to die. Also known as ogbanje.

Absál Nurse to Saláman, who died after their brief love affair.

Achilles The son of Peleus and the sea-nymph Thetis, who distinguished himself in the Trojan War. He was made almost immortal by his mother, who dipped him in the River Styx, and he was invincible except for a portion of his heel which remained out of the water.

Acropolis Citadel in a Greek city.

Adad-Ea Ferryman to Ut-Napishtim, who carried Gilgamesh to visit his ancestor.

Adapa Son of Ea and a wise sage.

Adar God of the sun, who is worshipped primarily in Nippur.

Aditi Sky goddess and mother of the gods.

Adityas Vishnu, children of Aditi, including Indra, Mitra, Rudra, Tvashtar, Varuna and Vishnu.

Aeneas The son of Anchises and the goddess Aphrodite, reared by a nymph. He led the Dardanian troops in the Trojan War According to legend, he became the founder of Rome.

Aengus Óg Son of Dagda and Boann (a woman said to have given the Boyne river its name), Aengus is the Irish god of love whose stronghold is reputed to have been at New Grange. The famous tale 'Dream of Aengus' tells of how he fell in love with a maiden he had dreamt of. He eventually discovered that she was to be found at the Lake of the Dragon's Mouth in Co. Tipperary, but that she lived every alternate year in the form of a swan. Aengus thus plunged into the lake transforming himself also into the shape of a swan. Then the two flew back together to his palace on the Boyne where they lived out their days as guardians of would-be lovers.

Aesir Northern gods who made their home in Asgard; there are twelve in number.

Afrásiyáb Son of Poshang, king of Túrán, who led an army against the ruling shah Nauder. Afrásiyáb became ruler of Persia on defeating Nauder.

Afterlife Life after death or paradise, reached only by the process of preserving the body from decay through embalming and preparing it for reincarnation.

Agamemnon A famous King of Mycenae. He married Helen of Sparta's sister Clytemnestra. When Paris abducted Helen, beginning the Trojan War, Menelaus called on Agamemnon to raise the Greek troops. He had to sacrifice his daughter Iphigenia in order to get a fair wind to travel to Troy.

Agastya A rishi (sage). Leads hermits to Rama.

Agemo (Yoruba) A chameleon who aided Olorun in outwitting Olokun, who was angry at him for letting Obatala create life on her lands without her permission. Agemo outwitted Olokun by changing colour, letting her think that he and Olorun were better cloth dyers than she was. She admitted defeat and there was peace between the gods once again.

Aghasur A dragon sent by Kans to destroy Krishna.

Aghríras Son of Poshang and brother of Afrásiyáb, who was killed by his brother.

Agni The god of fire.

Agora Greek marketplace.

Ahura-Mazda Supreme god of the Persians, god of the sky. Similar to the Hindu god Varuna.

Ajax Ajax the Greater was the bravest, after Achilles, of all warriors at Troy, fighting Hector in single combat and distinguishing himself in the Battle of the Ships. He was not chosen as the bravest warrior and eventually went mad.

Ajax of Locris Another warrior at Troy. When Troy was captured, he committed the ultimate sacrilege by seizing Cassandra from her sanctuary with the Palladium.

Aje (Igbo) Goddess of the earth and the underworld.

Aje (Yoruba) Goddess of the River Niger, daughter of Yemoja.

Akhet Season of the year when the River Nile traditionally flooded.

Akkadian Person of the first Mesopotamian empire, centred in Akkad.

Akwán Diw An evil spirit who appeared as a wild ass in the court of Kai-khosráu. Rustem fought and defeated the demon, presenting its head to Kai-khosráu.

Alba Irish and Scottish Gaelic word for Scotland.

Alberich King of the dwarfs.

Alcinous King of the Phaeacians.

Alf-heim Home of the elves, ruled by Frey.

All Hallowmass All Saints' Day.

Allfather Another name for Odin; Yggdrasill was created by Allfather.

Alsvider Steed of the moon (Mani) chariot.

Alsvin Steed of the sun (Sol) chariot.

Amado Outer panelling of a dwelling, usually made of wood.

Ama-no-uzume Goddess of the dawn, meditation and the arts, who showed courage when faced with a giant who scared the other deities, including Ninigi. Also known as Uzume.

Amaterasu Goddess of the sun and daughter of Izanagi after Izanami's death; she became ruler of the High Plains of Heaven on her father's withdrawal from the world. Sister of Tsuki-yomi and Susanoo.

Ambalika Daughter of the king of Benares.

Ambika Daughter of the king of Benares.

Ambrosia Food of the gods.

Amemet Eater of the dead, monster who devoured the souls of the unworthy.

Amen Original creator deity.

Amen-Ra A being created from the fusion of Ra and Osiris. He champions the poor and those in trouble. Similar to the Greek god Zeus.

Ananda Disciple of Buddha.

Anansi One of the most popular African animal myths, Anansi the spider is a clever and shrewd character who outwits his fellow animals to get his own way. He is an entertaining but morally dubious character. Many African countries tell Anansi stories.

Ananta Thousand-headed snake that sprang from Balarama's mouth, Vishnu's attendant, serpent of infinite time.

Andhrímnir Cook at Valhalla.

Andvaranaut Ring of Andvari, the King of the dwarfs.

Angada Son of Vali, one of the monkey host.

Anger-Chamber Room designated for an angry queen.

Angurboda Loki's first wife, and the mother of Hel, Fenris and Jormungander.

Aniruddha Son of Pradyumna.

Anjana Mother of Hanuman.

Anunnaki Great spirits or gods of Earth.

Ansar God of the sky and father of Ea and Anu. Brother-husband to Kishar. Also known as Anshar or Asshur.

Anshumat A mighty chariot fighter.

Anu God of the sky and lord of heaven, son of Ansar and Kishar.

Anubis Guider of souls and ruler of the underworld before Osiris; he was one of the divinities who brought Osiris back to life. He is portrayed as a canid, African wolf or jackal.

Apep Serpent and emblem of chaos.

Apollo One of the twelve Olympian gods, son of Zeus and Leto. He is attributed with being the god of plague, music, song and prophecy.

Apsaras Dancing girls of Indra's court and heavenly nymphs.

Apsu Primeval domain of fresh water, originally part of Tiawath with whom he mated to have Mummu. The term is also used for the abyss from which creation came.

Aquila The divine eagle.

Arachne A Lydian woman with great skill in weaving. She was challenged in a competition by the jealous Athene who destroyed her work and when she killed herself, turned her into a spider destined to weave for eternity.

Aralu Goddess of the underworld, also known as Eres-ki-Gal. Married to Nergal.

Ares God of War, 'gold-changer of corpses', and the son of Zeus and Hera.

Argonauts Heroes who sailed with Jason on the ship Argo to fetch the golden fleece from Colchis.

Ariki A high chief, a leader, a master, a lord.

Arjuna The third of the Pandavas.

Aroha Affection, love.

Artemis The virgin goddess of the chase, attributed with being the moon goddess and the primitive mother-goddess. She was daughter of Zeus and Leto.

Arundhati The Northern Crown.

Asamanja Son of Sagara.

Asclepius God of healing who often took the form of a snake. He is the son of Apollo by Coronis.

Asgard Home of the gods, at one root of Yggdrasill.

Ashvatthaman Son of Drona.

Ashvins Twin horsemen, sons of the sun, benevolent gods and related to the divine.

Ashwapati Uncle of Bharata and Satrughna.

Asipû Wizard.

Asopus The god of the River Asopus.

Assagai Spear, usually made from hardwood tipped with iron and used in battle.

Astrolabe Instrument for making astronomical measurements.

Asuras Titans, demons, and enemies of the gods with magical powers.

Atef crown White crown made up of the Hedjet, the white crown of Upper Egypt, and red feathers.

Atem The first creator-deity, he is also thought to be the finisher of the world. Also known as Tem.

Athene Virgin warrior-goddess, born from the forehead of Zeus when he swallowed his wife Metis. Plays a key role in the travels of Odysseus, and Perseus.

Atlatl Spear-thrower.

Atua A supernatural being, a god.

Atua-toko A small carved stick, the symbol of the god whom it represents. It was stuck in the ground whilst holding incantations to its presiding god.

Augeas King of Elis, one of the Argonauts.

Augsburg Tyr's city.

Avalon Legendary island where Excalibur was created and where Arthur went to recover from his wounds. It is said he will return from Avalon one day to reclaim his kingdom.

Ba Dead person or soul. Also known as ka.

Bairn Little child, also called bairnie.

Balarama Brother of Krishna.

Balder Son of Frigga; his murder causes Ragnarok. Also spelled as Baldur.

Bali Brother of Sugriva and one of the five great monkeys in the *Ramayana*.

Balor The evil, one-eyed King of the Fomorians and also grandfather of Lugh of the Long Arm. It was prophesied that Balor would one day be slain by his own grandson so he locked his daughter away on a remote island where he intended that she would never fall pregnant. But Cian, father of Lugh, managed to reach the island disguised as a woman, and Balor's daughter eventually bore him a child. During the second battle of Mag Tured (or Moytura), Balor was killed by Lugh who slung a stone into his giant eye.

Ban King of Benwick, father of Lancelot and brother of King Bors.

Bannock Flat loaf of bread, typically of oat or barley, usually cooked on a griddle.

Banshee Mythical spirit, usually female, who bears tales of imminent death. They often deliver the news by wailing or keening outside homes. Spelled *bean sí* in Gaelic.

Bard Traditionally a storyteller, poet or music composer whose work often focused on legends.

Barû Seer.

Basswood Any of several North American linden trees with a soft light-coloured wood.

Bastet Goddess of love, fertility and sex and a solar deity. She is often portrayed with the head of a cat.

Bateta (Yoruba) The first human, created alongside Hanna by the Toad and reshaped into human form by the Moon.

Bau Goddess of humankind and the sick, and known as the 'divine physician'. Daughter of Anu.

Bawn Fortified enclosure surrounding a castle.

Beaver Largest rodent in the United States of America, held in high esteem by Native American people. Although a land mammal, it spends a great deal of time in water and has a dense waterproof fur coat to protect it from harsh weather conditions.

Behula Daughter of Saha.

Bel Name for the god En-lil, the word is also used as a title meaning 'lord'.

Belus Deity who helped form the heavens and earth and created animals and celestial beings. Similar to Zeus in Greek mythology.

Benten Goddess of the sea and one of the Seven Divinities of Luck. Also referred to as the goddess of love, beauty and eloquence and as being the personification of wisdom.

Bere Barley.

Berossus Priest of Bel who wrote a history of Babylon.

Berserker Norse warrior who fights with a frenzied rage.

Bestla Giant mother of Aesir's mortal element.

Bhadra A mighty elephant.

Bhagavati Shiva's wife, also known as Parvati.

Bhagiratha Son of Dilipa.

Bharadhwaja Father of Drona and a hermit.

Bharata One of Dasharatha's four sons.

Bhaumasur A demon, slain by Krishna.

Bhima The second of the Pandavas.

Bhimasha King of Rajagriha and disciple of Buddha.

Bier Frame on which a coffin or dead body is placed before being carried to the grave.

Bifrost Rainbow bridge presided over by Heimdall.

Big-Belly One of Ravana's monsters.

Bilskirnir Thor's palace.

Bodach The term means 'old man'. The Highlanders believed that the Bodach crept down chimneys in order to steal naughty children. In other territories, he was a spirit who warned of death.

Bodkin Large, blunt needle used for threading strips of cloth or tape through cloth; short pointed dagger or blade.

Boer Person of Dutch origin who settled in southern Africa in the late seventeenth century. The term means 'farmer'. Boer people are often called Afrikaners.

Bogle Ghost or phantom; goblin-like creature.

Boliaun Ragwort, a weed with ragged leaves.

Book of the Dead Book for the dead, thought to be written by Thoth, texts from which were written on papyrus and buried with the dead, or carved on the walls of tombs, pyramids or sarcophagi.

Bors King of Gaul and brother of King Ban.

Bothy Small cottage or hut.

Brahma Creator of the world, mythical origin of colour (caste).

Brahmadatta King of Benares.

Brahman Member of the highest Hindu caste, traditionally a priest.

Bran In Scottish legend, Bran is the great hunting hound of Fionn Mac Chumail. In Irish mythology, he is a great hero.

Branstock Giant oak tree in the Volsung's hall; Odin placed a sword in it and challenged the guests of a wedding to withdraw it.

Brave Young warrior of Native American descent, sometimes also referred to as a 'buck'.

Bree Thin broth or soup.

Breidablik Balder's palace.

Brigit Scottish saint or spirit associated with the coming of spring.

Brisingamen Freyia's necklace.

Britomartis A Cretan goddess, also known as Dictynna.

Brocéliande Legendary enchanted forest and the supposed burial place of Merlin.

Brokki Dwarf who makes a deal with Loki, and who makes Miolnir, Draupnir and Gulinbursti.

Brollachan A shapeless spirit of unknown origin. One of the most frightening in Scottish mythology, it spoke only two words, 'Myself' and 'Thyself', taking the shape of whatever it sat upon.

Brownie A household spirit or creature which took the form of a small man (usually hideously ugly) who undertakes household chores, and mill or farm work, in exchange for a bowl of milk.

Brugh Borough or town.

Brunhilde A Valkyrie found by Sigurd.

Buddha Founder of buddhism, Gautama, avatar of Vishnu in Hinduism.

Buddhism Buddhism arrived in China in the first century BCE via the silk trading route from India and Central Asia. Its founder was Guatama Siddhartha (the Buddha), a religious teacher in northern India. Buddhist doctrine declared that by destroying the causes of all suffering, mankind could attain perfect enlightenment. The religion encouraged a new respect for all living things and brought with it the idea of reincarnation; i.e. that the soul returns to the earth after death in another form, dictated by the individual's behaviour in his previous life. By the fourth century, Buddhism was the dominant religion in China, retaining its powerful influence over the nation until the mid-ninth century.

Buffalo A type of wild ox, once widely scattered over the Great Plains of North America. Also known as a 'bison', the buffalo was an important food source for Native American tribes and its hide was also used in the construction of tepees and to make clothing. The buffalo was also sometimes revered as a totem animal, i.e. venerated as a direct ancestor of the tribesmen, and its skull used in ceremonial fashion.

Bull of Apis Sacred bull, thought to be the son of Hathor.

Bulu Sacrificial rite.

Bundles, sacred These bundles contained various venerated objects of the tribe, believed to have supernatural powers. Custody or ownership of the bundle was never lightly entered upon, but involved the learning of endless songs and ritual dances.

Bushel Unit of measurement, usually used for agricultural products or food.

Bushi Warrior.

Byre Barn for keeping cattle.

Byrny Coat of mail.

Cacique King or prince.

Cailleach Bheur A witch with a blue face who represents winter. When she is reborn each autumn, snow falls. She is mother of the god of youth (Angus mac Og).

Calabash Gourd from the calabash tree, commonly used as a bottle.

Calchas The seer of Mycenae who accompanied the Greek fleet to Troy. It was his prophecy which stated that Troy would never be taken without the aid of Achilles.

Calpulli Village house, or group or clan of families.

Calumet Ceremonial pipe used by Native Americans.

Calypso A nymph who lived on the island of Ogygia.

Camaxtli Tlascalan god of war and the chase, similar to Huitzilopochtli.

Camelot King Arthur's castle and centre of his realm.

Caoineag A banshee.

Caravanserai Traveller's inn, traditionally found in Asia or North Africa.

Carle Term for a man, often old; peasant.

Cat A black cat has great mythological significance, is often the bearer of bad luck, a symbol of black magic, and the familiar of a witch. Cats were also the totem for many tribes.

Cath Sith A fairy cat who was believed to be a witch transformed.

Cazi Magical person or influence.

Ceasg A Scottish mermaid with the body of a maiden and the tail of a salmon.

Ceilidh Party.

Cerberus The three-headed dog who guarded the entrance to the Underworld.

Chalchiuhtlicue Goddess of water and the sick or newborn, and wife of Tlaloc. She is often symbolized as a small frog.

Changeling A fairy substitute-child left by fairies in place of a human child they have stolen.

Channa Guatama's charioteer.

Chaos A state from which the universe was created – caused by fire and ice meeting.

Charon The ferryman of the dead who carries souls across the River Styx to Hades.

Charybdis *See* Scylla and Charybdis.

Chicomecohuatl Chief goddess of maize and one of a group of deities called Centeotl, who care for all aspects of agriculture.

Chicomoztoc Legendary mountain and place of origin of the Aztecs. The name means 'seven caves'.

Chinawezi Primordial serpent.

Chinvat Bridge Bridge of the Gatherer, which the souls of the righteous cross to reach Mount Alborz or the world of the dead. Unworthy beings who try to cross Chinvat Bridge fall or are dragged into a place of eternal punishment.

Chitambaram Sacred city of Shiva's dance.

Chrysaor Son of Poseidon and Medusa, born from the severed neck of Medusa when Perseus beheaded her.

Chryseis Daughter of Chryses who was taken by Agamemnon in the battle of Troy.

Chullasubhadda Wife of Buddha-elect (Sumedha).

Chunda A good smith who entertains Buddha.

Churl Mean or unkind person.

Circe An enchantress and the daughter of Helius. She lived on the island of Aeaea with the power to change men to beasts.

Citlalpol The Mexican name for Venus, or the Great Star, and one of the only stars they worshipped. Also known as Tlauizcalpantecutli, or Lord of the Dawn.

Cleobis and Biton Two men of Argos who dragged the wagon carrying their mother, priestess of Hera, from Argos to the sanctuary.

Clio Muse of history and prophecy.

Clytemnestra Daughter of Tyndareus, sister of Helen, who married Agamemnon but deserted him when he sacrificed Iphigenia, their daughter, at the beginning of the Trojan War.

Coatepetl Mythical mountain, known as the 'serpent mountain'.

Coatl Serpent.

Coatlicue Earth mother and celestial goddess, she gave birth to Huitzilopochtli and his sister, Coyolxauhqui, and the moon and stars.

Codex Ancient book, often a list with pages folded into a zigzag pattern.

Confucius (Kong Fuzi) Regarded as China's greatest sage and ethical teacher, Confucius (551–479 BCE) was not especially revered during his lifetime and had a small following of some three thousand people. After the Burning of the Books in 213 BCE, interest in his philosophies became widespread. Confucius believed that mankind was essentially good, but argued for a highly structured society, presided over by a strong central government which would set the highest moral standards. The individual's sense of duty and obligation, he argued, would play a vital role in maintaining a well-run state.

Coracle Small, round boat, similar to a canoe. Also known as curragh or currach.

Coyolxauhqui Goddess of the moon and sister to Huitzilopochtli, she was decapitated by her brother after trying to kill their mother.

Creel Large basket made of wicker, usually used for fish.

Crodhmara Fairy cattle.

Cronan Musical humming, thought to resemble a cat purring or the drone of bagpipes.

Crow Usually associated with battle and death, but many mythological figures take this form.

Cu Sith A great fairy dog, usually green and oversized.

Cubit Ancient measurement, equal to the approximate length of a forearm.

Cuculain Irish warrior and hero. Also known as Cuchulainn.

Cutty Girl.

Cyclopes One-eyed giants who were imprisoned in Tartarus by Uranus and Cronus, but released by Zeus, for whom they made thunderbolts. Also a tribe of pastoralists who live without laws, and on, whenever possible, human flesh.

Daedalus Descendant of the Athenian King Erechtheus and son of Eupalamus. He killed his nephew and apprentice. Famed for constructing the labyrinth to house the Minotaur, in which he was later imprisoned. He constructed wings for himself and his son to make their escape.

Dagda One of the principal gods of the Tuatha De Danann, the father and chief, the Celtic equivalent of Zeus. He was the god reputed to have led the People of Dana in their successful conquest of the Fir Bolg.

Dagon God of fish and fertility; he is sometimes described as a sea-monster or chthonic god.

Daikoku God of wealth and one of the gods of luck.

Daimyō Powerful lord or magnate.

Daksha The chief Prajapati.

Dana Also known as Danu, a goddess worshipped from antiquity by the Celts and considered to be the ancestor of the Tuatha De Danann.

Danae Daughter of Acrisius, King of Argos. Acrisius trapped her in a cave when he was warned that his grandson would be the cause of his ultimate death. Zeus came to her and Perseus was born.

Danaids The fifty daughters of Danaus of Argos, by ten mothers.

Daoine Sidhe The people of the Hollow Hills, or Otherworld.

Dardanus Son of Zeus and Electra, daughter of Atlas.

Dasharatha A Manu amongst men, King of Koshala, father of Santa.

Deianeira Daughter of Oeneus, who married Heracles after he won her in a battle with the River Achelous.

Deirdre A beautiful woman doomed to cause the deaths of three Irish heroes and bring war to the whole country. After a soothsayer prophesied her fate, Deidre's father hid her away from the world to prevent it. However, fate finds its way and the events come to pass before Deidre eventually commits suicide to remain with her love.

Demeter Goddess of agriculture and nutrition, whose name means earth mother. She is the mother of Persephone.

Demophoon Son of King Celeus of Eleusis, who was nursed by Demeter and then dropped in the fire when she tried to make him immortal.

Dervish Member of a religious order, often Sufi, known for their wild dancing and whirling.

Desire The god of love.

Deva A god other than the supreme God.

Devadatta Buddha's cousin, plots evil against Buddha.

Dhrishtadyumna Twin brother of Draupadi, slays Drona.

Dibarra God of plague. Also a demonic character or evil spirit.

Dik-dik Dwarf antelope native to eastern and southern Africa.

Dilipa Son of Anshumat, father of Bhagiratha.

Dionysus The god of wine, vegetation and the life force, and of ecstasy. He was considered to be outside the Greek pantheon, and generally thought to have begun life as a mortal.

Dioscuri Castor and Polydeuces, the twin sons of Zeus and Leda, who are important deities.

Distaff Tool used when spinning which holds the wool or flax and keeps the fibres from tangling.

Divan Privy council.

Divots Turfs.

Dog The dog is a symbol of humanity, and usually has a role helping the hero of the myth or legend. Fionn's Bran and Grey Dog are two examples of wild beasts transformed to become invaluable servants.

Dōshin Government official.

Dossal Ornamental altar cloth.

Doughty Persistent and brave person.

Dragon Important animal in Japanese culture, symbolizing power, wealth, luck and success.

Draiglin' Hogney Ogre.

Draupadi Daughter of Drupada.

Draupnir Odin's famous ring, fashioned by Brokki.

Drona A Brahma, son of the great sage Bharadwaja.

Druid An ancient order of Celtic priests held in high esteem who flourished in the pre-Christian era. The word 'druid' is derived from an ancient Celtic one meaning 'very knowledgeable'. These individuals were believed to have mystical powers and in ancient Irish literature possess the ability to conjure up magical charms, to create tempests, to curse and debilitate their enemies and to perform as soothsayers to the royal courts.

Drupada King of the Panchalas.

Dryads Nymphs of the trees.

Dun A stronghold or royal abode surrounded by an earthen wall.

Durga Goddess, wife of Shiva.

Durk Knife. Also spelled as dirk.

Duryodhana One of Drona's pupils.

Dvalin Dwarf visited by Loki; also the name for the stag on Yggdrasill.

Dwarfie Stone Prehistoric tomb or boulder.

Dwarfs Fairies and black elves are called dwarfs.

Dwarkanath The Lord of Dwaraka; Krishna.

Dyumatsena King of the Shalwas and father of Satyavan.

Ea God of water, light and wisdom, and one of the creator deities. He brought arts and civilization to humankind. Also known as Oannes and Nudimmud.

Eabani Hero originally created by Aruru to defeat Gilgamesh, the two became friends and destroyed Khumbaba together. He personifies the natural world.

Each Uisge The mythical water-horse which haunts lochs and appears in various forms.

Ebisu One of the gods of luck. He is also the god of labour and fishermen.

Echo A nymph who was punished by Hera for her endless stories told to distract Hera from Zeus's infidelity.

Ector King Arthur's foster father, who raised Arthur to protect him.

Edda Collection of prose and poetic myths and stories from the Norsemen.

Eight Immortals Three of these are reputed to be historical: Han Zhongli, born in Shaanxi, who rose to become a Marshal of the Empire in 21 BCE. Chang Kuo-Lao, who lived in the seventh to eighth century CE, and Lu Dongbin, who was born in 755 CE.

Einheriear Odin's guests at Valhalla.

Eisa Loki's daughter.

Ekake (Ibani) Person of great intelligence, which means 'tortoise'. Also known as Mbai (Igbo).

Ekalavya Son of the king of the Nishadas.

Electra Daughter of Agamemnon and Clytemnestra.

Eleusis A town in which the cult of Demeter is centred.

Elf Sigmund is buried by an elf; there are light and dark elves (the latter called dwarfs).

Elokos (Central African) Imps of dwarf-demons who eat human flesh.

Elpenor The youngest of Odysseus's crew who fell from the roof of Circe's house on Aeaea and visited with Odysseus at Hades.

Elysium The home of the blessed dead.

Emain Macha The capital of ancient Ulster.

Emma Dai-o King of hell and judge of the dead.

En-lil God of the lower world, storms and mist, who held sway over the ghostly animistic spirits, which at his bidding might pose as the friends or enemies of men. Also known as Bel.

Eos Goddess of the dawn and sister of the sun and moon.

Erichthonius A child born of the semen spilled when Hephaestus tried to rape Athene on the Acropolis.

Eridu The home of Ea and one of the two major cities of Babylonian civilization.

Erin Term for Ireland, originally spelled Éirinn.

Erirogho Magical mixture made from the ashes of the dead.

Eros God of Love, the son of Aphrodite.

Erpa Hereditary chief.

Erysichthon A Thessalian who cut down a grove sacred to Demeter, who punished him with eternal hunger.

Eshu (Yoruba) God of mischief. He also tests people's characters and controls law enforcement.

Eteocles Son of Oedipus.

Eumaeus Swineherd of Odysseus's family at Ithaca.

Euphemus A son of Poseidon who could walk on water. He sailed with the Argonauts.

Europa Daughter of King Agenor of Tyre, who was taken by Zeus to Crete.

Eurydice A Thracian nymph married to Orpheus.

Excalibur The magical sword given to Arthur by the Lady of the Lake. In some versions of the myths, Excalibur is also the sword that the young Arthur pulls from the stone to become king.

Fabulist Person who composes or tells fables.

Fafnir Shape-changer who kills his father and becomes a dragon to guard the family jewels. Slain by Sigurd.

Fairy The word is derived from 'Fays' which means Fates. They are immortal, with the gift of prophecy and of music, and their role changes according to the origin of the myth. They were often considered to be little people, with enormous propensity for mischief, but they are central to many myths and legends, with important powers.

Faro (Mali, Guinea) God of the sky.

Fates In Greek mythology, daughters of Zeus and Themis, who spin the thread of a mortal's life and cut it when his time is due. Called Norns in Viking mythology.

Fenris A wild wolf, who is the son of Loki. He roams the earth after Ragnarok.

Ferhad Sculptor who fell in love with Shireen, the wife of Khosru, and undertook a seemingly impossible task to clear a passage through the mountain of Beysitoun and join the rivers in return for winning Shireen's hand.

Fialar Red cock of Valhalla.

Fianna/Fenians The word 'fianna' was used in early times to describe young warrior-hunters. These youths evolved under the leadership of Finn Mac Cumaill as a highly skilled band of military men who took up service with various kings throughout Ireland.

Filheim Land of mist, at the end of one of Yggdrasill's roots.

Fingal Another name for Fionn Mac Chumail, used after MacPherson's Ossian in the eighteenth century.

Fionn Mac Chumail Irish and Scottish warrior, with great powers of fairness and wisdom. He is known not for physical strength but for knowledge, sense of justice, generosity and canny instinct. He had two hounds, which were later discovered to be his nephews transformed. He became head of the Fianna, or Féinn, fighting the enemies of Ireland and Scotland. He was the father of Oisin (also called Ossian, or other derivatives), and father or grandfather of Osgar.

Fir Bolg One of the ancient, pre-Gaelic peoples of Ireland who were reputed to have worshipped the god Bulga, meaning god of lighting. They are thought to have colonized Ireland around 1970 BCE, after the death of Nemed and to have reigned for a short period of thirty-seven years before their defeat by the Tuatha De Danann.

Fir Chlis Nimble men or merry dancers, who are the souls of fallen angels.

Flitch Side of salted and cured bacon.

Folkvang Freyia's palace.

Fomorians A race of monstrous beings, popularly conceived as sea-pirates with some supernatural characteristics who opposed the earliest settlers in Ireland, including the Nemedians and the Tuatha De Danann.

Frey Comes to Asgard with Freyia as a hostage following the war between the Aesir and the Vanir.

Freyia Comes to Asgard with Frey as a hostage following the war between the Aesir and the Vanir. Goddess of beauty and love.

Frigga Odin's wife and mother of gods; she is goddess of the earth.

Fuath Evil spirits which lived in or near the water.

Fulla Frigga's maidservant.

Furies Creatures born from the blood of Cronus, guarding the greatest sinners of the Underworld. Their power lay in their ability to drive mortals mad. Snakes writhed in their hair and around their waists.

Furoshiki Cloths used to wrap things.

Gae Bolg Cuchulainn alone learned the use of this weapon from the woman-warrior, Scathach and with it he slew his own son Connla and his closest friend, Ferdia. Gae Bolg translates as 'harpoon-like javelin' and the deadly weapon was reported to have been created by Bulga, the god of lighting.

Gaea Goddess of Earth, born from Chaos, and the mother of Uranus and Pontus. Also spelled as Gaia.

Gage Object of value presented to a challenger to symbolize good faith.

Galahad Knight of the Round Table, who took up the search for the Holy Grail. Son of Lancelot, Galahad is considered the purest and most perfect knight.

Galatea Daughter of Nereus and Doris, a sea-nymph loved by Polyphemus, the Cyclops.

Gandhari Mother of Duryodhana.

Gandharvas Demigods and musicians.

Gandjharva Musical ministrants of the upper air.

Ganesha Elephant-headed god of scribes and son of Shiva.

Ganges Sacred river personified by the goddess Ganga, wife of Shiva and daughter of the mount Himalaya.

Gareth of Orkney King Arthur's nephew and knight of the Round Table.

Garm Hel's hound.

Garuda King of the birds and mount Vishnu, the divine bird, attendant of Narayana.

Gautama Son of Suddhodana and also known as Siddhartha.

Gawain Nephew of King Arthur and knight of the Round Table, he is best known for his adventure with the Green Knight, who challenges one of Arthur's knights to cut off his head, but only if he agrees to be beheaded in turn in a year and a day, if the Green Knight survives. Gawain beheads the Green Knight, who simply replaces his head. At the appointed time, they meet, and the Green Knight swings his axe but merely nicks Gawain's skin instead of beheading him.

Geisha Performance artist or entertainer, usually female.

Geri Odin's wolf.

Ghommid (Yoruba) Term for mythological creatures such as goblins or ogres.

Giallar Bridge in Filheim.

Giallarhorn Heimdall's trumpet – the final call signifies Ragnarok.

Giants In Greek mythology, a race of beings born from Gaea, grown from the blood that dropped from the castrated Uranus. Usually represent evil in Viking mythology.

Gilgamesh King of Erech known as a half-human, half-god hero similar to the Greek Heracles, and often listed with the gods. He is the personification of the sun and is protected by the god Shamash, who in some texts is described as his father. He is also portrayed as an evil tyrant at times.

Gillie Someone who works for a Scottish chief, usually as an attendant or servant; guide for fishing or hunting parties.

Gladheim Where the twelve deities of Asgard hold their thrones. Also called Gladsheim.

Gled Bird of prey.

Golden Fleece Fleece of the ram sent by Poseidon to substitute for Phrixus when his father was going to sacrifice him. The Argonauts went in search of the fleece.

Goodman Man of the house.

Goodwife Woman of the house.

Gopis Lovers of the young Krishna and milkmaids.

Gorgon One of the three sisters, including Medusa, whose frightening looks could turn mortals to stone.

Graces Daughters of Aphrodite by Zeus.

Gramercy Expression of surprise or strong feeling.

Great Head The Iroquois believed in the existence of a curious being known as Great Head, a creature with an enormous head poised on slender legs.

Great Spirit The name given to the Creator of all life, as well as the term used to describe the omnipotent force of the Creator existing in every living thing.

Great-Flank One of Ravana's monsters.

Green Knight A knight dressed all in green and with green hair and skin who challenged one of Arthur's knights to strike him a blow with an axe and that, if he survived, he would return to behead the knight in a year and a day. He turned out to be Lord Bertilak and was under an enchantment cast by Morgan le Fay to test Arthur's knights.

Gruagach Mythical creature, often a giant or ogre similar to a wild man of the woods. The term can also refer to other mythical creatures such as brownies or fairies. As a brownie, he is usually dressed in red or green as opposed to the traditional brown. He has great power to enchant the hapless, or to help mortals who are worthy (usually heroes). He often appears to challenge a boy-hero, during his period of education.

Gudea High priest of Lagash, known to be a patron of the arts and a writer himself.

Guebre Religion founded by Zoroaster, the Persian prophet.

Gugumatz Creator god who, with Huracan, formed the sky, earth and everything on it.

Guha King of Nishadha.

Guidewife Woman.

Guinevere Wife of King Arthur; she is often portrayed as a virtuous lady and wife, but is perhaps best known for having a love affair with Lancelot, one of Arthur's friends and knights of the Round Table. Her name is also spelled Guenever.

Gulistan *Rose Garden*, written by the poet Sa'di

Gungnir Odin's spear, made of Yggdrasill wood, and the tip fashioned by Dvalin.

Gylfi A wandering king to whom the Eddas are narrated.

Haab Mayan solar calendar that consisted of eighteen twenty-day months.

Hades One of the three sons of Cronus; brother of Poseidon and Zeus. Hades is King of the Underworld, which is also known as the House of Hades.

Haere-mai Māori phrase meaning 'come here, welcome.'

Haere-mai-ra, me o tatou mate Māori phrase meaning 'come here, that I may sorrow with you.'

Haere-ra Māori phrase meaning 'goodbye, go, farewell.'

Haji Muslim pilgrim who has been to Mecca.

Hakama Traditional Japanese clothing, worn on the bottom half of the body.

Hanuman General of the monkey people.

Harakiri Suicide, usually by cutting or stabbing the abdomen. Also known as seppuku.

Hari-Hara Shiva and Vishnu as one god.

Harmonia Daughter of Ares and Aphrodite, wife of Cadmus.

Hatamoto High-ranking samurai.

Hathor Great cosmic mother and patroness of lovers. She is portrayed as a cow.

Hati The wolf who pursues the sun and moon.

Hatshepsut Second female pharaoh.

Hauberk Armour to protect the neck and shoulders, sometimes a full-length coat of mail.

Hector Eldest son of King Priam who defended Troy from the Greeks. He was killed by Achilles.

Hecuba The second wife of Priam, King of Troy. She was turned into a dog after Troy was lost.

Heimdall White god who guards the Bifrost bridge.

Hel Goddess of death and Loki's daughter. Also known as Hela.

Helen Daughter of Leda and Tyndareus, King of Sparta, and the most beautiful woman in the world. She was responsible for starting the Trojan War.

Heliopolis City in modern-day Cairo, known as the City of the Sun and the central place of worship of Ra. Also known as Anu.

Helius The sun, son of Hyperion and Theia.

Henwife Witch.

Hephaestus or **Hephaistos** The Smith of Heaven.

Hera A Mycenaean palace goddess, married to Zeus.

Heracles An important Greek hero, the son of Zeus and Alcmena. His name means 'Glory of Hera'. He performed twelve labours for King Eurystheus, and later became a god.

Hermes The conductor of souls of the dead to Hades, and god of trickery and of trade. He acts as messenger to the gods.

Hermod Son of Frigga and Odin who travelled to see Hel in order to reclaim Balder for Asgard.

Hero and Leander Hero was a priestess of Aphrodite, loved by Leander, a young man of Abydos. He drowned trying to see her.

Hestia Goddess of the hearth, daughter of Cronus and Rhea.

Hieroglyphs Type of writing that combines symbols and pictures, usually cut into tombs or rocks, or written on papyrus.

Himalaya Great mountain and range, father of Parvati.

Hiordis Wife of Sigmund and mother of Sigurd.

Hoderi A fisher and son of Okuninushi.

Hodur Balder's blind twin; known as the personification of darkness.

Hoenir Also called Vili; produced the first humans with Odin and Loki, and was one of the triad responsible for the creation of the world.

Hōichi the Earless A biwa hōshi, a blind storyteller who played the biwa or lute. Also a priest.

Holger Danske Legendary Viking warrior who is thought to never die. He sleeps until he is needed by his people and then he will rise to protect them.

Homayi Phoenix.

Hoodie Mythical creature which often appears as a crow.

Hoori A hunter and son of Okuninushi.

Horus God of the sky and kinship, son of Isis and Osiris. He captained the boat that carried Ra across the sky. He is depicted with the head of a falcon.

Hotei One of the gods of luck. He also personifies humour and contentment.

Houlet Owl.

Houri Beautiful virgin from paradise.

Hrim-faxi Steed of the night.

Hubris Presumptuous behaviour which causes the wrath of the gods to be brought on to mortals.

Hueytozoztli Festival dedicated to Tlaloc and, at times, Chicomecohuatl or other deities. Also the fourth month of the Aztec calendar.

Hugin Odin's raven.

Huitzilopochtli God of war and the sun, also connected with the summer and crops; one of the principal Aztec deities. He was born a full-grown adult to save his mother, Coatlicue, from the jealousy of his sister, Coyolxauhqui, who tried to kill Coatlicue. The Mars of the Aztec gods. In some origin stories he is one of four offspring of Ometeotl and Omecihuatl.

Hurley A traditional Irish game played with sticks and balls, quite similar to hockey.

Hurons A tribe of Iroquois stock, originally one people with the Iroquois.

Huveane (Pedi, Venda) Creator of humankind, who made a baby from clay into which he breathed life. He is known as the High God or Great God. He is also known as a trickster god.

Hymir Giant who fishes with Thor and is drowned by him.

Iambe Daughter of Pan and Echo, servant to King Celeus of Eleusis and Metaeira.

Icarus Son of Daedalus, who plunged to his death after escaping from the labyrinth.

Ichneumon Mongoose.

Idunn Guardian of the youth-giving apples.

Ifa (Yoruba) God of wisdom and divination. Also the term for a Yoruban religion.

Ife (Yoruba) The place Obatala first arrived on Earth and took for his home.

Igigi Great spirits or gods of Heaven and the sky.

Igraine Wife of the duke of Tintagel, enemy of Uther Pendragon, who marries Uther when her first husband dies. She is King Arthur's mother.

Ile (Yoruba) Goddess of the earth.

Imhetep High priest and wise sage. He is sometimes thought to be the son of Ptah.

Imam Person who leads prayers in a mosque.

Imana (Banyarwanda) Creator or sky god.

In The male principle who, joined with Yo, the female side, brought about creation and the first gods. In and Yo correspond to the Chinese Yang and Yin.

Inari God of rice, fertility, agriculture and, later, the fox god. Inari has both good and evil attributes but is often presented as an evil trickster.

Indra The King of Heaven.

Indrajit Son of Ravana.

Indrasen Daughter of Nala and Damayanti.

Indrasena Son of Nala and Damayanti.

Inundation Annual flooding of the River Nile.

Iphigenia The eldest daughter of Agamemnon and Clytemnestra who was sacrificed to appease Artemis and obtain a fair wind for Troy.

Iris Messenger of the gods who took the form of a rainbow.

Iseult Princess of Ireland and niece of the Morholt. She falls in love with Tristan after consuming a love potion but is forced to marry King Mark of Cornwall.

Ishtar Goddess of love, beauty, justice and war, especially in Ninevah, and earth mother who symbolizes fertility. Married to Tammuz, she is similar to the Greek goddess Aphrodite. Ishtar is sometimes known as Innana or Irnina.

Isis Goddess of the Nile and the moon, sister-wife of Osiris. She and her son, Horus, are sometimes thought of in a similar way to Mary and Jesus. She was one of the most worshipped female

Egyptian deities and was instrumental in returning Osiris to life after he was killed by his brother, Set.

Istakbál Deputation of warriors.

Izanagi Deity and brother-husband to Izanami, who together created the Japanese islands from the Floating Bridge of Heaven. Their offspring populated Japan.

Izanami Deity and sister-wife of Izanagi, creator of Japan. Their children include Amaterasu, Tsuki-yomi and Susanoo.

Jade It was believed that jade emerged from the mountains as a liquid which then solidified after ten thousand years to become a precious hard stone, green in colour. If the correct herbs were added to it, it could return to its liquid state and when swallowed increase the individual's chances of immortality.

Jambavan A noble monkey.

Jason Son of Aeson, King of Iolcus and leader of the voyage of the Argonauts.

Jatayu King of all the eagle-tribes.

Jesseraunt Flexible coat of armour or mail.

Jimmo Legendary first emperor of Japan. He is thought to be descended from Hoori, while other tales claim him to be descended from Amaterasu through her grandson, Ninigi.

Jizo God of little children and the god who calms the troubled sea.

Jord Daughter of Nott; wife of Odin.

Jormungander The world serpent; son of Loki. Legends tell that when his tail is removed from his mouth, Ragnarok has arrived.

Jorō Geisha who also worked as a prostitute.

Jotunheim Home of the giants.

Ju Ju tree Deciduous tree that produces edible fruit.

Jurasindhu A rakshasa, father-in-law of Kans.

Jyeshtha Goddess of bad luck.

Ka Life power or soul. Also known as ba.

Kai-káús Son of Kai-kobád. He led an army to invade Mázinderán, home of the demon-sorcerers, after being persuaded by a demon. Known for his ambitious schemes, he later tried to reach Heaven by trapping eagles to fly him there on his throne.

Kaikeyi Mother of Bharata, one of Dasharatha's three wives.

Kai-khosrau Son of Saiawúsh, who killed Afrásiyáb in revenge for the death of his father.

Kai-kobád Descendant of Feridún, he was selected by Zál to lead an army against Afrásiyáb. Their powerful army, led by Zál and Rustem, drove back Afrásiyáb's army, who then agreed to peace.

Kailyard Kitchen garden or small plot, usually used for growing vegetables.

Kali The Black, wife of Shiva.

Kalindi Daughter of the sun, wife of Krishna.

Kaliya A poisonous hydra that lived in the jamna.

Kalki Incarnation of Vishnu yet to come.

Kalnagini Serpent who kills Lakshmindara.

Kal-Purush The Time-man, Bengali name for Orion.

Kaluda A disciple of Buddha.

Kalunga-ngombe (Mbundu) Death, also depicted as the king of the netherworld.

Kama God of desire.

Kamadeva Desire, the god of love.

Kami Spirits, deities or forces of nature.

Kamund Lasso.

Kans King of Mathura, son of Ugrasena and Pavandrekha.

Kanva Father of Shakuntala.

Kappa River goblin with the body of a tortoise and the head of an ape. Kappa love to challenge human beings to single combat.

Karakia Invocation, ceremony, prayer.

Karna Pupil of Drona.

Kaross Blanket or rug, also worn as a traditional garment. It is often made from the skins of animals which have been sewn together.

Kasbu A period of twenty-four hours.

Kashyapa One of Dasharatha's counsellors.

Kauravas or Kurus Sons of Dhritarashtra, pupils of Drona.

Kaushalya Mother of Rama, one of Dasharatha's three wives.

Kay Son of Ector and adopted brother to King Arthur, he becomes one of Arthur's knights of the Round Table.

Keb God of the earth and father of Osiris and Isis, married to Nut. Keb is identified with Kronos, the Greek god of time.

Kehua Spirit, ghost.

Kelpie Another word for each uisge, the water-horse.

Ken Know.

Keres Black-winged demons or daughters of the night.

Keshini Wife of Sagara.

Khalif Leader.

Khara Younger brother of Ravana.

Khepera God who represents the rising sun. He is portrayed as a scarab. Also known as Nebertcher.

Kher-heb Priest and magician who officiated over rituals and ceremonies.

Khnemu God of the source of the Nile and one of the original Egyptian deities. He is thought to be the creator of children and of other gods. He is portrayed as a ram.

Khosru King and husband to Shireen, daughter of Maurice, the Greek Emperor. He was murdered by his own son, who wanted his kingdom and his wife.

Khumbaba Monster and guardian of the goddess Irnina, a form of the goddess Ishtar. Khumbaba is likened to the Greek gorgon.

Kia-ora Welcome, good luck. A greeting.

Kiboko Hippopotamus.

Kikinu Soul.

Kimbanda (Mbundu) Doctor.

Kimono Traditional Japanese clothing, similar to a robe.

King Arthur Legendary king of Britain who plucked the magical sword from the stone, marking him as the heir of Uther Pendragon and 'true king' of Britain. He and his knights of the Round Table defended Britain from the Saxons and had many adventures, including searching for the Holy Grail. Finally wounded in battle, he left Britain for the mythical Avalon, vowing to one day return to reclaim his kingdom.

Kingu Tiawath's husband, a god and warrior who she promised would rule Heaven once he helped her defeat the 'gods of light'. He was killed by Merodach who used his blood to make clay, from which he formed the first humans. In some tales, Kingu is Tiawath's son as well as her consort.

Kinnaras Human birds with musical instruments under their wings.

Kinyamkela (Zaramo) Ghost of a child.

Kirk Church, usually a term for Church of Scotland churches.

Kirtle One-piece garment, similar to a tunic, which was worn by men or women.

Kis Solar deity, usually depicted as an eagle.

Kishar Earth mother and sister-wife to Anshar.

Kist Trunk or large chest.

Kitamba (Mbundu) Chief who made his whole village go into mourning when his head-wife, Queen Muhongo, died. He also pledged that no one should speak or eat until she was returned to him.

Knowe Knoll or hillock.

Kojiki One of two myth-histories of Japan, along with the *Nihon Shoki*.

Ko-no-Hana Goddess of Mount Fuji, princess and wife of Ninigi.

Kore 'Maiden', another name for Persephone.

Kraal Traditional rural African village, usually consisting of huts surrounded by a fence or wall. Also an animal enclosure.

Krishna The Dark one, worshipped as an incarnation of Vishnu.

Kui-see Edible root.

Kumara Son of Shiva and Paravati, slays demon Taraka.

Kumbha-karna Ravana's brother.

Kunti Mother of the Pandavas.

Kura Red. The sacred colour of the Māori.

Kusha or Kusi One of Sita's two sons.

Kvasir Clever warrior and colleague of Odin. He was responsible for finally outwitting Loki.

Kwannon Goddess of mercy.

Labyrinth A prison built at Knossos for the Minotaur by Daedalus.

Lady of the Lake Enchantress who presents Arthur with Excalibur.

Laertes King of Ithaca and father of Odysseus.

Laestrygonians Savage giants encountered by Odysseus on his travels.

Laili In love with Majnun but unable to marry him, she was given to the prince, Ibn Salam, to marry. When he died, she escaped and found Majnun, but they could not be legally married. The couple died of grief and were buried together. Also known as Laila.

Laird Person who owns a significant estate in Scotland.

Lakshmana Brother of Rama and his companion in exile.

Lakshmi Consort of Vishnu and a goddess of beauty and good fortune.

Lakshmindara Son of Chand resurrected by Manasa Devi.

Lancelot Knight of the Round Table. Lancelot was raised by the Lady of the Lake. While he went on many quests, he is perhaps best known for his affair with Guinevere, King Arthur's wife.

Land of Light One of the names for the realm of the fairies. If a piece of metal welded by human hands is put in the doorway to their land, the door cannot close. The door to this realm is only open at night, and usually at a full moon.

Lang syne The days of old.

Lao Tzu (Laozi) The ancient Taoist philosopher thought to have been born in 571 BCE a contemporary of Confucius with whom, it is said, he discussed the tenets of Tao. Lao Tzu was an advocate of simple rural existence and looked to the Yellow Emperor and Shun as models of efficient government. His philosophies were recorded in the Tao Te Ching. Legends surrounding his birth suggest that he emerged from the left-hand side of his mother's body, with white hair and a long white beard, after a confinement lasting eighty years.

Laocoon A Trojan wiseman who predicted that the wooden horse contained Greek soldiers.

Laomedon The King of Troy who hired Apollo and Poseidon to build the impregnable walls of Troy.

Lava Son of Sita.

Leda Daughter of the King of Aetolia, who married Tyndareus. Helen and Clytemnestra were her daughters.

Legba (Dahomey) Youngest offspring of Mawu-Lisa. He was given the gift of all languages. It was through him that humans could converse with the gods.

Leman Lover.

Leprechaun Mythical creature from Irish folk tales who often appears as a mischievous and sometimes drunken old man.

Lethe One of the four rivers of the Underworld, also called the River of Forgetfulness.

Lif The female survivor of Ragnarok.

Lifthrasir The male survivor of Ragnarok.

Lil Demon.

Liongo (Swahili) Warrior and hero.

Lofty mountain Home of Ahura-Mazda.

Logi Utgard-loki's cook.

Loki God of fire and mischief-maker of Asgard; he eventually brings about Ragnarok. Also spelled as Loptur.

Lotus-Eaters A race of people who live a dazed, drugged existence, the result of eating the lotus flower.

Ma'at State of order meaning truth, order or justice. Personified by the goddess Ma'at, who was Thoth's consort.

Macha There are thought to be several different Machas who appear in quite a number of ancient Irish stories. For the purposes of this book, however, the Macha referred to is the wife of Crunnchu. The story unfolds that after her husband had boasted of her great athletic ability to the King, she was subsequently forced to run against his horses in spite of the fact that she was heavily pregnant. Macha died giving birth to her twin babies and with her dying breath she cursed Ulster for nine generations, proclaiming that it would suffer the weakness of a woman in childbirth in times of great stress. This curse had its most disastrous effect when Medb of Connacht invaded Ulster with her great army.

Machi-bugyō Senior official or magistrate, usually samurai.

Macuilxochitl God of art, dance and games, and the patron of luck in gaming. His name means 'source of flowers' or 'prince of flowers'. Also known as Xochipilli, meaning 'five-flower'.

Madake Weapon used for whipping, made of bamboo.

Maduma Taro tuber.

Mag Muirthemne Cuchulainn's inheritance. A plain extending from River Boyne to the mountain range of Cualgne, close to Emain Macha in Ulster.

Magni Thor's son.

Mahaparshwa One of Ravana's generals.

Maharaksha Son of Khara, slain at Lanka.

Mahasubhadda Wife of Buddha-select (Sumedha).

Majnun Son of a chief, who fell in love with Laili and followed her tribe through the desert, becoming mad with love until they were briefly reunited before dying.

Makaras Mythical fish-reptiles of the sea.

Makoma (Senna) Folk hero who defeated five mighty giants.

Mana Power, authority, prestige, influence, sanctity, luck.

Manasa Devi Goddess of snakes, daughter of Shiva by a mortal woman.

Manasha Goddess of snakes.

Mandavya Daughter of Kushadhwaja.

Man-Devourer One of Ravana's monsters.

Mandodari Wife of Ravana.

Mandrake Poisonous plant from the nightshade family which has hallucinogenic and hypnotic qualities if ingested. Its roots resemble the human form and it has supposedly magical qualities.

Mani The moon.

Manitto Broad term used to describe the supernatural or a potent spirit among the Algonquins, the Iroquois and the Sioux.

Man-Slayer One of Ravana's counsellors.

Manthara Kaikeyi's evil nurse, who plots Rama's ruin.

Mantle Cloak or shawl.

Manu Lawgiver.

Manu Mythical mountain on which the sun sets.

Mara The evil one, tempts Gautama.

Markandeya One of Dasharatha's counsellors.

Mashu Mountain of the Sunset, which lies between Earth and the underworld. Guarded by scorpion-men.

Matali Sakra's charioteer.

Mawu-Lisa (Dahomey) Twin offspring of Nana Baluka. Mawu (female) and Lisa (male) are often joined to form one being. Their own offspring populated the world.

Mbai (Igbo) Person of great intelligence, also known as Ekake (Ibani), which means 'tortoise'.

Medea Witch and priestess of Hecate, daughter of Aeetes and sister of Circe. She helped Jason in his quest for the Golden Fleece.

Medusa One of the three Gorgons whose head had the power to turn onlookers to stone.

Melpomene One of the muses, and mother of the Sirens.

Menaka One of the most beautiful dancers in Heaven.

Menat Amulet, usually worn for protection.

Mendicant Beggar.

Menelaus King of Sparta, brother of Agamemnon. Married Helen and called war against Troy when she eloped with Paris.

Menthu Lord of Thebes and god of war. He is portrayed as a hawk or falcon.

Mere-pounamu A native weapon made of a rare green stone.

Merlin Wizard and advisor to King Arthur. He is thought to be the son of a human female and an incubus (male demon). He brought about Arthur's birth and ascension to king, then acted as his mentor.

Merodach God who battled Tiawath and defeated her by cutting out her heart and dividing her corpse into two pieces. He used these pieces to divide the upper and lower waters once controlled by Tiawath, making a dwelling for the gods of light. He also created humankind. Also known as Marduk.

Merrow Mythical mermaid-like creature, often depicted with an enchanted cap called a cohuleen driuth which allows it to travel between land and the depths of the sea. Also known as murúch.

Metaneira Wife of Celeus, King of Eleusis, who hired Demeter in disguise as her nurse.

Metztli Goddess of the moon, her name means 'lady of the night'. Also known as Yohualtictl.

Michabo Also known as Manobozho, or the Great Hare, the principal deity of the Algonquins, maker and preserver of the earth, sun and moon.

Mictlan God of the dead and ruler of the underworld. He was married to Mictecaciuatl and is often represented as a bat. He is also the Aztec lord of Hades. Also known as Mictlantecutli. Mictlan is also the name for the underworld.

Midgard Dwelling place of humans (Earth).

Midsummer A time when fairies dance and claim human victims.

Mihrab Father of Rúdábeh and descendant of Zohák, the serpent-king.

Milesians A group of iron-age invaders led by the sons of Mil, who arrived in Ireland from Spain around 500 BCE and overcame the Tuatha De Danann.

Mimir God of the ocean. His head guards a well; reincarnated after Ragnarok.

Minos King of Crete, son of Zeus and Europa. He was considered to have been the ruler of a sea empire.

Minotaur A creature born of the union between Pasiphae and a Cretan Bull.

Minúchihr King who lives to be one hundred and twenty years old. Father of Nauder.

Miolnir *See* Mjolnir.

Mithra God of the sun and light in Iran, protector of truth and guardian of pastures and cattle. Alo known as Mitra in Hindu mythology and Mithras in Roman mythology.

Mixcoatl God of the chase or the hunt. Sometimes depicted as the god of air and thunder, he introduced fire to humankind. His name means 'cloud serpent'.

Mjolnir Hammer belonging to the Norse god of thunder, which is used as a fearsome weapon which always returns to Thor's hand, and as an instrument of consecration.

Mnoatia Forest spirits.

Moccasins One-piece shoes made of soft leather, especially deerskin.

Modi Thor's son.

Moly A magical plant given to Odysseus by Hermes as protection against Circe's powers.

Montezuma Great emperor who consolidated the Aztec Empire.

Mordred Bastard son of King Arthur and Morgawse, Queen of Orkney, who, unknown to Arthur, was his half-sister. Mordred becomes one of King Arthur's knights of the Round Table before betraying and fatally wounding Arthur, causing him to leave Britain for Avalon.

Morgan le Fay Enchantress and half-sister to King Arthur, Morgan was an apprentice of Merlin's. She is generally depicted as benevolent, yet did pit herself against Arthur and his knights on occasion. She escorts Arthur on his final journey to Avalon. Also known as Morgain le Fay.

Morholt The knight sent to Cornwall to force King Mark to pay tribute to Ireland. He is killed by Tristan.

Morongoe the brave (Lesotho) Man who was turned into a snake by evil spirits because Tau was jealous that he had married the beautiful Mokete, the chief's daughter. Morongoe was returned to human form after his son, Tsietse, returned him to their family.

Mosima (Bapedi) The underworld or abyss.

Mount Fuji Highest mountain in Japan, on the island of Honshū.

Mount Kunlun This mountain features in many Chinese legends as the home of the great emperors on Earth. It is written in the *Shanghaijing* (*The Classic of Mountains and Seas*) that this towering structure measured no less than 3300 miles in circumference and 4000 miles in height. It acted both as a central pillar to support the heavens, and as a gateway between Heaven and Earth.

Moving Finger Expression for taking responsibility for one's life and actions, which cannot be undone.

Moytura Translated as the 'Plain of Weeping', Mag Tured, or Moytura, was where the Tuatha De Danann fought two of their most significant battles.

Mua An old-time Polynesian god.

Muezzin Person who performs the Muslim call to prayer.

Mugalana A disciple of Buddha.

Muilearteach The Cailleach Bheur of the water, who appears as a witch or a sea-serpent. On land she grew larger and stronger by fire.

Mul-lil God of Nippur, who took the form of a gazelle.

Muloyi Sorcerer, also called mulaki, murozi, ndozi or ndoki.

Mummu Son of Tiawath and Apsu. He formed a trinity with them to battle the gods. Also known as Moumis. In some tales, Mummu is also Merodach, who eventually destroyed Tiawath.

Munin Odin's raven.

Murile (Chaga) Man who dug up a taro tuber that resembled his baby brother, which turned into a living boy. His mother killed the baby when she saw Murile was starving himself to feed it.

Murtough Mac Erca King who ruled Ireland when many of its people – including his wife and family – were converting to Christianity. He remained a pagan.

Muses Goddesses of poetry and song, daughters of Zeus and Mnemosyne.

Musha Expression, often of surprise.

Muskrat North American beaver-like, amphibious rodent.

Muspell Home of fire, and the fire-giants.

Mwidzilo Taboo which, if broken, can cause death.

Nabu God of writing and wisdom. Also known as Nebo. Thought to be the son of Merodach.

Nahua Ancient Mexicans.

Nakula Pandava twin skilled in horsemanship.

Nala One of the monkey host, son of Vishvakarma.

Nana Baluka (Dahomey) Mother of all creation. She gave birth to an androgynous being with two faces. The female face was Mawu, who controlled the night and lands to the west. The male face was Lisa and he controlled the day and the east.

Nanahuatl Also known as Nanauatzin. Presided over skin diseases and known as Leprous, which in Nahua meant 'divine'.

Nandi Shiva's bull.

Nanna Balder's wife.

Nannar God of the moon and patron of the city of Ur.

Naram-Sin Son or ancestor of Sargon and king of the Four Zones or Quarters of Babylon.

Narcissus Son of the River Cephisus. He fell in love with himself and died as a result.

Narve Son of Loki.

Nataraja Manifestation of Shiva, Lord of the Dance.

Natron Preservative used in embalming, mined from the Natron Valley in Egypt.

Nauder Son of Minúchihr, who became king on his death and was tyrannical and hated until Sám begged him to follow in the footsteps of his ancestors.

Nausicaa Daughter of Alcinous, King of Phaeacia, who fell in love with Odysseus.

Nebuchadnezzar Famous king of Babylon. Also known as Nebuchadrezzar.

Necromancy Communicating with the dead.

Nectar Drink of the gods.

Neith Goddess of hunting, fate and war. Neith is sometimes known as the creator of the universe.

Nemesis Goddess of retribution and daughter of night.

Neoptolemus Son of Achilles and Deidameia, he came to Troy at the end of the war to wear his father's armour. He sacrificed Polyxena at the tomb of Achilles.

Nephthys Goddess of the air, night and the dead. Sister of Isis and sister-wife to Seth, she is also the mother of Anubis.

Nereids Sea-nymphs who are the daughters of Nereus and Doris. Thetis, mother of Achilles, was a Nereid.

Nergal God of death and patron god of Cuthah, which was often known as a burial place. He is also known as the god of fire. Married to Aralu, the goddess of the underworld.

Nestor Wise King of Pylus, who led the ships to Troy with Agamemnon and Menelaus.

Neta Daughter of Shiva, friend of Manasa.

Ngai (Gikuyu) Creator god.

Ngaka (Lesotho) Witch doctor.

Niflheim The underworld In Norse mythology, ruled over by Hel.

Night Daughter of Norvi.

Nikumbha One of Ravana's generals.

Nila One of the monkey host, son of Agni.

Nin-Girsu God of fertility and war, patron god of Girsu. Also known as Shul-gur.

Ninigi Grandson of Amaterasu, Ninigi came to Earth bringing rice and order to found the Imperial family. He is known as the August Grandchild.

Niord God of the sea; marries Skadi.

Nippur The home of En-lil and one of the two major cities of Babylonian civilization.

Nirig God of war and storms, and son of Bel. Also known as Enu-Restu.

Nirvana Transcendent state and the final goal of Buddhism.

Nis Mythological creature, similar to a brownie or goblin, usually harmless or even friendly, but can be easily offended. They are often associated with Christmas or the winter solstice.

Noatun Niord's home.

Noisy-Throat One of Ravana's counsellors.

Noondah (Zanzibar) Cannibalistic cat which attacked and killed animals and humans.

Norns The fates and protectors of Yggdrasill. Many believe them to be the same as the Valkyries.

Norvi Father of the night.

Nott Goddess of night.

Nsasak bird Small bird who became chief of all small birds after winning a competition to go without food for seven days. The

Nsasak bird beat the Odudu bird by sneaking out of his home to feed.

Nüwa The Goddess Nüwa, who in some versions of the Creation myths is the sole creator of mankind, and in other tales is associated with the God Fuxi, also a great benefactor of the human race. Some accounts represent Fuxi as the brother of Nüwa, but others describe the pair as lovers who lie together to create the very first human beings. Fuxi is also considered to be the first of the Chinese emperors of mythical times who reigned from 2953 to 2838 BCE.

Nuada The first king of the Tuatha De Danann in Ireland, who lost an arm in the first battle of Moytura against the Fomorians. He became known as 'Nuada of the Silver Hand' when Diancecht, the great physician of the Tuatha De Danann, replaced his hand with a silver one after the battle.

Nunda (Swahili, East Africa) Slayer that took the form of a cat and grew so big that it consumed everyone in the town except the sultan's wife, who locked herself away. Her son, Mohammed, killed Nunda and cut open its leg, setting free everyone Nunda had eaten.

Nut Goddess of the sky, stars and astronomy. Sister-wife of Keb and mother of Osiris, Isis, Set and Nephthys. She often appears in the form of a cow.

Nyame (Ashanti) God of the sky, who sees and knows everything.

Nymphs Minor female deities associated with particular parts of the land and sea.

Obassi Osaw (Ekoi) Creator god with his twin, Obassi Nsi. Originally, Obassi Osaw ruled the skies while Obassi Nsi ruled the earth.

Obatala (Yoruba) Creator of humankind. He climbed down a golden chain from the sky to the earth, then a watery abyss, and formed land and humankind. When Olorun heard of his success, he created the sun for Obatala and his creations.

Oberon Fairy king.

Odin Allfather and king of all gods, he is known for travelling the nine worlds in disguise and recognized only by his single eye; dies at Ragnarok.

Oduduwa (Yoruba) Divine king of Ile-Ife, the holy city of Yoruba.

Odur Freyia's husband.

Odysseus Greek hero, son of Laertes and Anticleia, who was renowned for his cunning, the master behind the victory at Troy, and known for his long voyage home.

Oedipus Son of Leius, King of Thebes and Jocasta. Became King of Thebes and married his mother.

Ogdoad Group of eight deities who were formed into four male-female couples who joined to create the gods and the world.

Ogham One of the earliest known forms of Irish writing, originally used to inscribe upright pillar stones.

Oiran Courtesan.

Oisin Also called Ossian (particularly by James Macpherson who wrote a set of Gaelic Romances about this character, supposedly garnered from oral tradition). Ossian was the son of Fionn and Sadbh, and had various brothers, according to different legends. He was a man of great wisdom, became immortal for many centuries, but in the end he became mad.

Ojibwe Another name for the Chippewa, a tribe of Algonquin stock.

Okuninushi Deity and descendant of Susanoo, who married Suseri-hime, Susanoo's daughter, without his consent. Susanoo tried to kill him many times but did not succeed and eventually forgave Okuninushi. He is sometimes thought to be the son or grandson of Susanoo.

Olokun (Yoruba) Most powerful goddess who ruled the seas and marshes. When Obatala created Earth in her domain, other gods began to divide it up between them. Angered at their presumption, she caused a great flood to destroy the land.

Olorun (Yoruba) Supreme god and ruler of the sky. He sees and controls everything, but others, such as Obatala, carry out the work for him. Also known as Olodumare.

Olympia Zeus's home in Elis.

Olympus The highest mountain in Greece and the ancient home of the gods.

Omecihuatl Female half of the first being, combined with Ometeotl. Together they are the lords of duality or lords of the two sexes. Also known as Ometecutli and Omeciuatl or Tonacatecutli and Tonacaciuatl. Their offspring were Xipe Totec, Huitzilopochtli, Quetzalcoatl and Tezcatlipoca.

Ometeotl Male half of the first being, combined with Omecihuatl.

Ometochtli Collective name for the pulque-gods or drink-gods. These gods were often associated with rabbits as they were thought to be senseless creatures.

Onygate Anyway.

Opening of the Mouth Ceremony in which mummies or statues were prayed over and anointed with incense before their mouths were opened, allowing them to eat and drink in the afterlife.

Oracle The response of a god or priest to a request for advice – also a prophecy; the place where such advice was sought; the person or thing from whom such advice was sought.

Oranyan (Yoruba) Youngest grandson of King Oduduwa, who later became king himself.

Orestes Son of Agamemnon and Clytemnestra who escaped following Agamemnon's murder to King Strophius. He later returned to Argos to murder his mother and avenge the death of his father.

Orpheus Thracian singer and poet, son of Oeagrus and a Muse. Married Eurydice and when she died tried to retrieve her from the Underworld.

Orunmila (Yoruba) Eldest son of Olorun, he helped Obatala create land and humanity, which he then rescued after Olokun flooded the lands. He has the power to see the future.

Osiris God of fertility, the afterlife and death. Thought to be the first of the pharaohs. He was murdered by his brother, Set, after which he was conjured back to life by Isis, Anubis and others before becoming lord of the afterlife. Married to Isis, who was also his sister.

Otherworld The world of deities and spirits, also known as the Land of Promise, or the Land of Eternal Youth, a place of everlasting life where all earthly dreams come to be fulfilled.

Owuo (Krachi, West Africa) Giant who personifies death. He causes a person to die every time he blinks his eye.

Palamedes Hero of Nauplia, believed to have created part of the ancient Greek alphabet. He tricked Odysseus into joining the fleet setting out for Troy by placing the infant Telemachus in the path of his plough.

Palermo Stone Stone carved with hieroglyphs, which came from the Royal Annals of ancient Egypt and contains a list of the kings of Egypt from the first to the early fifth dynasties.

Palfrey Docile and light horse, often used by women.

Palladium Wooden image of Athene, created by her as a monument to her friend Pallas who she accidentally killed. While in Troy it protected the city from invaders.

Pallas Athene's best friend, whom she killed.

Pan God of Arcadia, half-goat and half-man. Son of Hermes. He is connected with fertility, masturbation and sexual drive. He is also associated with music, particularly his pipes, and with laughter.

Pangu Some ancient writers suggest that this God is the offspring of the opposing forces of nature, the yin and the yang. The yin (female) is associated with the cold and darkness of the earth, while the yang (male) is associated with the sun and the warmth of the heavens. 'Pan' means 'shell of an egg' and 'Gu' means 'to secure' or 'to achieve'. Pangu came into existence so that he might create order from chaos.

Pandareus Cretan King killed by the gods for stealing the shrine of Zeus.

Pandavas Alternative name for sons of Pandu, pupils of Drona.

Pandora The first woman, created by the gods, to punish man for Prometheus's theft of fire. Her dowry was a box full of powerful evil.

Papyrus Paper-like material made from the pith of the papyrus plant, first manufactured in Egypt. Used as a type of paper as well as for making mats, rope and sandals.

Paramahamsa The supreme swan.

Parashurama Human incarnation of Vishnu, 'Rama with an axe'.

Paris Handsome son of Priam and Hecuba of Troy, who was left for dead on Mount Ida but raised by shepherds. Was reclaimed by his family, then brought them shame and caused the Trojan War by eloping with Helen.

Parsa Holy man. Also known as a zahid.

Parvati Consort of Shiva and daughter of Himalaya.

Passion Wife of desire.

Pavanarekha Wife of Ugrasena, mother of Kans.

Peerie Folk Fairy or little folk.

Pegasus The winged horse born from the severed neck of Medusa.

Peggin Wooden vessel with a handle, often shaped like a tub and used for drinking.

Peleus Father of Achilles. He married Antigone, caused her death, and then became King of Phthia. Saved from death himself by Jason and the Argonauts. Married Thetis, a sea nymph.

Penelope The long-suffering but equally clever wife of Odysseus who managed to keep at bay suitors who longed for Ithaca while Odysseus was at the Trojan War and on his ten-year voyage home.

Pentangle Pentagram or five-pointed star.

Pentecost Christian festival held on the seventh Sunday after Easter. It celebrates the holy spirit descending on the disciples after Jesus's ascension.

Percivale Knight of the Round Table and original seeker of the Holy Grail.

Persephone Daughter of Zeus and Demeter who was raped by Hades and forced to live in the Underworld as his queen for three months of every year.

Perseus Son of Danae, who was made pregnant by Zeus. He fought the Gorgons and brought home the head of Medusa. He eventually founded the city of Mycenae and married Andromeda.

Pesh Kef Spooned blade used in the Opening the Mouth ceremony.

Phaeacia The Kingdom of Alcinous on which Odysseus landed after a shipwreck which claimed the last of his men as he left Calypso's island.

Pharaoh King or ruler of Egypt.

Philoctetes Malian hero, son of Poeas, received Heracles's bow and arrows as a gift when he lit the great hero's pyre on Mount Oeta. He was involved in the last part of the Trojan War, killing Paris.

Philtre Magic potion, usually a love potion.

Pibroch Bagpipe music.

Pintura Native manuscript or painting.

Pipiltin Noble class of the Aztecs.

Pismire Ant.

Piu-piu Short mat made from flax leaves and neatly decorated.

Pō Gloom, darkness, the lower world.

Polyphemus A Cyclops, but a son of Poseidon. He fell in love with Galatea, but she spurned him. He was blinded by Odysseus.

Polyxena Daughter of Priam and Hecuba of Troy. She was sacrificed on the grave of Achilles by Neoptolemus.

Pooka Mythical creature with the ability to shapeshift. Often appears as a horse, but also as a bull, dog or in human form, and has the ability to talk. Also known as púca.

Popol Vuh Sacred 'book of counsel' of the Quiché or K'iche' Maya people.

Poseidon God of the sea, and of sweet waters. Also the god of earthquakes. His is brother to Zeus and Hades, who divided the earth between them.

Pradyumna Son of Krishna and Rukmini.

Prahasta (Long-Hand) One of Ravana's generals.

Prajapati Creator of the universe, father of the gods, demons and all creatures, later known as Brahma.

Priam King of Troy, married to Hecuba, who bore him Hector, Paris, Helenus, Cassandra, Polyxena, Deiphobus and Troilus. He was murdered by Neoptolemus.

Pritha Mother of Karna and of the Pandavas.

Prithivi Consort of Dyaus and goddess of the earth.

Proetus King of Argos, son of Abas.

Prometheus A Titan, son of Iapetus and Themus. He was champion of mortal men, which he created from clay. He stole fire from the gods and was universally hated by them.

Prose Edda Collection of Norse myths and poems, thought to have been compiled in the 1200s by Icelandic historian Snorri Sturluson.

Proteus The old man of the sea who watched Poseidon's seals.

Psyche A beautiful nymph who was the secret wife of Eros, against the wishes of his mother Aphrodite, who sent Psyche to perform many tasks in hope of causing her death. She eventually married Eros and was allowed to become partly immortal.

Ptah Creator god and deity of Memphis who was married to Sekhmet. Ptah built the boats to carry the souls of the dead to the afterlife.

Puddock Frog.

Pulque Alcoholic drink made from fermented agave.

Purusha The cosmic man, he was sacrificed and his dismembered body became all the parts of the cosmos, including the four classes of society.

Purvey To provide or supply.

Pushkara Nala's brother.

Pushpaka Rama's chariot.

Putana A rakshasi.

Pygmalion A sculptor who was so lonely he carved a statue of a beautiful woman, and eventually fell in love with it. Aphrodite brought the image to life.

Quauhtli Eagle.

Quern Hand mill used for grinding corn.

Quetzalcoatl Deity and god of wind. He is represented as a feathered or plumed serpent and is usually a wise and benevolent god. Offspring of Ometeotl and Omecihuatl, he is also known as Kukulkan.

Ra God of the sun, ruling male deity of Egypt whose name means 'sole creator'.

Radha The principal mistress of Krishna.

Ragnarok The end of the world.

Rahula Son of Siddhartha and Yashodhara.

Raiden God of thunder. He traditionally has a fierce and demonic appearance.

Rakshasas Demons and devils.

Ram of Mendes Sacred symbol of fatherhood and fertility.

Rama or **Ramachandra** A prince and hero of the *Ramayana*, worshipped as an incarnation of Vishnu.

Ra-Molo (Lesotho) Father of fire, a chief who ruled by fear. When trying to kill his brother, Tau the lion, he was turned into a monster with the head of a sheep and the body of a snake.

Rangatira Chief, warrior, gentleman.

Regin A blacksmith who educated Sigurd.

Reinga The spirit land, the home of the dead.

Reservations Tracts of land allocated to the Native American people by the United States Government with the purpose of bringing the many separate tribes under state control.

Rewati Daughter of Raja, marries Balarama.

Rhadha Wife of Adiratha, a gopi of Brindaban and lover of Krishna.

Rhea Mother of the Olympian gods. Cronus ate each of her children, but she concealed Zeus and gave Cronus a swaddled rock in his place.

Rill Small stream.

Rimu (Chaga) Monster known to feed off human flesh, which sometimes takes the form of a werewolf.

Rishis Sacrificial priests associated with the devas in Swarga.

Rituparna King of Ayodhya.

Rohini The wife of Vasudeva, mother of Balarama and Subhadra, and carer of the young Krishna. Another Rohini is a goddess and consort of Chandra.

Rōnin Samurai whose master had died or fallen out of favour.

Rubáiyát Collection of poems written by Omar Khayyám.

Rúdábeh Wife of Zál and mother of Rustem.

Rudra Lord of Beasts and disease, later evolved into Shiva.

Rukma Rukmini's eldest brother.

Rustem Son of Zál and Rúdábeh, he was a brave and mighty warrior who undertook seven labours to travel to Mázinderán to rescue Kai-káús. Once there, he defeated the White Demon and rescued Kai-káús. He rode the fabled stallion Rakhsh and is also known as Rustam.

Ryō Traditional gold currency.

Sabdh Mother of Ossian, or Oisin.

Sabitu Goddess of the sea.

Sagara King of Ayodhya.

Sahadeva Pandava twin skilled in swordsmanship.

Sahib diwan Lord high treasurer or chief royal executive.

Saiawúsh Son of Kai-káús, who was put through trial by fire when Sudaveh, Kai-káús's wife, told him that Saiawúsh had taken advantage of her. His innocence was proven when the fire did not harm him. He was eventually killed by Afrásiyáb.

Saithe Blessed.

Sajara (Mali) God of rainbows. He takes the form of a multi-coloured serpent.

Sake Japanese rice wine.

Sakuni Cousin of Duryodhana.

Salam Greeting or salutation.

Saláman Son of the Shah of Yunan, who fell in love with Absál, his nurse. She died after they had a brief love affair and he returned to his father.

Salmali tree Cotton tree.

Salmon A symbol of great wisdom, around which many Scottish legends revolve.

Sám Mighty warrior who fought and won many battles. Father of Zál and grandfather to Rustem.

Sambu Son of Krishna.

Sampati Elder brother of Jatayu.

Samurai Noblemen who were part of the military in medieval Japan.

Sanehat Member of the royal bodyguard.

Sango (Yoruba) God of war and thunder.

Sangu (Mozambique) Goddess who protects pregnant women, depicted as a hippopotamus.

Santa Daughter of Dasharatha.

Sarapis Composite deity of Apis and Osiris, sometimes known as Serapis. Thought to be created to unify Greek and Egyptian citizens under the Greek pharaoh Ptolemy.

Sarasvati The tongue of Rama.

Sarcophagus Stone coffin.

Sargon of Akkad Raised by Akki, a husbandman, after being hidden at birth. Sargon became King of Assyria and a great hero. He founded the first library in Babylon. Similar to King Arthur or Perseus.

Sarsar Harsh, whistling wind.

Sasabonsam (Ashanti) Forest ogre.

Sassun Scottish word for England.

Sati Daughter of Daksha and Prasuti, first wife of Shiva.

Satrughna One of Dasharatha's four sons.

Satyavan Truth speaker, husband of Savitri.

Satyavati A fisher-maid, wife of Bhishma's father, Shamtanu.

Satyrs Elemental spirits which took great pleasure in chasing nymphs. They had horns, a hairy body and cloven hooves.

Saumanasa A mighty elephant.

Scamander River running across the Trojan plain, and father of Teucer.

Scarab Dung beetle, often used as a symbol of the immortal human soul and regeneration.

Scylla and Charybdis Scylla was a monster who lived on a rock of the same name in the Straits of Messina, devouring sailors. Charybdis was a whirlpool in the Straits which was supposedly inhabited by the hateful daughter of Poseidon.

Seal Often believed that seals were fallen angels. Many families are descended from seals, some of which had webbed hands or feet. Some seals were the children of sea-kings who had become enchanted (selkies).

Seelie-Court The court of the Fairies, who travelled around their realm. They were usually fair to humans, doling out punishment that was morally sound, but they were quick to avenge insults to fairies.

Segu (Swahili, East Africa) Guide who informs humans where honey can be found.

Sekhmet Solar deity who led the pharaohs in war. She is goddess of healing and was sent by Ra to destroy humanity when people turned against the sun god. She is portrayed with the head of a lion.

Selene Moon-goddess, daughter of Hyperion and Theia. She was seduced by Pan, but loved Endymion.

Selkie Mythical creature which is seal-like when in water but can shed its skin to take on human form when on land.

Seneschal Steward of a royal or noble household.

Sensei Teacher.

Seriyut A disciple of Buddha.

Sessrymnir Freyia's home.

Set God of chaos and evil, brother of Osiris, who killed him by tricking him into getting into a chest, which he then threw in the Nile, before cutting Osiris's body into fourteen separate pieces. Also known as Seth.

Sgeulachd Stories.

Sháhnámeh *The Book of Kings* written by Ferdowsi, one of the world's longest epic poems, which describes the mythology and history of the Persian Empire.

Shaikh Respected religious man.

Shaivas or Shaivites Worshippers of Shiva.

Shakti Power or wife of a god and Shiva's consort as his feminine aspect.

Shaman Also known as the 'Medicine Men' of Native American tribes, it is the shaman's role to cultivate communication with the spirit world. They are endowed with knowledge of all healing herbs, and learn to diagnose and cure disease. They are believed to foretell the future, find lost property and have power over animals, plants and stones.

Shamash God of the sun and protector of Gilgamesh, the great Babylonian hero. Known as the son of Sin, the moon god, he is also portrayed as a judge of good and evil.

Shamtanu Father of Bhishma.

Shankara A great magician, friend of Chand Sadagar.

Shashti The Sixth, goddess who protects children and women in childbirth.

Sheen Beautiful and enchanted woman who casts a spell on Murtough, King of Ireland, causing him to fall in love with her and cast out his family. He dies at her hands, half burned and half drowned, but she then dies of grief as she returns his love. Sheen is known by many names, including Storm, Sigh and Rough Wind.

Shesh A serpent that takes human birth through Devaki.

Shi-en Fairy dwelling.

Shinto Indigenous religion of Japan, from the pre-sixth century to the present day.

Shireen Married to Khosru. Her beauty meant that she was desired by many, including Khosru's own son by his previous marriage. She killed herself rather than give in to her stepson.

Shitala The Cool One and goddess of smallpox.

Shiva One of the two great gods of post-Vedic Hinduism with Vishnu.

Shogun Military ruler or overlord.

Shoji Sliding door, usually a lattice screen of paper.

Shu God of the air and half of the first divine couple created by Atem. Brother and husband to Tefnut, father to Keb and Nut.

Shubistán Household.

Shudra One of the four fundamental colours (caste).

Shuttle Part of a machine used for spinning cloth, used for passing weft threads between warp threads.

Siddhas Musical ministrants of the upper air.

Sif Thor's wife; known for her beautiful hair.

Sigi Son of Odin.

Sigmund Warrior able to pull the sword from Branstock in the Volsung's hall.

Signy Volsung's daughter.

Sigurd Son of Sigmund, and bearer of his sword. Slays Fafnir the dragon.

Sigyn Loki's faithful wife.

Símúrgh Griffin, an animal with the body of a lion and the head and wings of an eagle. Known to hold great wisdom. Also called a symurgh.

Sin God of the moon, worshipped primarily in Ur.

Sindri Dwarf who worked with Brokki to fashion gifts for the gods; commissioned by Loki.

Sirens Sea nymphs who are half-bird, half-woman, whose song lures hapless sailors to their death.

Sisyphus King of Ephrya and a trickster who outwitted Autolycus. He was one of the greatest sinners in Hades.

Sita Daughter of the earth, adopted by Janaka, wife of Rama.

Skadi Goddess of winter and the wife of Niord for a short time.

Skanda Six-headed son of Shiva and a warrior god.

Skraeling Person native to Canada and Greenland. The name was given to them by Viking settlers and can be translated as 'barbarian'.

Skrymir Giant who battled against Thor.

Sleipnir Odin's steed.

Sluagh The host of the dead, seen fighting in the sky and heard by mortals.

Smote Struck with a heavy blow.

Sohráb Son of Rustem and Tahmineh, Sohráb was slain in battle by his own father, who killed him by mistake.

Sol The sun-maiden.

Soma A god and a drug, the elixir of life.

Somerled Lord of the Isles, and legendary ancestor of the Clan MacDonald.

Soothsayer Someone with the ability to predict or see the future, by the use of magic, special knowledge or intuition. Known as seanagal in Scottish myths.

Squaw A Native American woman or wife (now offensive).

Squint-Eye One of Ramana's monsters.

Squire Shield- or armour-bearer of a knight.

Srutakirti Daughter of Kushadhwaja.

Stirabout Porridge made by stirring oatmeal into boiling milk or water.

Stone Giants A malignant race of stone beings whom the Iroquois believed invaded their territory, threatening the Confederation of the Five Nations. These fierce and hostile creatures lived off human flesh and were intent on exterminating the human race.

Stoorworm A great water monster which frequented lochs. When it thrust its great body from the sea, it could engulf islands and whole ships. Its appearance prophesied devastation.

Stot Bullock.

Styx River in Arcadia and one of the four rivers in the Underworld. Charon ferried dead souls across it into Hades, and Achilles was dipped into it to make him immortal.

Subrahmanian Son of Shiva, a mountain deity.

Sugriva The chief of the five great monkeys in the *Ramayana*.

Sukanya The wife of Chyavana.

Suman Son of Asamanja.

Sumantra A noble Brahman.

Sumati Wife of Sagara.

Sumedha A righteous Brahman who dwelt in the city of Amara.

Sumitra One of Dasharatha's three wives, mother of Lakshmana and Satrughna.

Suniti Mother of Dhruva.

Suparshwa One of Ravana's counsellors.

Supranakha A rakshasi, sister of Ravana.

Surabhi The wish-bestowing cow.

Surcoat Loose robe, traditionally worn over armour.

Surtr Fire-giant who eventually destroys the world at Ragnarok.

Surya God of the sun.

Susanoo God of the storm. He is depicted as a contradictory character with both good and bad characteristics. He was banished from Heaven after trying to kill his sister, Amaterasu.

Sushena A monkey chief.

Svasud Father of summer.

Swarga An Olympian paradise, where all wishes and desires are gratified.

Sweating A ritual customarily associated with spiritual purification and prayer practised by most tribes throughout North America prior to sacred ceremonies or vision quests. Steam was produced within a 'sweat lodge', a low, dome-shaped hut, by sprinkling water on heated stones.

Syrinx An Arcadian nymph who was the object of Pan's love.

Tablet of Destinies Cuneiform clay tablet on which the fates were written. Tiawath had given this to Kingu, but it was taken by Merodach when he defeated them. The storm god Zu later stole it for himself.

Taiaha A weapon made of wood.

Tailtiu One of the most famous royal residences of ancient Ireland. Possibly also a goddess linked to this site.

Tall One of Ravana's counsellors.

Tammuz Solar deity of Eridu who, with Gishzida, guards the gates of Heaven. Protector of Anu.

Tamsil Example or guidance.

Tangi Funeral, dirge. Assembly to cry over the dead.

Taniwha Sea monster, water spirit.

Tantalus Son of Zeus who told the secrets of the gods to mortals and stole their nectar and ambrosia. He was condemned to eternal torture in Hades, where he was tempted by food and water but allowed to partake of neither.

Taoism Taoism (or Daoism) came into being at roughly the same time as Confucianism, although its tenets were radically different and were largely founded on the philosophies of Lao Tzu (Laozi). While Confucius argued for a system of state discipline, Taoism strongly favoured self-discipline and looked upon nature as the architect of essential laws. A newer form of Taoism evolved after the Burning of the Books, placing great emphasis on spirit worship and pacification of the gods.

Tapu Sacred, supernatural possession of power. Involves spiritual rules and restrictions.

Tara Also known as Temair, the Hill of Tara was the popular seat of the ancient High-Kings of Ireland from the earliest times to the sixth century. Located in Co. Meath, it was also the place where great noblemen and chieftains congregated during wartime, or for significant events.

Tara Sugriva's wife.

Tartarus Dark region, below Hades.

Tau (Lesotho) Brother to Ra-Molo, depicted as a lion.

Taua War party.

Tefnut Goddess of water and rain. Married to Shu, who was also her brother. She, like Sekhmet, is portrayed with the head of a lion. Also known as Tefenet.

Telegonus Son of Odysseus and Circe. He was allegedly responsible for his father's death.

Telemachus Son of Odysseus and Penelope who was aided by Athene in helping his mother to keep away the suitors in Odysseus's absence.

Temu The evening form of Ra, the Sun god.

Tengu Goblin or gnome, often depicted as bird-like. A powerful fighter with weapons.

Tenochtitlán Capital city of the Aztecs, founded around 1350 CE and the site of the 'Great Temple'. Now Mexico City.

Teo-Amoxtli Divine book.

Teocalli Great temple built in Tenochtitlán, now Mexico City.

Teotleco Festival of the Coming of the Gods; also the twelfth month of the Aztec calendar.

Tepee A conical-shaped dwelling constructed of buffalo hide stretched over lodge-poles. Mostly used by Native American tribes living on the plains.

Tepeyollotl God of caves, desert places and earthquakes, whose name means 'heart of the mountain'. He is depicted as a jaguar, often leaping at the sun. Also known as Tepeolotlec.

Tepitoton Household gods.

Tereus King of Daulis who married Procne, daughter of Pandion King of Athens. He fell in love with Philomela, raped her and cut out her tongue.

Tezcatlipoca Supreme deity and Lord of the Smoking Mirror. He was also patron of royalty and warriors. Invented human sacrifice to the gods. Offspring of Ometeotl and Omecihuatl, he is known as the Jupiter of the Aztec gods.

Thalia Muse of pastoral poetry and comedy.

Theia Goddess of many names, and mother of the sun.

Theseus Son of King Aegeus of Athens. A cycle of legends has been woven around his travels and life.

Thetis Chief of the Nereids loved by both Zeus and Poseidon. They married her to a mortal, Peleus, and their child was Achilles. She tried to make him immortal by dipping him in the River Styx.

Thialfi Thor's servant, taken when his peasant father unwittingly harms Thor's goat.

Thiassi Giant and father of Skadi, he tricked Loki into bringing Idunn to him. Thrymheim is his kingdom.

Thomas the Rhymer Also called 'True Thomas', he was Thomas of Ercledoune, who lived in the thirteenth century. He met with the Queen of Elfland, and visited her country, was given clothes and a tongue that could tell no lie. He was also given the gift of prophecy, and many of his predictions were proven true.

Thor God of thunder and of war (with Tyr). Known for his huge size, and red hair and beard. Carries the hammer Miolnir. Slays Jormungander at Ragnarok.

Thoth God of the moon. Invented the arts and sciences and regulated the seasons. He is portrayed with the head of an ibis or a baboon.

Three-Heads One of Ravana's monsters.

Thrud Thor's daughter.

Thrudheim Thor's realm. Also called Thrudvang.

Thunder-Tooth Leader of the rakshasas at the siege of Lanka.

Tiawath Primeval dark ocean or abyss, Tiawath is also a monster and evil deity of the deep. She took the form of a dragon or sea serpent and battled the gods of light for supremacy over all living beings. She was eventually defeated by Merodach, who used her body to create Heaven and Earth.

Tiglath-Pileser I King of Assyria, who made it a leading power for centuries.

Tiki First man created, a figure carved of wood, or other representation of man.

Tirawa The name given to the Great Creator (*see* Great Spirit) by the Pawnee tribe who believed that four direct paths led from his house in the sky to the four semi-cardinal points: north-east, north-west, south-east and south-west.

Tiresias A Theban who was given the gift of prophecy by Zeus. He was blinded for seeing Athene bathing. He continued to use his prophetic talents after his death, advising Odysseus.

Tirfing Sword made by dwarves which was cursed to kill every time it was drawn, be the cause of three great atrocities, and kill Suaforlami (Odin's grandson), for whom it was made.

Tisamenus Son of Orestes, who inherited the Kingdom of Argos and Sparta.

Titania Queen of the fairies.

Tlaloc God of rain and fertility, so important to the people, because he ensured a good harvest, that the Aztec heaven or paradise was named Tlalocan in his honour.

Tlazolteotl Goddess of ordure, filth and vice. Also known as the earth-goddess or Tlaelquani, meaning 'filth-eater'. She acted as a confessor of sins or wrongdoings.

Tohu-mate Omen of death.

Tohunga A priest; a possessor of supernatural powers.

Toltec Civilization that preceded the Aztecs.

Tomahawk Hatchet with a stone or iron head used in war or hunting.

Tonalamatl Record of the Aztec calendar, which was recorded in books made from bark paper.

Tonalpohualli Aztec calendar composed of twenty thirteen-day weeks called trecenas.

Totec Solar deity known as Our Great Chief.

Totemism System of belief in which people share a relationship with a spirit animal or natural being with whom they interact. Examples include Ea, who is represented by a fish.

Toxilmolpilia The binding up of the years.

Tristan Nephew of King Mark of Cornwall, who travels to Ireland to bring Iseult back to marry his uncle. On the way, he and Iseult consume a love potion and fall madly in love before their story ends tragically.

Triton A sea-god, and son of Poseidon and Amphitrite. He led the Argonauts to the sea from Lake Tritonis.

Trojan War War waged by the Greeks against Troy, in order to reclaim Menelaus's wife Helen, who had eloped with the Trojan prince Paris. Many important heroes took part, and form the basis of many legends and myths.

Troll Unfriendly mythological creature of varying size and strength. Usually dwells in mountainous areas, among rocks or caves.

Truage Tribute or pledge of peace or truth, usually made on payment of a tax.

Tsuki-yomi God of the moon, brother of Amaterasu and Susanoo.

Tuat The other world or land of the dead.

Tupuna Ancestor.

Tvashtar Craftsman of the gods.

Tyndareus King of Sparta, perhaps the son of Perseus's daughter Grogphone. Expelled from Sparta but restored by Heracles. Married Leda and fathered Helen and Clytemnestra, among others.

Tyr Son of Frigga and the god of war (with Thor). Eventually kills Garm at Ragnarok.

Tzompantli Pyramid of Skulls.

Uayeb The five unlucky days of the Mayan calendar, which were believed to be when demons from the underworld could reach Earth. People would often avoid leaving their houses on uayeb days.

Ubaaner Magician, whose name meant 'splitter of stones', who created a wax crocodile that came to life to swallow up the man who was trying to seduce his wife.

Uile Bheist Mythical creature, usually some form of wild beast.

Uisneach A hill formation between Mullingar and Athlone said to mark the centre of Ireland.

uKqili (Zulu) Creator god.

Uller God of winter, whom Skadi eventually marries.

Ulster Cycle Compilation of folk tales and legends telling of the Ulaids, people from the northeast of Ireland, now named Ulster. Also known as the *Uliad Cycle*, it is one of four Irish cycles of mythology.

Unseelie Court An unholy court comprising a kind of fairies, antagonistic to humans. They took the form of a kind of Sluagh, and shot humans and animals with elf-shots.

Urd One of the Norns.

Urien King of Gore, husband of Morgan le Fey and father to Yvain.

Urmila Second daughter of Janaka.

Usha Wife of Aniruddha, daughter of Vanasur.

Ushas Goddess of the dawn.

Utgard-loki King of the giants. Tricked Thor.

Uther Pendragon King of England in sub-Roman Britain; father of King Arthur.

Utixo (Hottentot) Creator god.

Ut-Napishtim Ancestor of Gilgamesh, whom Gilgamesh sought out to discover how to prevent death. Similar to Noah in that he was sent a vision warning him of a great deluge. He built an ark in seven days, filling it with his family, possessions and all kinds of animals.

Uz Deity symbolized by a goat.

Vach Goddess of speech.

Vajrahanu One of Ravana's generals.

Vala Another name for Norns.

Valfreya Another name for Freyia.

Valhalla Odin's hall for the celebrated dead warriors chosen by the Valkyries.

Vali The cruel brother of Sugriva, dethroned by Rama.

Valkyries Odin's attendants, led by Freyia. Chose dead warriors to live at Valhalla. Also spelled as Valkyrs.

Vamadeva One of Dasharatha's priests.

Vanaheim Home of the Vanir.

Vanir Race of gods in conflict with the Aesir; they are gods of the sea and wind.

Varuna Ancient god of the sky and cosmos, later, god of the waters.

Vasishtha One of Dasharatha's priests.

Vassal Person under the protection of a feudal lord.

Vasudev Descendant of Yadu, husband of Rohini and Devaki, father of Krishna.

Vasudeva A name of Narayana or Vishnu.

Vavasor Vassal or tenant of a baron or lord who himself has vassals.

Vedic Mantras, hymns.

Vernandi One of the Norns.

Vichitravirya Bhishma's half-brother.

Vidar Slays Fenris.

Vidura Friend of the Pandavas.

Vigrid The plain where the final battle is held.

Vijaya Karna's bow.

Vikramaditya A king identified with Chandragupta II.

Vintail Moveable front of a helmet.

Virabhadra A demon that sprang from Shiva's lock of hair.

Viradha A fierce rakshasa, seizes Sita, slain by Rama.

Virupaksha The elephant who bears the whole world.

Vishnu The Preserver, Vedic sun god and one of the two great gods of post-Vedic Hinduism.

Vision Quest A sacred ceremony undergone by Native Americans to establish communication with the spirit set to direct them in life. The quest lasted up to four days and nights and was preceded by a period of solitary fasting and prayer.

Vivasvat The sun.

Vizier High-ranking official or adviser. Also known as vizir or vazir.

Volsung Family of great warriors about whom a great saga was spun.

Vrishadarbha King of Benares.

Vrishasena Son of Karna, slain by Arjuna.

Vyasa Chief of the royal chaplains.

Wairua Spirit, soul.

Wanjiru (Kikuyu) Maiden who was sacrificed by her village to appease the gods and make it rain after years of drought.

Weighing of the Heart Procedure carried out after death to assess whether the deceased was free from sin. If the deceased's heart weighed less than the feather of Ma'at, they would join Osiris in the Fields of Peace.

Whare Hut made of fern stems tied together with flax and vines, and roofed in with raupō (reeds).

White Demon Protector of Mázinderán. He prevented Kai-káús and his army from invading.

Withy Thin twig or branch which is very flexible and strong.

Wolverine Large mammal of the musteline family with dark, very thick, water-resistant fur, inhabiting the forests of North America and Eurasia.

Wroth Angry.

Wyrd One of the Norns.

Xanthus & Balius Horses of Achilles, immortal offspring of Zephyrus the west wind. A gift to Achilles's father Peleus.

Xipe Totec High priest and son of Ometeotl and Omecihuatl. Also known as the god of the seasons.

Xiupohualli Solar year, composed of eighteen twenty-day months. Also spelt Xiuhpōhualli.

Yadu A prince of the Lunar dynasty.

Yakshas Same as rakshasas.

Yakunin Government official.

Yama God of Death, king of the dead and son of the sun.

Yamato Take Legendary warrior and prince. Also known as Yamato Takeru.

Yashiki Residence or estate, usually of a daimyō.

Yasoda Wife of Nand.

Yemaya (Yoruba) Wife of Obatala.

Yemoja (Yoruba) Goddess of water and protector of women.

Yggdrasill The World Ash, holding up the Nine Worlds. Does not fall at Ragnarok.

Ymir Giant created from fire and ice; his body created the world.

Yo The female principle who, joined with In, the male side, brought about creation and the first gods. In and Yo correspond to the Chinese Yang and Yin.

Yomi The underworld.

Yudhishthira The eldest of the Pandavas, a great soldier.

Yuki-Onna The Snow-Bride or Lady of the Snow, who represents death.

Yvain Son of Morgan le Fay and knight of the Round Table, who goes on chivalric quests with a lion he rescued from a dragon.

Zahid Holy man.

Zál Son of Sám, who was born with pure white hair. Sám abandoned Zál, who was raised by the Símúrgh, or griffins. Zal became a great warrior, second only to his son, Rustem. Also known as Ním-rúz and Dustán.

Zephyr Gentle breeze.

Zeus King of gods, god of sky, weather, thunder, lightning, home, hearth and hospitality. He plays an important role as the voice of justice, arbitrator between man and gods, and among them. Married to Hera, but lover of dozens of others.

Zohák Serpent-king and figure of evil. Father of Mihrab.

Zu God of the storm, who took the form of a huge bird. Similar to the Persian símúrgh.

Zukin Head covering.

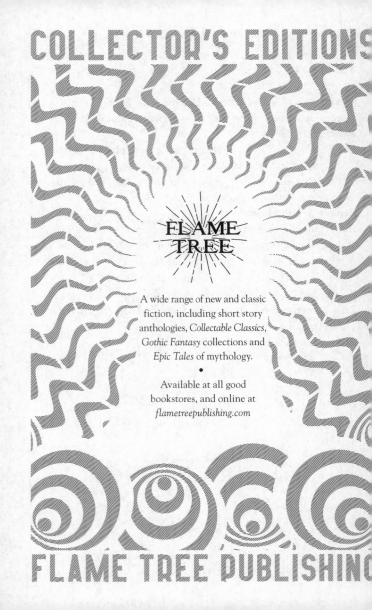